THE MIGHTY WAR
MACHINES OF EMPIRE

Over a rise there came a terrifying roar. Lumbering forms appeared, unearthly in the masking dampness. Travelling abreast, five of them filled the meadow from cliff wall to mountainside. Lights twinkled along their flanks. There was a sound as if a blanket covering the entire valley were being ripped in half. Indian warriors began to fall like the fat raindrops that spattered Sedrich's bloodied shoulders.

The giant forms approached rapidly. A hurricane roared in their wake.

The war machines of the Crystal Empire had arrived.

L. NEIL SMITH

THE CRYSTAL EMPIRE

A TOM DOHERTY ASSOCIATES BOOK
NEW YORK

THE CRYSTAL EMPIRE

Published by arrangement with Bluejay Books

A TOR Book
Published by Tom Doherty Associates, Inc.
49 West 24 Street
New York, NY 10010

Cover art by Michael Whelan

ISBN: 0-812-55425-6   Can. ISBN: 0-812-55426-4

First Tor edition: February 1989

Printed in the United States of America

0 9 8 7 6 5 4 3 2 1

The phrase in Chapter XXIII, "The Sword of God", is used with the consent of my friend, colleague, and so-far-unindicted co-conspirator, J. Neil Schulman.

FOR PHILIP B. SULLIVAN,
wherever you are

CONTENTS

Sura the Third: 1420 A.H.—
Sedrich Fireclaw

Sura the Fourth: 1420 A.H.—
The Voyageurs

Sura the Fifth: 1420 A.H.—
The Saw-Toothed Sword

Sura the Sixth: 1420 A.H.—
The Crystal Empire

Sura the Seventh: 1420 A.H.— The Hollow-Handled Knife

The Rat Crusade

And he that owneth the house shall come and tell the priest, saying, it seemeth to me there is as it were a plague in the house. Then the priest shall command that they empty the house . . . that all that is in the house be not made unclean. . . . And he shall cause the house to be scraped within round about, and they shall pour out the dust . . . into an unclean place.

—Leviticus 14:35–41

They obliged the carpenters to watch.

Gathering his robe against the January cold, Wilhelm of Glarus was likewise an unwilling witness, the prisoner of his own eyes. They refused to tear themselves from the fine new house—a remarkable, windowless structure of two stories' height—standing, daubed with pitch instead of plaster and unpainted, upon a rocky islet where the Rhine bent itself toward the faraway ocean. Neither were the scraps and shavery of its making cleared away, instead being swept beneath its open foundation, augmented with many a wicker basket of forest-gathered kindling.

1

Snowflakes, impelled by savage, pine-laden gusts, stung exposed flesh. Wilhelm's rough-woven garment afforded scant protection. Yet the marktplatz above the river overran with a multitude little better clothed, under no such compulsion as the house-carpenters suffered—save, perhaps, of the variety that tormented Wilhelm.

Before the Rathaus, which dominated the wind-drifted square, city fathers, arrayed in heavy furs and ornate neck-laces, nodded. A ring-mailed officer shouted; armsmen low-ered long-shafted pikes, shepherding a clot of shivering, bedraggled forms—not members of the waiting throng—toward the century-old stone bridge. The bridge was the city's proudest achievement, the first in history to span the Rhine.

The community of Basle's unbelievers would this day make penitence for the Great Mortality.

Even as a third part of the town's inhabitants—indeed, a third of all Christendom—were being thrown into shallow common trenches, warning had arrived from Savoy, in the form of confessions extracted by torture. Messengers from Toledo, the tale was told, bore poison in little leather packets for sprinkling in the wells and springs of Europe. In the Rathaus, a decree was passed forbidding Jews to settle in the town for two hundred years. The problem, it was understood, was what to do with those hundreds whose fathers had been born here, who possessed shops, tools, property—and a wealth of gold and silver.

Wilhelm shuddered. He was a small man, of fragile build, with awkward hands and feet, a narrow, bony chest. His pale blue eyes, watering in the cold, were set too close beside the prominence of his nose. Yet there was kindness in them, wisdom beyond his twenty-three years. Almost he regretted his tonsure, which hadn't been required of him absolutely. His head ached where the freezing wind rasped across his shaven scalp.

In Avignon, Pope Clement VI, in the sternest of promulga-tions, had forbidden, upon pain of excommunication, mea-sures like the one this moment transpiring before the young priest's horrified eyes. Still, Clement was just one Pope of two, and Avignon further away than the ocean.

The march across the ancient span began.

It was difficult to stand against the merciless wind, which roared unimpeded along the water, without leaning into it. The cold was terrible, the armsmen ungentle. Yet only the children cried as pike-points pricked them, as frozen stone cut unshod feet. Their mothers made to quiet them, but it was effort wasted.

Reaching a point where rough siege ladders slanted against the footings, they were compelled to climb in their hundreds onto the barren surface of the island. Several lost their grip upon the crude-lashed poles, falling to the cruel rock. The armsmen forced the living to drag the shattered dead until they came to the house, into which, by pairs and dozens, many were already crowded. When it was full, and none save armsmen and a single carpenter stood visible upon the rock, that unlucky artisan raised his hammer and let it fall, again and again, nailing the one door shut.

Some armsmen had brought torches, wind-whipped and showering sparks against the pitch-daubed windowless walls. These they thrust beneath the foundation, amidst the scraps and kindling. The house caught, flame lashing out and upward. Even across this distance, and the river, Wilhelm could feel the heat of it upon his face.

More than the wind was moaning now. He could hear the victims calling upon their god. Their prayers sounded distressingly like his own (and were received with the same divine indifference). Noise—the shrilling sound of hundreds of trapped men, frightened women, helpless children, screaming out their last breath as muscles shriveled, twisted, hair singed into glowing beads upon their scalps, burning its way to the bone, their very eyes bursting in the furnace—

2

"Willi! Willi!"

Rough hands shook his shoulders. Drenched with foul-smelling sweat and a fatigue untouched by stolen sleep, Wilhelm sat up on a narrow pallet, propping his elbows

beneath him. He blinked—standing over him was an armsman, like the ones who had . . . but that had been a year
ago, he realized with returning consciousness. He'd been
suffering again through one of his recurring nightmares.

This wasn't his familiar cell, but a broad, high-ceilinged
·chamber which in the daytime would fill with light from arch-
topped many-colored windows. At present they tossed back
scattered shards of candlelight, absorbed by the amorphous
writhing forms which covered the flagging of the minster
nave. The place reeked of burnt tallow, fevered bodies,
incense, and death. To think how he'd complained within
himself when it had merely smelled of mildew!

Weight settled upon his chest. These lumps were people, his
parishioners, now Father Albert was gone. Sounds of doomed
souls suffering and dying filled his every waking hour, as well
as every moment of his sleep. Yet there was naught he could
do for the still-living whose plague-racked bodies surrounded
him, crowding the ancient church. He had tried. Having fallen
at last into a guilty and exhausted sleep, during frantic
attempts to comfort victims of this freshened onslaught of the
Mortality, he admitted to himself that his limited strength
would have been best spent attempting to dispose of the
mounting dead.

There was a cough.

He looked up at the travel-stained warrior who'd awakened
him. "What wish you of me, soldier?"

The nightmare had evaporated, giving way to the horror of
reality. Still, this was no faceless, obedient murderer. He knew
this man, and well. Despite their mutual weariness, each
afforded the other a grin.

"By the good God, Willi, I've ground five horses into
butcher-bait getting here. You'd damned well better recognize
me!"

"Profaning in a sanctuary," answered Wilhelm, shaking his
head. "So this is what has become of my big brother Emil.
Like every young Swiss youth he longed to go away from his
native Glarus years ago, questing for wealth and glory. Unlike
most, he managed to accomplish it—the leaving, anyway.

Now he is a mercenary, spreading death and destruction in a world already overflowing with it.''

Wilhelm wasn't certain whether he spoke in seriousness or in jest. He was too tired to decide.

Pulling a soiled helmet-coif over his sweaty head, Emil responded, "For the moment, good friar, I'm a simple messenger—though 'tis mine to wonder what's become of my *little* brother. 'Twould seem I've been sent here, bearing personal regards—for him alone—from none other than the Pope in Avignon. Nor shall he—Willi, not the Pope—receive the least syllable of them till he explains—to the head of his family, I might add—how such a thing can come to pass!"

It was an old joke between them. Emil was elder by less than a year. Their father had died before the younger brother had been born, his death a gangrenous agony from a wood-cutter's accident.

With great effort, Wilhelm climbed to his feet, muscles stiff not so much from overuse as from months of working their owner's will against a steady burden of futility. He felt terrible. Nor, despite deepest wishes to the contrary, could he keep from examining himself, minute to minute, tongue, throat, armpits, and groin, for the signs of incipient disease. He supposed it was more commendable than fleeing to a country villa, refusing, as many priests and doctors were doing elsewhere, to enter the presence of victims of the Mortality.

Emil at his side, he left the cavernous nave, at last finding a quiet alcove. Here they could talk.

Unlike his brother, Emil was a big man, hardened by combat, his height and breadth exaggerated by soldier's trappings. Bits and pieces of the uniform Wilhelm recognized as French. A scabbarded two-handed sword—another sacrilege in this place—slapped at Emil's thigh. A crescent-guarded basilard, insignia of the Swiss mercenary, spanned the small of his back.

He was dirty; also, he smelled of the last animal he'd ridden to death getting here.

The monk was too exhausted for much curiosity about the message from Clement VI, too exhausted to explain it had been unexpected only in its means of being delivered. But he was too exhausted for many of the things which each day he'd accomplished nonetheless.

Relating to his brother the events upon the island in the Rhine, he complained, "I was cursed, Emil! Although I prayed for no more than to be a humble servant to my God, I was burdened with a selfish lust to *know*. I returned from the fire with two strange notions. The first was that the Great Mortality represented neither the curse of God upon Man, nor a Jewish 'well-poisoning' plot against Christians, but a natural affliction of some kind.

"The second was that there ought to be some way to prove it."

3

Old Father Albert had never uttered a word of protest. He, too, had been horrified by the mass incineration of the canton's Jews, against the specific injunction of the Holy Father.

In the next days, Wilhelm spent much time meditating upon the Mortality. The boys' mother had always hated rats, believing them a source of illness and corruption. It was, at the least, a place to begin. Wilhelm resolved to put his mother's belief to trial.

With the greatest imaginable pains, he caused the minster to be sealed, flushing the cellars with fire and water, following in the wainscoting with vinegar and pungent incenses, bribing small boys to maintain a constant vigilance against the rodents, killing a few which had escaped the purge—the many which chewed their way back in—with their little crossbows, burning the remains without touching them.

The building was scoured after each Mass. During this time, not one soul who resided upon the minster site—other friars, the sexton's family, servants and retainers—was afflicted.

Realizing some would claim it was the holiness of the church which protected its inhabitants, he persuaded others in the town—some few who suffered the same pangs of conscience he and Father Albert did—to repeat the prophylaxis upon their own houses, quoting Scripture where plain argument failed. The results, save those whose occupations took them into buildings unprotected, were the same as at the minster.

With the approval of his abbot, he wrote a letter to the Holy Father in Avignon. The reply Wilhelm received exceeded his most sanguine expectations. Having tried in vain to stem the tide of anti-Jewish sentiment himself, Clement was overjoyed to receive Wilhelm's suggestion that, whatever its unknown fundamental nature, the Mortality was transmitted neither by Jews nor evil spirits, but somehow by rats.

By that time, Wilhelm, suspecting fleas rather than the rodents who carried them—*"And he that is to be cleansed . . . shall shave all his hair off his head and his beard and his eyebrows, even all his hair he shall shave off, and he shall wash his clothes, also he shall wash his flesh in water, and he shall be clean"*—had begun to devise experiments afresh.

4

"Our mother is dead, Willi, three weeks since. The house lies empty, the door swinging upon a single hinge."

Emil coughed again, spat upon the floor.

"This sheds some light upon one mystery, at least." He rubbed his temple. "Not much. Willi, I was instructed by the Pope himself to tell you a peculiar story of my own."

The corridor of which their alcove was a part was still in darkness. At its ends, however, Wilhelm discerned the light of the coming dawn. Together, they rose and walked, coming to an unglazed window which overlooked the flagstones of a parapet-walk below, and, past it, the valley of the Rhine.

The air was clean and cold. Wilhelm needed it.

Almost a year had gone by since the fire, since the nightmare began coming. He'd labored toward its exorcism, yet still it came. Perhaps it always would.

But perhaps what Emil had to say might banish it.

"A private army—of which your big brother happened to be part—was called upon July last to ring the wicked port of

Marseilles. D'you know where that is? You do? You surprise
me with your worldliness, little brother. Anyway, we marched
inward with great clamor, beating weapons upon shields, with
the object of driving rats, hundreds of 'em, thousands,
numbers which I in my ignorance don't know how to name,
through cunning wicker chutes into the hold of an ancient-
hulled old tub at the quayside."

He leaned out the window to spit.

"We were paid off and dispersed, but some time afterward
your Clement requested of our captains lists of men among the
Free Companies at Marseilles who were from Switzerland, in
particular Basle or Glarus.

"There was I, of course, and here I am."

Lifting his leg with an effort, he tucked thumb and
forefinger into an age-darkened boot-top, levering out a folded
scrap of soiled parchment.

"I can attest," he told his brother, "this is a letter from
Clement, for he wrote it as I stood before him, there, 'twixt
those great blasted braziers he keeps going day and night to
fend off the plague. He gave it thus into my hand to give to
you.

"Here it is."

There was no signature, no salutation. Wilhelm recognized
the writing:

*I eschew certain proprieties, valued friend, with an inten-
tion to preserve the sanctity of our converse from prying
eyes—also, as you'll see, your esteemed person. My messenger will relate a tale of the Marseilles "campaign." Others of
my court discerned in your inquiries the opportunity of
accomplishing what no Crusade has.*

*The vessel, I've determined by distasteful methods, was
crewed with convicts who'd survived the Pest and were
thought immune. Its destination was the Saracen shore, the
object to bring the Pest upon the people there. The vessel itself
was no great loss, a derelict, its keel full of Cornish ballast,
the detritus of ages in the tin trade.*

Yet, once put to sea, in some mysterious fashion the

character of the Pest malevolently altered. Each soul aboard perished in the most horrible manner—I've seen their dead faces. Storm-driven, the death-ship fetched up on the Genoese coast, its nonhuman passengers escaping to sow new terror which we suffer in increased numbers.

Wilhelm paused.

Before this evil intervention, the Mortality, what Clement called "the Pest," had been slaying between a third part and half of the population. Sometimes it seemed that rats and fleas had naught to do with it, that one could breathe it in and die before the victim one took it from. There were rumors of calamity from Iceland to the farthest eastern reaches of the known world.

Wilhelm, struggling now to save a pitiable handful of villagers, knew the New Death, unlike the old, was killing horses, cattle, even housecats, emptying the land.

I've excommunicated the instigators [Clement continued], *cursing their souls to eternal damnation. Too late it is to prevent the perversion of your discoveries, my son, but from what I believe to be my deathbed I've ordained publication of our correspondence, of the truth concerning the attempted extermination, not of the Saracens alone, but of Christendom, of the known world, and beyond.*

The universe we know disintegrates about us. Those "Crusaders" beyond my reach spin superstitious fantasies that such things as the use of clockworks, waterwheels, and gunpowder are responsible for the raging Pestilence. Every manner of tale is being placed in currency to oppose the truth. Of those who still care, many prefer the lies.

I caution you, friend, against the possibilities of assassination. Those there are who wouldn't have their story contradicted. They may have followed my messenger to you, but I believed it important you hear the truth from me.

"Know you the contents of this letter, Emil?" Wilhelm asked after he had read it through twice.

Looking up as if just awakened, his brother shook his head. "When have I'd time to learn reading? What's it say—or ought I ask?"

Wilhelm read the letter to his brother, the grim expression on his face soon matched by strain upon Emil's countenance.

"If this be true," the friar mused, "it would explain why so many more are afflicted than was the case ere now."

Emil coughed. "The land's passing empty, Willi, 'tween Avignon and this place, with naught but ragged penitents whipping themselves from town to town."

Wilhelm frowned. Flagellants appeared everywhere, trying to expiate the sin of all mankind—and perhaps the Mortality itself—through self-mortification. Authorities considered it heresy, an attempt at direct intercession, rather than through office of the Church.

"In truth," Emil continued, "Basle's well off by comparison. 'Tis as if an invisible army'd murdered all of Christendom. The world's dying. 'Tis the end."

Wilhelm shook his head. "Yet the world began once with a single man and woman. If a single man and woman should survive, my brother, it can begin again, can it not?"

The soldier pushed away from the window.

"Don't speak to me of such things, brother. I left a woman—did you know I'd married?—I left Jeannette to do this errand for your Pope. I don't know whether she or our two small children yet live. Knowing's more important than you can imagine."

Wilhelm placed a hand upon his brother's shoulder. "I did not know that you had married." He shook his head. "But I am a man, am I not? Though I be bound by vows of celibacy, I can imagine—"

"No, Wilhelm, you can't." Steadying himself against the window casement, Emil looked into his brother's eyes. "You see, I'm hoping—for I'll no longer pray—that they're safely *dead!*"

Wilhelm stepped backward, aghast. "May god forgive you, Emil! Why?"

"Because"—Emil peered up the corridor and down, left

hand reaching for the crescent pommel of his basilard—"your friend Clement's correct. 'Twas a near thing, my making it here. An assassin's indeed come with the intention of silencing you.

"God be damned!"

In a single fluid motion, Emil thrust his broad-bladed dagger upward, to the bar-guard, through the arch of his brother's lower jaw. Wilhelm was almost relieved when the blow fell.

Emil spoke to one who could no longer hear him. "You see, Willi, 'twas his own messenger, this assassin. Jeannette and our babies're prisoners of his enemies, threatened with torture."

Tears streaming down his face, Emil gave one more cough, spat blackened blood.

He fell across his brother's body and was still.

It was the *last* Year of Our Lord, 1349.

SURA THE FIRST: 1395–1400 A.H.—

The Land-Ship

. . . so let those who go against His command beware, lest a trial befall them. . . .
—The *Holy Koran*, Sura XXIV, *Light*

I:

Young Sedrich

Prosperous are the believers who in their prayers are
humble . . . and who preserve their trusts and their
covenant. . . . Those are the inheritors. . . .
—The *Koran*, Sura XXIII

"I *won't!*"

The boy stood half inside the rowboat, one bare foot within
the green translucent hull, the other on the dampened planking
where the little craft lay canted. Scattered about him on the
dock were his father's tools. Like a quarterstaff clutched in his
hands—one anchored at his left hip, the other outthrust before
him—he wielded the long sculling oar he'd hoped his idea
might make unnecessary.

The still air smelled rich with salt and iodine, the spicy
stench of marine decay. The sun was hot, for a summer
morning with the dew just off the sparse sand grass. Skipping
from unrippled water, it assaulted unprotected eyes. The boy's
fair skin was reddened by it, lightly blistered and peeling, as
seemed natural to him.

Better than the fish-belly pallor of this foul-odored old man who confronted him.

Answer there came, crack-voiced and wheedling: "Here, boy, stay thy hand! Too young thou art to pay the penalty thou beg'st for!"

The speaker was an undersized, wizened individual, his bony figure draped in unbleached fabric. His narrow-crested skull, with its ink-and-needle imprints at the temples, was scraped smooth. Where his simple garment left a shoulder bare, a crosshatch of ancient scars offended the eye. Two others, likewise swathed, tattooed, and shaven, stood behind him. They were younger, differing in their greater bulk—as well as in the lesser number of their scars.

Their leader leaned forward, stretched out a ropy-veined hand. "Give me that oar!"

Overhead a gull wheeled, mocking them both with its squeals.

Sedrich Sedrichsohn was big for a boy of eleven. He complied with the order—after his own fashion—thrusting the blade-edge into his tormentor's solar plexus. Making retching noises, the small man folded, staggering backward, his hands clutched over the insulted portion of his anatomy.

The man's companions each took a threatening step forward.

Sedrich recovered from the thrust, assumed a firmer stance straddling the gunwale.

He let the oar whistle in a defiant circle over his head.

They stopped.

Still doubled, the man looked up, hatred burning in his yellow eyes. "Why," he gasped, "you young—"

Behind them, heavy footsteps vibrated through the pier.

"What in the name of Exile d'you think you're about, Oln Woeck?"

It was a rich, rasping bass which interrupted them, followed by the whispery ring of hammered steel leaving a brass throat. Making more noise with his moccasin-shod feet than necessary, a giant form strode past the corner of the village boatshed. The wolfhide shoulder band of an empty half-scabbard crossed his shaggy chest.

From one huge fist he swung a length of polished metal, high as a tall man's breastbone, broad as a big man's hand, sharp-edged as an old man's memories of yesterday.

Beside him trotted a pair of huge black curly-pelted dogs.

Scar-backed Oln Woeck straightened with visible effort.

"I greet thee, Sedrich Owaldsohn, renowned slayer of Red Men, *and* thy greatsword *Murderer*. This contraption of thy son's devising"—he indicated the boat, upon which young Sedrich had begun to work some alterations—"is forbidden by the mandate of His suffering."

Ignoring the formal salutation, Old Sedrich ran a free hand through his curly gray-blond mane, where a pair of eagle feathers, bound at their bases with bright thread, replaced the warrior's braid he'd once worn. His nose was a great sunburned hook, his eyes the color of the frozen hearts of icebergs which sometimes passed this coastline in the springtime.

They flared, now, at the robe-draped man.

"What pigshit nonsense is this, skinny one?"

Like his younger namesake, he wore only a leather breechclout with matching vest, the latter decorated with buttons fashioned from the points of deer horn.

"Forbidden? Tell me where you see its fire-burning machinery, Oln Woeck!"

Both canines sat, tongues lolling, their faces curiously intelligent and ironic. Keeping a wary eye on the animals, as well as the end of Sedrich's makeshift weapon. Oln Woeck stepped toward the boat.

He pointed at a black iron shaft which lay among the clutter of tools and parts.

"This was fashioned in thy forge, was it not, blacksmith, by *fire*?"

Owaldsohn laughed. "As well you know! Each moon-quarter I pay fire-tithe for the privilege! You ignorant dung-ball, there's no more forbidden art in this thing than's to be discovered in a cart-axle!"

He slammed the greatsword back into its half-scabbard, a gesture more intimidating than its unsheathing.

One of the dogs gave a good-natured bark.

"Be hush, Willi! Leave the boy to his tinkering, Oln Woeck—or, by my forge, *you'll* pay a tithe, in bone and blood!"

"How darest thou speak to me thus!"

Oln Woeck's face flushed red, veins standing out upon his forehead. Foam formed upon his lips, whence sprayed small gobbets.

"I care not a whit that this be no combustible machine," he spat. "Ask the boy thyself, Owaldsohn—what is it for, boy, what purpose doth it serve?"

Still braced, Sedrich looked down at the boat, perplexity wrinkling his features. Across the gunwales stretched the iron bar which seemed to be the focus of the older man's objections, bent at right angles in four places to produce a two-handed crank. Where it passed outboard, at the previous locations of the rowlocks, small wooden paddle wheels of four blades each were attached.

"Why, no more than to make the rowing easier, Oln Woeck."

The old man grinned as if this were a confession, looking back over his disfigured shoulder at his companions, then at Owaldsohn.

"And why should rowing be made easier, young Sedrich?"

Perplexity turned to exasperation.

"So more can be accomplished in a given time, that the livelihood of fisherfolk—"

Oln Woeck stamped a callused, naked foot.

"Thou'st no calling to make life easier, impious brat! 'Tis the purpose of our lives to ease His suffering in Hell, by sharing it with Him on this earth!"

"So you say, *priest*!" the boy retorted.

One of the great hounds growled.

The three robed figures stepped backward, mouths agape, eyes widened at the insult.

"This new idea is *mine,* old man, not yours to dispose of!" the boy continued. "Before I let you interfere, I'll smash this boat and burn the splinters!"

Oln Woeck eyed first the fearsome father, then the brace of war-dogs, then the boy. He peered down at the rowboat with its half-finished innovations.

"*Thy* new idea, eh? What makest thee think we want new ideas? 'Tis new ideas've brought on every calamity a sinful mankind's suffered for a thousand years!"

Wry humor danced in Sedrich's eyes, the image of his father's.

"All the better to 'ease the suffering' of your precious . . ."

The boy let it end there, feeling he had gone too far.

Indeed, the word "blasphemy" had begun to form upon Oln Woeck's lips, but he silenced it.

A calculating look appeared in the old man's yellow eyes.

"Tell me, boy, who first thought of rowboats? Who first thought of iron cranks? Who first thought of thee? This idea of thine resteth upon the inventions of others. It belongeth to the community who made boats and iron and thyself.

"Destroy it, thou committest theft, since thou've invented naught!"

Once again the boy was puzzled. He remembered well conceiving of the idea, persuading his father to help him with it at the forge, testing it for the first time across a barrel in the shop.

Unable to answer, he let the oar drop, until its blade-end rested on the pier.

Owaldsohn laughed, thrusting Oln Woeck's companions aside. Dogs trotting behind him, he covered the distance between him and his son in an easy stride. Bending, he took hold of the paddle-crank at its center, strained, and, iron straps and nails flying, wrenched it from its attachments to the gunwale. Straightening, he gave it a casual toss.

It sailed far out upon the mirror-surfaced estuary and disappeared with a splash.

"Now," the big man declared, "Sedrich's dangerous idea's gone forever from your 'community.'"

"Gather up the tools, boy—if we've your permission, Oln Woeck. Willi! Klem! Let's be going."

As he followed his father's instructions, the boy watched Oln Woeck's hands clenching into fists, the veins of his forehead threatening to explode. The boy knew what was going on in his mind. Sedrich Owaldsohn was a hero of the western wars, a pillar of the community. He was even famous for a new idea of his own—folding two grades of steel under the hammer to create a sword unequaled elsewhere in the New World.

They daren't make trouble with him.

At present.

As the two Sedrichs left the end of the dock, setting foot on solid turf, Owaldsohn laid a gentle hand upon his son's shoulder.

"You did well with that sculling oar. You've learned the lesson well, that aught about you is a weapon.

"Howe'er . . ."

"Yes, Father?"

The older man ruffled the boy's dark hair, bleached at the ends by exposure to sea and sun.

"If that muttonhead upon Master Thee-thou's right hand had brought his wits with him, you'd be fishbait. Children're too rare and valuable to waste by neglecting their instruction. And you're too right-handed. You must put some work into your off-side."

Sedrich grinned up at the shaggy giant. "Yes, Father."

There was a long pause. "Father, about my idea being lost . . ."

Owaldsohn growled. "I'll speak a word with Hethri Parcifal. A good idea's rare and valuable, too. The village won't permit the Cult to have its way in this."

"'Tis all right, Father." The boy smiled craftily. "I needs must start all o'er again, anyway."

The big man stopped, stared at his son, a puzzled expression on his broad, bearded face.

Sedrich's eyes were calculating. He reached down to tousle one of the animals between the ears.

He didn't have to reach far.

"Yes, Father, the paddle wheels need to rotate independent of each other, so the boat may be steered.

"I'll make a drawing after supper."

II:

Mistress of the Sisterhood

We have charged man, that he be kind to his parents; his mother bore him painfully, and she gave birth to him; his bearing and his weaning are thirty months.
— The *Koran*, Sura XLVI

Sedrich Owaldsohn was a blacksmith, as anyone could tell from the ebon lines imprinted upon his palms, his fingertips, underneath his stubby fingernails.

Had the man purified himself ten times a day, instead of the required five—Owaldsohn was ne'er one to permit cleanliness to lapse into empty ritual, as his son would attest, presenting well-chafed skin as evidence—his vocation would have marked him nonetheless. It had been thus since he was himself a boy. When yellow iron bellows in the quenching bath, be it oil or water or icy brine, the outer layer is transformed into ink, giving the blacksmith his name.

By the time the pair were hungry for the evening meal, Young Sedrich's arms were black from the shoulder down—a first intimation he'd follow in his father's profession. They'd spent the remainder of the day heat-treating steel billets for shoulder-bow prods, replacement parts for hunting weapons fashioned from hair-fine glass, bound together with tree sap hardened with a substance which was a secret of the village resiner. The stock would be of bonded wood, even linen.

There had been talk of renewed trouble with the Red Men. The canton was in the throes of grim preparation.

Owaldsohn claimed his greatsword from a nail driven in the shed-rafter where it hung when he was working. Whistling up the dogs, they began walking the hundred yards separating the smithy from their family home.

It was a warm evening in the summer. Owaldsohn's claimstake, defined on this side by a sea-cliff, overlooked the eastern ocean, upon whose surface the slanting sun, low over fields and forests to the west, picked out an occasional whitecap. Partway to the house they paused, hoping to glimpse an iceberg, or, perhaps, to catch the rarer sighting, even more fascinating, of a spouting whale.

"Father, *look!*" the boy shouted. "A *ship,* at the edge of the world! It must be passing tall! It twinkles, flashing and fading in a rhythm, as if . . . as if—"

"I see it, son, although just."

Owaldsohn put a hand on Sedrich's shoulder, peering with middle-aged eyes in the direction his son was pointing.

"As if what?"

"As if the sails were somehow turning like . . . like windmill blades, only—"

He paused, lacking words to continue.

"Horizontal," his father supplied. "As if in the same plane as a gristmill. I believe you're right, now you point it out."

He looked at the boy.

"To what purpose, d'you suppose?"

Sedrich screwed his face up, concentrating.

He shook his head.

"Think about your own boat, Sedrich."

The boy laughed. "Why, you could gear such a contrivance to a pair of paddle wheels, Father! You could—"

Owaldsohn joined his son in laughter. "And what a stench old tattooed Woeck would raise o'er that!"

The glittering alien vessel disappeared.

They resumed walking.

"Hello, the house! Ilse, we're home!"

As they trod the walkstones leading to the long log structure, Sedrich saw what his father had. His mother had arrived already. Her staff lay propped against the doorframe, a sign she was available if needed.

The staff was as tall as she, a finger's width in breadth, fashioned of copper. His father would have given much to learn its secret, brought by Mistresses of the Sisterhood from the Old World, sacred to ceremonies of forging from which all save Mistresses were excluded. Ilse herself had fashioned it, as was required. At one end it tapered for some distance to a needle-sharp point. At the other, a crook, also sharp-ended, presented a broad surface, back of the bend, which could be used, and often was, as an effective club.

Sometimes Owaldsohn would, with a grin, offer to fashion her a better one. In equal humor she would, of course, refuse. Annoying, for a blacksmith to see butter-soft alloy ensorcelled into something rivaling honest metal in steel-hard durability. It wouldn't have been impossible to learn its secret. Yet, not for immortality itself would Owaldsohn have violated the trust which lay between them.

Just now, both crook and pointed end were lacquered with dried blood. Both dogs sniffed curiously and growled.

"Mother'll be in a bad mood," Sedrich observed.

His father grimaced in agreement, reaching for the latch-rope.

The stoop-stone had been scrubbed and was already drying. Thus Sedrich understood that little Frae Hethristochter had already gone for the day. He surprised himself by feeling disappointed. Frae was a neighbor-girl who helped Ilse with the house. An unusual arrangement it was, a potential source of jealousy among the village women had it not been for his mother's sacred duties. The child's widowed father, for all he was closer to Sedrich's age than Owaldsohn's, acted by mutual consent as a local arbiter. He often spoke for the village in regional councils.

"He is also a cheap son of a bitch," Owaldsohn growled as if in answer to Sedrich's unspoken comment. "Willing to put an infant to profitable labor!" He shook his head.

Sedrich knew what he was thinking. Apprenticeship was one thing—any child must learn a trade. However, in this village of a hundred houses, Sedrich and Frae were the only children between babyhood and marriageability. Of all the loose confederation upon the eastern shoreline—or at least those hundred villages within a week's energetic walk—this one was considered fortunate. Neighbors were inclined to offer an opinion—if they did nothing else—regarding how a child was raised.

Owaldsohn laughed as he perceived that Sedrich's thoughts paralleled his own. "Well, son, it could be worse. To a man of Oln Woeck's beliefs, for example—Fiery Cross and Sacred Heart—our practices of cleanliness are empty rituals, imposed by a community which would burn him out did he not make some visible concession to them."

"Thou shalt not suffer a rat to live," intoned Sedrich, echoing the teachings of an admittedly brief lifetime.

Ah, well. Hethri Parcifal held to the customs. Mother esteemed Frae a bright girl, learning the way of the Sisterhood from simple exposure to Sedrich's family. She'd turn out proper e'en if she lacked a mother of her own to teach her.

"As in the days of our fathers," Owaldsohn responded, *"so ne'er mote it be again."*

They entered.

The small house was spotless, walls scrubbed until, had the bark not been peeled in the building of the place, there would have been none left in any case. Curtains, clothing, bedding were changed each morning. Despite the day's warmth, flames rolled in an enormous hearth.

Sedrich scarcely noticed.

Twin models of decorum, Willi and Klem took places flanking the great door. They were as clean as the house itself, having spent most of the day, as was the wont of their breed, bathing in the salt-surf.

Hanging the greatsword on the wall beside a massive

shoulder-bow—from this weapon's cranequin had young Sedrich got the idea for his boat-crank—Owaldsohn strode across the polished hardwood floor to embrace his wife.

"Put this day aside," he murmured, "now we're home together."

"How is it you always anticipate my mood?"

Ilse Sedrichsfrau, initiated Ilse Olavstochter, was a small woman, slender, dark-haired with a tracery of gray, her cheekbones high and prominent. Unlike the blue eyes which marked her husband, hers were dark, set like those of Red Men, slanted, with foldless lids in oval framing. She wore a homespun shift, her flower-decorated hair bound back with patterned ribbon in anticipation of the evening ritual. She was more often visible to neighbors in robes of the Sisterhood, her hair unbound, flowing over her shoulders toward the small of her back.

"Your staff outside," replied her husband, peeling off his work-stained vest, "wants cleaning."

She shook her head, a sour look on her face.

"Let the night air cleanse it first. Perhaps then 'twill be fit to touch."

"Gunnarsohn's house blessing?" Sedrich asked.

She nodded. "I don't understand what people think about."

"You speak of Ivarsohn, the house-carpenter?" Owaldsohn sneered. "A Pest upon him!"

Ilse chuckled. Used to her husband's language, she didn't flinch at the obscenity.

Owaldsohn skinned off his knee-length moccasins, placed them in a cabinet on an outside wall with vest and breechclout. Ilse put in Sedrich's garments before she closed the door.

Sedrich himself, bare and shivering, padded off to another room.

From a table candle—dinner was already laid but would wait until after the ritual—she lit a stick of pungent incense, placing it before a grille below the cabinet. A draft drew it, through the wire racks and the clothing they held, out into the evening stillness to mingle with incense from other dwellings. Compounded by the Sisterhood, people could breathe it with the mildest discomfort. Yet no insect could live within its fragrant embrace.

Owaldsohn growled, pulled the eagle feathers from his tangled hair. Holding his breath, he tossed them into the cabinet, slamming the door behind them.

The puff of smoke he released thus dissipated.

Ilse laughed. "Ivarsohn left the place with open spaces along the walls and under the roof. Gunnarsohn failed to notice. The house is sawdust new, Husband, yet I killed three large rats before the blessing could be completed!"

He wrinkled his nose. "Hence the stains upon your crook. Well, isn't it what the blessing—and the Sisterhood—are for, my love?"

"Ivarsohn's a Cultist," she replied with ill humor. "Each year grow they in number and influence. 'Tis a bad omen."

"A pox," Owaldsohn roared, "upon Thor Ivarsohn, Oln Woeck, the whole smelly gaggle of superstitious shave-pates!"

He told her of Sedrich's morning confrontation.

She shook her head. "No Mistress ought to criticize the Cult, nor would the Cult in theory take issue with the Sisterhood. 'Tis no matter of choosing 'tween them. Each has its place in the way of things, preserving tradition, protecting the present—"

"Caring not a fart for the future!"

"*Sedrich!*"

He laughed a wicked laugh. Heaping more charcoal into the already blazing fireplace, which jutted, open upon three sides, into the broad room, the naked blacksmith climbed five tiled steps, easing his grimy body into the tub above it. The younger of the massive canines, Willi, whistled wistfully. It had taken the family months to discourage both dogs from joining in the family bath.

Owaldsohn groaned with pleasure as the near-boiling water sloshed about him.

"Did you speak to me, Mother?"

The boy had reappeared, a towel wound about his loins, displaying a recent adolescent modesty. His father sometimes teased him, threatening to invite Frae to bathe with them some evening.

The boy's blushes were soon lost in the color the hot bath brought to his skin.

"No, dear." Ilse was the last to join them, bearing a tray of colorful tumblers beaded with condensation. "To your father, who often says things in haste he oughtn't." Her vocation wouldn't permit her to partake of fermented or distilled beverages, and Sedrich, she maintained, was too young. Nor would Owaldsohn drink alone. Thus did they imbibe—the blacksmith in a grudging spirit—of cold peppered fruit juice, as steam from the heated waters rose about their shoulders.

As always, when there were rumors about the sighting of a ship—today's was the first he'd himself seen—Sedrich begged to hear again of the Invaders of the Elder World. It had been his favorite bedtime tale in infancy. Now it was his favored conversation at the evening time.

"We've no way of telling truly whether they be Invader vessels," Ilse cautioned, "or those fashioned by some other stranger."

Fumbling beneath the scalding water, Sedrich produced the towel he'd worn, wrung it out, and set it on the tile beside the bath.

"This I know, Mother, for they ne'er make landfall in the New World."

"So 'tis said. . . ." She pursed her lips, thinking, Sedrich knew, of those two items which, more than any others, made life as it was lived in their village possible—cotton cloth and iron pipe—and of the generally accepted explanation that they originated in villages much like this one, "far to the south."

"Likeliest"—his father turned the tap to cool the tub, watching his son from the corner of his eye—"they be not Invaders, for then they'd come ashore, wreaking conquest as of old."

Sedrich wriggled in the hot water, delightful shivers of terror traveling up his backbone.

His mother continued. "All we possess are legends, Sedrich, of which the Sisterhood—"

She looked to her husband. "Yes, and the Cult, after its own fashion—are custodian."

Owaldsohn gazed through the steam, out the great windows to the sea beyond.

"Those legends speak of times in Eldworld when great men dared greater deeds."

"Yet," answered Ilse, "they were cut down in their pride, nine hundred nine and ninety out of every thousand. In weakened numbers, those remaining could venture naught but to retreat before unnamed and numerous Invaders from the south."

"Unnamed," repeated Sedrich, almost to himself.

His mother heard.

"No tale or book I know of names them."

She nodded toward a case of volumes across the room, each hand-lettered, passed down to fewer heirs each generation by their predecessors.

"See for yourself, young sir."

Sedrich made a face.

"I am a blacksmith, Mother. I want naught to do with books."

"Yet you show a talent for them 'twould be sinful to neglect. Pity poor Frae who, unmothered and unlettered, must needs learn to read and write from me five years later than she ought."

"Frae is a girl!"

Owaldsohn chuckled, then assumed serious aspect.

"Would I had time for learning, son, though most men cannot. 'Twould be a help in the forge—fashioning springs, for instance. As is, I need remember size and heat and quench and draw for a thousand which were better marked down.

"Should something e'er happen to me—"

All three rapped on the resin-impregnated tub-edge.

"—you'd at least possess the writing of it."

Ilse spoke. "Sedrich, you should value Frae more. She is intelligent, no ordinary barren female falling into the Sisterhood for aught else better. Hers is a powerful gift."

She mused, " 'Twould be a merry thing to induct my own marriage-daughter."

Owaldsohn made a noise which was half laugh, half growl.

"Sedrich is too young by far for such discussion to be decent, Ilse!"

"Ne'er any harm in discussing, dear," his wife replied. "Plans for Sedrich's future are important. He was such a long time coming! We won't be with him long to guide his footsteps."

Young Sedrich's ears reddened as his parents spoke of him thus in his presence. As before, the embarrassed reaction was disguised by the heat of the bath.

"Nor should we be, woman, for, by St. Willem and St. Klemmet"—by the doorway, both dogs perked their ears at mention of their names—"he'll soon be a man in his own right!"

"Which was my point." Ilse overlooked Owaldsohn's self-contradiction. "Husband, always you force me to consider truths I might not otherwise confront. I'll return the favor: I see no reason not to begin learning letters, e'en for one of your venerable years!"

Bested, Owaldsohn made a sour face.

Sedrich laughed.

Spilling both their drinks in the doing of it, his father seized the boy and pressed his head beneath the water, holding him there as he flailed. Of a sudden, Sedrich fell limp, lying thus, face below the surface, for a long time.

Owaldsohn, in alarm, hauled him up and shook him.

A moment passed.

Then Sedrich's breath exploded into his father's face. He laughed until his own turned redder even than it had been.

III:

The Cult

"I take refuge with the Lord of the Daybreak from the evil of what He has created, from the evil of darkness when it gathers, from the evil of the women who blow on knots, from the evil of an envier when he envies."
—The *Koran*, Sura CXIII

Beneath the slanted beams of a loft he'd claimed as his own upon first leaving his baby crib, Sedrich pondered his parents' words as he prepared for sleep.

The room was small, cluttered with the many artifacts of imaginative boyhood.

From the center joist dangled an artful miniature rowboat equipped with crank and paddle, which he'd pieced together from parchment scraps and bits of wire.

Where one wall was vertical the boy had hung a dozen facsimiles of knives, swords, axes, edged weapons customers had ordered, which Owaldsohn had first try-fashioned out of wood. One or two more fanciful in form young Sedrich had carved out, which had not yet found a life in steel.

That would wait until his eye and hand were surer.

No thought had he given to marriage, being but eleven—although precocious. This last he understood with an unmodest certainty few adults carry away from childhood. He was aware no Helvetian was allowed to marry until a child of the union-to-be had been conceived. From a boy's point of view, marriageable girls were mercifully rare. In their village of a hundred houses, but two families boasted of children Sedrich's age—Owaldsohn and Parcifal. Of families with younger infants there were perhaps another three or four.

The full moon, orange on the horizon, poured itself through the round leaded window set into the other vertical end-wall. Sedrich blew the candle out and slid between the worn, familiar blankets of the low pallet he was accustomed to sleep upon. He lay back, arms folded behind his head, and thought about his village as if it were the dwelling-place of strangers he, a visitor from far away, must strive to understand.

Rather a lot of couples, he knew—and knew he wasn't supposed to know—had conceived, married, and suffered disappointment which the village women gossiped of afterward, but which Sedrich couldn't quite fathom. What was a "stillbirth"?

One or two households had grown children yet unmarried.

One or two there were whose children had found mates.

He knew of various widows and widowers—of these, Old Roger the resiner was crossing customary barriers by teaching Sedrich something of his arcane craft.

He reminded himself also of the arrangements made for Sisters—likewise, he supposed, for Cult Brothers—who, despairing at last of finding someone to love, or of making a child, had given themselves to their beliefs. They were many, living in open compounds, one at the west end of the village, another at the south, rows of simple cabins centered about common structures of gathering and meditation. Each cabin door faced outward, for the sake of privacy, from the center of the compound.

No one, Sedrich realized with sudden insight, ever gave up entirely.

His own mother had been one such before the surprise of Sedrich's quickening.

Thus the population of the world which Sedrich knew lay somewhere between an uncounted four hundred and five hundred. When the proper time arrived—oh, but that was a long way off yet!—did he show interest in some one someone (for well he understood his parents, never expecting at their hands an arrangement against his own inclinations), this "someone" would be invited for visits, at first family dinners, then the bathing ritual which preceded the meal (he blushed again to contemplate his father's threat regarding Frae), and then at last, did all proceed aright, for the entire night.

The colloquial expression, Sedrich squirmed to recall, was "bundling," every precaution taken to assure that the young couple was left unattended, undiverted save by one another's presence. The tasteless hazing would come later, when a young man led his pregnant bride before a Sister who would sanctify what already existed.

The whole idea filled him with foreboding—with the oddest feelings, like a deep-down itch, somehow pleasant, somehow demanding, somehow mysterious.

It made sleep difficult.

Yet not impossible . . .

2

He awoke a while later to a rattle-pounding which shook the house.

"Sedrich! Sedrich! Wake up! Wake up!"

At their posts beside the door downstairs, Willi and Klem began barking.

The cries were for his father.

He recognized the voice.

Wrapping a blanket about him, Sedrich seized his dagger—this being no mere wooden model—where it lay beside his pallet, and placed a foot upon the folding ladder. The steps swung beneath his weight, coming to rest in the hallway below.

Already his mother and father were descending the short fixed flight to the ground floor.

Tossing aside the small pillow-sword he'd carried from their bedroom, Owaldsohn took his great blade *Murderer* from the wall. As he quieted the animals, his free hand reached to give his wife the shoulder-bow.

"Yes, yes," he shouted at the ironbound door, more from annoyance than lack of recognition. "Who is it?"

"Your neighbor!" came a muffled voice. "Let me in! I bear ill tidings!"

" 'Twas e'er true," the blacksmith muttered.

He let his hand drop to the latch, which he unfastened.

"What cause have you to rouse us up this late, Hethri Parcifal?"

The oaken door swung to reveal a night-robed figure somewhere between the two Sedrichs in years, tall, and— thought the younger—odd-shaped. From stooped, narrow shoulders Parcifal tapered under purple draping to wide-set hips and plump behind. With the old green scarf about his neck, he resembled an eggplant, although he lacked, as yet, a belly to match the hips. The green-wrapped neck was skinny, the narrow head balding.

Parcifal blinked as he stepped inside. The candle-lantern Ilse carried dazzled him.

"Speak of rousing," he began, "whate'er have you done to rouse the Brotherhood?"

Listening, Ilse carried candle to hearth and began laying a fire. She fetched a kettle, hanging it on a hook as flames crackled up to reach its blackened bottom.

Owaldsohn answered, "Whene'er did those blotchheads want something to rouse them, Hethri?"

He tossed a glance at his son, whose hands still gripped the dagger, then looked back to Parcifal.

"Tell me what they're doing, and I'll tell you, if I can, what we have done."

As if from exhaustion, Parcifal sat upon a chair Ilse kept by the door. He ran a hand across his forehead and looked up at the blacksmith.

"Oln Woeck," he groaned, glancing in apology at Sedrich, "has been sowing hints about the character of your son."

Owaldsohn shook his shaggy head. "Also, no doubt, about those who are bringing him up."

He found a chair of his own, placing the scabbarded *Murderer* between his knees as if it were a cane. The strap crossed his hairy thigh, trailing to the floor.

Both dogs arose, settling themselves again at his feet.

"But 'tis naught new. Why the midnight visit, Hethri?"

The man opened his mouth to speak. He was interrupted by a low rolling growl from Klem. Willi shambled to the door, where he began pacing uneasily back and forth.

Parcifal stopped, cocking an ear toward the door.

"Too late!" he whispered, eyes focused somewhere other than the room he sat in. "It has begun!"

It could indeed be heard before it could be seen. No night-bird sang, no insect chirped in the dew-wet grass. The still air carried a dull thrumming which might at first have been mistaken for no more than the rush of blood through straining ears.

Soon, however, there was no misinterpreting it, a deep rumbling, more felt than heard, and more by the feet than by the ears, pulsing through the earth in an unhuman rhythm. Even across the sleeping village, through the forest at its margin, greasy smoke and wind-fanned flames were visible half a mile away, sparks wafting into the now-moonless sky like condemned souls fleeing corrupted bodies.

The apparition drummed nearer, a colossal fire-exhaling serpent winding toward them, relentless, unstoppable.

Next came real noise: hissing, shuffling, groaning, all in a cadence timed to the clash of metal against naked metal, multiplied ten thousandfold until a river of moving steel racketed by their door.

The flames grew brighter, the very windows rattling as if with the passage of some infernal forbidden engine.

"We believe— (Clash! Clash!)
We believe—(Clash! Clash!)

We believe in the Father,
Maker of heaven and earth,
Who hath turned His face away. (Clash!)

We believe— (Clash! Clash!)
In Jesus Christ, His only son,
Born of the Virgin Mary,
Crucified, dead, and buried. . . .
He descended into Hell. (Clash!)

There shall he suffer
Till he be redeeméd,
And sitteth on the right hand
Of God the Father Almighty,
Whence shall he come— (Clash!)
To judge the quick and the dead! (Clash!)"

Yet, if it were an engine of some kind, it fueled itself on human blood, flagellants, marching in their hundreds from house to house, sometimes from village to village, as ever they had since the legend-misted centuries of the Old World.

Together, the family and their visitor crowded into the open doorway.

Blood was all Sedrich noticed at first, glistening black in the torchlight, sprayed upon the face and forehead, down the arms, breast, and thighs of each marching flagellant. Each splashed the man behind him with his steel-linked whip as it cut his flesh. Even the man in front was covered with it, as, at regular intervals, he'd migrate to the rear of the column, leaving someone else to lead it.

To one side of the gore-stained horde Oln Woeck strode, unsullied by any blood save his own, the thumb-sized markings upon his temples blackly visible in the torchlight.

As if one being, the Brothers halted at his shouted command in the road between the houses of Owaldsohn and of his neighbor, Harold Bauersohn, the fletcher.

Silence crashed down about them.

Oln Woeck separated himself from the others, advancing to Bauersohn's threshold. The arrow-maker, a fellow veteran, with Sedrich's father, in the wars with the Red Men, came not to the door. It was opened to the leader of the Brotherhood by Helga Haroldsfrau, the man's wife.

Even at this distance across the road, Sedrich could make out the whine and buzz of Oln Woeck's voice.

It spoke.

It paused.

It spoke again.

At each utterance, the nightclothed woman in the torch-lighted doorway bobbed her head.

Sedrich seized Ilse's sleeve.

"She's informing, Mother! Upon her own husband!"

"Hush, son," Ilse replied, a grim expression making her face look like a stranger's.

She stroked Willi's head to calm him as well.

" 'Tis the custom of our people."

The talking continued. Whine-buzz, the unheard murmur of Helga's answers.

Another whine-buzz.

Toward the end, she gave a loud sob.

As if this were a signal, half a dozen of the flagellants broke from the column, rushing past into the house. There was a shout, the unexpected sound of muffled thunder. One of the robed figures reeled backward, howling like a kicked dog, carrying his mates with him, the bent shaft of a shoulder-bow quarrel hanging where the fleshy part of his upper arm had been. Now there was naught save charred bone and sinew, smoldering. He was replaced by half a dozen more.

The augmented force charged back into the house.

Silence.

Amidst a flurry of shouted curses, Harold was dragged out by the Brothers, flung into the dirt at the feet of Oln Woeck. The fletcher tried to push himself upward, into a sitting position. It was all the man could manage. He had been crippled, captured by the Red Men and tortured, long before young Sedrich had been born. He'd spent his days since sitting in the cross-legged pose his wife put him in each morning, fashioning arrows with a small, flywheel-operated lathe.

He turned the best quarrels, bolts, and arrows in the canton.

Oln Woeck kicked the man's hand from under him. The fletcher fell forward upon his face. Some decision having been come to, Harold's wife screamed, *"No!"*

From the house one of the Brothers brought an ax. Another seized Harold's right wrist, twisted a bit of cord about it, stretched it out before him, while a third kept a bare, bloodied foot in the middle of the victim's back.

In their own doorway, Willi and Klem growled.

Sedrich Owaldsohn took a step forward, the iron tendons of his wrists flexing along the handle of the greatsword.

Ilse placed a gentle hand upon his naked bicep.

"No, Husband, we can't interfere."

Oln Woeck himself swung the ax.

The cord flew free, carrying some terrible cargo. One of the Brothers put the torch to Harold's mutilated arm.

The fletcher uttered not a sound. His wife continued sobbing.

Casting the ax aside, the Cult leader strode, without a backward look, across the road to the threshold of Sedrich Owaldsohn. The boy could smell him, ancient body odor mixed with the fresher iron tang of blood, where he stood, Fiery Cross imprinted upon the right side of his naked skull, flame-enveloped Sacred Heart upon the left.

Without preamble, at the top of his lungs, he gloated, "Harry Bauersohn hath paid the price for dabbling where the blessed daren't. Be there one among thy number who hath grinded good charcoal fine as flour?"

Parcifal shrank back into the shadows of the room.

Owaldsohn strode forward, flanked by his great bearlike dogs, *Murderer* still in his hand, as much to bar the way as greet a visitor. This nightmarish parade was no routine occurrence—although they'd been known to happen in the past—but was intended for his benefit.

Lips compressed with rage, red color showing in his face, Owaldsohn answered, "No."

His wife stood by him, crook-bent staff in hand, no

implication in her manner, or the way she held the copper shaft, that its Mistress was a shepherdess of any kind.

Oln Woeck spoke again. "Be there one among thy number who hath pitchforked beneath dungheaps for the evil crystals to be found there?"

Owaldsohn lifted an elbow, exposing a hand's width of razor steel at the scabbard throat.

"A petty way to even up the morning's confrontation, Oln Woeck. And dangerous—"

Ilse placed a hand again on Owaldsohn's huge-muscled arm.

"Hush, Husband, mind the ritual."

"Answer, *blacksmith* Sedrich, son of Owald! Be there *any* one among thy number who hath pitchforked beneath dung-heaps for the evil crystals to be found there?"

"No, Goddess blind you!"

Oln Woeck ignored the epithet.

"Be there one among thy number who hath delved in the earth in search of brimstone ore?"

"No!"

"Be there one among thy number who hath mixed the three together, leavening with water?"

"No!"

"Be there one among thy number who hath dried the black cakes, breaking them asunder and, so doing, sifting them?"

"No! Go away, you scabrous creature! We're no practitioners of your cursed Cult, attempting to take the weight of what you imagine to be the world's sin upon your own self-lacerated shoulders! We don't belong—"

The spatter-visaged baldpate sneered.

"Have a care for public utterances of heresy, blacksmith! No one 'belongs,' yet everybody doth—to his neighbors and fellowmen who must be protected from the likes of thy vile little—"

Klem gave a mind-curdling snarl.

Steel rang as it leapt from brass-lined leather. Owaldsohn hurled the wolfhide scabbard aside.

"Have a care yourself, loosemouth! Are you saying because

my son has found a better way to row a boat, he's the sort to play at compounding the forbidden substance?"

"On the contrary, Owaldsohn, 'tis just the other way round!"

Forgetting the sword in his right hand, Owaldsohn lunged forward, wrapping a black and mighty left about the Cult leader's throat, lifting him from the ground. As a pair of Brothers stepped out of the column to assist their leader, they were met at the front margin of the yard by a pair of slavering, curly-pelted guards who brought them to a halt.

Oln Woeck's eyes bulged, but there was no terror to be found in them, only derisive laughter which, shut off, could not escape his lips.

Ilse pounded her husband's back with the copper staff before he flung the robed man away.

Oln Woeck staggered back but didn't fall.

He coughed long and rackingly.

For his part, Sedrich had listened carefully to the ritual questions. His mother had been wrong, he thought, very wrong to hold his father back. If only someone would stand up to these crazy-men—and great Owaldsohn was just the man to do it—life would be different. Better.

It was the first time it had occurred to Sedrich that his mother could be wrong about anything. He didn't much welcome the revelation, nor what it told him of the Sisterhood she was sworn to.

Still, she had been right, after all, about reading and writing.

Charcoal . . . easy enough, "ground fine as flour," the man had said. And dungheap crystals—mother called it nitre, keeping a supply for healing purposes, along with what Oln Woeck in his ignorance had referred to as brimstone ore.

He wondered about the proportions. He knew he could expect no help from his mother or from anybody else. They were all too frightened of Oln Woeck and of the Brotherhood of the Cult of Jesus in Hell. He could only depend upon himself. As soon as these meddlesome old men had gone along their way, he'd take advantage of what they'd unintentionally given away. Perhaps he'd borrow a little from the fear which froze everyone about him into inaction, transforming it into appropriate precautions. Most of all, he'd take advantage of what his mother had insisted he learn.

Exploding shoulder-bow quarrels—what an idea!

Some hiding places—that's what he'd need for the experimental materials he would assemble, for the notes and drawings which must precede them. He'd hurry upstairs to his loft and write down the ingredients the Brotherhood had so thoughtfully listed for him!

Frae Hethristochter

No man can change the words of God . . . and if their
turning away is distressful for thee . . . so be not
thou one of the ignorant. Answer only will those who
hear. . . .

—The *Koran*, Sura VI

"Common wisdom"—Sedrich lowered his preadolescent
voice to a timbre he imagined sagelike—"when it speaks upon
such matters, has it they were sorcerers who drove the real
human beings out of Eldworld long ago."

Dust coiled itself in hair-thin sheets in the narrow rays of
afternoon sunlight pouring through the rafter-gaps at the front
of the shed. Sedrich, for the moment, had been left alone with
his dangerous dreams. Owaldsohn had departed with the
dawn, leading a two-dog cart laden with fresh-finished
shoulder-bow prods for a neighboring village.

Nine-year-old Frae Hethristochter sneezed, blinking tears,
and took a step backward, out of Sedrich's dust cloud. The
little girl shaded her blue eyes, a faint chill nuzzling the back
of her neck as she looked toward the ocean, imagining the

squat vessels of evil magicians lurking just beyond her safe, familiar horizons.

At last she turned toward her grime-covered friend with something resembling benediction. "What manner of people are they, Sedrich, d'you think?"

Sedrich set the bonded glass container, huge as a pumpkin, down on the bench. He stepped round the piled-up parts of what someday might become a spare dogcart. Somehow, they set a nagging tingle loose inside his mind. He'd thought of trying to apply his boat-crank to the thing—the reason for its having been reduced to constituent components—but the effort he foresaw, of propelling the resulting contrivance, was matched solely by the mechanical difficulty of fitting a high-mounted crank-shaft to a low-mounted axle.

This had been no problem with the little boat; it's gunwales had been just the right height above the waterline.

He frowned, dismaying Frae. Why, whenever he tripped over this junkheap, did he think upon the ocean—and of rippling yellow prairies westward, where his father's name had become known to all Helvetii? It was a region of forbidding, blood-soaked reputation.

Sedrich covered his consternation with a gruffness learned from Owaldsohn, his adolescent maladroitness adding insult to an injury he'd no idea he inflicted.

Over his shoulder he observed, "Mother says in Eldworld the Cult of Jesus, or something like unto it, was that powerful—all must belong, or else—and the Sisterhood small and powerless and hidden."

"In olden days," Frae agreed (she, too, echoing what Ilse had taught her), "there were a lot more people. The world was crowded."

In absent concentration, she picked at a splinter in one of the weathered shed uprights, watching with big eyes as the boy went about his mysterious boylike business.

From the corner of his own eye Sedrich watched the only friend he owned of his approximate age. Had he thought to, he'd have admitted—with reluctance—in the end he'd likeliest find himself wedded to her. That she pleased his eyes—though such be true—no one might have extracted from him with red-hot pliers. He was curious—shy to the point of paralysis—about the way of men with women.

Frae might satisfy his curiosity, and more.

Yet he resisted such thoughts, not for his age alone, but because it was natural to resent being forced, by circumstance or other people.

In particular, by other people.

In general, he'd learned—was learning, there was still this silliness with the rowboat—to keep wary silence regarding his ambitions. That he shared a bit of them with Frae betrayed beginnings of a certain feeling toward her which, in truth, confused him. It, too, might prove a mistake—or lead to one.

Ah, well, even great grim Owaldsohn had embarrassing failures, did he not, as was the fate of all who aspired to new things? The gravest of the ropy scars which marked his massive torso came not from mortal encounters with the Red Men westward but from an ill-fated attempt to accustom an unwilling whitetail to dogcart harness.

Not looking up again, Sedrich said, "And there were all kinds of strange animals: horses—sort of like a big deer without horns, so big you could climb on—unicorns, cats . . ."

Frae wrinkled her brow. "Cats?"

"Sure. They killed rats we have ourselves to kill now. Something bad happened to them—I don't know as I believe what books say of them, anyway. But oxen there were, and gryphons . . ."

All of these existed now, both children knew, only in Ilse's many illustrated volumes and in talismanic carvings venerated by the superstitious. Sedrich wasn't certain he believed any such had ever in truth existed.

On a block of granite which served as one of his father's anvils he began making circular motions with the pumice he'd been using to sand the resin smooth. Before long, the softer stone was flat again. Not quite aware how closely his companion watched him, Sedrich went back to the jar, hoping this time he'd finish, the curved walls of the lightweight container would be uniform and smooth, before the pumice block, growing hollow in his hand, needed truing up again.

There wasn't much left.

It was expensive.

Sedrich knew his curious aptitudes were frowned upon, not by the Cult alone, but by most Helvetii. His parents—each for a particular reason—had encouraged him since first he'd shown interest in tinkering. Owaldsohn himself was bothered in the middle of the night by more ideas than ever he would, in his lifetime, have opportunity to explore. Ilse felt, among a people dominated by legends of the long ago, it was time something new got written into her books and those of her Sisters—and, of course, there was the visible joy with which the doing of these things filled her son.

"But how," asked Frae, thinking Sedrich something of a sorcerer himself, "can you catch lightning in that thing?"

Motherless, with her father being the sort he was, the little girl had been neglected in the matter of her education. Unconsciously she twisted her fingers in the front of her simple shift. It was an honest question, without a trace of whine, disbelief, or disapproval. If Sedrich said he could do a thing, he could do it. Frae simply wanted to know how such a thing was possible.

Meanwhile, if he, at age eleven, sometimes demonstrated an outward, boyish indifference, even unwitting cruelty, toward her, neither realized it consciously.

He inspected his handiwork. "I don't know. Last winter did my blankets crackle with a faint blue light when shaken in a dark room. Yestermorning I awoke with an idea that I might make miniature lightning thuswise."

He looked up, his dark eyes intent upon a sky he couldn't see within the shed. "Perhaps the clouds are like blankets. They look woolly enough. And the greater lightning they make as they tumble can be trapped."

He shook his head, returned attention to his work. "Anyway, I mean to try."

Frae nodded meekly, golden curls bobbing. She remembered that people struck by lightning perish, at the least fall deaf or blind. Should aught ill befall *her* Sedrich—she pushed the thought away, and with it the incriminating possessive.

At the quenching bath the boy washed the last of the sanding dust off the big jar which Old Roger had given him. It had come off the mandrel a bit lopsided, with odd bumps and sticky patches where the trade-secret hardener hadn't been mixed into the resin evenly. Sedrich would have been well pleased to have it, experiment or none.

There were always uses for such.

While the jar dried by the forge, he turned to a pile of soft-tanned doe leather upon another bench. Unfolding it, he peeled up a corner of the lead-tin alloy he'd beaten to paper thinness inside its folds—this trade secret being one of his father's—with a rawhide hammer whose rounded face was near the size of his own.

"Anyhaps, when all those olden people died, the few left—those the Invader didn't slaughter, I guess—discovered the New World. Don't ask me how. In the year 1078, it was, o'er three hundred years ago."

"And what," asked Frae, "happened thirteen hundred ninety-five years ago? Why count we the years thus?"

" 'Twas not the Goddess' birthday, for She is timeless and forever young, the Sisters say. Nor e'en of the Brotherhood's Lord Jesus, whom they reckon came into the world more than two millennia ago. Father avows 'tis the way that the Invader calculates the years, from some event significant to them and no one else—that having lost everything first to the Death and then to them, our people took their calendar and brought it with them here. Nobody knows for certain," the boy concluded. "Not e'en my mother. Perhaps 'twas then the world began."

Planting a loose confederation of settlements upon the eastern shoreline of the new continent, the survivors, Sedrich knew, of the Mortality, of the Invasion, and of the desperate journey across the great ocean, had come to owe much, for their initial survival and eventual prosperity, to the teachings of another people they'd found here, Iroquois and other nations of Red Men.

"Not those we Helvetii fight with now upon occasion," he told the little girl, "but others, with whom we trade, from whom we first obtained our plainest, most wholesome foods."

When the pliant hide was spread upon the bench, he began with care to separate it from the foil he'd made. Enough was there to cover his jar twice over, just as he'd planned.

He began applying it to the inside of the container, molding and smoothing as he went.

There were, indeed, other Red Men. As the Helvetii trickled westward toward a legendary range of Great Blue Mountains no white man had seen and lived to tell of, they'd discovered—the discovery resulting in a series of violent small-scale wars—the presence of another culture.

"Native tribes," Sedrich explained, mimicking Owaldsohn now. "Their mechanic arts are superior to our own—though none could stand long before my father's war-dogs or his greatsword *Murderer*."

Having covered the inside of the jar, Sedrich applied foil to the outside. He'd turned a wooden stopple for it on his father's lathe. Into this he now inserted a short, thick bit of wire to which he'd fastened a length of copper chain.

"Father's told me there are rough, peculiar tracks across those plains, well worn. Frae, I am most curious about those, for, by description, they were beaten out neither by human feet nor by dogcarts."

He assumed a crafty expression. "And I think I know what made them."

He set the foil-covered container on the bench nearest the same lathe upon which he'd fashioned its cover. In its jaws he'd clamped a stranger contraption, a pair wooden dowels glued into a cross. At the ends of its arms were rods of the same resinous material the jar was fashioned from. These were hidden by a yard of wool he'd stitched into a broad, circular band, now hanging from the rafters.

Copper wire ran from the rods, down the wooden arms to the center, along the central shaft toward the chuck. A stiff length of copper lay on the shaft where it came into occasional contact with the revolving wire.

Its other end he fastened to the jar-chain.

"This won't work quite as well as in the wintertime," he observed, putting his foot on the treadle. "The air seems to need to be dry. Perhaps it won't work at all in the daytime."

The lathe began to spin, rubbing the resin rods round in their belt of homespun wool. To Sedrich's satisfaction, he heard the fabric crackle. At least he was making *miniature* lightning— and in a more efficient manner than by shaking blankets. He hoped he was capturing it in his jar. It ought to work, he thought, with two layers of foil to ensure it couldn't leak out.

Resting his hand upon the great iron anvil of the smithy, Sedrich reached across the complicated apparatus, making sure of its connection to the jar. A fat blue spark flashed from the container to his outstretched fingers. With a scream of convulsed muscles, he was tossed across the shed like a toy, slamming against the splintered wall where he slid to the dirt floor.

"Sedrich!" Frae shouted, running to him. She seized his hand, laying her cheek upon it. "Are you still alive?" she asked in a small voice, tears streaming down her face.

Sedrich grunted.

He fluttered his eyelids.

He looked up at her.

He shook his head.

"Methinks"—he grinned—"I've discovered a new means of transportation."

As a timid smile began to creep into her expression of concern, a shadow fell across the front of the shed.

" 'Twould be thought you were more capable of learning, young Sedrich." Hethri Parcifal's voice was deep and apologetic. "Not a week has passed since Oln Woeck led his followers through our village on your account. Your family's troubles with the Cult continue e'en now!"

Confusion wrote itself upon young Sedrich's countenance. He knew his mother was away this afternoon—as was usual. Had there been another incident of some kind with Oln Woeck?

Parcifal passed a weary hand over his eyes. "I see you don't know what I speak of. Ilse takes the Sisterhood's part in conflict 'tween her maternal, nurturative vocation and the paternalistic Cult, concerning a colony of rats discovered upon the latter's unsanitary compound."

He shook his head. " 'Twould *be* no dispute, were her authority not compromised by the mischief you think of to be doing."

Sedrich levered himself to his feet. Involuntarily his eyes went to the deep-shadowed back of the shed where, beneath a tarp, he'd hidden the mortar and pestle in which he'd ground a mixture of charcoal, sulfur, and nitre. There'd been no time, yet, to carry that experimentation further.

"But I was only—"

Parcifal sighed. "It has come to me—believe me, son, I didn't look for it—to be a go-between in life, disputes to resolve among my fellows and to keep the peace. 'Tis a path of moderation."

Bending, he took Frae's elbows, gently lifting the child to her feet.

"I've imperiled my reputation—not to mention my neck, boy—interfering with the Brotherhood on your account and on your father's. Ne'er mind. Like him, 'tis a mad bare-chester you are, boy, a seer of the blood-haze. In the Brotherhood you've earned an enmity which must culminate in disaster, for yourself, your family, for anyone else unfortunate enough to be present when it arrives.

"Come, daughter, we'll leave this young demon—and his corrupting influence—to himself for the time being."

He turned, almost tripping over the pile of dogcart parts. Regaining his balance, to Sedrich he said, "And your *dreams,* boy—yes, I heard you speaking of them ere now—your dreams would accomplish naught save disturb an unspoken truce 'tween our people and the Red tribesmen west. A truce won in your father's time, at a price beyond your powers of imagining."

They left the shed.

As the boy watched their backs diminishing in the twilight, one young and upright, the other bent beyond its years, his eye lighted upon his mother. Ilse Sedrichsfrau stood apart, thin hands folded across the top of her staff, an expression of pain upon her face as she contemplated what had transpired between the man Hethri and her son.

For the first time in Sedrich's memory, she, too, looked old.

V:

Murderer

Marry the spouseless among you, and your slaves and
handmaidens that are righteous. . . .
—The *Koran*, Sura XXIV

In time, as Sedrich somehow knew it would, Hethri Parcifal's
frightened anger passed away. He wasn't the sort long to keep
a grudge—nor, the boy conceded to himself, much of any
other feeling. Such wasn't the manner of "moderation." This
quality in him made a decent neighbor.

Perhaps it would make an amiable father-in-law.

Following that one terrible night, there was, for a time,
peace. The Brotherhood soon discovered others to call upon.
In one respect, at least, Oln Woeck was wrong: fisherfolk, not
from their village alone, but from many neighboring settlements along the coast, found use for Sedrich's "dangerous"
innovation.

Seldom needing to be shown something twice, the boy
forged another boat-crank, without Owaldsohn's help. Then
another. And another. Small thanks to Parcifal, in whose
friendship Sedrich in any case came to feel his father's

51

confidence misplaced, an exception was made where interests of the belly outweighed Helvetian conservatism.

In time, great Owaldsohn's help became necessary. Soon after, it was indispensable. By the following season, the smithy was producing more of Sedrich's simple marine equipment than the remainder of their custom accounted together. Before another twelvemonth was out, father and son were required to find a carpenter to fashion wooden paddle wheels. They'd no time for it themselves.

Three more summers passed in this prosperous, happy wise.

2

"Now the left hand!"

One ankle crossing the other, Owaldsohn lounged against the shed, bearlike arms folded, a malicious grin buried in his white-shot beard. The sun glowed orange atop the razor-edge of the horizon. Klem, beginning to grow old himself, dozed in the afternoon warmth. Willi watched Sedrich's labors with interest.

Sedrich groaned, sweat-drenched, trembling, but obedient to his father's command. His weak wrist ached, bruised in the marrow with what already he'd demanded of it this morning. By turns, he wiped wet palms upon the clout which was all he wore. Shifting the great weapon for another two-handed assault upon a creosoted post planted in the smithy yard, the youth, grown man-tall with time's passage, changed his stance.

Whirling *Murderer* high above his head, he suddenly lengthened his reach with a roar which was half agony, half fury, letting the gleaming steel lash out.

No wood-chips flew. Though the edge bit deep, the heavy tarring upon the post preserved its life somewhat. Whittled remains of a dozen predecessors did dot the yard, making hazardous navigation of a moonless nighttime. They'd have to be dug out ere long.

Levering the great blade free, Sedrich watched the blackened timber "heal" itself for another attack. Cleaning creosote off his father's sword had become almost as arduous as the effort which put it there. In sun, snow, and rain, summer heat and winter cold, he'd repeated these painful motions a hundred times each dawning the last two years. Given another five, his wrists would come to resemble bundled iron staves, his forearms outsizing the calves of many another man.

Another whirl, another scream of unleashed power, another bite into the unyielding butt Sedrich had come to view as a personal enemy. Shock sang up the blade into his tortured wrists.

Yet, with each swing of the legendary *Murderer,* he'd come to appreciate his father's genius more. Seven winters in the forging, beginning when the apprentice smith had been little older than his fifteen-year-old son, the sword was enormous, for grim Owaldsohn was a big man, bigger than Sedrich would ever be. The naked blade spanned a handwidth, its guard three times as wide. When *Murderer* was rested upon its point (which neither Sedrich would think to do in practice), the fist-sized pommel stood even with the younger blacksmith's chin. When the sword was slung across his back, handle high above his head, with the broad guard at his right shoulder, the scabbard-tip slapped the back of his knee.

The grip—fashioned not from leather windings, as was customary with the Helvetii, but of iron disks separated by mandrel-wound glass washers—constituted a third of the entire greatsword, allowing leverage necessary to swing the thing. The broad iron cross-guard tips pointed straight forward, splayed to trap an opponent's weapon. And trap it was, a broad path leading along the flat, polished edges of the unground "forte" onto a wedge of case-hardened steel inset upon the guard-face. This would notch another blade. With a hearty twist of the wielder's wrist, the dinted blade would snap like dried sea-oat.

Survival then became a matter of avoiding the other fellow's jagged stump as it flashed off the guard.

Only half the blade was ground—the foible, Owaldsohn called it, a flimsy naming, Sedrich thought, for such a length of deadly steel as this—sharpened to the whispery keenness of a blade of grass along both edges all the way round its leaf-shaped point.

Yet Owaldsohn's truest genius lay in the fact that, the handwidth blade notwithstanding, *Murderer* balanced at the apex of the breaking-wedge. This miracle had he accomplished only in part by means of the weighted "four-hand" grip. The "fuller," a broad, round-bottomed channel extending from a finger's width behind the point the full length of the foible and halfway down the forte, was responsible. Where it was deepest, the blade felt parchment-thin. Yet in a single stroke (a more practiced stroke than Sedrich yet was capable of delivering), *Murderer* could hew down a tree the diameter of the boy's head.

After decades of war against the western savages, the weapon's sheen betrayed neither nick nor scratch. *Murderer* was a perfect implement. Try as he might, Sedrich could think of no innovation, no alteration of form or fabrication—save perhaps in its monumental proportions—which might have improved it.

This annoyed him.

"Now the right hand for a while, and back to the left!"

But not as much as his father's persistence.

3

Afternoon found Sedrich at the village boatshed, where the weathered pier jutted into the estuary. Save for the young blacksmith, the place was deserted. It was too late in the day for any boats to be departing, too early for any to be coming home.

His tools lay spread about him.

At the request of some of the fishermen, Sedrich was attempting to determine whether it was practical to fit half a dozen of his devices to the steeply curved gunwales of a dory, presently hauled up for repairs. He wasn't the only one, they'd told him, who could get new ideas. Each crank, forged wide for what came close to being a small ship, would be turned by two men, creating a craft which could run swift upon calm water as a whitetail through a forest clearing, keeping its bow into the nastiest swell if caught in unexpected storms.

Sedrich had his doubts about the latter.

Across the water, wading-birds called raucously.

The young man had come to shoulder much responsibility for one of his short years, always busy, his few idle moments filled with sketches, acquiring scrap, altering its shape and composition, pursuing boyhood dreams his custom might have doubted, as he doubted theirs. Despite persistent clamor for more boat-cranks, there was idle time to fill. Ilse, making certain of it, pressed this wisdom upon her men: labor must give way to rest and play, else accomplish less and less. That her husband's "rest" and her son's "play" resembled what they did for a living, she could but shrug to herself about and live with.

Thinking himself alone, he knelt beside the huge canted dory with his stick measurer. A shadow fell across the hull, startling him. He whirled, the stick becoming *Murderer* in his reflex-guided hands. This he acted to control before the newcomer could notice.

"Good day, Sedrich, son of Sedrich," a silvery voice commented. "Pray do not slice me with yon mighty weapon, warrior, for I assure you I mean no harm."

Frae smiled shyly and then laughed. Sedrich joined her, flinging the stick aside as he rose.

"Good day, gentle neighbor. 'Tis no warrior I am"—he flexed his much-abused wrist, remembering the morning's pointed comments to that effect from his father—"but tradesman and artisan." He grinned. "Hast need of my talents?"

A soft salted breeze lifted her unbound golden hair. Falling past her shoulders, it framed a smooth, well-boned and pink-cheeked face, full-lipped, with an upturned nose. Her teeth were white and even. Her eyes, beneath long lashes, reflected the glory of the afternoon sky. Improving upon it, Sedrich found himself thinking, and not only because there were storm clouds cluttering the seaward horizon.

Frae's shift was of blue-dyed cotton reaching to her knees, rope-fastened at the waist. A pair of ribbons tied in bows held

the simple garment upon her shoulders. From her rope belt
hung scissors, token that she was mistress of her father's
household. Sedrich had fashioned them himself, the first gift
he'd given anyone outside his family.

Jest still twinkling in her eye, she began, "Methinks——"

Never knowing whence the impulse came, in a swift and
certain gesture he seized her by the wrist, pulled her close,
kissed her upon the mouth, feeling her body pliant against his,
back straight and slender, hips rounded. To his bewilderment,
she didn't return the kiss—the first for both—but stood as if
nailed to the spot, then burst into tears. Confused, Sedrich
stepped back awkwardly, catching his heel upon the dory.

He all but fell.

Frae advanced, placing a white hand upon his forearm.
Wiping her eyes, she smiled, the truest smile, Sedrich would
have sworn, he'd ever seen of her, unreserved and gay.

"I'm this night to be inducted into the Sisterhood. Your
mother will perform the ceremony. It means I'm a woman
grown."

Laying his brown hand over hers, Sedrich scowled at the
gray pier-planking, then looked into her eyes. Enormous they
seemed, and infinitely trusting. Induction might mean naught
but that she was another childless woman—were she not being
groomed to succeed Ilse.

Aloud, he answered, "Frae, I'm glad for you. Were men
permitted, I'd stand witness myself."

"Dear my Sedrich, I'd in mind another ceremony. 'Tis said
among women it's bad luck to be inducted as a . . . as a
virgin."

She reached for the rope at her waist, pulling it free.

He caught her scissors before they slid to the ground.

"Bad luck?" he croaked, watching his fingers, living their
own life, pull the knot from one of the ribbons which held her
shift up. The hair stood out upon the back of his neck as a
wash of prickly weakness coursed through his body. A corner
of the fabric fell in a diagonal, exposing a soft, small, rounded
breast. She kept her eyes on his, blushed as he touched the
nipple with a trembling finger and it came erect. With a
tremor, her flesh reclothed itself in goosebumps.

Frae had indeed become a woman.

With clumsy hands, Sedrich pushed the shoulder of her shift back into place, casting his eye about to see if they were watched.

"My own boat's at the end of the pier. We won't be noticed upon the estuary."

A few minutes later, Frae sat in the bow, a hand upon her undone shoulder—for she refused to tie it up again—while Sedrich labored at the paddles. He was glad of the work, as he couldn't will his hands to stop shaking. All of his strength seemed concentrated in one lone embarrassing place. Moments later—what seemed hours to the youth—the spun glass of the hull brushed through upthrust vegetation near a sandbar a hundred yards from the pier. The far shore was unoccupied by man or beast.

The wading-birds had long since fled at their approach.

"The trouble with your invention," the girl observed, taking the end of the other shoulder-ribbon between forefinger and thumb, "is that we can't lie down in this boat." She sighed, smiling up at him from beneath her lashes. "Thus progress claims its price."

He'd been thinking through this problem himself. "I, er, brought some tools. I can unship it."

"Stay, good blacksmith, I've a better idea."

Pulling at the ribbon, she stood, letting the shift drop to the floor, and, after a single delicious instant before the boy's widened eyes, vanished over the side with a salty splash.

Sedrich followed her.

The water was deeper than their toes could reach. They played about for a time, at last treading together in the pale shadow beneath the translucent boat, out of the glare of the sun. Sedrich had his right hand upon the gunwale, she her left. Once again, an arm about her waist, he pulled her close.

Her nipples brushed his chest.

This time she didn't weep but returned his probing kiss. This time there was no shift, however sheer, to prevent him knowing the woman she'd become. As she hung before him, his free hand roved with a demanding and joyful will of its own.

His wrist no longer pained him.

For her own part, in their first magic hour together, Frae wasn't shy. She began to know him as he knew her, taking the same delight in the learning. When he pulled her body against his, guided only by a boyhood knowledge of animals and what he'd seen in books, she tried to help.

"This isn't going to work," he acknowledged in frustration as they hung from the side of the boat. "Not with one hand apiece. I think we're supposed to be lying down."

Frae touched his cheek and giggled. "I've an idea," she told him. "You hold on to the boat for both of us, and I'll hold on to you."

So she did, lowering her body, wrapping both her arms about his neck, her legs about his waist. She gasped, surprised less by the pain she had awaited than by its absence. For some while, Sedrich was quiet, shocked at new sensations coursing through him, reflexes of lower back and thigh he'd not known he possessed. Frae closed her eyes, brushing her mouth upon his, upon his cheeks, his neck, his shoulders, sighing.

She bit gently at his lips.

Abruptly, an explosion in his loins disminded him, wiping away memory and ego, the very instinct for survival. With an openmouthed exclamation, he lost his purchase on the boat-edge, plunging them both into the water over their heads.

The next he knew, he was back in the air, both hands locked under one of hers upon the gunwale, while she pounded his back.

"*Sedrich! Sedrich!*" Frae demanded, fear filling her voice. "Are you all right?"

He coughed, freeing one of his hands, then turned to gaze upon the loveliest face the world had ever seen.

"Love," he told her, caressing a wet strand of hair back into place at her temple, "I misdoubt that e'er I'll be all right again!"

4

That night, a sleepless Sedrich followed his mooncast shadow out into the smithy. The rent in the cloud-cluttered sky was temporary. A few stars twinkled through, but it would rain again before morning.

They'd made love again that afternoon, he and Frae, a second, third, and indescribable fourth time under his up-turned rowboat, beached across the estuary from the village while a summer deluge hammered upon its keel. The third time, Frae found out what had almost drowned her Sedrich and was grateful to be lying upon her back upon solid, if somewhat sandy, ground.

Thunder grumbled to the west.

Lighting a candle, Sedrich inspected the "tiller" of his vehicle: a fifth wheel trailing a man's height behind the other four, controlled by a bar stretching from the bow of the machine. As with his rowboats, he'd given up the idea of independent gearing. It had proven beyond his mechanical capability to produce such a system which didn't suffer fragility.

Outside, lightning flickered.

As he crawled beneath the hull, he espied, at the shed-front, a pair of small, moccasin-shod feet. For an instant, his heart leapt within his chest. Then he saw they were not Frae's.

"Sedrich?"

"Yes, Mother? I'll be out in just a moment."

He'd have to do something about the pinion gear. One thump from a rock or tree-stump as the machine traveled across country, he'd be afoot again.

Ilse didn't wait. "Dear, your father and I discussed this. We decided I should be the one to tell you. . . ."

Sedrich seized the front axle, hauled himself from beneath his machine and rose, wiping imaginary grime upon his breechclout.

"Mother, I know the village disapproves of my land-boat. Give them time. They came round where my rowboat was——"

Ilse set her glass-paned hurricane lantern upon a bench, strode into the shed. She took Sedrich's right hand in both of hers.

"My son, this does not concern your work. Naught wouldn't I give to avoid telling you this. I wish now I'd listened to your father. He's courageous. He argued with me o'er it."

The wind had quickened, driving rain-spatter a few paces into the shed. Sedrich shook his head in confusion, unnamed fear beginning to creep within him. Was there something amiss with his father's health? Owaldsohn was slowing down a little. Natural, but——

" 'Tis about Frae, Sedrich." Ilse's face contorted with the pain she imagined her son was about to feel. "We inducted her into the Sisterhood tonight, as you know. Then . . ." She looked away from the youth's questioning expression, saying forcefully, "You must forget her, Sedrich. Leave her be. There are other girls——"

"What are you talking about, Mother? Not in this village, none of them *Frae!*"

"All right, in other villages. You're young, dear, there's plenty of time."

Sedrich's fear was turning into a hard, fiery knot in his midsection. He would, in future time, come to think of this moment as that in which a lifelong fury had begun.

"But, Mother, I thought you and——"

"We do, dear, we love her as much as you do. In a sense, I brought her up, right alongside you. She was practically my daughter already. In the eyes of the Sisterhood, she *is* my daughter."

Dread etched its acid pathway through him. Had they—had he injured her in some manner?

"What's amiss? She isn't sick, or——"

"No, Sedrich, naught such. We've but just heard, dear. Oh, my poor, darling Sedrich, Hethri's been 'keeping the peace' again. He's promised Frae in marriage—*to Oln Woeck!*"

VI:

The Twisted Sails

I see you are prospering and I fear for you the
chastisement of an encompassing day.
—The *Koran*, Sura XI

"Dear my Sedrich," Frae pleaded, "calm yourself."

A dozen gulls played catch me with each other, diving,
tilting in their awkward, stiffened way as they turned.

" 'Tis but for a little time, and then . . ."

"Then *what?*" he responded bitterly.

She watched him test the edge of his dagger upon the fine
golden hairs of his left forearm. It always made her nervous.
He frowned, returned to honing it upon a pair of angled stone
rods he'd brought with him, set into a block of walnut.

"Dagger" was a relative expression. The blade was a model
Sedrich's father had made before the forging of the greatsword
Murderer. It stretched from the tip of the young man's middle
finger to his elbow, in form a perfect miniature of the fabled
weapon.

Frae twisted both slim hands in the loose fabric of her shift,

61

lifting the hem in the front, an unconscious gesture she'd brought with her from childhood.

If only she could make him understand!

"I'll stave Oln Woeck off, beloved, I promise. I'll delay him, make excuses. I'll not be fourteen for a month yet, perhaps 'twill serve. You'll see . . ."

He turned toward her, his face colored and distorted with hatred. "I'll see his rat's blood covering this blade e'er he touches you!" Once again he ran the sharpened foible between the stones. "If that old tattoo thinks he can . . ."

The pair were at their favorite meeting-place along the estuary, across the brackish water from the village, well away from observation by their neighbors. Above, the sky was sullen-looking, but it wouldn't rain today, nor even yet tomorrow—save perhaps in Sedrich's heart, Frae thought. Why was it aught he loved, aught he desired of life, was denied him by the beliefs of their kind? Why couldn't people leave him, and his dreams, alone? Why couldn't they . . .

But it was useless.

'Twas like reasoning with the Red savages Owaldsohn's sword had been created for. Some men—on both sides of any argument—comprehended naught but steel. If she couldn't reason *her* man out of it, she was certain that he'd kill Oln Woeck, believing they could escape to another village. Perhaps even to his beloved, mysterious west. That wouldn't be the end of it, however. Wherever they went, whatever they did, they'd finish hating one another for the evil they'd each taken part in. Aught they'd fought for would be lost. This she knew.

Or at least felt she knew.

Sedrich slammed the dagger back into the brass-throated scabbard at his waist, disassembled the sharpener, tucked it in its quilted deerskin bag, and tossed it into the boat which they'd drawn up on the beach. Frae sat down beside the boat, legs folded beneath her, drawing meaningless lines in the sand with her slim fingers.

"Sedrich." She looked up at him, his gaze striking her with what felt like physical force, somewhere just below her navel.

Her voice she kept mild as always, but she could feel that she was blushing.

"Aye, love?" he answered, despite their troubles breaking into a grin at the sight of her—or perhaps at the sound of her voice. He really did love her, then, she thought to herself. She'd grown up beside this . . . this miraculous creature, seen him daily, always adored him, and yet each day he was like a new and wonderful stranger to her. Sometimes, as now, a frightening one. "What?"

She gathered courage. "I've a way for us. And 'tis a matter of giving life, not, as you contemplate, taking it."

He scowled at her, then, seeing its effect upon her, softened his expression, explaining, " 'Tis more from puzzlement than irritation, dearest. I can feel no irritation where you're concerned—even when I ought—but I can feel puzzlement."

"I often do."

"Silly," she laughed, "we could make our *own* child! No one could part us afterward, for we'd have proven our love."

Sedrich reacted in mock astonishment, clapping a hand to his forehead. "Of course! Why hasn't this occurred to me?"

He joined her in laughter, blushing as well, then reached across the small distance separating them. In a moment her shift fell away.

He began assisting her with her plan.

2

Thus passed many happy months for Frae Hethristochter and Sedrich Sedrichsohn, yet with a cloud hovering over them. She turned fourteen, he sixteen soon after. Together they labored with a loving will to escape her father's intentions—and the foul-smelling clutches of yellow-eyed Oln Woeck.

For his part, Old Woeck seemed content to be patient. To be sure, the customary usages of the Helvetii were observed. He brought himself to frequent dinners at Hethri Parcifal's house. He was at all times accompanied by his pair of bodyguards—or whatever they were. In discussion of this, Sedrich told her of a long-ago conversation overheard at his father's forge.

They'd been working, waiting as an order of leaf-springs slow-cooled in clay jackets.

The customer had waited with them.

"Aye," Owaldsohn observed, testing the outer layer of clay with a bit of straw, "some Red Men be our friends. Others our foes." He turned toward the customer, beetling his shaggy brows at the man. "'Tis a longevous fellow knows the difference."

There was a disbelieving snort.

"There be but two sorts of Red Man, live ones and good ones," insisted the customer, a captain-of-one-hundred from a village militia to the south. "The heathens believe not as we. Thus you've said of them yourself, son of Owald, red-handed Slayer of the Plains."

Owaldsohn grimaced. He'd never liked the titles given him in honor of his crimson deeds. Looking at Sedrich rather than the captain, the blacksmith observed, "Nor often do neighbors, such as our good friend Hethri Parcifal, nor e'en your mother and I, at times."

With a wink at his son, he turned to the other adult. "Yet we seem to get along, don't we?"

Sedrich had doubts, as always, about Parcifal. He ran a hand through Willi's coat, the fingers coming away oily.

Old Klem slumbered by the forge, snoring quietly.

The captain said in answer, "They worship neither God nor Goddess!"

The blacksmith mused. "Thus 'tis said—wrongly. We be the heathens in their eyes. Red Men worship powerful beings dwelling among the Great Blue Mountains, far to the west. I've not seen the like myself, mind you—the mountains I mean, for no one e'er sees any god—still, I've witnessed many a stranger sight."

The militiaman looked first to Sedrich, then his father, lowering his voice. "I've heard it said that among the Red devils, some are wont to couple with other men."

He gave an elaborate shiver, folding his arms as if this settled the matter of the Red Man's fitness for extermination.

Owaldsohn tossed his son a look of concern. Some months

would pass yet before Owaldsohn would acknowledge knowing of his son's first afternoon upon the estuary with Frae. Meanwhile, as with many fathers, even good ones like the son of Owald, his offspring's readiness to hear about such things was a matter to him of embarrassed conjecture.

"Aye, 'tis rumored," he said at last, his voice soft, "as are many things."

Sedrich spoke up, his face reddening. "The same's true among the Brotherhood, Father. Or thus I've heard whispered."

"Aye, boy," replied the captain with a sour grin, glancing round to see if they were overheard. "Such things are best *always* whispered."

3

Now, months later, Frae wondered still about that conversation. It had ceased, of late, being a matter of idle speculation, for her or Sedrich. If such whisperings about the Brotherhood—or at least its local leader—were truthful, then she was confused.

There would come a day, no doubt, when Oln Woeck would be invited to bathe with the Parcifals. Later yet . . .

Sedrich said he didn't care if Oln Woeck buggered he-goats, observing that the old man certainly smelled as if he did. Frae would have agreed had she been clearer about the meaning of the word "bugger." To be sure, the Cultist never walked out without his retinue of underwitted, overmuscled—yet somehow soft-looking—young men.

But if men were what Oln Woeck preferred to bed, what did he want with her?

Frae shuddered, imagining obscene rites in secret places.

Between sweet stolen moments together, Frae watched Sedrich sharpen his knife. At nights she often glimpsed him keeping watch upon her from the house next door.

Meantime, week by week, Sedrich's land-boat began assuming its proper shape. He'd abandoned his experiments with the awkward dogcart, converting a rowboat contributed by his friend Old Roger the resiner, one considered by its former owner to be beyond repair. For his purpose, its parchment-thin translucent fiberglass hull was perfect.

Wheels she'd watched him fashion, taking the lightest, strongest design their people possessed—more trade secrets, this time from the wheelwright, Hillestadt—doubling the diameter, halving the thickness. This was necessary, he explained, determined by his boyhood experiences with the wheelbarrow in his mother's garden. The bigger a wheel, the bigger the bumps it could get over. The roads round their village were nothing to brag of, having taken their courses from the sheep driven over them for hundreds of years.

At the stern of the little craft, she helped him step his peculiar mast. Sedrich had fashioned it from resin-filled glass fabric, upon a long, greased hardwood mandrel. A hollow tube, in diameter the width of his palm and mounted in a block of laminated hardwood, he'd begun fashioning sails for it, using broad strips of cloth likewise stiffened with resin. These rode upon half a dozen booms, above and below, which, in turn, were fixed to lightweight steel rings encircling the mast.

They'd spent many a day together—days she ought to have spent indoors with the housework—while he lathe-cut the cylindrical bearings which bore upon the mast, letting the rings turn without friction.

The machinery wasn't complicated. Sedrich's genius lay, Frae realized, in having conceived such a thing in the first place. The lower ring sat upon a great hollow gear intermeshing with a worm—the middle section of the boat's rear axle. The upper ring he raised and lowered by means of a line passing through the hollow mast.

There came at last a day when all he wanted for a first ride was a good stiff breeze. Such were plentiful where they lived, courtesy, each dawning and sunset, of the great ocean upon whose shores their little village sat. That first morning, thinking Frae home asleep, Sedrich pushed his craft to a bluff where a sandy pathway tipped over toward the water. From behind a dune she watched as he raised sails, waiting for the wind to begin turning them, for the gear to move the worm which moved the wheels. He glanced about, obviously worrying about Oln Woeck—among others—hoping, at this time of the morning, no one would see him. But for Frae, concealed by sand and seaside plant growth, no one did. It was a good thing for his pride, if not his safety.

Nothing happened.

The sails filled, straining the mast, tautening the guyline running from a sprit aft, slacking that which ran to the bow. Nothing else came to pass. Humiliated, he furled his sails, pushed his useless craft back to the shed. He sat down to think. As much beyond her years, in her own way, as her lover, Frae crept home unseen.

She never mentioned his first failure to him.

Next morning, Sedrich and Frae were in the same places at the same time. Realizing the feature which allowed him to lower the upper set of booms also allowed him to raise the lower set, he'd contrived a lever, with a spare bearing at its end, to lift the hollow gear from engagement with the worm. Freed of their load, the sails began to turn. Round and round they turned, faster and faster, the ends of the booms they strained against becoming an indistinguishable blur.

He let the lever rise in his hand to engage the gear.

Disaster exploded round him as the course teeth struck the worm. Sedrich had expressed worries about the stresses his hollow gear would endure. He'd built well. It tore the worm from the gunwales, hurling it a hundred paces—just as Owaldsohn had once done with the boat-crank—showering splinters, metal scrap, and fiberglass debris.

"Sedrich!"

This time, despite herself, Frae ran forward, driven by despair. He was too stunned to protest. Even together, they'd had to get his father's help—Willi and Klem trotting along for the fun—to haul the ruin back to the shed.

With greater patience than most children his age, and with the passage of much time, Sedrich improved upon his boat. Sometimes enthusiastic, sometimes afraid, Frae watched and helped. He learned that the lower and upper boom-rings must be somehow connected to keep the sails from twisting about the mast—which had been the second most obvious result of his most disastrous experiment. He contrived clever arrangements of gears, enabling him to engage the system without destroying it.

In the next trial he acquired a scar across his back which he'd carry to the grave.

Frae sewed him back together in the manner Ilse and the Sisterhood had taught her, stifling tears of sympathetic anguish and unfulfilled terror. This disaster taught him that he must redesign his steering system. Thus he abandoned the fifth wheel, learning to turn those upon each side of the craft at differing speeds.

This led to inventing a way to move the boat backward. On one good, windy afternoon, he'd driven it into a thicket whose spines he'd to endure to push the boat back by hand.

Frae watched all this with horrified fascination. As the machinery grew more reliable, she took rides with him as he labored to increase the land-boat's speed.

Meanwhile, she'd encountered less difficulty putting off Oln Woeck than she'd thought possible. Sedrich said the old man was loath to take a bath of any kind, ritual or aughtwise. Time passed, and it was upon one such ride across the back roads of the village, at the exhilarating speed of a doddering oldster, that she explained to the one man she loved how in the winter she'd give birth to his child.

Sedrich slammed the clutch out, kicked the brake-lever, bringing the vehicle to a halt.

"Out of the boat!" he ordered.

Fear seized at the girl. "Sedrich, have I thus displeased you?"

Seeing he'd frightened her, Sedrich placed a gentle hand upon her arm. "No, dearest, I'm not displeased. But riding in this contraption is too dangerous. I'll not have you hurt yourself or lose our child."

Frae fumed aloud, protesting.

Still, inside her was a warm glow—only partly because of their child-to-come.

VII:

The Sacred Heart

Is there not in Gehenna a lodging for those that are proud?

—The *Koran*, Sura XXXIX

"With me"—Ilse laughed—" 'twas sardines."

She folded the knitting in her lap and gazed up at the ceiling, her thoughts focused not upon flickering shadows thrown there by the great fireplace—where a kettle of sweet cider simmered—but seventeen years in her past.

"I'd thought tales women told of such yearnings were mere jest. Yet, I trow, had Owaldsohn not found a fishmonger willing to be awakened many a night, methinks I'd have died of longing."

Beside her upon the divan, Frae laughed, taking another bite of the great red onion she'd just set upon an end-table.

"Aye," remembered Owaldsohn, "people roundabout've been saying e'er since there's something fishy about me!"

The blacksmith grinned, scratching black Klem between the ears. The dog turned blind adoring eyes upon his master. Owaldsohn, his legs outstretched before him, lounged in a broad-backed chair before the fire, doing nothing. It was for him a rare moment of relaxation. His long hair was nearly white, as was his furry chest, but muscles bulged with latent power where they were exposed by his sleeveless vest. Across the carved wooden arms of the chair lay *Murderer* in its wolfhide scabbard. He'd just finished oiling the great blade.

Frae's blue eyes twinkled in the firelight, dimples showing. She, too, had knitting in her lap. Both women were preparing tiny clothing, impelled, no doubt, by the sight of the blizzard piling up outside to the halfway point of the night-blackened window.

"I don't know what we'd have done, had we not come to you." Sedrich nodded to his parents.

Out of grudging self-protection, he, too, took a bite from Frae's gigantic onion before returning to his work. Willi whimpered, wanting some as well.

It was denied him.

"Knowing all we know of such things, we'd have been in utter darkness about what was happening with her. I still am, half the time."

The young man sat cross-legged at the girl's feet, a yard of thin, soft deerskin in his own lap. In his hands were a bit of dull-tipped antler and a fist-size lump of glassy stone. With the horn, he bore down hard upon a corner of the flint.

There was a crackle.

"Damn!" he shouted, throwing stone and horn down, sucking at a knuckle where dark blood welled from a small, straight-sided cut. "How do the Red Men do it?"

"They don't"—Owaldsohn guffawed—"Whene'er they can get steel trade-points from us. What make you there, anywise?"

Sedrich gave the man a brief, peculiar look. "Why, naught of import, Father. Another experiment."

2

Outside the snowbanked window, with little save his misery to keep him warm, Hethri Parcifal listened.

Things were coming to a critical pass. He couldn't pretend much longer that he didn't know his daughter was with child. Already the village women were looking at him in the same wise as just before his wife, Frae's mother, had . . .

No use thinking about that.

Nor could he pretend the fact that Frae spent all her time with the next-door neighbors—instead of with the man he'd chosen for her—had aught to do with her employment.

Peering through the dense-steamed window, he watched Sedrich, intent upon his mysterious flint-knapping, wondering what vile mischief the young devil was preparing now, there in that same lap where he'd ruined Parcifal's only child.

Just like her faithless—no!

Backing upon his frozen belly through the snowdrift, Parcifal was grateful to Owaldsohn for the oversolicitude the blacksmith was wont to show his dogs. He'd not leave them out upon a night like this, bred to it though they be. As they baked, indolent, before the fire, Parcifal could approach without risk of their fangs and listen.

And plan.

A prudent distance away, he rose, brushing wet, heavy snow from his clothing. Racing to his own house, cold and dark by contrast to the Owaldsohns', lonely, he dragged his own dogs from the kennel, hitched them to their cart. They snarled and nipped at one another, tangling their traces. Seating himself in the cart, he whipped them to attention, drove them out into the road.

Too far it was to trek this night afoot to the compound of the Brotherhood of Jesus in Hell.

The ride, five minutes' walk upon a summer's day, took more than an hour, the dogs just able to haul the cart through the wind-drift, their master squinting through the driven flakes to steer them. He reached the village headquarters of the Cult sooner than he knew, however, passing between the gateposts without seeing them. Aside from the few candles the penurious flagellants allowed themselves, no other light was there to tell him he'd arrived.

In the middle of the compound yard, he stopped, handing

the reins to the sick-looking probationary in a dirty robe who'd unwittingly served as a milepost.

The tattoos at the fellow's temples were as yet seeping raw.

"Take these animals somewhere. Let them warm up." He indicated the cart. "There is food for them there. See you give it to them, instead of distributing it among your number."

"As always, Hethri Parcifal, thou'rt the soul of generosity," a voice behind him wheezed in the darkness.

Parcifal turned to see Oln Woeck watching him, soiled robe pulled up against the cold, a humorless half-smile upon the old man's thin lips. Behind him, more shadow than substance, were his eternal pair of young, husky companions.

"As always, Oln Woeck, your order pays as little as it can get away with for aught it takes. And that is plenty. I bear it— and you—few charitable thoughts."

"There we differ, dearest friend. In my heart, I've naught but the most cordial thoughts for thee and thine, *good* Hethri Parcifal, peacekeeper and paragon."

Parcifal shuddered in response, perhaps only with the cold.

The sole illumination in the yard streamed from the open double doors of the common central building, where a circle of Brothers knelt about the reclining form of one of their own number. The man rested upon a raised platform, the focal point of light from tallow candles resting in every niche and wall-projection visible. Even out here in the frozen air, the odor of putrefaction was unmistakable.

Curious, Parcifal repressed an urge to retch and stepped closer. Inside, the victim gave a feeble moan, tossing his head. Clearly, he suffered from gangrene, the undressed fracture at his ankle swollen glossy black, bone fragments thrusting white through outraged flesh. Mumbled prayers rose from the group round him, slipping out the door like smoke, and drifting into the unseen overcast sky.

Astonished, Parcifal realized he'd known men injured worse than this to recover with the proper care. Why didn't the Brothers—that quick with the axe when they encountered "blasphemy"—do something? He turned to make some comment to Oln Woeck. He saw the leader's face. Three hundred candles blazed inside the room. Not a flicker lit the compound yard. What it wouldn't give to life, the Cult squandered upon death.

Perhaps one fewer of them by daybreak might be a blessing.

Oln Woeck beckoned Parcifal to the front of one of many huts surrounding the bleak establishment. His companions followed. In the tradition of the Brotherhood, the leader's was no better than any of the other huts, being of rammed earth, not perhaps the best choice for this climate. It showed sign of continuous incompetent repair.

As he shut the raw planked door, Oln Woeck began to fumble with a tinderbox, purposing to light a candle, while Parcifal clapped his hands upon his upper arms in vain attempt to keep them warm. Oln Woeck's companions disposed themselves in the shadows at two corners of the room. As one sat cross-legged and vacant of expression, picking his nose, the other sprawled, rooting through the clothing at his loins. He commenced a crude rhythm, grunting in time with the motion of his cupped hands. *"We believe—unh, unh—we believe—unh, unh—we believe in the Father, Maker of Heaven and earth, and in . . ."*

Disgusted, Parcifal sat upon a worn, tilt-legged wooden stool. There was no fire, not even a hearth for it, such being forbidden by several stringent doctrines of the Cult, nor was any other hospitality offered the visitor—who'd no reason to appreciate the outrageous profligacy the single candle represented.

He reflected upon the leader's earlier, peculiarly cordial greeting, finally replying, "As long as you get what you want—what you extort from me!"

"What'st thou say? Ah, yes, I recall." Oln Woeck made clucking sounds with his tongue. "Now, now, Hethri Parcifal, the price of silence is high. Wouldst thou liefer face the open wrath of our Brotherhood in this affair, or continue reaping thy illicit benefits—benefits I've not e'en asked thee to share—"

"Yet!"

"—yet, with us?"

Old anger flared within the younger man, squeezing his eyes shut against his will. For a moment, he wished he could feel the blood-haze which sometimes possessed warriors such as Owaldsohn, rendering them omnipotent, invulnerable.

Alas, when he opened his eyes again and looked down, all he saw was himself.

"I recall no teaching which forbids trade with foreigners!"

Oln Woeck chuckled. "With the Invader, Hethri, with the Invader. Nor do I, in God's truth. But wouldst thou like it common knowledge? We've been o'er this before. In the end, thou reckoned it worth the price. How *is* thy little daughter, anywise? I see her—and thy grandchild-to-be—that seldom these days."

A father's outraged horror swept through Parcifal, but the diplomat within him stifled it.

"E'en now I fail to understand what you want with her. Would you sire offspring in your dotage you couldn't before now—"

"Silence, thou base hypocrite!" Oln Woeck rasped, his yellow eyes afire, the markings standing out upon his shaven temples. Abruptly he mellowed. "Thou speakest aright, good Hethri. I'm an old man, with an old man's craving for a woman's warm young body. Though my usage with her shall be the same—*exactly* the same—as for these"—he indicated his companions, slouched against the earthen wall, with a contemptuous flip of a veiny hand—"who pleaseth me no longer."

He shook his head. "At one time in my life I thought it well to have their temperament, shall I say, ameliorated—why, thou appearest puzzled, friend Parcifal. Could it be I've let a little secret of our Brotherhood slip by to an unbeliever? But look'st thou upon them, upon the sigil of our order."

Controlling his unease, Parcifal bent aside upon his stool, examining the Sacred Heart tattoo upon the left side of the companion's head. The blue dye concealed a small, deep, circular scar.

He turned to Oln Woeck, a terrifying suspicion growing within him, "What does it signify?"

"Compliance." Oln Woeck chuckled. "Pure, disminded compliance, to the Brotherhood, to my e'ery whim."

Parcifal sprang up, knocking the stool over. *"You'd do this to my daughter?"*

Oln Woeck made patting motions at the air in front of him. "Sittest thou, *merchant*. And what if I intended so? We've a bargain, haven't we? Yet be not afraid. E'en that chirurgical improvement will not be foisted upon her. I should prefer her, um, somewhat resistant—at least in the beginning."

"But what excuse can I offer the village, Oln Woeck, for giving her wholly to you? You can't father children upon her, and in any case, young Sedrich—"

"Aha! Now thou perceivest, dost thou not, the reason for my recent tolerance? Get thee home, Hethri Parcifal. Upon the morrow wilt thou make announcement that I and my betrothed have conceived a child and are in haste impetuous but seemly to be wed."

3

As the single smoky candle flickered, scattering grotesque shadows, the men at the battered table spoke a while longer, in particular concerning young Sedrich Sedrichsohn and his warrior sire. Oln Woeck had given the matter much thought.

After a time, a reassured Hethri Parcifal burrowed back out into the night, no longer fearful of the naked steel-edged wrath of the Owaldsohns. As he latched the door behind the unbeliever's back, Oln Woeck rubbed his bony hands together before he caught himself at it. Likewise he fought—and defeated—a look of unrestrained glee which had threatened to settle itself upon his taut-stretched features.

"So mote it be!"

From a corner, one of his young companions looked up in dull incomprehension.

Oln Woeck nodded. "It beginneth. Let the parasite attribute my designs upon his tender youngling to the stirrings of senescent lust. The wisest lie hath yet an admixture of truth; the wisest conspiracy is a conspiracy of one—ne'er forgetting thee, of course, who shareth my every thought."

Bringing the candle-stub, Oln Woeck took the young man

by the hand, bidding him arise. He led him over to the pallet where the other young man dozed now, blew the candle out, and settled himself between the two warm bodies.

" 'But what of the Sisterhood?' " he mocked Parcifal, more to himself than to companions incapable of understanding. " 'Twas aught that simpering craven could ask about, did we no sooner dispose of the question of the stripling father. As well he might."

Flesh slapped naked flesh.

There were other noises.

" 'A boy-baby,' reasoneth our mendacious merchant, 'can someday be sealed safely unto the Brotherhood.' " Oln Woeck caressed a scarred and tattooed temple. "Doubtless he contemplated thy decorations with some comfort. 'But a girl-baby'd be of special interest to that witch-woman Ilse and thus constitute a threat.' "

Staring at the unseen ceiling in the dark, Oln Woeck addressed the night: "Hethri Parcifal, e'er I use what I will of her—if there be aught left—I'll pass thy little Frae on to many well-deserving others. She is but a step-stone toward fulfullment of my strategies."

Among the three there was some squirming, grunting rearrangement.

Oln Woeck took a sudden breath.

"But observest thou: B'time her bawling calf becometh problematic—should it survive the uses I make of its mother—there'll *be* no Sisterhood to threaten anyone!"

VIII:

The Fiery Cross

Surely We will try you with something of fear and hunger and diminution of goods and lives and fruits. . . .

—The *Koran*, Sura I

"I *won't!*"

"Your will in this," replied Frae's father, weariness slurring his voice, "shall be without question to behave as I bid, in cheerful obedience, and *now.*"

Late as he had been arriving from the compound, he'd awaited hours before his daughter had crept home. His body trembled with humiliated fury. Still, in a corner of his mind, he took pride that he'd not raised his voice to her.

Nor yet his hand.

Frae answered, "You're mistaken, Father."

Dawn brushed pale color, brightened by the snowfall, across their whitewashed ceiling. Standing across the room from one another, neither was warmed by it. In this house, not otherwise unlike the one next door, no fire glowed in the hearth. No candle had been lit. It seemed to both as if nobody lived here. Frae's heart was with the Owaldsohns. Parcifal's plans lay elsewhere, as well.

"I'm a woman." She spread her hands upon her belly. "Tell me I'm not! My life belongs to me! I'll do with it as I—"

"Your life belongs to *me!*" He took an angry step forward, she, a step back, until her heel met a wall. "Afterward, to whomsoe'er I should deliver you unto!"

Hot tears sprang forth unbidden in her eyes. Hating the weakness they betrayed, she made fists of her small hands, regaining the half-pace she'd given up.

"Do I belong to anyone beside myself, 'tis to my love, Sedrich Sedrichsohn, and to this child of his I carry."

Parcifal strode forward of a sudden, seized his daughter's upper arms in both hands, bruising her. Between clenched teeth he whispered, " 'Tis Oln Woeck's child you carry! 'Tis what everyone will believe. What everyone believes is the truth.

"As for Sedrich Sedrichsohn . . ."

Frae looked up, terror in her eyes. "He'll come for me! He'll take me away!"

Releasing her, Parcifal snorted. "When your betrothed finishes with him, he'll rescue no one. Not e'en himself!"

2

The late-afternoon light was beginning to fail as Sedrich looked upon his handiwork. It was the smallest arrow he could fashion, half the length of his little finger, the shaft of bronze, tipped with razored steel and fletched with tiny copper vanes. With a grunt of satisfaction, he tried what he'd begun calling the shoe—a half-cylinder of resin-impregnated softwood, grooved upon its flat diameter for the little arrow. It was the second such he'd fashioned with painstaking care. Together they encased the small projectile, only the tip of its lethal broadhead projecting beyond their rounded ends.

Sedrich breathed.

It was time for testing.

Rummaging in the spiderwebbed spaces behind the forge's

hardwood pile, he extracted a doeskin bundle, obtaining from it an iron tube the length of his forearm, closed at one end with a plug of steel—which had itself been pierced through with the finest twist his father possessed. Halfway along the tube, at right angles to its long axis, he'd fastened the handle of a block-plane, using castoff metal strapping.

He glanced over his shoulder.

In the forge lay a length of iron wire, its end glowing red in the coals. From the leather bundle he took a small resin container of irregular granules, gray-black, foul-smelling. Sedrich unstoppered it, poured out a measure in his palm, tipped it into the open end of the tube. He started the softwood cylinder in behind it, taking care that the two carved pieces stayed in place along the tiny shaft. Using the brass rod, he rammed the cylinder home over the granules.

It was, he thought to himself, now or never.

The front end of the tube was equipped with a crude sight, like that of a shoulder-bow. At the rear, the double peaks of a shoulder-bow's rear sight had been attached. Taking aim upon the largest log-end in the pile, Sedrich reached for the coiled "handle" of the wire in the forge, plunging its hot end, now glowing yellow, into the small hole behind the rear sight.

The tube moved in his hand with an orange flash, a soft *boom!*

Casting it aside upon the bench, Sedrich hurried to examine the log. As he'd planned, the wooden shoes lay upon the floor between him and the target, stripped off by air resistance. The arrow itself was buried past its vanes in the hard wood of the log.

He'd improved, he told himself, upon the old fletcher's idea. Better to let the explosive *push* the arrow than to carry the substance to the mark. Now to install the flint-striker which had been the most difficult portion of this project to conceive. In this wise, his new weapon would be free of the forge or some other source of fire.

"Sedrich!"

The anguish in Frae's voice clamped a cold hand about Sedrich's insides. He threw the tube aside, along with his musings. Running the muddy pathway toward her, he watched the girl tear through the snow-covered hedge at the margin of their properties, her face red-blotched, streaming with tears. At her wrists, blood dripped.

"Sedrich!" Throwing her arms about his neck, she buried her face in his shoulder. "They're going to steal our child!"

"What?"

Pulling back a little, she looked up at him. "My father. Oln Woeck. They're going to say our baby's his!"

The cold hand was replaced by a burning one. Placing an arm about Frae's shoulders, he led her back to the warmth of the forge. "It makes a demented sort of sense," he told her. "But I promise you, they'll not get away with it."

In the shed, he swept the clutter off a low bench. "Here, you must calm yourself, and not only for your own sake." He placed a gentle hand upon the girl's swollen abdomen. "What's wrong with your wrists?"

Frae glanced down, as if just aware of the injuries which covered her hands with blood. "Father tied me in my room." She shook her head. "I got loose."

Sedrich thought, did his fury build higher, he'd die of it. Taking his own advice, he breathed deep several times, then fetched the water jug with which he and his father were used to refresh themselves in the forge-heat. He was washing the girl's wounds, which were superficial, when she looked up at him. "Sedrich, what is that noise?"

Outside, far away, the young man heard the drumming of feet. He had heard its kind before. It was not long before his first, most dismal guess was confirmed.

> *"We believe—* (Clash! Clash!)
> *We believe—* (Clash! Clash!)
> *We believe in the Father,*
> *Maker of heaven and earth,*
> *Who hath turned His face away.* (Clash!)"

"The Botherhood of Man, love."

Striding across the shed, he retrieved the dagger he'd put

aside. Thrusting it through his belt, he proceeded to charge his iron tube with granules once again. He'd another arrow to spare, and the spent shoes lay easy to hand upon the floor.

"I'd wondered why your father didn't pursue you. He's Oln Woeck's Brotherhood to do it for him."

> *"We believe—* (Clash! Clash!)
> *In Jesus Christ His only son,*
> *Born of the Virgin Mary,*
> *Crucified, dead, and buried. . . .*
> *He descended into Hell.* (Clash!)
>
> *There he shall suffer*
> *Till he be redeeméd,*
> *And sitteth on the right hand*
> *Of God the Father Almighty,*
> *Whence shall he come—* (Clash!)
> *To judge the quick and the dead!* (Clash!)"

Just as Sedrich completed his preparations, they arrived in full panoply, surrounding the forge with a wall of robe-clad bodies. The air stank with their presence. Awaiting their shouts for him to show himself, Sedrich was surprised to see Oln Woeck's companions drag some burden onto the property, struggling it into an erect position. It was a pole, the thickness of a man's thigh, wrapped with burlap about straw ticking. Across the pole, set perhaps a quarter of its length from the top, was a shorter spar. It was a cross, he realized, symbol of the martyr they worshipped.

But why the straw and burlap?

In the growing shadows, Sedrich could feel Frae behind him, one hand at his hip, the other at her throat. Wondering where his mother and father were, he tightened his grip upon the handle of his tube, watching as Oln Woeck put torch to the cross. Soon, in the failing light, the yard was full-illumined with its burning.

"*Sedrich, son of Sedrich who is called Owaldsohn! Surrender thyself to the justice of Him who burneth for thy sake in Hell!*"

Sedrich stepped into the roaring light of the cross. "Go there yourself, Oln Woeck! I've no truck with your cross-god, nor has he with me. Leave us alone!"

With his bodyguard, Oln Woeck strode forward. Light glared from the ring of robes surrounding the yard.

"Thou'st no right to be left alone, boy. Not when thou've kidnapped my bride, nor in any case at all! Give thyself over! Cast off thy iniquities. Surrender thyself to His mercy!"

Sedrich raised his tube, aligning it upon Old Woeck's shaven head. "She's *not* your bride, you vile, scum-sucking—"

There was an orange flash, a soft *boom!*, just as one of the bodyguard stepped into the arrow's path. The bronze projectile took him in the base of the throat. He screamed, spewing blood, and fell convulsing to the muddy ground where he kicked himself silent.

Two tubes, Sedrich was amazed to find himself thinking. I should have fashioned two of these things, lashed side by side.

He'd just drawn his dagger when a dozen of the Brothers, rushing forward, seized him. An overwhelming press of bodies descended upon him. The dagger was torn from his hand. Sedrich was aware they'd taken Frae. She called his name but wouldn't scream. They held him against the wall. Others took her outside into the firelight. Like a dog, they dragged him through slushy snowmelt into the yard. When he attempted to regain his feet, a sharp blow in the small of his back pinned him to the ground.

Looking up, Sedrich could see Oln Woeck, one hand buried in Frae's hair as, upon her knees, she struggled against his grasp.

" 'Tis my pleasure to announce I'm about to be a father!" the old man shouted, mouth-fog making his vile words visible against the torchlight. "My betrothed is with child!"

Once again Sedrich attempted to struggle erect. Once again the foot upon his back held him helpless in the mud. *Where was his father?*

"You're a liar, Oln Woeck," the young man shouted. "The child is mine! Ask its mother!"

Frae opened her mouth. Oln Woeck released her hair for a moment. As she staggered, he struck her with all his strength, backhanded, across the face. To keep her from falling further, he seized her hair again.

"Best," the old man suggested, "ask her father!"

From between two of the Brothers ringing the property Hethri Parcifal stepped forward, holding his cloak clear of the sodden ground. " 'Tis so," he answered. "All the formalities have been observed. The child is of Oln Woeck. This insane kidnapper must be punished."

"More," Oln Woeck shouted at the world, "he dabbleth in the forbidden! His parents both have tutored him in the fiery arts mechanic."

Several Brothers pushed Sedrich's land-boat from the shed. Its wheels cut deep furrows in the snow.

"Here be the first indication," Oln Woeck shouted, waving a skinny arm in the vehicle's direction, "and here"—he pointed toward the motionless body of the Brother Sedrich had shot—"is yet the worst! *Firearms!* He'd bring the Death upon us again!"

He looked down at the mud-bespattered girl.

"By the power of our Lord who suffereth for our sake, I declare this woman and myself to be lawfully wed. Let him who dareth speak now or fore'er hold his peace!"

Sedrich shouted, "I speak against it, you scabrous—"

"Hearing no one *fit* to speak—" Oln Woeck began. He was interrupted by a cry from Frae.

"*No!* Do not leave me with this creature! I beg—"

"*Silence!* This is childish hesitation, hysteria, brought about by her condition! We are man and wife!"

"*Sedrich!*"

The shout came this time from the house. "Sedrich, your father—"

Rolling beneath the imprisoning foot, Sedrich seized the naked ankle of the distracted monk—Oln Woeck's other bodyguard. He kicked upward, hard, his heel stopping in the man's crotch. The side of his fist took the man's knee. The joint crumpled with a crackling noise. Leaping to his feet, the young man brought one of them down upon the anguished face, hearing bone crackle again.

He ran the well-worn pathway toward the sound of his mother's voice.

Ilse met her son as he pushed past her through the open door, wet soil dripping in his wake. In the room beyond, great Sedrich Owaldsohn lay sprawled in a chair, eyes blankly open, his head half shaven, the remaining lock already braided for mortal combat.

He was dead.

Before him, upon a low setee, lay *Murderer*, unsheathed and oiled. Rubbing wet and dirty hands on his scarcely cleaner breechclout, Sedrich swept the weapon up, unnoticing of its great weight. Time enough to mourn his father later, if he were still alive to—

A sudden commotion arose behind him.

Sedrich turned to see Hethri Parcifal push past Ilse into the room, seizing her copper staff. He pushed her against the heavy door. With an unearthly snarl, Willi leapt at Parcifal's throat. He didn't reach it. The sharp end of Ilse's staff penetrated the dog's body, slamming Parcifal against the wall, where he barely kept his feet. Willi fell, awkward with the weapon through his body, silent as his master.

"No, Klem!" Sedrich shouted as the older dog advanced upon Parcifal. He strode forward. Almost unbidden, *Murderer* swept up in a glittering crescent, descending with all of Sedrich's conscious strength behind it, cutting the screaming man at the collarbone, silencing his screams as it clove him to the waist, spilling him across the polished hardwood floor. The flesh which had been Hethri Parcifal fell over the furry inert form of the dog. Where it had been sundered, it steamed in torchlight coming through the door.

Oln Woeck had followed to the house.

Behind him, his remaining body-servant, eyes crossed with pain, was supported on his ruined leg by a pair of Brothers. Mindless fury filled the old man's face, lashed by shadow and torchlight. Frae lay sobbing, propped upon one arm, at his feet, her long tresses still wrapped about his bony fist.

"This day, young Sedrich, thou'st proven thyself twice a murderer, likewise many times a dabbler in forbidden art." The Cult leader turned to address those behind him. "Our laws stateth not which is worse, but holdeth they're the same. The punishment—"

"You'll do the being punished, Oln Woeck! You've killed my father!"

Oln Woeck whirled to face the threat. A dozen men stepped between their leader and the young sword-wielder, armed with long, heavy staves. Where their robes fell clear of their bodies, Sedrich could see heavy muscles. Oln Woeck sighed, assuming an air of tired patience.

"Be your father dead, 'tis of thy mischief. Now acceptest thou the judgment of thy fellowmen, Sedrich Sedrichsohn. The punishment for thy crimes is merciful. Moreo'er, 'tis voluntary—thou'rt to make the Choice."

One overzealous among Oln Woeck's company stepped forward, leveling his staff at Sedrich. Almost unthinking, Sedrich sliced the man's weapon in half with a short swipe of *Murderer*.

The man stepped back.

"The Choice?" Sedrich echoed. "The Choice 'tween what and what?"

" 'Tween exile," intoned the old man, "from home, family, village, canton, to go where no man knoweth thy crime, and . . ."

It wouldn't do, thought Sedrich. His gentle Frae lay full upon the ground now, her sobs having given way to the ungentle sleep of failed strength.

He *must* stay to fight this—

". . . and mutilation. The loss of the hand which hath offended us, as is the custom."

Sedrich blinked. "As once you did to Harold Bauersohn, the fletcher?"

Oln Woeck grinned a skull's grin. " 'Twould end thy tinkering forever. Thou'd best be upon thy way, boy."

Sedrich stepped a measured pace to the doorway of his dead father's home. Shifting the greatsword to his left hand, he spoke for all to hear. "Oln Woeck, you're a liar. You'll not escape such punishment as I've in mind for you. Let this be token of it!"

Without further word, he slapped the doorframe with his right hand, swung the greatsword with his left. Oln Woeck's eyes grew wide with shock. The blade bit deeply into wood as Sedrich's hand parted from the wrist and fell into the mud.

There was a gout of blood.

He was surprised to feel no pain.

Behind him, his mother screamed until a scarlet gossamer descended over his eyes.

He lost consciousness.

IX:

Fire-Tithe

"O unbelievers, I serve not what you serve. . . ."
—The *Koran*, Sura CIX

" 'Tis useless, Helga," Ilse muttered, "we've lost her."

Sedrich awoke in black, furious confusion, senses sharpened like those of a hurt and hunted animal. What was this he overheard of losing *her*? His father, he remembered — with an agony not much less painful than being cloven by the greatsword *Murderer*—was dead, struck down by the shock and rage of what had been done to his only son. Willi, too, was gone, fierce, faithful Willi, he whom Sedrich had expected would outlive his own sire, Klem, by at least a decade.

The next words which came to Sedrich bathed his heart in ebon flame. "And the child, Sister Ilse?"

"Come two moons early, and no nurse to give it sustenance, e'en did it survive? I fear me 'tis but a matter of a few hours, good Helga. We've done our uttermost, thanks to you for your aid, but . . . what am I going to tell my son?"

The neighbor-woman made clucking noises.

Struggling to arise from where he lay, the young man took

87

first note of his surroundings. He was in his parents' chamber, lying on their great bed, the draperies so close-drawn he couldn't tell the hour of the day. A pair of chimneyed oil-lamps burned before the mirror upon a dark, carven chest, throwing redoubled light, quadrupled shadows, about the room. He lay helpless, he discovered, unable to do more than lift his head, and this but feebly.

The shadows writhed upon the walls.

Gathering his strength—blackness boiled within him, driving out weakness—he tried again. A sharp, painful constriction across his chest caused him to think once more in anguish upon his father. Fears for himself were groundless: a rope had been passed round the bed to hold him down. Without thought, he reached toward the knot. He felt a tug against the motion, heard a clatter—

—and remembered his right hand was gone.

In its place, he wore a heavy bandage, reaching past his elbow. The ruined limb had been bound, likeliest by his mother, and suspended from its wrappings upon a nail, driven without care for the ornate bedstead from whence it hung, wrist uppermost, elbow down. He thought it odd that he felt but little pain. Perhaps that would come later. He could flex the fingers of his missing hand as if they still existed.

Sedrich rolled, loosening the bindings with his left hand. He untied the rope holding him to the mattress. The ends fell to the floor, where they passed beneath the bed. Sitting up, he observed even these small efforts had not been without cost: a red stain had sprung forth upon his bandage, spreading. Sweat rolled down his cheeks, his forehead, trickling to the base of his neck.

No matter.

Setting bare feet upon the carpet, he arose, supporting himself upon one of the tall posts at the foot of the bed. After a time, he staggered across the room to the doorjamb, where he leaned, breathing. His breechclout, vest, and dagger lay upon the dresser, between the lamps. He realized for the first time that, save the dressings of his wound, he was naked. With a clumsy gesture, he swept up his possessions, making his way out through the open door.

Waves of nausea became Sedrich's world for a nameless time. His journey along the short upper hallway, down the stairflight to the main floor, whence he'd heard his mother's voice, he accomplished in a hazy dream. When he arrived, it was to a room rearranged almost beyond recognition. A fire blazed high in the three-sided hearth. Daylight outside—early morning, judging by the yellow light filtering through the snow-cloud overcast—filled the room with a sick, shadowless glare. Yet every lamp the family possessed, save the pair upstairs, shone bright.

Furniture had been pushed out of the way, against the whitewashed walls, the great dining-table draped in linen white as the snow still falling outside the windows.

Her eyes open wide, Frae lay, motionless and silent, upon the table.

Blood was everywhere.

Staggering across the room, Sedrich knew before he reached her that, whatever had animated this beloved face, those slim hands he knew so well, it was gone forever. At her side, he touched her still-warm cheek, bent to kiss her upon unmoving, waxen lips.

"Sedrich!"

Ilse Sedrichfrau, Mistress of the Sisterhood, looked up from where she sat beside the table, lifting her sweat-matted head from her blood-bespattered forearms.

Helga Haroldsfrau slumped in a corner of the room by the great window, staring at the snowfall which concealed the ocean. She held a small, still bundle in her arms, crooning to it as tears streamed down her fat, care-weathered face.

Sedrich felt no wish to examine what she held.

" 'Twas too early, too long in coming"—Ilse sighed in weariness—"and little Frae too young to withstand it."

"What?" Sedrich had heard the words. Somehow they'd failed to carry any meaning to him.

Pushing up from the table, his mother arose from her seat, a stool Owaldsohn had been used to prop his feet upon before the fire.

She wiped stained hands along her robe-clad thighs.

" 'Tis the curse of our people, my son." She spread a hand toward the table. "Birthing comes hard upon us—when it comes at all. E'en the Red Men, who know little of medicine or cleanliness outbreed us ten to one. Each year, methinks, our numbers dwindle a little."

Sedrich caught his mother's eye and knew she was lying— or, at the least, attempting to distract him. If Frae were lost to him, what mattered any of this talk?

The blackness inside him boiled and boiled.

"Where," he asked in a voice the evenness of which he marveled at, "is Oln Woeck?"

"Sedrich, this is the blood-haze speaking, else you'd not e'en be standing up now upon your own. 'Tis rest you need, contemplation to control it, lest it take you o'er, kill you as it did your . . ." She stopped a moment. ". . . as it did your father. 'Twill do no one any good to take revenge now."

"Yes, Mother, my father—your husband—is dead. 'Twas not the blood-haze killed him either. My love is dead, and ere long—or thus I overheard you say to Helga—likewise the child she tried to bear me. *Where is Oln Woeck?*"

Snow fell outside, quiet as a fall of feathers.

"Gone south. 'Tis rumored, to confer with other Brother-hoods. But Sedrich, vengeance—"

He raised what had been his right hand as if to stay her speech. This it did, with more effect than he'd anticipated. Realizing his nakedness once again, Sedrich slipped an armhole of his vest over his bandage. The wound had stopped bleeding. Never taking his eyes from his mother, he tucked the clout between his legs, awkward as he fastened the belt about his waist.

"And Hethri Parcifal," he asked, "Where is our *good* neighbor?"

Ilse glanced at Helga, as if for support. The woman dozed now, her face still turned toward the window. When his mother turned back, there were terror and wonderment in her eyes.

"He's dead, Sedrich, by your own hand. D'you not remember?"

"Yes. Now I do."

Sedrich crossed the few paces between himself and his mother. He bent, kissing her upon her graying hair. He turned for the door, taking naught save the dagger he still carried, stopping to lift *Murderer* from its pegs. Who had returned it to its place, he wondered.

He tucked the small blade into his belt, slung the scabbard of the greatsword across his back, slanted for a left-hand draw. He didn't know how he'd wield his father's sword. It had been too much for him, in truth, even before he was a cripple.

Ilse rushed to wrap a bearskin robe about him. Her eyes held an appeal she knew was useless and would not utter again.

Sedrich paused in the doorway. "Aught I wanted, Mother—aught Frae wished for—was to be left alone. Oln Woeck wouldn't grant us e'en this. Nor will he in the future, do I know him.

"Revenge? Vengeance? I'll give you a promise, Mother, strike a bargain. For in all the world, you're aught I've left of what I love. Likewise I'm aught that remains of what you had. So certain am I that I know Oln Woeck, so sure am I that, even with all that's come to pass he cannot rest till one of us is dead or has submitted, that, for the peace of your mind I'll make you this pledge: I'll not take Oln Woeck's life till he comes to me, offering it."

A long speech, it was, for the young son of the blacksmith Sedrich Owaldsohn, even longer for the man he'd been forced, overnight, to become.

No further word passed between them.

Wind had swept the front garden clean of snow, heaping it against the picketing which surrounded it. At the end of the stone-flagged path, where it joined the village road, old Klem caught up with Sedrich, whistling in fierce supplication, wagging his tail.

He'd not be left behind.

Why not, thought Sedrich, why not let the old dog spend his last days as he wishes? 'Tis more than was given Frae and me!

He rubbed the dog's great head between the ears, thinking for the first time since regaining consciousness about the living Frae—not the pale mound of ashes, clay, and dust back there upon his mother's blood-soaked table, but the living, breathing being whom he'd loved. Even through the furry pelt he wore, the wind was bitter cold—yet not enough to cool the roiling blackness deep inside him.

Frae would have agreed with his mother, he thought, begging him to set aside this dark lust for revenge, approving of the promise—of the bargain—he'd made.

Klem following, he left the pathway for the road, heading not south toward vengeance, but westward to oblivion.

SURA THE SECOND: 1410–1418 A.H.—

The Agreement of Islam

In the alternation of night and day,
and what God has created in the heavens and the earth—surely there are
signs . . .

The *Holy Koran*, Sura X, *Jonah*

X:

Ayesha

And the king said, "I saw in a dream seven fat kine, and seven lean ones devouring them; likewise seven green ears of corn and seven withered. My counselors, pronounce to me upon my dream, if you are expounders of dreams."

"A hotchpotch of nightmares!" they said. "We know nothing of the interpretation of nightmares."

Then said the one who had been delivered, remembering after a time, "I will myself tell you its interpretation. . . ."

—The *Koran*, Sura XII

As if its own teeth were not enough, a mountain wind whipped sand into her face.

When her eyes ceased watering, her first thought was for her weapon—a reflex born of bitter experience. It had been conceived for harsh treatment, but there were limits. Their Enemy—whose weapon it had been only a few days before—was not the most exacting of manufacturers. Perhaps this was why he had come to steal from her people.

At this moment, his objective was limited: to clear them from a strategic area. His ultimate goal, destruction of their homes, of the food they ate, the society they defended, could be accomplished piecemeal. He had discovered—as he shipped his dead home thousand by thousand—that he could not achieve it overnight.

Pulling a rag-wrapped finger from the trigger-guard, she flipped a catch, tipping out a long, curved magazine. She drew the operation handle back until she could see a cartridge—one of fifteen she had left.

The bolt moved with a gritty sound.

Hers was an older weapon, of a decent caliber—not one of the little ones their Enemy had brought in later. This made her happy, although ammunition was becoming harder to obtain. When her people had captured enough new weapons, their Enemy would, in probability, begin importing a third, then a fourth. Laa thaghthaam, no matter. Weapons were easy enough to come by—take them from the dead Enemy.

In the beginning, they had rejoiced at the childish ease with which these last could be produced, not thinking of endless numbers of slave-soldiers brought each day into their country to replace them. Now it was becoming clear that their Enemy would bury them beneath a mountain of his own conscripted dead if that was what it took to gain an upper hand. This sort of suicidal warfare was difficult for her people—slaves only to their God—to comprehend.

And counteract.

Today they would try again, her people. Information from the capital—relayed to them from one the Enemy believed reliable—was that he would be pushing many trucks through these hills, laden with supplies for a forthcoming winter offensive. Winter was a good time for their Enemy. Her people, limited to foot-travel, were bogged down by weather so bad it was renowned the world over. He could fly high above it or burrow through upon cleated treads.

These trucks would be making for a supply depot, high in the mountains, well protected. They would travel behind a column of tanks, followed by armored troop carriers.

Overhead, mechanical birds of prey patrolled a barren sky.

They were not omnipotent birds, however. It was difficult for them to fly as high as the peaks to which her people climbed, from which they unleashed their own fury upon the vulnerable backs of the helicopters. Their Enemy knew that the machines which protected his column needed protection themselves.

Thus, to these peaks he would send his best fighters—in flying machines straining at the limit of their capabilities—who would occupy advantageous positions until the supply column had passed, then jump to the next series of peaks, until the heavy-laden trucks had reached their destination.

This time, thanks to their man in the capital, her people would be upon the peaks to meet them, while others of her kind, far below, filled the front of the column with stolen rockets, it rear with sliding rocks started into motion by explosives already planted—and its middle with blazing death.

This winter, their Enemy would starve.

There was a shout. Someone heard a thud-thud-thud of an Enemy warship as it clawed itself peakward. She huddled between two rocks, waiting.

The noise grew louder.

Of a sudden, fluttering aircraft noise was replaced by an explosion as a helicopter fired rockets into their position, scattering flaming death. Had their man betrayed them, or was he himself betrayed? Screams, hurried footfalls, inevitable confusion. The Enemy was among them, wearing masks, spraying bullets. She turned, saw an old friend fall, another neighbor writhing upon the ground, his belly torn open. Not a whimper did he utter. He had been a weaver of carpets.

A bullet spanged off rock beside her.

Then she was up, returning shot for shot in measured cadence, using her remaining ammunition. An Enemy soldier, said to be of the best his country had to offer, fell, spilling his guts upon the same ground where partisan blood was running like a mountain freshet.

Another fell, and another.

Out of ammunition, she seized up one of the new weapons. With no place to hide, it was a matter of fight or die.

Conscripts seemed to prefer the latter. Their mountaintop battlefield grew emptier while a handful of her neighbors still stood to hold it. The helicopter, unable to hover long at this altitude, had departed, stranding its former passengers, sentencing them to death.

It would be back. By then she, with her people, would be gone.

At last their final Enemy—at least in this place, at this time—was dead.

With others, she began gathering up weapons of the Enemy. These new ones were lighter. She could carry four where she had managed three before. Down she climbed with her remaining comrades, from flat-topped peaks into a steep, brush-choked ravine which spilled itself into a barren, boulder-tumbled valley where they would, for a time, be safe. Dried branches crackled, snatching at her head-scarf.

Safe.

Again a thud-thud-thud, this time overhead.

She screamed, threw up her arms in futile reflex as slow-rolling flying-machine wheels passed within touching distance. Tossing all but two captured weapons aside, she held their triggers back until they emptied themselves into its belly.

It did not notice.

She heard a plopping, hissing noise. A yellow fog, fanned by backwash of the departing helicopter, spread among them. She tried to run but found that her full skirt had become entangled in a sharp-thorned shrub. Too late, she knew that village tales she had heard were true.

Deadly vapor reached her. She felt it burn her eyes, the insides of her mouth and nostrils. Blisters formed upon the backs of her hands. As blackness descended about her, she heard a comrade call to her, "Ayesha! Ayesha!"

2

As usual, she woke up screaming in the palace of her father.

"Ayesha! Ayesha!" a voice from her dreams continued. "*Manlayagh*, all is well, my child, be hush!"

The voice was softer now, empty of the despairing panic which her dream had given it. It was still a voice of someone she loved well.

"David?"

Her own voice was very different, a little one, that of a ten-year-old child, small for her age.

"*Nanam,* Princess, it is I. Sit up a moment. See a firm familiar world about you. You have had another of your dreams."

Strong, articulate hands lifted her, propped her up with plump, colorful silken pillows. These same hands rearranged her golden brocade coverlet across her, brushing away sheer lavender bedcurtains in which she had become entangled. Through the pointed arch of a nearby window she heard nightwatchmen calling.

Other hands turned a gilded valve inset beside a door, bringing gaslights up until Ayesha could see a concerned look becloud dark eyes, behind thick lenses, in a thin, dark-bearded face she knew belonged to her favorite tutor, David Shulieman, rabbi, scholar, counselor to her father. Behind him, framed in the doorway like a formal portrait-of-state, stood Marya, one her less favorite nurses.

Rabbi David should not have been here, in family quarters, at this hour. Such was unseemly. Some recent wives of her father were quite orthodox and old-fashioned, yearning for the ancient niceties of purdah. Either there had been some trouble—requiring his presence and advice—or there would be.

The little girl, in fact a Princess, firstborn of Shaatirah, retired consort to Abu Bakr Mohammed VII, Sword of God, Keeper of the Faith, His Pan-Islamic Holiness, Caliph-in-Rome, sat up to accept the glass of water David offered her.

XI:

Rumors of War

Gross rivalry diverts you, even till you visit the tombs.
                                    —The *Koran*, Sura CII

"*Sapaagh chalhghayr*, good morning, Da—Your Holiness!"
"*Sapaagh chalhghayr*, Ayesha. Is it The Day, then?"
Ayesha closed her book over a finger, shaded her eyes with a small hand. Sitting under a bright sky, upon a stone balustrade overlooking the Tiber and six hills of the ancient capital, she smiled, sensing one of her father's frequent jests in the offing.
" 'The Day,' Your Holiness?"
In the gloom of a point-arched doorway leading from the palace, displacing the nurse Marya, who normally played chaperon to her small charge, a pair of grim-faced uniformed guards, shortswords and stubby pistols ready, kept watch over their Caliph, awaiting his will—or the suicidal foolishness of some assassin.
Far at the other end of the balcony, a dozen pigeons, startled by some sudden noise or passing shadow, fluttered heavenward.
"*Nanam*, the Dreaded Day upon which Our favorite daughter ceases calling Us 'Daddy'—"

100

The Caliph strode across the sun-warmed geometric flagging of the balcony. He poured himself a cup of fragrant coffee from a silver service standing upon a table beside a wall.

"—and Our desire to walk the surface of this trouble-weary planet is at an end."

Aside: "*Sapaagh chalhghayr,* David."

Many floors below, in some unseen courtyard, palace guardsmen were changing shifts with what seemed to Shulieman something more than their usual military enthusiasm. There were hoarse shouts, followed by jingle-stamping from booted feet, a clack-clack-clack of inspected breech-loading chambers slamming shut, then the clattering thunder of rifle-buttstocks hitting pavement.

The young rabbi set his own cup down, annoyed a bit by this interruption of the lessons of his only pupil. At another court he might have been an old man, dressed in formal vestments for the morning tutoring of the favorite daughter of the Caliph—and afraid to feel annoyed. In this one, brilliant, Byzantine, sometimes bizarre, renowned the world over for its respect of knowledge, exploration, and innovation—without any of the empty trappings of pedantry or piety—his thin form was adorned in sturdy blue-dyed cotton trousers, a short-tailed tunic open at the throat, untucked into his belt. His curly hair and beard were clean but, as usual, unkempt.

His thick spectacles gave back twin miniature images of the Caliph.

"Good morning, sir."

Abu Bakr Mohammed VII, Sword of God, Keeper of the Faith, was a tall man, yet he gave everyone he met the opposite impression. Twinkling of eye, jocular of temperament, rotund of form, he possessed hard, capable hands, not those of a king or philosopher but of a potter or stonemason. In fact, following a dictum of the Prophet—may his name be blessed—that a man should have a manual trade, whatever his official station in life, be dabbled, in what had once been palace dungeons, at carpentry. Family quarters were filled with the furniture he had constructed with those hands—while listening to reports from agents, advice from counselors, over the rasping buzz of saw and scraper.

For one so great of girth, he trod very lightly upon an earth whose surface he now threatened to depart. His voice was that of a singer-of-tales, a bit higher than most individuals remembered of him, rich and clear. Though he was nominal ruler of half the world, the broad, blue-black-bearded face he wore adorned no coin, no plaque, no statue. Yet his word went everywhere, and, being heard, was heeded.

"Ayesha." The Caliph addressed himself more to David Shulieman than to his daughter. He had taken a sip of dark, sweet coffee, finding, beside the pair, a place upon the broad stone railing for his even broader fundament. "Marya informs Us that you had another bad one last night. Did you not take your medicine?"

"Why, *thapnan*, of course, Your—Daddy!"

Ayesha shuddered in undimmed memory of her dream—likewise of a time not long ago when, for lack of extracts from a certain obscure desert plant her doctors had later compounded, nightmares had threatened to destroy her young mind altogether.

Her voice an octave lower, she nodded, "I always do."

"Very well," Abu Bakr Mohammed answered. "We shall speak again to Our physicians—provided that you add a big hug to that 'Daddy.'"

Gathering her yellow silks about her, the little girl jumped up giggling and complied, almost upsetting the cup her father held. For a moment or two, he shared her smile, as she shared his dark complexion and darker eyes. From the beginning, she had been an unusual child, he thought, sweet, affectionate, her waking hours marked by quiet study and reflection, rather than boisterous play as with her brother and her many sisters.

She was pretty and would one day be beautiful

She was clever and would one day be brilliant.

When she stepped away, he asked, "What is David having you study this morning?"

"History, Daddy. The Consultation of 878 A.H."

The Caliph nodded, then looked gravely at Shulieman. "Incidentally, while Our female household may raise Gehenna about your presence in their quarters last night, We Ourselves thank you. *Sghuhran jazeelan*. We should have been there Ourselves, had not Commodore Mochamet al Rotshild, arriving late from—"

It was at this moment Shulieman first noticed that the Caliph wore military garb, rough-tailored trousers, save in coloring not unlike those Shulieman himself wore, a long, many-pocketed tunic the color of wet sand, knee-length high-heeled cavalry boots. Pistol and dagger swung from his broad leather belt.

"But, then," the Caliph continued, "that is none of your concern. You know what *is,* which is why We overpay you so well. Get yourself more coffee, boy, *relax!*"

Shulieman, incapable of obeying the latter of his sovereign's commands, obeyed the former. Save upon occasions of marksmanship practice—the Caliph had insisted that his daughter learn to shoot both rifle and pistol—he had never seen Abu Bakr Mohammed armed before, nor shadowed quite so closely by guards. His was a happy reign, an enlightened one, if Shulieman were any judge of history—and he had best be, for this was his chief value both to the Caliph and to his daughter.

He wondered what had happened in the night.

To Ayesha, the Caliph said, "The Consultation, eh? Always been rather fond of that period, Ourselves. One of a very few demonstrable instances of reason defeating stupidity. Humph. Or at least fighting it to a draw. Or maybe it is just that its hero—one of them—shared Our name: Abu Bakr Mohammed III.

"Tell Us, then, about the Consultation."

Having taken her place atop the rail, Ayesha sat up, back straight, hands folded in her silk-draped lap. She closed her eyes, taking her lower lip between her teeth.

"*That* Abu Bakr Mohammed was a mighty Sunnite Caliph who worried a lot, for Moslems could not seem to get along with one another, even though they shared the same faith."

Pigeons began drifting back to the other end of the balcony. The present Caliph laughed, driving them away again.

"Darling daughter, as you will learn all too soon, it is often far more difficult to obtain peace within your own family than with foreigners, even in these troubled times. Nevertheless, you are quite correct: in those days there were long-standing factional disputes within Islam between Sunnite and Shiite (which was in essence a simple family argument over inheritance), Fatimite and Druse."

He gave David Shulieman a questioning look before continuing, wondering whether the palace tutor, discontent with answers expected to be satisfying in the public schools, had taken his little girl to the next level of analytic sophistication.

"Also he worried that one particular tenet of his denomination—that the Nazarene Carpenter was the Mahdi foretold to return at the end of time—had been discredited and would destroy his own people, even as the ancient Christians were destroyed."

"*Nanam*, Daddy, that is just what David has told me. So he wisely persuaded all the leaders of all the other sects, under the Doctrine of . . . of . . ."

"*Ijma*," the rabbi provided, sipping coffee, "'Agreement of Islam,' in which that which is believed by most of the Faithful is to be believed by all."

Ayesha nodded. "*Ijma*. Abu Bakr argued that neutral referees should be obtained to resolve their disputes."

"The Consultation with Rabbis," Shulieman offered, "marked the beginnings of a new, vigorous, hybrid culture, more progressive and humane than any our world has ever known heretofore."

"Never overlooking that a little blood got spilled along the path toward establishing our Great Consensus," added the Caliph with a wry expression. "We would not have Our daughter tutored in anything other than the plain, unvarnished truth. But it built a *dually* Semitic civilization which came to span our globe from Irland to the Steppes, from Skandinavia to the Cape at World's End."

"And you are boss." Ayesha beamed up at her father.

The Caliph frowned, skeptical of any naïveté his precocious daughter displayed, wondering, with a small, anticipatory ache, whether this was a cynical ploy of a kind he had never seen her exercise before or just a subtle joke.

He motioned David Shulieman to answer.

Shulieman, the consternation of the Caliph visible to him, suppressed a grin. "It is a little-appreciated fact that your father is leader of half the Moslem world only through his wise and continuing moral example. He is not a king, such as ancient Christians had."

They all sat silent with that eloquent phrase a moment, "half the Moslem world," Abu Bakr Mohammed thinking about the other half, of the ironic term "consensus," and of young men dying at this moment in faraway places at his express command.

Rabbi David Shulieman thought about the historic place of his own people in the scheme of things.

"Or your people," Ayesha thought to say at last.

"What?" Shulieman laughed. He knew more about the unholy talents which held this little girl in their clutches than anyone. Still, she managed to startle even him with embarrassing frequency. "Yes, well, I suspect they should best have listened to their prophet Samuel, who tried very hard to warn them about kings."

Little Ayesha, slyly or not, was far from finished asking unexpected, difficult questions of her elders. "But *limaadaa*, why only half, Daddy? I thought that—"

"Once upon a time," the Caliph answered, taking fond revenge by talking down to her, "far away eastward, all of Great Asia was ruled by a wily Mongol fellow by the name of Kublai Khan. Grandson of the mightiest of conquerors, Genghis, he possessed the mind of a philosopher, the heart of a desert chieftain. His passing might be regretted even by a civilized folk such as ourselves. The world of today contains no remnant of his once-vast empire, which must have been swept away in the same disaster which removed the ancient Christians from Europe."

The rabbi added, "Just as Sunnites came to dominate Europe, so Afghan inheritors of Zahirud-din Mohammed Babar, claiming descent from mighty Tamerlane, launched a dynasty which soon—in Mongol absence—dominated the largest continent of the earth.''

Abu Bakr Mohammed nodded. "His people, calling themselves Mughals, do not recognize unitarian reforms wrought by us Moslems here in Europe with Judaic advice. Perhaps they wish to re-create the splendor of ancient Khans. Perhaps—"

Far off, near an unseen ocean horizon, came a rolling boom which was not that of thunder, for the sky remained bright. The Caliph, knowing what it was, sighed.

"Well, *laa thaghthaam*, never mind. We do not believe they understand it any longer, themselves. When God's proper time arrives, they always say to themselves, generation after generation, this heresy—we, child—will be wiped out."

He fell silent.

Shulieman continued. "Until this moment, however, ruling a myriad intransigent people of Asia has been sufficient to keep Mughal overlords occupied for centuries. They have a saying: 'Time enough for housecleaning later.'"

He looked up at his sovereign.

"If I understand your father aright, that dreaded time has at long last arrived."

"*Nanam*, yes, Rabbi, that is what We came to tell Ayesha. And you. We received word from Our Admiralty yesternight that Mughal forces have fallen upon our colonies in the Island Continent, destroying them. They pressed the survivors into slavery. We have just dispatched our mighty Pan-Semitic Fleet. Those were their guns we heard just now, performing departure drills. We are to have war, perhaps the greatest and the cruelest war our world has ever witnessed."

Far away, the thin voice of a muezzin rose above the lower rumble of the city.

"And may God," said the Caliph, "have mercy upon all the Faithful."

XII:

Mochamet al Rotshild

Were it a gain near at hand, and an easy journey, they
would have followed thee; but the distance was too far
for them. Still they swear by God, "Had we been able,
we would have gone out with you" . . . and God
knows that they are truly liars.

—The *Koran*, Sura IX

A man with a gun in his hand sat near the stairs, as far away
from the bar as possible.

Mochamet al Rotshild tightened his grip upon the small
two-barreled breech-loader he always carried in his pocket,
grateful for the darkness of this damp and dirty place. One
could not see the vermin certain to be crawling underneath the
tables. He sat, waiting, listening to the music, watching
women dance, pretending to drink his drink. The music was
raucous, off pitch. The women (he was inclined to shout out
"Put it back on!") were almost as old as he was. When he left
this place—if he were allowed to leave alive—he intended
donating his drink to those vermin he was glad he could not
see.

107

Where was that girl?

While he waited, Mochamet al Rotshild thought about many things. He had lived, and for the most part enjoyed, a long, eventful life which had left him many things to think about. One of these was the Caliph he now served, His Holiness Abu Bakr Mohammed VII.

A canny, pragmatic ruler following the legendary tradition of Haroun al Raschid, Abu Bakr Mohammed had made it his custom to surround himself whenever possible with an unusual mixture of counselors and administrators, assuring himself that they came from every conceivable walk of life within his vast, varied domain. This made certain security risks inevitable; still, upon occasion it produced an individual such as Mochamet al Rotshild, whom the Caliph insisted upon calling Commodore.

"I was the unlooked-for consequence of an unsanctified union," the merchant had explained to the Caliph, when they had first met many years before, "between one of your Saracen noblemen and a lady of Judaic heritage—and what her kin considered easy virtue."

Within himself, Mochamet al Rotshild smiled over memories of that first meeting. The Caliph had journeyed to Marseilles, among other reasons to confer an honor upon a rising merchant prince. Each had come away with what he had reason to believe was a new friend. Concerning his past, the "Commodore" had found himself being uncharacteristically open with Abu Bakr Mohammed.

A young Mochamet al Rotshild might have been doomed, even in this enlightened world of Judaeo-Saracen Europe, to a lowly status, menial labor, a lifetime of social invisibility. His mother, abandoned by her lover, cast out onto frozen streetcobbles by her penurious and puritanical family, had expired—he believed of nothing more than despair—just six years after he had been born.

At an early age, however, he had stumbled into a profession in which he could make a mark through brave intelligence, solely by his own efforts, independent of whatever fate polite convention might otherwise have decreed for him. Having fallen prey to a press-gang, he had shipped out from his native Iskutlan ("I myself have seen that mighty, mysterious serpent of Loch al Ness," he had lied to the Caliph decades later), from Glasgow, down the Firth al Claid, as a common seaman.

It had been an age of discovery, not only for the boy but for his entire civilization. He himself had witnessed many strange and wonderful sights, trading with white barbarians, presumed to be the final remnant of the ancient Christians, upon the eastern shore of the Savage Continent, with the mighty and decadant Incas in the south, even with hostile and suspicious Mughals in ports from Sakhalin to the Red Sea. Growing up, he had supplemented what he saw with book-wisdom, aspiring to everything a human being could learn of the universe he lived in.

Cabin-boy to deckhand, deckhand to mate, Mochamet al Rotshild climbed the endless ladder, at long last a master, then owner of his own vessel. Sails it had been in those days, canvas, line, great rotary wings turning side-paddles bigger than houses, taking him to worlds beyond imagination. Now all of his numerous fleet were run by steam—he had been first in his business to convert—as were railroads everywhere, crisscrossing Europe and Africa.

There was occasional talk of slaveless sedan chairs.

The merchant sighed. Not in his time, he found himself half hoping—then, in an abrupt reversal, chiding himself for that same conservatism which kept his competitors from catching up with him. Slaveless sedans run by steam, indeed! A fortune there, just waiting to be made! Not only would he be the first in Islam to purchase one, but, when he found time—perhaps after this current political unpleasantness was over with—he would see about hastening their invention!

Make a note of it!

Thus it was scarcely fear of the unkown but a familiar expectation which caused Mochamet al Rotshild now to grasp his concealed weapon with his left hand while pretending to drink with his right. He knew this sort of establishment very well. That is was buried deep within a landlocked city, was a gathering-place for draymen, day-laborers, off-duty palace drudges, rather than barefooted sailors, reeking of creosote and coal-smoke, made little difference. He was aware of probabilities, not only of having been followed here but of being accosted by a simple robber. For this rendezvous, he had borrowed the oldest, most disreputable clothing of his oldest, most disreputable servant. He had put aside his jewelry. A worn and dirty burnoose concealed the flaming red hair which, even at his age, remained something of a trademark with him.

Was that confounded woman ever going to show up?

There was a lull as the musicians laid ouds and concertinas they had been torturing aside, seeking whatever respite they were accustomed to. Dancing-women (he could hardly call them girls) circulated among their custom, selling drinks along with cynical promises. Mochamet al Rotshild poured his own drink upon the floor beneath his table, then bought a second from a half-naked harridan who could have been his mother— or at least his sister—and looked around him.

Charles Martel they called this basement, in reference to an inscription graven over the nearby entrance of a grander building which, centuries before, had become the Caliph's palace. It had not been built by the Faithful. *Charles Martel,* the inscription demanded in flowing cursive, *where are you now?*

Protected from that very Mortality originally ordained to the wholesale destruction of their Faith—it was their conscientious practice of ritual sanitation which had afforded their salvation—dark-complected strangers with curve-bladed swords had, once upon a time, and on their way to greater conquest, marched into a deserted, undefended Tours with that sardonic question upon their lips.

They had received no answer.

Their ancient enemy was gone forever.

The Old World did not long lie empty, although the merchant gathered from the histories he had read that a greatly increased barrenness, as compared to earlier times, had been one consequence of the Death his ancestors had not entirely escaped. Population everywhere was small and very slow-growing, yet it made a certain prosperity possible for those who had survived and been fruitful.

Today, not one citizen of Rome in five thousand could tell you who Charles Martel had been. *Laa thaghthaam,* it mattered but little. His had become name to an illegal drinkery where low-status palace servants came daily to break the laws of God and man. Mochamet al Rotshild had been required to give a password ("Open Sesame") to some low-browed thug behind a slitted window before being allowed to descend into this temporary Gehenna. Unlike some of his predecessors, the Caliph left it alone, certain its eradication would spawn worse places, better hidden.

If the former were possible.

The sweet-sour odors of *thanpaah* and *ghashish* drifted toward him upon stale, *ouiskeh*-tainted air. Mochamet al Rotshild, bastard son of poor-but-proud Iskutish Jewry and a slumming Moslem aristocrat, had in his youth avoided such deadfalls for the destitute hopeless. He pulled his cloak about him, wrinkling his nose.

"Charjooh, Siti, nabhwan thismaghly . . . ?"

There came a soft, female voice behind him. He must be getting very old not to have sensed her approaching. He turned to see a close-veiled face, that of a woman, too well dressed to be safe in this establishment. A dram of the perfume she wore, pilfered no doubt from her mistress, might have bought this entire place.

"Sit down, girl!" he growled, "I am *not* your Lord—I am a 'sir,' if that makes you feel more comfortable. How do I know that you are who you are supposed to be?"

"Artichoke," the woman asserted, as if this reply she gave made perfect sense. It did, the merchant thought, indeed. More passwords, this one not quite so foolish as it sounded, grimly appropriate, a much-better-kept secret than "Open Sesame."

"Very well, Marya," Mochamet al Rothshild answered. "Wait till the music starts again—if you wish to dignify it by that name—then tell me of the Princess' most recent nightmare."

2

Later, when the old man had wasted yet another *ouiskeh* upon a patch of crumbling, filth-encrusted brick, he was even less satisfied than he had been before.

The girl Marya was less wasteful. Lifing her veil modestly at immodest intervals, she gulped her vile portion, as if this could somehow protect her from the potential consequences of being caught at spying upon the Caliph's family.

Or at least from contemplating them.

Mochamet al Rotshild muttered, disappointment in his tone, "I have never heard of those particular thorn shrubs growing in the Island Continent. It was not a prophetic dream at all."

"Yet," offered an alcohol-emboldened Marya, "the Holy Koran teaches—"

"I *know* what the Koran teaches, child!" He looked at her empty cup, a sneer ill-concealed behind his beard. "Better than you, to appearances. Yet that strange flying machine . . . those weapons. Firing fifteen or twenty cartridges without reloading? It may be prophecy after all, of a time far in future, when—"

"She often sees machines that fly, fan-bladed hoverers, slant-winged shiny screamers, bright-plumed little buzzers, disk-shaped glowing warblers—a veritable aviary of them. What of it? If flying machines could be made, they'd all look alike, wouldn't they?"

He gave his head to a reluctant nodding which grew more vigorous with each cycle. "You are right, woman! I will not succumb to superstition! There was a chance, that is all, a chance, that something of interest to my principals might be happening with our Princess, perhaps a chance to test it, with war flaring southward. But it has come to nothing, as was to be rationally anticipated."

He reached into his cloak, extracting a gold coin.

"There—go back to the palace. Keep your eyes and ears

open. Let this be a lesson: there is much to learn, but just one way to learn it. The difficult, mundane way."

The treacherous girl was gone before he had poured his last drink out upon the floor. Climbing the stone steps, passing through the guarded, slitted door himself, he wondered for a moment to whom she would report *this* conversation for a coin of gold.

Palace intrigue: always the weak of mind and spirit gathered around power, attempting to jog the elbow of anyone who held it in hopes of catching a little of it when it spilled. It was inevitably the tiniest dribblings of power which produced the greatest betrayals. He himself, Mochamet al Rothshild, well-known adviser to the Caliph, pirate, merchant prince, and spy, ought to know!

As did a cloaked and veiled figure which detached itself from the criminal shadows, following him up the stairs and away from the Charles Martel.

XIII:

The Artichoke

Your Lord knows you very well; if He will, He will have
mercy on you, or, if He will, He will chastise you.
—The *Koran*, Sura XVII

Time passed, thought Rabbi David Shulieman, and with its
passage, each man's youthful hopes (yes, and his accumulated
fears as well), leaving nothing in its turbid wake but
dispassionate, useless knowledge—and aching emptiness.

This morning's lesson with Ayesha had not gone well at all.
He had not been himself. She had been gracious, quite
understanding and forgiving, but he had felt too distant, too
abstracted to concentrate, focused upon one particular moment
in the past they shared.

Eight years had gone by in a twinkling, while war with the
Mughal Empire had somehow swollen from what had been at
best a moment of stirring adventure, enjoyed vicariously by
all, at worst an equally to be borne annoyance—shortages,
rationing, disrupted personal plans—into something gray and
terrible which had come to dominate the days, the nights, the
entire lives of everyone within Islam's embrace.

Men in the tens of thousands had been called to duty. Europe was becoming a continent of women's villages. Taxes had become unbearable, burdening, as all taxation must, whatever the intention or the mandate, those who could afford them least. Vaster, more potent battle fleets were launched southward. Sometimes they even returned. Link-treaded steam-chuffing titans roamed the lifeless central deserts of the Island Continent—an invention which, at another time, might have filled him with enthusiasm for the future—sinfully wasting any genius which had created them by hurling shells at one another.

Saracen surgeons were becoming most adept at pulling shards of steel and bronze and lead from the writhing, shrieking, blood and excrement-smeared bodies of male children old enough to wear a uniform and carry guns. For that reason, if for no other, the cultivation of poppies was becoming quite as important a war-industry as the mass production of explosive projectiles. Win or lose the war, they would not soon see an end to what this sort of agriculture portended.

The scholar shook his head.

He sat, now, upon the selfsame balustrade where, the best part of a weary decade ago, he had first received news of the war from the lips of the Caliph himself. Below, Islam's Eternal City was fog-enshrouded. Invisible. Reflecting his mood, the sky was mournful today, a light fall of chilly moisture keeping the stone flagging slippery, muffling city noises, forcing the very birds into hiding. It made his spectacles opaque, then stream with condensation. Inside the palace, it would be warm and dry, approaching time for the midday meal. Shulieman, however, would not go inside. He drew his thin cloak about himself, listened to his stomach grumble, and continued thinking gloomy thoughts.

Had it been nighttime, the city below would have been invisible in any case, strict martial orders to snuff out street and window lighting having been issued. Thus, from the near-miracle of his boyhood, citywide gas lighting, civilization had returned once again to the dimness and danger of candles and oil-lamps. Not that the capital of Islam was in peril—from Mughal artillery, sabotaged gas lines, or from anything else—but it must be seen by all the Faithful to share inconvenience with other of the Caliph's cities which were.

Like ancient Romans before them, Saracens regarded the Mediterranean as "our sea," fortified, impassable at Gebr al Tarik, likewise sealed at the Bosporus. The long, mountainous border shared with Mughals eastward was quiet. This, after all, was not a war for land—such a war had not been fought since the Mortality—but, in a sense, for the heart and mind of God. The Lesser Ocean had not seen much fighting—the Mughals' lines of supply were too long to mount much of an effort there, their ships inferior to those of the Caliph.

If one could believe reports these days.

Thus the bitterest conflict centered upon the Island Continent, as if it had been chosen arbitrarily as a neutral battleground, a vacant lot selected by two brawling schoolboys. If there were already a people there, primitive but wise, who knew—who cared—nothing for the dispute of foreign invaders which reshaped them into injured innocents, well, they were not of the Faithful, were they?

Of *anybody's* Faithful?

Feeling damp, he shivered. Not enough sense to go in out of the rain. Perhaps this was the essence of all human folly, he thought. Mankind lacked sense to go in out of the rain, be it a harmless urban drizzle or a torrent of lethal machinery hurled by an anonymous enemy who suffered an identical shortcoming.

Unbidden, almost unwelcome in his present mood, came a more comforting thought that these eight joyless years had produced one thing of uncompromised preciousness. The Princess Ayesha had grown into young womanhood, eventempered, graceful-limbed, beautiful by any standard of any time or any civilization.

Thanks to himself, to other of her teachers—no less than to her own innate intelligence—she had come to grasp each of the sciences, theology, and mathematics. August visitors to the Roman court, even resident artists, philosophers, rabbis, holy men, were upon frequent occasion dumbfounded by the girl's astute observations—offered gravely, in the beginning with a childish lisp. Most were not aware that her sleeping hours were punctuated by nightmares. Her screaming, however, still awakened the entire palace at times. Awake, she chorded her oud, handled animals and servants well. If her nightmares had endowed her with any talent for soothsaying, however, it was an erratic, useless one.

He ought to know.

For some time, now, he had been keeping a compendium of his young charge's dreams, in an attempt to sort them out, make some sense of them. In her visions, she often glimpsed people of extinct races, in alien array, many curious beasts, impossible machines, fantastic cities that could never have existed.

Only last week, for example, "she"—from the viewpoint of her dream—had been chauffeured about in a wheelless vehicle, one of a myriad skimming grass-covered big-city thoroughfares at ridiculous velocities—guided by a shaggy, manlike animal of some variety in colorful attire.

Sometimes she dreamed of horses.

In a more recent dream, she had been married to a humble scholar, much like himself—bury that thought deep, old friend!—suffering with his fellow citizens through a widespread economic dislocation, who was nevertheless gifted by some patron with a double-breeched pistol, its barrels fashioned of glass, muzzles molded together into the shape of a roaring lion's head.

This odd weapon she had seen in much detail, even to twisted rifling in its pentagon-sectioned bores. That she could retain her dreams with such vivid clarity was thanks, in the main, to efficacious medicines compounded for her by her father's physicians from, if one could credit it, dried hearts of the common artichoke.

Scientific efforts to determine what it was in artichokes that did the work had been interrupted by the war—so much for any thesis that war is good for progress—but the same medicine was being given now to soldiers who had survived the conflict southward, but whose experiences had left them shambling mental wrecks.

It seemed to help.

There was a certain aptness here. Thus far, Shulieman had found no pattern to Ayesha's dreams which made sense of them. Upon occasion, she predicted future events with startling accuracy. Yet her strongest-felt premonitions in most instances proved groundless. It was as if she possessed a private peephole upon what-might-be, as if the universe itself resembled that artichoke of which her medicine was compounded, the real world in which she spent her waking hours one slender threadlike leaf, deep inside its very heart, surrounded by near-identical leaves which grew larger, coarser, more *different* from the original as they grew further from the familiar core, until, at its outer circumference, they were unrecognizable distortions of what had been begun with.

Universe as artichoke. You are a poet, Rabbi Shulieman, or a madman. Perhaps both: a Jewish Sufi.

"Do you think thoughts too deep for me, David, or can you share them with a humble nursemaid?"

Shulieman took off his spectacles, polished them upon his robe, replaced them, then looked up with annoyance. It was Marya, Ayesha's companion, dressed for warmth, veiled more against dampness than against the lustful eyes of men.

"I ramble in my thoughts as if overnight I had become an old man. What in the name of the Merciful and Compassionate are you doing out here in this drizzle, Marya?"

She curtsied. "It was my intention, sir, to ask the same of you."

She came closer. Unfastening the veil at one side of her face, she let it drop. The years had given to the corners of her eyes a faint network of fine lines.

"There is a fire upon the hearth in my quarters, also sweet tea laid, hot and thick. Will you not join me?"

Within himself, Shulieman smiled a rueful smile. This was not the first time, over the years he had known Marya, that she had approached him thus. Always he'd had better things to do, and insufficient time to do them in: his own studies, his duties to the Caliph, to Ayesha. Always he had rebuffed Marya, as he made a habit of rejecting others, in gentleness, and not because she was unattractive—she was not, even now—nor even owing to any sort of scandal he might fear. At heart, he thought, he was a romantic. The fear of scandal would not have stopped him had he been so inclined.

In plain truth—he cursed himself for a foolish pickishness which had cost him many another such opportunity he might well regret when he really had become an old man—she appeared to be rather stupid, and this spoiled her for him, although what the quality of her intellect might have to do with casual flirtation, something less causal, or even a hot cup of tea before a blazing fire upon a cold, rainy afternoon, he was himself uncertain. Was it her fault she could not measure up to a standard he had set, despite himself, long ago and far too high?

Resolving that he could not be a fool all the time, he rose. "Yes, thank you, Marya, I believe I shall."

2

She invited Shulieman to sit upon a low, cushioned divan before the fire. Marya stirred coals in the small grate, poured them each a colorful porcelain cup from the matching pot which sat upon a worked-brass end-table, then reclined upon a silken cushion at his feet.

She looked up at him.

"Scholar Shulieman, always thinking. What are you thinking about this miserable morning, Scholar Shulieman?"

Shulieman sipped at the tea she had given him. Even just beneath his nose, its aroma was overmatched by her perfume. Much like his hostess, it was too sweet, yet promising of a bitter aftertaste. He considered long before replying.

"I was thinking about the war, Marya, for the most part. How it seems to have grown while we were not looking, from a brief holiday excursion of splendid, gay-uniformed young Moslems and Jews into a nightmarish grind of muddy bloodshed."

She smiled, as he thought she might have done at any answer he offered. She had removed her veil, and with it, it seemed, at least half of her clothing. From this vantage she had contrived, he could peer down into the heavy-scented abyss between her ample, tautly rounded breasts, if he wished it, to her jewel-bedecked navel.

He found, as usual, that he did not wish it.

She folded her white arms across her belly, ripening what was to him already overripe. "Do you not worry, David, about not being in the fighting?"

He laughed, tapping the nosepiece of his spectacles. "Saying I was nigh unto being blind, they would not take me. Nor am I much interested in great adventures, Marya, save those purely of the intellect. I believe that, if enough individuals thought about the problem long enough, we would not now be threatened by destruction in this war or any other. That would be adventure enough for me."

Still, like many another man, he wondered privately how he would acquit himself challenged thus. Would he be brave? Could he kill another man? These were not thoughts which he could share with someone like Marya, nor, for different reasons, with anyone else. Bespectacled and sedentary scholar that he was, too fast approaching middle age, something wild within him did yearn for physical adventure.

Marya, ignoring her own cup, which she had left unsipped upon the ornate table, flowed closer to him, placing one white, freckled, ring-laden hand upon his knee.

"Still, I sometimes try imagining what it would be like, fighting for the greater glory of God against the heretic."

She fluttered her long eyelashes at him.

"I fear that the place of women in the scheme of things precludes their playing at being soldiers, rulers, or even advisers to the rulers of the world."

Her index finger began making tiny circles upon his knee.

"Men always make the rules," she murmured, her voice now a husky whisper. "They play their glorious games with warnings posted, No Girls Allowed. There are times—not now, though, dearest David—when I would that it were different."

Understanding well that he lacked any charms which were not resistible, Shulieman began to worry about what Marya was after. Concealing any alarm he felt, he answered with caution. "Women play at different games, Marya, games which seem to have no rules at all."

She sat up, brushed long, dark auburn hair back from her eyes, but did not take her hand from his body. Her movement raised one rounded breast until he thought it would erupt from its covering. Fine hairs prickled along the back of his neck.

"Yes, David, there are indeed those women who find their own way in the world, rules or not."

"Women such as?"

She purred, her tone belying the content of her words. "Such as our mutual charge, the Princess Ayesha, who feels no qualm intruding upon the councils of men."

"So that is it," he answered, somewhat relieved. "Marya, a thousand axes are ground each day in this court of our enlightened sovereign Abu Bakr Mohammed VII . . ."

In Ayesha's case, it was a choice among four current stepmothers, more than a dozen "honorably" retired wives (including Ayesha's mother) proven incapable of providing the Caliph with male heirs, her only brother Ali, sisters, numberless grandparents, uncles, aunts, cousins, nephews, nieces, all struggling for a tiny share of prominence. Uninterested in power, Ayesha might become a pawn in such struggling, and he, uninterested in power himself, had likely slighted her in failing to prepare her against such a contingency. He looked down at Marya's exploring fingers.

"Whose whetstone are you cranking at this moment?"

"I?" the woman protested, placing her free hand in a modest pose across her bosom. Her other hand slid from Shulieman's knee halfway along inside his thigh. "You are asking such a question of Ayesha's dearest lifelong friend?"

In defense, he placed a hand over hers, a gesture which made him feel silly, like a reluctant virgin. She responded by taking his cup, placing it upon the bright-polished table, then rising a little to face him, one hand upon each of his legs.

She looked into his eyes, sliding her soft hands higher. "But of what earthly worth can her counsel be, when she herself borders each night upon raving madness?"

She passed a pink tongue across her lips.

He cleared his throat.

Become somewhat the pedant, he heard himself replying, "Marya, we both know that, despite the unreliability of her dubious gift—which her father, in an exercise of his own considerable intelligence, rightly distinguishes from the rational operations of her mind—he finds her easy to communicate with. He has come to rely upon the calm wisdom behind those night-tortured eyes of hers."

To the rest of her "family," all but her father—also her favorite teacher (she had few other friends at court)—she was something of an embarrassment, regarded with increasing awe, even fear, by her own otherwise sophisticated people.

Marya had moved forward again, so that her breasts were between his knees, her hands as high as they could go without leaving his thighs. "Perhaps you are right, David darling, perhaps there is wisdom to be gained from pain. Do you like pain, David darling, do you, too, find wisdom in it—or do you prefer inflicting it?"

Again she licked her lips as one of her hands moved for his waistband. He seized them both, holding them in one of his.

"And you, Marya," he said hoarsely, "inconspicuous little mouse in the wainscoting that you pretend to be, have always and ever acted as an all-around snoop and outright spy against full half Ayesha's family, in service of the other."

She rocked back, eyes wide, eyebrows arched in astonished outrage.

"In our complicated social, political, and religious situation—very like an artichoke I seem to have been thinking about all morning—with countless groups of individuals playing every side of every issue out of every conceivable motivation, *which* particular half of the family you serve seems somewhat inconstant."

Examining her at arm's length, he sighed to himself. Yet another missed opportunity.

It was going to be a long, rueful, bitter old age.

He continued. "Perhaps you are not so stupid after all, my dear, as I believed, but simply preoccupied, keeping track of all your lies, all your deceptions, all your trickeries, all your betrayals, each layered upon a contradictory predecessor. Now, what have you to say to that? Nothing? Well, then . . ."

Tossing her hands back at her, he levered himself from her over-upholstered divan, leaving her upon the floor, balanced upon her heels. As he opened an ornate, carven door into the family-quarters hallway outside, he turned once more.

"My thanks for the tea, Marya. Your life must be bewildering."

XIV:

A Suitable Token

Hast thou not regarded those who were forbidden to
converse secretly together, then they return to that
they were forbidden, and they converse secretly together in sin and enmity . . . ?
—The *Koran*, Sura LVIII

The instant that her door shut with a soft whoosh behind David
Shulieman's back, Marya hurled herself to her feet, breathing
harshly. No oath came to her lips. She was incoherent with
insulted rage, frustrated, desperate to fight back tears.

Behind her, a door opened. A woman, rich-clad, subtly
perfumed, and perhaps ten years older, stepped from a nearby
room.

"Well, Marya, are your charms beginning to fail you—and
me?"

The younger woman whirled toward the voice behind her, a
scorching epithet at last upon her lips, but one which, under
the circumstances, might well have cost her her life.

"Lady Jamela! A person that hairy could not be celibate,
could he, ma'am? Perhaps he prefers boys."

Abu Bakr Mohammed's current senior wife chuckled. "Perhaps he prefers Princess Ayesha. I marked the color in his face when you were working your, er, magic upon him—or attempting to. He is no celibate, I assure you, and he prefers girls."

Forgetting courtesty, Marya sank to the divan, feet and knees together, her face buried in her hands. Jamela let it pass. She might have suffered this indignity herself, had she not been wiser at an earlier age and begun employing surrogates like Marya.

"The trouble, my dear, is that you are no longer a girl."

Jamela sighed, more to herself than to her servant. Turning to a nearby window, she pulled back its heavy drapings to look out upon a gray fogbound landscape. Idly she played with one of the many rings upon her long-nailed fingers.

"Nor am I, I am afraid. We have reached a point in our lives when we shall have to depend upon something other than our looks. If you cannot extract information one way, I shall have to do it another. I go now, to wait upon my husband and his guest."

Turning, Jamela walked toward the door. "Upon occasion I have made you lavish promises, Marya, which none has power to abrogate as long as I am here in Rome, and you to be rewarded."

Marya looked up, sudden fear written into her eyes.

Jamela raised a hand. "*Laa, laa.* Read no irony into my words, child, for, unlike some others, I am ever faithful to them, believing it good business.

"I suggest, for sake of your confidence and self-esteem, that you test your wiles upon some other victim, for practice. Try Lady Shaabbah's new lover, the guard-lieutenant Kabeer. I may require your abilities again in future—I do not wish them blunted by any uncertainty."

2

When Jamela arrived, voices were raised in her husband's study.

"Bu, you are an optimist," one of them was saying, "and a bloody fool! Just look at this!"

As she entered, Jamela gasped. A small, shiny gun was out, being pointed straight at the undefended belly of Abu Bakr Mohammed VII, Sword of God, Defender of the Faith, the Caliph of Rome, by the elderly—and equally fat—merchant, Mochamet al Rotshild. Yet it was this latter who appeared indignant.

"Your guard did not search me so much as once upon my way up here!"

Grinning, the Caliph sat forward in his chair, put a hand out, palm up, to receive the weapon. Jamela relaxed, turned to a tea service already laid out, listening.

"Mo," the Caliph replied, "you have carried this lethal trinket with you for as long as We have known you. I must say, We would enjoy watching any ten guardsmen trying to take it away from you."

He turned Mochamet al Rotshild's weapon over in his hand.

"My, my, such a tiny thing—with such great big holes at the front! Here, take it back before We hurt Ourselves."

He handed the gun back to his friend.

"Besides," he continued, "—*Sghuhran,* thank you, my dear, why do you not pour yourself a cup, sit down, you look tired—what good would searching a determined assassin do? We have seen you deliver lectures upon how to kill a man with nothing more than the binding of a book."

He waved a hand about a room which, save for its windows and doors, was lined in nothing but books.

"*Laa,* a hundred bodyguards could not stay your hand, Mo, if you could not be trusted."

Unsatisfied, the merchant frowned. His friend the Caliph observed this and laughed.

Jamela found a place to sit, discomfited at being required to listen to a conversation openly.

Still, there was always something to be learned. Looking at the two men, one might almost think them brothers, identical in some ways, twin-opposites in others. Both were heavy and bearded, somewhere between fifty-five and sixty-five years of age, although neither showed it. The Caliph's ebon hair and beard were close-trimmed and thick, the merchant's fiery red, long and unruly. Abu Bakr Mohammed spoke with the cultured accent of a Roman, Mochamet al Rotshild with the glottal burr of his native Iskutlan. The Caliph wore no jewelry save the sunburst upon his breast which marked him Supreme Commander of the military. The merchant wore many rings, bracelets, the crossband and hanger for a cutlass which he had surrendered at the palace gate, and a piratical single earring. He was an enormous man. The Caliph was enormous-minded.

The latter continued. "As for those such as Marya and others you have been keeping an eye upon, We want them left where they are. They can be trusted, too, in their own way. Better a spy you know . . ."

Jamela suppressed an astonished gasp, recovering her cup before it spilled in her lap. So this was why the old bastard had forced her to be here, acting like a servant wench for this . . . this tradesman. Her husband put a hand up, stifling Mochamet al Rotshild's protest before it could be uttered.

"That is Our best security, Mo, friends—and enemies— who can be trusted."

Had he turned his gaze upon her for a moment when speaking the word "enemies"?

"Venerable as you are—Our age, almost to the day, as We recall—you are much like the best of Our personal guard, but better. Yet, for all that, 'merely' a merchant."

Mochamet al Rotshild grumbled, "Mine was a rough upbringing, Bu. Good preparation. A merchant learns to defend himself, in places where every other hand may be turned against him. He has motivation; no one will do it for him half so well as he himself."

"Indeed. A life of far-reaching voyages, rising from fore-castle to quarterdeck, thence to owner of a trading fleet with business and political connections around the globe. Success. A testament not alone to self-defense but to many skills. We hope you will retain them all where We are about to send you."

Mochamet al Rotshild subsided, resigned to a change of

subject. "We have spoken of this before. Yet, Bu, in all that time, I never before landed upon the *western* coast of the Savage Continent. Nothing crosses into that land or ever seems to come out of it. One hears fascinating, horrible tales."

"And sees, We gather, fascinating, horrible things?"

The merchant nodded. "Bu, let me tell you a story. I was offshore upon one occasion when . . .

"But I should explain. As a youth, I sailed upon many vessels, practicing at many positions. A merchantman I had signed upon was captured by a squadron of Mughal corsairs, those of us who survived their shelling and subsequent boarding pressed into service for a time until we died or could escape.

"Upon this voyage, a cooper's apprentice had already died, of some pox he had picked up from a dancing-girl in Hindi, so they told me—*charjooh,* I beg your pardon, Lady Jamela, for a rough old sailor's anecdote. Little good it did him, for he was a Mughal, with no need of death as an alternative to escape!"

The merchant laughed, as if this were a great joke. The Caliph motioned for him to go on.

"*Nanam,* yes, well, I was appointed cooper's helper, and spent much time thereafter making barrels. I believe I could still do it today, were there a need. Our squadron sailed about the Greater Ocean, from Attu down to Hawaii, thence to the Island Continent, doing a little trading and a deal of adventitious plundering, until a storm blew up one day, driving us hard upon the coast we spoke of earlier."

Mochamet al Rotshild shivered at his memories.

"I swear to you the storm had cleared and skies were sparkling as we made for what we took to be an uninhabited island where we could lay up to patch our bodies and our boats. Of a sudden, we were struck by lightning—not a brief blue-yellow flash as one is used to, but a long, blood-colored stroke which carried yards away as a feather singes in the hearth. It sank every one of seven ships in our squadron, leaving me the sole survivor. The very ocean boiled about the place where our ships had gone down."

The merchant rose, pacing as he spoke.

"I clung to a barrel I had hidden in during the onslaught. New white oak it was, lined with copper sheet for holding oil. Then I snagged a drifting lifeboat. I rigged a sail, making back for the last of those islands we had called upon. A long voyage it was, nor was I much welcomed when I got there, having helped to burn their largest town. I swore to them by God and by His Prophet that I had been a slave. Whereupon I found myself fashioning barrels for them until a Saracen vessel happened to call there. I eventually returned home."

These words had brought him to the window. He stood, his hands locked behind him, his back to the room, staring at the rain. Then he turned back to the Caliph and his wife.

"No one believed me about scarlet lightning, but I saw it myself. I remember it as if it were yesterday. The barrel which saved my life was reduced to charcoal outside. What it did to a squadron it could have done to a fleet.

"What was it, you ask? I have no idea. An act of God? Black magic? Forgive me, Your Holiness, Lady Jamela, but in all truth I do not believe in either one. A freak of a storm long past? I do not know. I have seen many other strange things, in my long life, but nothing like that before or since. I would like to know what it was."

The Caliph had arisen to join his friend. He placed a hand upon Mochamet al Rotshild's shoulder. He turned his face, however, to Jamela.

"Indeed, such a thing might end a war. This is our hope. And now Mochamet al Rotshild, old man that he has become in service to his Caliph since last seeing the western shore of the Savage Continent—yet not an old man in spirit—is about to serve Us once again by embarking upon another voyage, by sea *and* land, this time a diplomatic mission to the very center of that barbarian world."

To Mochamet al Rotshild: "For a subtle, multifaceted trader, this need not be an altruistic venture in entire. Nor, for the sake of its success, should it appear so.

"You may leave Us, Jamela. You have heard that which We would have you hear. Doubtless you have errands of your own you wish to see to. We shall stay here a while, making plans.

Send Ayesha to Us, will you? We believe her advice might
prove helpful."

Jamela rose. "*Massach chalhghayr*, Your Holiness; good
day, Mochamet al Rotshild."

"*Massach chalhghayr*, Lady Jamela; may God, most
Merciful and Compassionate, go with you."

3

As soon as she was able, Jamela returned to her own
apartments, ticking liabilities and assets off upon her fingers as
her slippers scuffed down the thick-carpeted hallway.

Let old men worry themselves, she thought, about global
politics. Scarlet lightning, indeed! Toys—fantasies of children. Her problem, as always, was a domestic one. Her
husband had called her there for but one reason: to let her
know he knew that for the sake of her son, his only legal heir,
she schemed against his favorite Princess at the risk of his
displeasure. Abu Bakr Mohammed might think he valued that
crazy little brat of his for her strange visionary "wisdom."
Jamela knew better.

Jamela always knew better.

Ayesha was the very image of her absent mother. Shaatirah
had not only been the Caliph's first wife but his first love, as
well. Retiring her, even in an elegance which she had
refused—such had been a letter of the law to which a ruler is
more subject than any of his citizens—had aged him by
decades.

Even the name of Malta, whither she had been sent, was, by
mutual agreement among inhabitants of the palace, forbidden
to be mentioned in the Caliph's presence.

Ayesha's presence, then, the reminder she represented,
weakened the power, not just of Jamela herself, but of others
with whom she was engaged in a shifting complex of
alliances. Ayesha, too, must be "retired," some *proper* use
found for her.

Perhaps an advantageous marriage, or as a suitable token in
the making of a treaty.

Nodding to a hallway guard, Jamela entered her own door.

Tea had been laid there by a servant, but this she ignored, going first to an adjoining room to look in upon her son.

Twenty-year-old Ali sat in his pen, a diaper about his loins, playing with a carven butterfly suspended from the ceiling on a cord. At the sound of the door opening behind him, he twisted his fat neck around and favored her with a gummy, crooked smile.

The ever-present nurse-servant sat knitting in a corner. Jamela walked across the carpet, leaned into the pen, and tousled Ali's hair. His eyes were tiny, his ears very slightly pointed and carried low upon the sides of his overly broad head. He smiled again and reached for her. She leaned back beyond his grasp—he was immensely strong.

She wondered if this thing she felt for Ali might be love. She had never felt the like for anyone else. A fierce protectiveness, mingled with the knowledge that, whatever else he might be, Ali was the Caliph's only heir—had she not bribed and blackmailed enough midwives, and at terrible risk, to be sure of it?

With an aged Caliph out of the way—he was an old man, after all, and could not last forever—Jamela would be Ali's regent. These thoughts and feelings were so mixed in her, love, hate, greed and pity, that she examined them but seldom.

She refused to do so now.

Returning to the first room, she strode to a locked cabinet, whence, by means of a key suspended from a fine gold chain about her neck, she removed a small lacquered box.

Throwing herself upon a pile of cushions, she took from the box a small packet of white papers, a pouch containing dried, shredded leaves of an illegal and unholy weed. With deft fingers she rolled both into a slender cylinder, placing it between her lips. She thrust its other end into a brazier beneath the teapot.

The feel of nicotine surging through her blood was a benediction, after so many hours without it.

Now she could think. Even an absolute ruler, Jamela reasoned, must bow to the necessity of keeping peace in his own household. The Caliph's objections to a rational disposition of his bothersome girl-child should prove easy to overcome.

Again she considered assets she could bring to bear upon her problem. Marya's failure this morning was another reminder, one which could not have come too soon. Pretty little Shaabbah might serve, the Caliph's wily and seductive youngest wife. She would do as her senior bade her. Perhaps not *gladly*—but she supposed Jamela alone knew of her affair with the Caliph's guardsman.

Other obstacles?

Ayesha's teacher, *maa ismugh*, what was his name again? Shulieman-something.

"Shulieman counts for less than nothing," she heard herself saying aloud. "He is only a hireling Jew."

Hirelings, she thought, often were required to travel with those they served. If he truly loved her, if a rigorous journey sapped him of resolve to conceal that love . . . Either way, he could be disposed of as easily as the girl.

Ayesha's own protests, should she be foolhardy enough to give voice to them, could lead to her more direct undoing.

At long last, Jamela poured herself a cup of tea, settling back. Lighting her second *seekaaragh*, she began sorting through her mind for names of foreign dignitaries—*thapnan*, also their children, of course—of a marriageable disposition.

And the further away, the better.

XV:

By Arrangement of the Caliph

Whomsoever God will, He leads astray, and whomsoever He will, He sets him on a straight path.
—The *Koran*, Sura VI

Prairie stretched in all directions, much like the south of Faransaa, infinitely emptier. A tireless wind bore the same rich spices. The sky had the same look: bleak where it was still clear, cloud-mountains clenched in towering fists, blue-black, seamed by lightning.

She lay in soap-odored dirt, breathing hard from terror and exertion, trying—for her life—to keep still. Yellow flies buzzed about, drawing crusty patches of blood where they bit. Her clothes were drenched with the effort of doing nothing. Figures either side of her lay even more still, splintered war-shafts protruding from their bodies, scarlet mingling with alkali soil.

High above, upon widespread fringe-tipped wings, scavengers circled, wary and patient. It was not yet their time. A random arrow thudded into the dirt, a finger's width from her side. She lay still, trying to control her fear.

"Ayeeeah!"

Her world filled with an idiot screaming for the fifth time that afternoon, the gloating whoop of victory-to-come, savage voices raised into falsetto. Through the earth at her ear, she heard the pounding of many feet. She lay with her arms beneath her body, something small and hard folded in her hands.

With deliberate care—and both thumbs—she turned back the hammer of a small, two-barreled pistol. It was difficult. The thing had been made for a strong man. Trying not to think, she bent its muzzle upward, beneath her jaw, remembering at the last moment to put it in her mouth to avoid half-measures too hideous to contemplate. She tightened both index fingers upon the trigger.

Almost too late, she heard the screams cut off.

Pulling the gun away from her face, she risked rising upon an elbow. Bodies—those of friends and enemies alike (including the man who had given her his pistol as a desperate last resort)—lay everywhere in the dry prairie grass. Others, a pitiful few, strained with her to see what had stopped the attack.

A cloud of yellow dust boiled upon the horizon with a thundering which might have come from the angry clouds overhead. In seconds, she could hear something else, a caterwauling whine, like musicians tuning up in the bazaars of Rome—a paralyzing wave of homesickness chose that moment to wash over her—then she saw them.

In form, they were like brown helmet-crabs she had played with upon girlhood trips to the beach, they of the many tiny legs and long-barbed tail. These monsters were a hundred times larger. There were a score of them, skimming across the plain.

Heedless of broken gunfire coming from the few survivors they had left, the savages fled. One archer screamed as the leading creature drew him beneath its advancing carapace, then fell as silent as his own victims.

He disappeared.

2

As usual, Ayesha awoke with a start.

"Merciful God," she sighed to herself, "that was a strange one!"

Placing her small feet upon a parqueted floor beside the divan, she ran a hand across her forehead. One might believe, she thought, that a person would get used to waking up like this. She never had. For some reason, it was worse when she slept during the daytime, her dreams more alien and vivid, her awakening a hot and dizzy one.

She arose, tucking her day-robe about her, and, barefoot, crossed the comfortable study which was a part of her personal suite. Not waiting for a servant, she drew back draperies from windows which comprised one wall of the room. She was startled for a moment by the sight of one of the palace handymen outside, half naked, the skirt of a burnoose wound about his face, scrubbing at her window-framing with a dry brush. Removing old paint, she assumed. His box of cleaning supplies hung suspended by a strap over his shoulder.

She waved and smiled, a habit she was certain all of her father's wives would have disapproved, then crossed to a huge brass-barred cage suspended upon a gilt-threaded rope from the high ceiling. She tapped one of its bars with a dainty, short-trimmed fingernail.

"Sagheer, are you ready to come out now, little one?"

There was a stirring inside the cage.

Taking a key from the drawer of a nearby stand of ebony and inlaid mother-of-pearl, she unfastened a padlock hanging from the small cage door. It had been necessary to resort to this. Sagheer could unfasten every other sort of closure she had tried.

Inside, a brown, furry form reached tiny fingers toward her. Its eyes glistened in the shadows of a quilted satin cozy which covered half the cage. The animal leaped off its swinging perch, rushed to the door, forcing it open with sheer weight as soon as Ayesha could remove the lock. No larger than her two fists put together, it jumped into her arms.

"Sagheer, Sagheer!" she crooned, smoothing the small, round head between rounded ears. The creature's great eyes regarded her as it twined its fingers in her hair. From the drawer she took a peanut, offering it to him. He slapped it from her fingers. It hit the floor, skidding beneath the stand. Most times, he took it in both hands, dismembered its hull with his teeth, which were tiny and pointed.

"*Chanaa muthachassibh*. I only meant it to be a little nap, Sagheer. Studying for examinations I shall never take is a stern test of one's resolve. I hope Father and David appreciate it."

Sagheer looked up at her, almost, she thought, as if he could understand what she was saying. A second offering he accepted. She laughed, then crossed the book-lined room in a different direction, passing a great globe of the world, a beloved and battered rocking-dog she refused to let them put into storage, to an enormous well-lighted desk, weighted down with volumes and implements of writing.

Scattering bits of broken shell behind him, Sagheer rode upon her shoulder as he had since Ayesha had been eleven. The pygmy marmoset had been a gift from her father's friend, that fabulous merchant captain (some whispered pirate) Mochamet al Rotshild.

He himself preferred (as pirates were wont to do, she imagined) a parrot, a gray-white roc of a bird with yellow eyes, a shiny black beak, and a bright orange tail, which he sometimes brought with him when he came to the palace. It rode upon *his* shoulder, expressing sentiments, in its harsh, raucous voice, which would have embarrassed anyone else (save perhaps the captain, who must have taught him) even to *think* about.

Still, Ayesha's one regret about Sagheer was that he could not talk to her. She loved her father, and he her. Yet he was the most important man in the world, not to her alone, but to every one of the Faithful. He had little time to spare her. For a like reason, her father's power, nobody offered open friendship to her, untainted with ulterior designs, nor could she have accepted if they had.

Even David, she had understood since she was a very little girl indeed, must be careful to maintain a professional attitude toward her. He was a good friend, seeming unimpressed with anyone's power, social importance, or wealth. What mattered to him was one's intelligence, perhaps even more, one's ethics. This made him even lonelier than she was, she supposed (he had never married), and—for different reasons than any lack of intelligence or ethics she might have suffered—kept the two of them at more than arm's length.

3

"Princess?"

Late that afternoon, as outdoor light had begun to fail her, Ayesha was surprised by a timid rapping at the arched frame of the open door between her study and the sitting-room connecting with the family-quarters corridors outside her suite. She turned from her book to see Marya standing in the doorway.

"Princess," the woman offered with uncharacteristic diffidence—she had never bothered to knock before, either—"your presence is requested in the Caliph's library as soon as is convenient. I am instructed to accompany you there."

What was that odd look in Marya's eyes, Ayesha wondered. Smugness, perhaps, mingled with what . . . fear? Perhaps it came from being commanded by too many high-placed masters. Marya was her servant, to be ordered about by no one else. She had exchanged well-measured words with Lady Jamela over this very topic not many days ago. In any event, it was certainly an unattractive combination of expressions.

Ayesha arose from her desk, brushing at her robe, which had become wrinkled from long hours of sitting, cupped a palm over the chimney of a reading lamp she had just lit, blowing it out.

"Have I time to change, Marya?"

The woman swallowed. "Princess, I have relayed to you all the message I was charged with."

Ayesha nodded. "*Jayyit*, let us assume, then, that good manners are still called for. *Min bhatlah*, please lay out my green velvet with gilt at the shoulders. Perhaps Father has company. In any case, I should want to look my best for him."

Through the curtain Ayesha had redrawn when night began to fall, neither of them noticed the turbaned handyman, removing something from the glass, making minute adjustments within his shoulder-slung toolbox. Satisfied, he climbed down from the window, leaving the vicinity of the Princess' quarters as they did.

4

When she arrived at her father's library, not more than half an hour later, Ayesha saw that her guess had been correct. In addition to herself and Marya, and a lieutenant-of-the-guard, there were His Holiness himself, the Lady Jamela, the Lady Shaabbah, Rabbi David, and the "Commodore," Mochamet al Rotshild.

He had not brought his parrot.

Curtsying, Ayesha glanced at each person in the room, attempting to divine from their expressions why she had been called here. Observing Mochamet al Rotshild, whom she knew least well of all those here, she would have described his expression as studiedly neutral. He was seated in a high-backed chair beside her father's, a steaming mug of coffee in his enormous, freckled hand.

David stood behind the old pirate, not leaning against the bookcases. There was an odd look upon his face which she could not interpret, but the gloating in Jamela's eyes was unmistakable. Seated upon a hassock by the Caliph's right knee, she had broken all precedent by bringing Ali with her, dressed in his finest, which he had soiled sometime in the last few minutes. He sat upon the carpet at Jamela's feet, sucking a finger and whimpering a little around it.

Her father's bearing was dignified, betraying no sign of his sense of humor. He wore another of those unadorned uniforms he had taken to wearing since war had been declared. He was sitting in his own chair, almost at attention. It was as if he were, for some as-yet-unspoken reason, hiding grief.

This frightened her very much. What had she done?

Marya curtsied. "The Princess Ayesha, Your Holiness, as you commanded."

Abu Bakr Mohammed VII grunted, for a moment something of his true self showing through his stiff exterior.

"We did not command, girl, We requested. Even with a Caliph, there is a difference. Now We command you to be seated and be quiet. You are enjoying this too much, and We shall not forget it."

He extended a broad hand, palm upward. "Our daughter We *request* to sit—Rabbi, kindly get her a chair, will you?—for We have consequential matters to discuss with her, nor do We relish watching her participate upon her feet."

Stepping around Mochamet al Rotshild, David Shulieman brought her a straight-backed but comfortable wooden chair which her father himself had fashioned. He then returned to his original place, giving her no sign of what was about to happen.

The Caliph glanced at his senior wife, failed to suppress a sour expression, then turned back to Ayesha.

"Ayesha, you are an intelligent, farsighted individual. You have been educated all your life to anticipate what it might mean to be the Caliph's daughter, to serve Almighty God, His Faithful, and their civilization as We serve them."

Ayesha nodded, still not understanding. "*Nanam,* yes, Your Holiness, I have, indeed, been thus educated."

"*Jayyit,* very well, then. There has, this past month, come to Our attention a unique opportunity for you to perform that service, an opportunity which could end this war we endure, impose a lasting peace upon the entire globe. Such is a worthy cause upon which to spend a life. Such is the cause upon which, in service of Almighty God, His Faithful, and their civilization, We now command you to spend yours."

Afterward, she was never able to describe the feeling which

started in the center of her being, spreading along her limbs into the tips of her extremities. It made her scalp prickle.

"*Chanaa la chabhgham,* I do not think I understand, Father. Am I to die, then?"

The look of anguish which swept across the Caliph's face was undisguised. "*Laa,* daughter, no. Although you may very well *risk* death in performance of this service. That is sometimes the lot of a woman. You are—and We assure you We take no pleasure in decreeing that it should be so—to go away from Us, into a foreign land, there to be married to its ruler, that an alliance might be forged to overcome the Mughal. For such were you born, child, for such were you ordained."

Ayesha wanted to ask her father, *But what of my mind, can that be of no service to Almighty God, His Faithful, and their civilization,* but she did not. She could not. She had known, as long as she could remember, that this might happen someday. She had not thought about it much. Ah, well, another court, another ruler, a loyal subordinate to her father. She would continue her studies, perhaps even travel back and forth, leaving Rome neither altogether nor forever.

"May I be permitted to ask, Your Holiness, to which ruler I am to be married? The Sultan of 'Inglitarrah has four wives and two male heirs. Faransaa's ruler has taken a vow of celibacy. Hoolandaa—"

The Caliph stopped her with a hand.

"We do not know whom you are to wed, girl. . . ."

There was a roughness in his voice which spoke of tears suppressed.

"You are to travel with Mochamet al Rotshild, here, also with your tutor, to the western coastline of the Savage Continent, there to be married to whomsoever rules there."

A small voice shrilled within Ayesha's mind. *What am I supposed to feel at this moment? What am I supposed to feel?* Her rigid posture suggested to the outer world what she did feel: nothing. Even one of her nightmares, she thought, was preferable to this numbness.

The Caliph turned his head, looking first at Mochamet al

Rotshild, then at the Lady Jamela, his expression changing as he did so.

"Each of those who have labored so diligently to persuade Us of this course—shall it prove successful or otherwise—shall reap an appropriate reward. We shall begin with Marya. You, too, are to accompany Our daughter, never setting a treacherous foot in Our court again as long as you live!"

Marya gasped and closed her eyes.

"But there are others well deserving of reward, Ayesha. As the future consort of a ruler—not to mention Our favorite child—We wish you to hear it meted out."

He turned in his chair to look upon the Lady Shaabbah, who paled under his prolonged gaze.

After a time, he spoke. "We have not forgotten, for example, Our young, pretty, *faithless* junior wife, who helped Lady Jamela persuade Us of your disposition. She will be retired in disgrace—unless, within a year, she can provide Us with a healthy male heir, one she can prove beyond question was sired by Us. We leave it up to her to provide a method, satisfactory to Us, of guaranteeing its pedigree."

Shaabbah blinked, a small and timid smile flirting about the corners of her mouth. She took a breath and straightened, a certain determination visible in her bearing, Ayesha thought, a certain pride. A glance at the amused twinkle—others might have called it a savage glitter—in Mochamet al Rotshild's eye told the Princess that he shared her observation and opinion. Cast loose from Jamela, Shaabbah would make something of herself. Shaabbah would triumph.

Ayesha wondered why she cared.

"As for her lover," Abu Bakr Mohammed went on, "guard-lieutenant Kabeer. You, sirrah, are to be reduced in rank and sent along to the Savage Continent, to serve another mistress. But 'mistress' in name alone, We are afraid, as you are first to be relieved by the executioner of those portions of your nether anatomy which got you into trouble. Performed under anesthesia in the Palace infirmary, the process should be relatively painless."

Kabeer swayed, his face gone gray.

The Caliph grinned. "Now that you know where you stand, Kabeer, We shall rescind Our order for your castration upon grounds of Caliphitic mercy, to inspire you to more faithful service in future—also because you are too liable to worsen your situation by buying off Our executioner. That is, if We still kept an executioner around.

"Jamela—" Her eyes empty of fear or hope, the Caliph's senior wife looked up again when her name was mentioned. He refused to look upon her, keeping his eyes instead upon Ayesha. "Jamela is to be retired, penniless, to that shabby Persian village whence she came."

"But what of my son?" she demanded. Her voice was level, stripped of emotion. "*Your* son, Bu, your only legal heir?"

"*Min bhatlah*, David, will you please explain to the Lady Jamela, as once We heard you explain to the Princess, that, contrary to popular belief, there is no automatic inheritance of the Caliphate?"

Stunned by this swift turning of events, and by a certain hideous brilliance in the Caliph's judgments which he found himself both loathing and admiring, the rabbi could but nod in confirmation.

"In any case, Our former dear," the Caliph continued, turning to face his senior wife at last, "that point shall soon be moot. As We were at some pain explaining to Ayesha, there is a war. Everyone—even poor, mindless Ali—is expected to serve."

He glanced up at the guard-lieutenant, his voice sharper. "Put that *thing* into a uniform. Have it sent out with tomorrow's troop shipment to the Island Continent!"

XVI:

A Party of Every Section

It is not for the believers to go forth totally; but why should not a party of every section of them go forth, to become learned in religion, and to warn the people when they return to them, that haply they may beware?
—The *Koran*, Sura IX

In the dusty stillness of a service corridor behind the Caliph's library, a young man, tanned and turbaned, carefully removed a slim metallic wand from a hole he had drilled into the wall.

Daubing the aperture with a bit of spackling which he carried in his toolbox, now resting upon the floor, he gave the stuccoed wall an absent swipe to smooth it down. He played the hair-fine cord, leading from the wand into the box, back and forth into his palm until the elliptical hank could be fastened with another bit of wire and put away.

Glancing up the dimly gaslit hall, he stooped to the box. There was a small, shrill squeal, then:

". . . *point shall soon be moot . . .*"

A colorful miniature image of the Caliph was visible in a tiny window deep within the box.

". . . *As We were at some pain explaining to Ayesha, there is a war. Everyone—even poor, mindless Ali—is expected to serve. Put that* thing *into a uniform. Have it sent—*"

There was a *click*. The young man arose once again, dusting his hands off upon one another.

Smiling, he slung the toolbox over his naked shoulder and proceeded at a brisk pace down the corridor, satisfied that, at long last, he had something of substance for the evening transmission homeward.

SURA THE THIRD: 1420 A.H.—

Sedrich Fireclaw

The evildoers shall have their portion,
like the portion of their fellows; so let
them not hasten Me!
                        —The *Holy Koran*, Sura LI,
                              The Scatterers

XVII:

The Silver Chest

". . . We shall roll up heaven as a scroll is rolled for the writings. . . ."

—The *Koran*, Sura XXI

She sat waiting in a sidewalk restaurant in the busy heart of Rome, sharing a stained composition-covered table with three shabby foreigners. Young black men they were, perhaps students. They were of a correct age, speaking with heavy accents. One had brought a book-sized silver-colored chest. From twin, mysteriously screened apertures upon its face there issued a barbaric chant:

"Dancin' in the dark, to the radio of love . . ."

This dubious miracle she took for granted. For her, at least at this particular moment, it was a common, sometimes pleasant, often irritating phenomenon. At this particular moment, she did not mind it. To her left, heavy traffic squeezed by through a self-consciously quaint and cobbled street inadequate to handle it properly. There was a rumbling hiss of rubber-tired wheels, a not totally unpleasant odor of burning petroleum fractions inefficiently consumed.

Facing south, toward the Eternal City's largest and most famous mosque, she realized that mounted sets of crossed bars, exactly like those worshipped by the ancient Christians, defiled the building. Moreover, people walked through its high-arched portals without so much as leaving their shoes upon the steps outside.

Any indignation she felt at the sacrilege seemed unreal, far away from her immediate concerns.

One of these was that she was about to meet David. Bored with waiting, with the present randomly acquired company and location, she was looking forward to seeing him. All around her hung an atmosphere of stagnant poverty, of a depression in which she was somewhat better off than the average. Absently she wondered what it was she did for a living. No Caliph's daughter would brazen unescorted into the streets of this strange, transformed city. David, she felt, was off somewhere, not very far away, in a general southeasterly direction.

The silver box continued pouring primitive music into the air.

She saw a police officer approaching from her right, a fortyish, pale blonde, almost plump woman, with rather short, curly hair. Not even the impossible phenomenon of a female law-enforcer surprised the girl. The woman wore a black cap with a short, highly polished visor extending halfway around her head, a light blue, epauletted tunic of cotton, a dark blue skirt, wool and scandalously short. Wrapped about her waist was a black leather pistol belt, stamp-tooled to resemble basket-weaving. There was no buckle—nor did Ayesha notice any other insignia.

Ayesha recalled having shared a casual word with the policewoman fifteen or twenty minutes earlier, upon her arrival at the café. Now she worried, not so much about the weapon the woman carried as about her own—a gray-black boxy little implement of death, rapid-fire, illegal in the extreme, slung by a black webbed nylon strap from one shoulder and concealed beneath her baggy overcoat.

Her right hand slipped through a hole cut in her coat pocket, tightening about its plastic-paneled grip.

Nearing Ayesha, the policewoman drew her own weapon, a short, heavy-barreled revolver, very dark and therefore new. As its barrel rose, Ayesha could see its stubby front sight, its convex muzzle crown, even the faint, annular tool-markings about its bore. Thinking that perhaps the woman planned to arrest her, Ayesha felt frustration rather than fear. The Cause—whatever cause that might happen to be—was too urgent to be thus inconvenienced.

As the woman reached Ayesha's side, she pressed the cold muzzle of her revolver to the girl's right temple. Ayesha felt a gentle bounce before it made firm contact. To her utter surprise, just as the mysterious silver chest shouted "Lights out!", the woman spat, "Goodbye, terrorist!"

She pulled the trigger.

Ayesha heard the explosion in the center of her brain, not particularly loud. There was no pain. Her vision blacked abruptly—with some lingering granularity. More than anything, it was this loss of vision which made her angry.

She had time for two other thoughts: "Now I shall find out for certain" and "I was having such a good time with David. I am not yet ready to leave him."

Child of her culture, child of many cultures, she somehow expected to begin drifting heavenward.

2

Instead, she awakened feeling depressed and shaken—something to which she was accustomed—with the blood vessels throbbing in the right side of her head.

Usually, when she had dreams like this one, she awoke just before she died. It was a long, long time before she felt like sitting up, longer still before she thought to brush her porthole curtain aside to see where this odd vehicle had brought her upon this new and sunny day.

When at last she did, light fluttered harshly past the speed-blurred spokes of one of the great wind-driven wheels just outside. It was a strange and wonderful contrivance, this vessel she rode aboard, half ship, half sail-powered locomotive, superior in some way to its rail-bound European counterpart, since it was independent of all but the crudest of road-beds.

Bowing to Mochamet al Rotshild's overprotective insistence that she sleep at night—while everyone else on board took their rest during the heat of the day—had been a mistake, not solely in that it made her feel that much more lonely. For Ayesha, loneliness was itself an old, familiar companion, whose presence depended not upon the absence of others. But it established an evil precedent, that of obedience—as if Mochamet al Rotshild occupied her father's place—to the pirate's will.

Or to anyone's save her own.

Then again, she corrected herself, that precedent had been well set long before this voyage had begun.

Letting the short, pleat-folded curtain fall back into place before the porthole, she summoned up the memory of a darker morning, several months before, at the quayside resting-place of a more conventional vessel, where her father had come, unexpectedly and incognito, to see her off. Out of a briny-odored Marseilles fog, his stout figure had materialized upon the creaking gangway, spoken for a moment with a weapons-laden Sergeant Kabeer, then, coming aboard, turned aside at the rail to seek the cabin Mochamet al Rotshild had assigned her aboard his *Daghapy Wezza,* upon which bloody and famous ship the merchant prince had already thrice circumnavigated the globe.

From the opposite end of the ship, Ayesha saw her father, immediately recognizing him despite the common robe which he affected and the wrappings which concealed his broad and bearded face. She herself was better disguised by the weather, standing high upon the fog-shrouded foredeck, watching the hard-muscled laborers below her, reeking as they did of *thanpaah* and *ouiskeh,* loading cargo.

Now she hurried down a rope-railed flight of stairs, along

the weather-dampened planking of the main deck, following, although he knew it not, the Caliph aft.

He knocked upon her door.

"Enter, Your Holiness."

Startled, he turned to face her.

"One customarily says that from within doors, daughter. *Limaadaa,* why are you out upon deck, in this pestilential soup, among all these ruffian sailors?"

"*Jayyit jittan, sghuhran,* Father, since you see fit to ask, I am very well, sir, no thanks to you. And yourself?"

He shook his head in resignation.

Sliding past him, she turned the fog-dewed brass handle, cold and slippery in her hand. Together, they stepped into the light and warmth of the owner's cabin. The owner had displaced the captain, and the captain the first mate, and so on, down the ladder of authority, until she had speculated to herself that one of the stokers, pitiable fellow, would this night be forced to sling his hammock from the anchor-flukes.

She turned, pulled the shawl from around her shoulders, tossed it upon the single bunk, sitting in one of two chairs bolted beside a small table, began asking questions of her own.

"*Maadaa thureet, Siti?* Have you not left it a bit late to play protective parent? Or do you worry that this western potentate, whoever he may be—if he indeed exists—might receive his little gift in damaged condition?"

The Caliph stood without speaking, feeling the deck roll gently beneath his feet, watching a green-shaded kerosene lamp swing gently back and forth from the rafter-beam, wondering why his heart continued, in indecency, to beat.

Without awaiting answer, Ayesha added, "I have just this past hour overheard a sailor's tale that the western coast of the Savage Continent is lorded over by women." Savoring the dual salaciousness of this confession, she laughed, sarcasm carried in an undertone. "Of what good will be your offering then, Your Holiness?"

Turning to face his daughter, the Caliph thrust his hands deep within his pockets, looking at her over the folds of a patched and soiled muffler he had not yet removed. His eyes were those of a starveling. Even through the woolen windings, his sigh was audible.

"Our informants advise Us that he styles himself Sun King, scarcely an appellation for a female ruler."

Taking a step toward her, he shook his head. "Ayesha, so well closed is his entire domain that there is precious little more Our informants *can* tell Us. We have spent many a life—which will join thousands of others to haunt Our conscience forever—merely learning that much.

"Our concern, daughter, is for you—although, *manlayagh*, you have scant reason at this moment to believe it."

The girl just managed to suppress a snort of derision.

"Ayesha, child of my heart, I did not journey all this distance merely to give you tantalizing half-hints of your destiny."

At last he discarded his shabby cloak, letting it fall in a soggy bundle to the polished floor, and with it the noble plural she had never heard him set aside before.

"Nor shall I argue further with you over it. Nor make excuses for myself. I am required, God help me, to perform a Caliph's deeds, albeit I am just a man. And, as with those agents whom I sent to certain death upon the Savage Continent, or that multitude slain elsewhere, there can be no excuse, not from your point of view, nor, speaking as a simple man and not a Caliph, from my own. If He will not help me, in his mercy and compassion, perhaps He will at least forgive, for He knows I cannot forgive myself. I came . . ."

He stopped, having for the moment run out of voice. She saw that his eyes were sunk in blackened pits. Familiar furrows upon his face seemed vastly deeper this morning. Almost, she was tempted . . . almost . . .

"I came, this morning, as a simple man, to wish *man assalaamagh* to the only living human being I love. May God's peace go with you, dearest child, beloved daughter. May—"

Ayesha stood, a sudden chill running up her back and down through her limbs. "The only *living* human being? *Maa manna,* what does that mean, Father, the only *living* human being?"

He took a step and, turning, sank at last into the other chair beside the table. With one hand upon his knee, he rested his forehead in the palm of the other, keeping his eyes upon the floor as he spoke.

"It means, my darling, that your mother, the Lady Shaatirah, the only woman, besides yourself, who ever meant a thing to me, has been dead and buried this fortnight past, the life impersonally smashed out of her by Mughal artillery in a surprise shelling of Malta." And I, he thought, continue living. Where is the mercy and compassion in that?

He looked up, raised a hand, then let it fall back to the chair-arm.

"No one thought to tell me about it until this afternoon, when I received a coded wire aboard the train."

"But how?"

For a moment, Ayesha's voice had become that of a little girl again. A very frightened little girl. With a considerable effort, she regained some measure of control, so that she fell to her knees beside him as an act of volition. She placed a hand over his.

"I thought we had this sea of ours locked up. Does our fight go that badly, Daddy?"

For his favorite daughter Abu Bakr Mohammed, the Sword of God, Protector of the Faith, Caliph of Rome, summoned up a pained smile.

"*Laa,* my darling, *Inshallagh* and the creek don't rise, our 'lock,' as you have put it, remains intact. As these things are reckoned militarily, it was nothing more than a minor tactical escapade, a strategically pointless sally past the Gebr al Tarik of one cheerless, fogbound morning exactly such as this."

Eyes filled with sadness, he shook his head, returning it to the palm of his hand.

"Those there are who, for a variety of reasons, might reckon otherwise. The Mughal, it would now appear, have found a way to plank-in a whaleboat, caulk its seams, weight it down with ingots of lead, and propel it a few feet beneath the water's surface, whilst crew and engine suck the breath of their life through a tube.''

The Caliph seemed to shake himself, to sit up straighter. "This boat carried a breech-loading mortar. Our own engineers advised Us some years ago that such a thing was possible, using hand-pumped tanks for rising and sinking. Now We fear we shall have to fashion such a terrible vessel to cope with theirs.''

"Progress," Ayesha answered, one portion of her mind wondering whether there was purpose in his telling her all this. Perhaps he sought to dedicate her more to the ending of this war her fate was shaped for. There had been a time when she believed him incapable of such a cynical usage with her. She rose and stood away from him. Did people ever truly know one another? Would her father use her, then, as he used soldiers? Would he expend her like a rifle cartridge? Well, she was here, wasn't she?

The Caliph shook his head again, as if in denial of her unspoken accusation.

"*Nanam.* Yet truly We never intended to burden you needlessly with this news about your mother's death. What We would say to you, instead, is this: should an alliance come about, as is Our fondest hope, some regular communication must be established, as one condition to the treaty which the Commodore carries with him.''

He put out a hand, tacitly begging her, she thought, to place her own within it. Ignoring it, she stood where she was, realizing that, in this sudden and unwelcome perception of her father as an ordinary man, desperately in need of her approval and affection, she had at last—and perhaps it was not such a good thing as she had looked forward to these many years— grown up.

He shrugged and dropped his hand to his side.

"All of your life, my daughter, you have experienced terrible—and ofttimes revealing—visions. Your struggle to discern their meaning has given you command of such a knowledge of the science of the mind as We possess. Now We bid you, both as daughter and as subject, offer to interpret the dreams of this unknown ruler you are being given to, after the manner of Joseph in the Holy Koran—and afterward convey what you learn thus of him and his domain back to your own people."

Why did this suggestion of betrayal within betrayal abruptly fill her with an interest she had not found in life since learning of this voyage? Was she becoming like the rest of them at court, a cynical intriguer?

Or was it something else, some hope she sensed in her father which had nothing to do with his official hopes of ending the war?

"Mo will instruct you in the methods of enciphering information within innocent-sounding phrases. Keep Us informed. Perhaps, when a happier time shall come to pass, visits home will not be beyond thinking.

"Do you serve Us, and in any case, your name will be remembered in every mosque, in every square and city within Islam, for as long as *this* Caliph reigns in Rome."

He placed his stubby hands upon the chair-arms, pushed himself to his feet with a grunt, then, clapping his hands together, rubbed the palms upon his chest.

"Now, dear, *min bhatlah*, could you find it in your heart at least to offer an old man a hot cup of *shaay* before he once again must expose his poor dilapidated carcass to the cold?"

3

The ship struck some minor obstruction which sent a shudder through its keel.

Wind flapped at her porthole curtain.

Bitter memories giving way to an even more bitter reality, Ayesha rose at long last to her feet. This ship which bore her—no longer the pirate Commodore's *Daghapy Wezza* but a different conveyance entirely, by previous arrangement fashioned for her party by a strange, barbaric people—now seemed in a terrible hurry.

Outside, a wave-tossed ocean of man-high yellow grass rippled with its passing.

What sets mankind apart, she thought, from all other organisms is that mankind seeks pain and avoids pleasure—and is proud of it. Now she herself was doing so at an unprecedented velocity. At this headlong speed, the great curved springs upon which each wheel's axle rested failed to soften the roughness of the rutted road they rolled upon, as they had at a more temperate pace.

There was a hoarse shout of alarm just outside her louvered cabin door.

A buzzing shadow passed by her window.

In his swinging cage, little Sagheer chittered out his uneasiness. Ayesha crossed the small room in a single pace to comfort him. Through the space she had occupied just a heartbeat before, an arrow flashed through the open porthole above her bunk, burying itself with a dull thud in the wall across her tiny cabin.

Outside, Mochamet al Rotshild shouted an order.

The land-ship picked up even more speed.

XVIII:

The Pillar of Fire

But as for the ungodly, their refuge shall be the Fire; as often as they desire to come forth from it, they shall be restored into it, and it shall be said to them, "Taste the chastisement of the Fire. . . ."

—The *Koran*, Sura XXXII

"What is it, old fellow? What d'you hear?"

For Fireclaw, it began that cloudless morning with a squirming animal, its whistle-whimpering protests just at the upper limits of human audibility, and the not-quite-sound of muffled explosions somewhere near the razor-straight horizon.

They were followed soon after by an underlying thunder which pricked memories he'd thought long buried.

Looking up from his work—one of Ursi's great yellow-gray talons, too long unwatched, had curled upward into the pad, cruelly splitting it and causing the black woolly beast considerable pain—Fireclaw patted the animal upon its shaggy head and ducked out of the low earthen shed they occupied to see what the commotion was about.

Ursi barked, struggled to his feet, and limped to his master's knee.

Upon the eastern skyline, brushed into crimson brilliance by the rising sun, there stood a pillar of fire.

"Husband?"

At the same moment, Fireclaw's wife, Dove Blossom, drying her brown, capable hands upon a homespun apron, appeared in the kitchen doorway across the yard, drawn by the same disturbances as her husband. Her ears were, at most times, much sharper than his. The noise of running water at the kitchen sink must have given him the advantage.

She stood upon her moccasined toes—a small woman, she needed all the height she could obtain thus—one hand resting upon the large, scabbarded knife at her waist, the other shading her eyes, straining to watch the apparition upon the flat, grass-covered prairie.

"Best we take the usual precautions," was his only answer to her unasked question, yet his tone and posture spoke to her—as such things are communicated, man to woman—of an inward excitement less stoic than his countenance.

Bending under the low wooden lintel once again, Fireclaw stepped back into the machine shed, his mind considering at once the rare occurrence of visitors—unwelcome, dangerous ones in all possibility—and the everyday pragmatics of ranch life which those visitors, and that possibility, had just interrupted.

He swept his proud, proprietary gaze across the clutter of machinery: wire-spoked wheels and rubber tires, disembodied drive-trains shimmering with lubricant, small dismantled engines, the gleaming rustless and dust-free forms of metal lathe and horizontal mill, compound vise and drill-press, all of which he'd fashioned for himself, one square and clean-edged component at a time. The loving labor of twenty good years.

He thought of visitors to come, and of how much easier—and quicker—it was to destroy than to build.

Ursi would be fine, although for a few days he and Dove Blossom would have to be watchful for infection. One of her mother's herbal drawing poultices, applied this night ere bedtime—whenever that turned out to be—would solve that problem for a while.

He was their most valuable and prolific breeder, in his own right something of a legend among Dove Blossom's people, and almost a full partner in the couple's various enterprises. His own sire, gray about the ears and muzzle, and very nearly toothless, had gone down valiantly—before a pack of timber wolves wintering one harsh season upon the frozen plains— defending the very litter from which Ursi himself had sprung. 'Twas a good line, Fireclaw thought now, as he had often thought, and Ursi, just like his father before him, well trained and eager.

Ursi growled uncertainly, sensing changes in his master's mood, his own brown, liquid eyes too poor to make out what the man had just seen, many miles away.

Fireclaw patted the animal, ran five stub-nailed and callused fingers through his own graying mop.

He was a big man in his middle years, his great strength and unrelenting character the subject of many a harrowing tale among the translucent resined hides and spun-glass lodgepoles of his adopted prairie tribe. Ever was he accompanied, in real life as well as in the tales, by Ursi (or another who, from countless retellings by a myriad of tongues, now bore the same name), his huge black, curly-pelted "bear-dog."

Snapping the plier-like toenail-cutters from their socket with his left hand, Fireclaw reached for the great double-edged blade he'd leaned in its scabbard against the cluttered workbench. This he slung over his shoulder where it would hang ready—although its chiefest value nowadays lay in its powers of intimidation—for the thrust-twist which would lock it to his right wrist. More than aught else about Fireclaw, this gleaming and terrible weapon, his skill in wielding it, and the grisly work to which, in years gone by, he'd put both, were the focus of his reputation among a hundred tribes of native plains-dwellers.

Briefly he inspected the smaller but more potent article of hand-wrought weaponry slapping, handle forward, at his left thigh. Unlike the gleaming greatsword and the matching dagger which had been his father's only tangible legacy, this he never laid aside. The dagger, too, he loosened in its scabbard, then gathered up, from the pegs upon which they hung above a tool-covered bench, a quiver of stout, featherless arrows and his four-limbed longbow, a peace-offering from Knife Thrower, his former mortal foe, now trusted ally and good friend, Dove Blossom's brother.

And this, too, brought certain memories to his mind.

2

Cold and exhausted as he was, young Sedrich Sedrichsohn shook his head in wonder, staring, as he'd done a thousand times thus far, at the scar-ridged stump of his right hand.

Many weeks had passed—he wasn't exactly certain how many—still, whene'er he willed it, and often when he willed it least, he could feel the fingers of the hand he'd left lying on the bloody sill-stone of his dead father's doorway curl themselves into a fist, even flex his nonexistent thumb toward the intangibly tangible palm.

Perhaps 'twould e'er be thus, he thought. Perhaps he'd e'er be haunted by the ghost of a hand severed from his body to no good purpose, for the gain of naught and to the loss of everything he loved.

He shook his weary head again—sprinkling his already white and shivering shoulders with rainwater—as if to rid himself of such thoughts. Painful they were, and of no more use to him than was the phantom hand which continued to mystify him. At this particular moment they were a distraction and a danger to his life.

Spring was surging northward onto the Forbidden Plains, bringing with it sudden storms which transformed arid gullies into rivers, rivers into swollen, deadly seas. A gust-lashed rain was falling now, and he'd been caught out in the open.

The rabbit Willi had managed to kill for them—he himself couldn't have drawn and aimed a shoulder-bow if he'd brought one, nor even thrown a rock in any reasonable hope of hitting something with his left hand—was two days gone, and they were both hungry. That Willi, well trained as he was, had shared it with him—they'd been as hungry as this at the time—had been surprising and a stroke of luck.

The rabbit's untanned pelt now cushioned Sedrich's bleeding feet within his travel-worn moccasins and covered the end of his right wrist. Willi's pads were bruised and bleeding as well, but the dog had chewed off every dressing Sedrich had applied. The rotting skin wouldn't last long. What clothing Sedrich still retained, after a river crossing which had cost him most of his possessions, hung in shreds.

His only other luck had come upon the second—or had it been the third?—day after leaving home. Outside a neighboring settlement, a former member of the local Sisterhood, rejected by her husband after losing her one child to some feverish illness, and refusing to rejoin the compound of the Sisterhood, had found him wandering in delirium near her hermitage, instinctively avoiding villages upon a back trail, headed ever west.

He didn't remember that part very well.

She had cared for him, in the way of her training cleansed and sewn his burned and bleeding stump. She had fed him, sheltered him, begged him afterward to stay with her. He could not. He was of an age which made it unclear what it was she wished of him, to take the place of her dead child or that of her unfeeling mate. Perhaps she hadn't known, herself.

Why begin again in a village no different from the one which had, in its complacence, witnessed the destruction of everything he loved? Would the Cult of Jesus shrink from persecuting unbelievers in this place? Would the Sisterhood defend him here, as it had failed to do at home?

And if he stayed here, something told him he would never learn the secret of what lay to westward of Helvetia. That secret, the curiosity it still piqued in him, was all that remained to animate him now.

Making good his escape from her woods-hidden cottage hadn't been easily accomplished. One thing he did owe Ursula Karlstochter: following a practice held by but a few among the Sisterhood, she'd given him a sleeping potion. He'd scarcely needed it (although he still shuddered at the chance of having awakened prematurely in the middle of her ministrations). Before sealing his flesh, free now of the stinking black and yellow discharge which had itself come near to killing him, she'd pulled the ravaged muscle-ends into place and sewn them to the bones where they belonged, using a tiny hand-driven brace and drill he or his father might have fashioned for the trade. This had restored the normal tensions and relationships among the parts of what remained of his right forearm, speeding the healing of it, allowing him greater use of the limb than might have otherwise been possible.

Later, when she thought his stomach capable of bearing it, she'd demonstrated for him what it was she'd accomplished, upon a chicken she was preparing for dinner. He almost smiled at the memory. She'd misjudged what he could bear to witness. Afterward, he'd been unable to choke down a bite of that chicken. Huddling with a wet and odorous Willi against a slight overhang in the rocks of a waist-high ridge—nothing resembling a cave—he wished he had it now, e'en without a fire.

Of a sudden, Willi looked up, snuffling into the damp breeze. Rain still fell in stifling curtains all about them, limiting vision to a few paces in three directions. Sedrich kept his back to the rock, although it blinded him upon one side and sucked the heat out of his body. While he was wishing, he wished for flint and steel and tinder—e'en without the chicken. As he shivered and pulled the big dog closer, the pommel of his father's greatsword scraped against the overhang.

Abruptly a wiry hand thrust itself down over the blind lip of the rock, seizing Sedrich by the hair, dragging him upward against the slanting ceiling of the overhang.

Out of boyhood reflex, he grabbed for *Murderer*'s handle with the hand that wasn't there. By the time he'd overcome this impulse, it was too late to correct it. Instead, he took a firm grip upon the rain-slick wrist above his eyes and *pulled*.

A youth, no older than himself, tumbled over the rock onto his back, twist-jerked himself into a crouching posture, and slashed at Sedrich with a rusted knife, deep-worn in the center of the blade from being honed upon random stones.

The boy shouted something at him and spat.

Sedrich kicked him in the crotch.

The Red boy stumbled back, just retaining his balance, eyes filled with an agony he bore in stoic silence. The rage Sedrich had felt so long began to boil over within him. Oblivion stretched black and greedy talons up to drag him downward, into the depths. He did not resist. Instead, heedless and unconscious of what he was doing, he advanced, swatted at the knife with his pelt-covered forearm, seized the stranger by the throat with his one good hand. With unnatural strength he squeezed, letting his thumb and fingers find the thin, ribbed cartilage beneath the skin.

Sweat stood out upon his forehead, mingling with the streaming rain.

His opponent dropped his knife, tore frantically with both hands at Sedrich's fingers, but to no avail. He squirmed, twisted, but couldn't escape the energy of surprise he'd given Sedrich and which, within an instant, had turned to blood-haze.

A few paces away, black Willi snarled and bristled. Sedrich was unaware that he was being watched. Indeed, he was unaware of anything at all. Half a dozen other boys, who'd by now forgotten both their weapons and their duty to a friend, were frozen by the terror of the moment and by Sedrich's rage which appeared to them a palpable entity in itself. The dog's growling threats were secondary. A killing, so ruthless as to defy description, so cruel as to stun the sensibilities of any decent warrior, was occurring before their horror-fascinated eyes. They were held as helpless by it as their companion, whose soul, stopped in its outward journey by Sedrich's hand upon his throat, would be trapped within a dying body, never to escape.

Only demons fought in this wise.

Rain fell.

Sedrich's enemy had fallen limp, but it was long before the young Helvetian let the inert body slip onto the muddy ground.

When he did, a tiny movement caught the attention of whatever it was that looked out through his eyes. Another leather-clad boy with black and braided hair was watching him, openmouthed.

And another.

Four, five, or maybe six of them altogether. Faithful Willi stood his ground between him and the enemy, fangs bared, muzzle pleated, eyes insane, keeping them at bay.

Unsheathing *Murderer* left-handed, Sedrich stepped forward.

The Red boys turned and, scattering their handheld possessions, fled screaming.

Time passed.

As his mind at last began to clear, Sedrich looked down at the dead one. Doubtless he would feel something about this— what little he remembered of it—later. At present, he felt nothing. Clothing—the boy's loose-fitting buckskins covered him from collarbone to ankle. And new moccasins, if they fit. And he could always use an extra knife—

What was this? A brassy oblong shimmered in the wet grass where it had fallen from the beaded pouch his enemy had worn. Picking it up, Sedrich turned his back to the rain to examine it, discovering that about a third of the rectangular object could be hinged away from the rest, exposing a perforated steel cylinder, a serried steel wheel—and a wick!

The thing reeked of alcohol.

Minutes later, a warmly clad Sedrich Sedrichsohn huddled against the stony outcrop once more, considerably more watchful than he'd been ere now, basking in the joyous radiation of a fire which raised steam from Willi's wet, crinkly coat.

The big dog's eyes twinkled merrily, and he drooled: he'd found a brace of arrow-punctured ruffled grouse one of the boys had dropped. Both birds were gutted, plucked, and roasting now, upon green sticks cantilevered over the fire.

Elsewhere, frightened children spoke to their temporarily unbelieving parents of giant demon-dogs and invincible strangling spirits. Sedrich's one step forward hadn't merely saved his life.

It had begun a legend.

3

"Who kills a dozen of us is our enemy," Knife Thrower had told Fireclaw long ago, making him a peace-gift of the four-limbed longbow after five scarlet-stained years of continuous warfare between a single crippled stranger and the best fighters of an entire warrior nation. Grinning, the young Comanche war chief had added, "Who kills a hundred of us *must* become our friend."

Fireclaw had by that time dispatched five hundred.

Now the legendary killer strode between his ranch buildings toward the front gate of a broad, well-swept, foot-hardened yard, delineated by a low fence of the same stacked sod the buildings were constructed of. In cool prairie stillness, the first breath of morning rippled their close-trimmed grassy coverings.

Eastward, an orange sun hung low over dew-damp plains. The Great Blue Mountains, showing a more gentle, violet hue this time of day, at sunset would stand against the flame-colored western sky in blackened silhouette, like the jagged teeth of some unimaginable monster.

At times, Fireclaw wondered still what lay beyond them, although for some years, for the most part, he'd been content with wondering, nothing more. Now, a bit ashamed at his abated curiosity, he wondered about something else: whether he was growing old.

Ursi, joined by some of the other dogs, came with him. Sniffing the air, the great beast uttered a low, threatening mutter which was taken up by the rest of the pack. Tucking bow and quiver beneath his sword-arm, Fireclaw reached down, took one of creature's ragged, oily ears between left thumb and forefinger, massaged it with absent affection until the animal was quiet again.

The pillar of fire drew nearer.

A series of all-too-familiar whoops and shrieks could be heard now above the less frequent explosive pops and low thundering. The former sounds had filled a thousand sleepless nights when he'd first come to this place; they'd echoed all round him as he later fought the enemies of his adopted tribe. He himself fought in an icy silence punctuated only by the drumming of his heart, the sizzle of frozen fire through his veins. Comanche tales marked this silence—and nothing of what Sedrich felt within it—another legend born of naught more than his own unselfconscious nature, the grim, unvarnished necessities of survival. Whate'er he did, breathe in this wise, move a weapon-bearing hand thus, legend seemed to stalk him like his own shadow.

He spat.

Far away, the thundering continued.

Concentration wrinkling his weathered features, Fireclaw strained to recall where he'd heard yon latter noise ere now, that headlong clattering rumble. 'Twas something like unto the echoes from a nearby canyon when he "shot the anvil"—set off a charge of black powder beneath it, flinging it high into the air each Midsummer's Day to the delighted terror of the children of Dove Blossom's tribe.

Out of long proprietary reflex, he glanced toward his powder mill, two thousand measured paces from the ranch, of deliberately flimsy construction. Each loose-driven nail, every tool within, was fashioned out of beaten, sparkless copper. He'd lost the first two such buildings before learning to grind and sift the sun-dried cakes from a safe distance, employing braided ropes running about lathe-turned wooden pulleys. Each accident had added to his many scars. He felt grateful that was all they'd added—or carried away. This mill had stood some seven years, thus far, but was a source, for him, of constant apprehension.

He shook his head. This new noise came not from the mill but from the opposite direction, far to the eastward, rolling on and on, unlike a powder accident, being felt now, even through the soles of his knee-length moccasins.

The memory, however, wouldn't come. Wondering about

his age again, he acknowledged failure with a shrug, shielding his eyes with his left hand against the bright morning sky.

By now, Dove Blossom was ensconced, with two of the dogs, upon the grassy roof of their home, well armed with a split-limbed bow of her own, a full cache of arrows they kept beneath cover there. Glancing away from the troubled horizon, he waved at her. She could kill a rabbit at a hundred paces, urging one and all to name which eye the arrow entered. She'd be safe upon the roof, well-trained, fierce retainers at her back, but no intruder would be safe from her.

In the east, about where a rutted native road crossed the skyline, curving from its ancient, original course toward their ranch, Fireclaw could see that the pillar was in fact a squat, rapid-moving cloud.

At least there could be no mistaking it, he thought with some relief, for the twist-storm it had at first resembled. This was the wrong time of year for them. They seldom struck this watershed in any case. And the weather wasn't right.

'Twas the rising sun had given it the appearance of a column of flame.

A troop of his brother-in-law's warriors, pursuing an antelope or a foolhardy trespasser from a rival tribe, might well produce such a cloud, but it would have been much smaller, colored brown or yellow.

This, at its heart, flash-danced with fire.

Without being able to say why, the long-suppressed image of tall, rotating sails came into his mind, as he'd seen them upon the sea-horizon of his boyhood home.

Memory flooded back into him.

Of a sudden, he knew strangers were traveling this direction in the greatest of haste.

And they were under attack.

XIX:

The Ship of the Desert

And of His signs are the ships that run on the sea like
landmarks; and if He wills, He stills the wind . . . or
He wrecks them for what they have earned. . . .
                              —The *Koran*, Sura XLII

Ayesha blinked at the unfamiliar-looking arrow quivering in
the paneled wall before her face. For the most fleeting of
instants, for reasons she could never afterward discover, it
struck her as funny. Then indignation filled her heart, and,
close upon that, curiosity. She felt little fear: those who have
already died a thousand times—and have nothing left to live
for—do not fear death.

Outside, above the steady rumble of the land-ship's giant
wheels, she could hear the erratic pop and crackle of Saracen
gunfire, the demented, murderous shriek of savages.

Through the open door to the adjoining tiny cabin, she could
see that it was empty.

She wondered where Marya was.

Assuring herself that Sagheer was secure in his little cage,
she opened the outside door a cautious crack—only to find

herself become the immediate target of several arrows which whistled past her eyes, rattling off the doorframe or sprouting in the wall behind her.

One flailed sideways against the cage bars with a peculiar thrumming ring. Unhurt, the huge-eyed pygmy marmoset chittered fear and anger at the world.

Ayesha threw herself to the floor, crawled out the door, along the short, narrow deck of the land-ship.

Above her head, the very air seemed streaked, thick with missiles whispering of death. Peeking over the arrow-studded rail, she saw that the land-ship was rolling swiftly—if not as smoothly as before—across an endless mustard-colored prairie which reminded her of the south of Faransaa. Its twelve tall, white-bellied sails, six to a mast, flashed round and round almost indistinguishable from one another. Its four great steel-shod wheels left a spark-punctuated, impenetrable cloud of dust billowing behind for leagues to dim the morning sunlight.

In the greater distance, edging the broad prairie to the west, tree-clad foothills shouldered one another in blurred and purple humps before a still-shadowed horizon serried by pale blue, insubstantial-looking peaks. Ayesha thought that they appeared somehow less real than the mountains painted in the background of a palace mural.

"May your children call your worst enemy Father!"

"*Father! Father!*"

Grinning into the wind, orange-maned Mochamet al Rotshild stood upright, exposing himself to peril at the land-ship's tiller, one freckled, broad and hairy hand upon the gear lever, laughing and cursing at their assailants as his parrot flapped upon his shoulder, echoing his vile language. His loose, bright-colored clothing snapped and crackled, like the sounds of gunfire all around him.

"*May your mother find a treatment for the disease she contracted conceiving you!*"

"*Mother!*" came the parrot's raucous squawking. "*Mother!*"

One brown-skinned native guide, the skinny one Mochamet al Rotshild had hired in a grimy tavern shortly before departing the eastern shore, huddled at the pirate's knee beside the binnacle, pointing and shouting advice. The captain shouted back and nodded, hauled upon the tiller or pushed it away from him as was appropriate. Against the wind and sounds of warfare, Ayesha could not hear a word they uttered.

The native's squat, scar-faced companion lay upon his belly at the opposite end of the hurtling craft, high upon the foredeck, loading and discharging a crossbow into the tormenting pack. These two were, in appearance, quite unlike the fair-skinned east coast villagers of the Savage Continent—they much more closely resembled the attacking horde surrounding them—but had been stranded sailors whom the Commodore had picked up along the way.

She could not see the third man, the old one, they had recruited from among the villagers, but she knew enough of him by now to be assured that he had seen to his own safety.

Rabbi David Shulieman, as well, knelt close by the tiller, struggling in tight-lipped silence to reload the enormous four-barreled pistol he had seen fit to acquire in Rome, and to learn to use, and bring along. All the deadly while, he made the same frequent, unconscious stabs with a forefinger at the bridge of his spectacles as he had while conducting lessons all her life, shoving them back into place before his eyes.

Once again Ayesha was tempted to laugh, and wondered if this was what people meant by hysteria.

Traveling even faster than the land-ship they harried, uncounted red-skinned naked men, faces painted up in hideous colored patterns, each straddled the saddle of a small, two-wheeled machine, decorated as garishly as its rider.

They zoomed past the land-ship's bow, flashing aft to cut behind its stern, then forward once again to complete the circle, shouting, as they rode, in high, bloodcurdling voices, bouncing across the road-ruts, steering with their knees as they launched a sleet-storm of deadly missiles into the land-ship and those aboard her.

Ayesha caught a glimpse of a blood-red handprint slapped upon the flank of one such machine, a flash of unclothed flesh, a flurry of streaming coal-black hair and eagle feathers, just before a sudden volley of arrows forced her to duck behind the rail.

Amidships, Abu and Ali, the retainers her father had sent along, fired back with issue military-rifles, trying, as they did so, to avoid the land-ship's whirling lower sail-booms as they whistled overhead. They were aided by Mochamet al Rotshild's young female . . . what? Body-servant? Traveling companion? In any case, she was an endless subject of scandalized indignant muttering upon Marya's part, who, with Sagheer and the parrot, completed their expeditionary party of thirteen.

Not far from Ayesha's cabin door—she had not noticed him before—Sergeant Kabeer lay face down upon the hardwood decking, his lifeblood staining the well-scrubbed planks.

Disregarding the hail of lethal objects showering all about her, Ayesha crawled toward the fallen man. The land-ship pitched and wallowed over uneven ground, slowing her progress, tossing her from side to side, and bruising her elbows.

Kabeer groaned as she approached, trying to turn over. The long, ugly protruding shaft of an arrow, one end tangled in a basket-sized coil of rope beside the gunwale, stopped the motion.

The other end was buried in his chest.

Ayesha freed the arrow-end from the rope pile. It was a strange artifact, quite without the feathering she was used to. Its hollow rear length was filled with tiny drill-holes which lightened it, providing stabilizing resistance to the air. The front, almost half its length, was shod in metal.

The deadly implement had passed through Kabeer's leather ammunition bandoleer, the heavy woolen layers of his tunic, into his body, and out again just above the shoulder blade, exposing a broad, sharp-edged, spade-shaped tip, much like the point of a dagger, save for the outward-curving barbs at its rear corners.

Both entry wound and exit welled scarlet about the intruding shaft in short, regular surges. The tubular, perforated rear half of the shaft encouraged the flow. The sergeant groaned again, relieved of some part of his pain, then closed his eyes.

With trembling fingers, Ayesha broke the arrow where it entered. Odd, how she could feel fear for someone else but not herself. Opening his tunic, she stuffed the corner of a sheer and beautiful silk handkerchief from her sleeve into the open end of the projectile, and the rest of it about the entry wound, trusting to his heavy coat to hold it. She was afraid to do more, afraid that she had done too much. The shaft was solid where it left his back, the bleeding not quite so profuse there. She put her face near his, feeling his breath, warmly even upon the sensitive skin between her nose and upper lip.

For the moment, then, he was still alive.

An arrow smashed through the lightweight railing wall above her head, scattering splinters through her hair. She was surprised to feel a wave of anger washing fear away.

The unconscious sergeant's long, hammerless army rifle lay smoking upon the deck beside him. Sitting up, she unfastened one of a dozen flaps upon the broad leather diagonal which encircled his body. She extracted three finger-length brass cartridges from their loops. She placed them between the fingers of her left hand in the regulation manner which her father had insisted upon teaching her.

With the same hand she supported the wooden fore-end of the rifle—its round, blued, tapered barrel was too hot to touch, and much heavier than the cut-down target weapons she was used to—while with her right she grasped the gracefully curving underlever, yanked it downward, lowering the breech-block at the rear of the receiver.

A spent casing sizzled past her, bouncing off her shoulder. It rattled across the deck.

She slid one of the fresh rounds into the breech, slammed the lever shut, and rested the muzzle of the long-barreled weapon upon the deck rail. That was better.

Another arrow lashed past her face, ruffling her hair.

Keeping both eyes open, as she had been taught, she laid her right cheek upon the polished walnut stock, wrapped her right hand about its wrist. She leaned forward, peering through the tiny hole in the rear sight toward the slim, bead-topped post atop the muzzle.

The movement of the howling, motorized savages was so rapid it was difficult to get one of them lined up in her sights, let alone to keep him there. Inspired, she pivoted her barrel toward the land-ship's undercut bow, holding her sights upon an imaginary space just to its port side.

A different sort of howl unnerved her momentarily as the land-ship gave a slight lurch, grinding one unlucky rider and his machine beneath its giant iron wheels as he crossed the bow.

The instant she saw a second blurred flickering of movement—she had been taught, and properly, to focus her eyes upon the front sight—she squeezed the trigger, aiming to the left, giving the traversing Red Man an arm's-length lead.

The heavy weapon roared, its all-consuming bellow becoming her entire universe for a moment which seemed to stretch into eternity. The rifle's curved steel buttplate smashed cruelly against her frail, thin-clad shoulder, stunning her as if she had been shot herself. Her vision was obscured by shock and by infernal-odored smoke.

There was a scream, at first ahead of her. It drifted backward as the land-ship thundered onward. When it had passed out of the smoke, she looked back to see one naked savage struggling to get his machine upright, blood streaming down his chest.

He shook his fist at the land-ship.

She caught herself grinning, wondering whether—no, *hoping* that—he was the one she had shot at.

"Princess!"

Ducking behind the rail, Ayesha levered the breech open. Smoke curled from the chamber. Marya's hysterical shout she ignored, concentrating instead upon the task of handling the awkward weapon without burning herself upon its overworked and overheated metal parts.

The extractor flung the empty cartridge casing from the chamber with a cheerful *ping,* repeated as it struck a hatch-cover behind her. Before it had bounced a second time, she took a new one from between the fingers of her left hand and reloaded.

The servant woman elbowed and kneed her way across the blood-slippery, arrow-cluttered deck from wherever she had been hiding, her breath coming in ragged, frightened gasps.

"Princess, you must stay inside! We shall all be killed!"

"Marya, do not distract me!" Ayesha shouted over the clatter and roar of battle. If her maidservant's fractured logic was correct, she would rather be killed outdoors than in. "Go inside yourself—or find a gun!"

One of her father's hired retainers—Abu, she thought it was—fell on his face a dozen paces ahead. Seeing his impact with the deck drive a reddened arrow shaft through his back, Marya began to whimper, then curled herself into a ball, her back against the railing wall.

This time, when Ayesha stroked the smooth curve of her weapon's trigger—she was long past noticing its recoil—the rifle's mind-shattering roar was matched by a secondary, louder bellow and a blinding burst of light. She had struck one of the riding-machines instead of its rider. There was an explosion. Something thudded heavily to the deck-planking just in front of her.

She glanced down briefly, expecting to be rewarded with the sight of a scorched, distorted fragment of the machinery she had just destroyed. Perhaps the boiler.

Instead, she saw a brown-ankled human foot, severed high upon the limb, still writhing, encased in lightweight bead-fringed suede.

She swallowed back an ugly taste.

With the greatest moral effort she could ever remember expending, the Princess Ayesha, cloistered daughter of the Caliph, emptied and reloaded the rifle once again, obtained three more fresh cartridges from the wounded sergeant's bandoleer—he was still breathing, she observed absently—then sought yet another target.

She fired, uncertain this time whether she had hit her mark, took a calming breath, reloaded, and fired again.

Until this moment unaware of how her companions fared

about her, she was suddenly conscious of a change. The rumble of the land-ship's giant wheels had dropped in pitch. Its hull groaned mightily with the strain as, for some reason, its pace began to slow.

Past her rifle's brass front sight, the air above it shimmering and dancing with the barrel's metallic heat, Ayesha now made out a number of low sod buildings.

A big man, heavily bearded—unlike those smooth-faced savages upon their machines—yet accoutered and deep-tanned in an identically indecent manner, stood in the broad gap of a grass-topped earthen wall, his hands upon his hips, complacently watching the Saracen vessel as it began circling round the buildings. She was reminded of an ancient saying of her mother's people: "In my weakness, I fled into the desert to escape my enemies—and the desert gave me strength to defeat them."

Armed with undrawn sword and unpulled bow, scabbarded dagger and holstered pistol, he waved what seemed a casual gauntleted hand at one of the savage riders, who gave a shrill whoop, wrenched his speeding machine up on its rear wheel, and waved back.

A nearby sound distracted her.

Marya sat staring with dull surprise at an arrow buried half its length in her silk-covered thigh. There did not seem to be much blood, and whatever pain she was suffering could not compete with such uncomprehending terror as she had already endured.

Enough.

Aligning her sights upon the bearded man, Ayesha pulled the trigger.

XX:

The Botherhood of Man

Had there not overtaken him a blessing from his Lord
he would have been cast upon the wilderness, being
condemned. But his Lord had chosen him. . . .
                                        —The *Koran*, Sura LXVIII

Enough, thought Sedrich Fireclaw, *is enough*.

The breathless morning silence was over. A brisk, sage-
laden high-plains breeze gusted away the brimstone odor
lingering in a dense cloud about the ranch yard, leaving behind
an underlying metallic smell of freshly spilled blood.

It wasn't that the carmine-handed killer, always present,
leering like a freshly unearthed skull deep within him, in any
wise begrudged his painted cycle-riding brothers their innocent amusements. And, after all, this was their land, their
home, their place apart from all others in a world where every
living thing and every force of nature conspired to end the
lives of the hesitant and unwary.

Moreover, in some spiritual sense he'd never fully understood himself, he knew that, in keeping the golden prairie
swept clean of interlopers—in particular those intruding from

the east—they were performing what they solemnly considered a sacred duty to the unforgiving gods who dwelt in mystery across the Great Blue Mountains.

But when a projectile whirred past *his* face, the survival sense he'd acquired at a terrible price upon the untender breast of that same prairie told him it was time now—and perhaps time well past—to put a stop to the tribesmen's harassment of the alien vessel circling round and round his freehold.

At least until he learned for himself something of the reasons which had brought it here.

Besides, he was discovering that he was curious again. His vision of long ago—and the bitter memories of its near-destruction—had been vindicated. This apparition, pressing wheel-marks wider spread and deeper than any vehicle before it into the cycle-rutted road before his gate, was a rotary-sailed land-ship of the very sort he'd himself conceived and been forced to abandon twenty years before.

More than that, he recognized certain details, solutions to the problems of mechanics which had been born in his mind alone. These had merely been expanded to accommodate the admittedly grander scale of the giant vessel now arriving at his doorstep amidst a sleet of arrows from his adopted relatives. He'd reason to appreciate such differences in engineering style: the Comanche warriors pursued the land-ship astride knee-guided steam-cycles he'd no hand himself in designing, but which he and Dove Blossom had spent many of their days, for fifteen years, repairing and maintaining for them, and with which he was thus intimately familiar.

Wheels roared past him, spattering him with sand.

Come to think upon it, one of those little machines—ridden, he thought, by his wife's cross-cousin Porcupine Eater—had sounded a bit rough as it had passed him, its rider sending a flying shaft into the eye of one of the foreigners. Likeliest the drive-chain had gone a bit slack. Trail-wear in each of the bearing-holes of not more than a fine hair's width, multiplied times the number of links in the chain, quickly added up to fingers' widths, loading the engine at stops and starts, and each time the gears were shifted to a different ratio.

Have to see to it soon, ere it cause other difficulties.

Another gun barked. Elsewhere somebody screamed with pain.

But service to the Comanche was an everyday consideration, to be put aside for later. Now it was the land-ship which held his fascinated attention, and another, similar machine which occupied his thoughts.

There were differences, of course: the experimental vessel of his adventurous boyhood had been little larger than a rowboat. This two-masted monster was incomparably greater, a veritable mobile village. Its two dozen spinning sail-booms, twelve per mast, six up and six down, stretched wider, tip to bronze-shod tip, than his entire ranch house. Its sails—each resin-saturated expanse was greater than Dove Blossom's garden. The glass-fiber masts themselves soared into the prairie sky, straight and tall as mountain evergreens. The great spoked wheels, rimmed in iron, stood three times the height of a tall man.

Fireclaw watched with interest as its desperate and motley complement discharged breech-loading rifles at their whooping tormentors, one slow and awkward loading after another. And to considerably less practical effect, he observed, than the tribesmen with their optically sighted longbows, quick to load and quick to reload.

Here was yet another surprise. He'd believed he possessed the sole firearm within many months' journey of this place, perhaps upon the entire continent. They seemed to be forbidden or unknown to every culture he encountered.

Now here came a *boatload* of the things.

Nonetheless, these oddly clad assorted foreigners hadn't learned a lesson yet which he himself had absorbed even before the first blood-drenched twelvemonth he'd settled here upon the western plains—that in order to survive, a lone warrior must be capable of fighting like many. This meant with a repeating weapon of some kind, like the fat-cylindered revolving pistol hanging now upon his left hip.

He scanned the land-ship with a practiced tactical sweep,

complex ideas and images flowing, twining, braiding together wordlessly within his mind in fractions of an eyeblink.

Three upper decks the land-ship boasted, those at bow and stern a few steps higher than the center where the masts were stepped. At the tiller there growled and bellowed a shaggy laughing giant, long-barreled pistol and curved dagger thrust into his colorful sash, a man who might well have been his own father, Sedrich, dead these many years, save for the tangled orange of his hair and beard.

Some sort of gray exotic bird perched screaming upon his shoulder. A flash of crimson showed among its tail feathers.

By either side of this outlandish, noisy pair there crouched another man. One slight, blue-clad, and darkly bearded foreigner wore transparent coverings, set in polished metal frames, before his eyes. Even as the Helvetian watched, two barrels of his huge four-barreled pistol belched, generating twin balls of flame.

One of the riders fell, his face a ruin.

Another of them, slightly wounded several places in the same one-man volley, screamed with something more than pain and pointed at the shooter, cursing. Multiple projectiles, Fireclaw nodded approvingly, most likely pellets of iron or lead.

An angry flock of arrows coursed toward the eyeglass wearer.

He ducked behind a rail, untouched.

The Comanche—despite, or perhaps *because* of, their familiarity with telescopic sights—might well be taking the fellow's eye-coverings for a sign of sorcerous capability. Fireclaw realized, in a flash of intuition, that these small windows compensated for short-sightedness such as Owaldsohn had complained of near the end of his life. He remembered, with a sad, hidden smile, watching his father hold his mother's books at arm's length, struggling to extract some meaning from the letters he was trying so hard to learn as an example to his son.

The window-wearing man fired another volley and reloaded.

The other figure beside the tiller was lean and brown, bereft

of facial hair save for a thin, drooping mustache, almost naked
and well muscled. Something deadly in this fellow's posture
seemed familiar, promising of reserves untapped. He fought in
silence, defending the red-haired steersman with a weapon
Fireclaw had never seen before, fitting a series of small
spears—or perhaps large arrows—into a curve-ended stick,
hurling them with surprising force at the enemy.

One such pierced a steam-cycle from side to side as
Fireclaw watched, penetrating fuel tank and boiler. Another,
following in its wake, trapped itself between two wheel-
spokes, snapping the tautly adjusted wires, chewing the wheel
free of its hub. Amidst a clattering uproar, the gutted machine
ground itself into the prairie floor, flipping end over end in a
spectacular cloud of dust and small parts. Porcupine Eater's
successor would need more done to this machine he inherited,
after this day, than a simple tightening of the drive-chain.

That was it! This spear-launching fighter reminded Fireclaw
in some way of his own brother-in-law, Knife Thrower. The
Helvetian chuckled to himself, resolving to keep a wary corner
of his eye upon the man as he took in the rest of the ship.

Besides the oddly assorted valiants upon the afterdeck,
Fireclaw watched three others forward. Another brown,
mustached, and loinclothed man with the squint eyes of a hired
killer was armed, to Fireclaw's astonishment, with a well-
worn Helvetian shoulder-bow which he or his father might
once have forged the prod for. He used it clumsily—an
unfamiliar task which he was learning—missing shot after
shot, yet kept reloading and discharging it as if he were
himself a machine.

Fireclaw realized that this battle, a furious and desperate
struggle for most of the participants aboard the land-ship, was
merely finger-practice for the squint-eyed shoulder-bow man.
When things are slack enough, a professional needs must
acquire familiarity with as many outlandish weapons as one
finds practical.

A swarthy rifleman beside the bowman was dressed much
like the shaggy shouter upon the tiller deck, in bright, loose-
hanging pants and jacket, weapon-heavy sash.

And—was not yon third rifle-wielder, more slender in vest and pantaloons, a woman? Little matter. She handled her gun as if she knew what she was doing.

Amidships was the one who'd shot at him. Also a woman.

Her shining eyes were big for the rest of her face, black as a moonless midnight sky. A slight blood trickle drew a thin and ragged sinuosity from her hairline to a gracefully arched eyebrow, although she appeared not to have noticed it as yet. This one, thought Fireclaw, looked pale 'neath the olive cast of her flawless skin, inexperienced in combat, frightened into fearlessness, but determined. In his experience this made a dangerous and unpredictable mixture.

What was worse, her gaze never left him. Nor the front sight of a smoking breech-loader near as big as she was.

She'd bear watching, too.

He wondered whether there was anyone else aboard, belowdecks or behind the rail. Well, time enough to find out later. Glancing back past his shoulder to make certain Dove Blossom knew what he was about, and leaving his own weapons conspicuously untouched, he stepped out, empty-handed, into the very middle of the onslaught.

Delighted shrieks arose from one of the war-painted forms slashing by upon wire-spoked wheels. *Hi-yi!* A day to remember in lodge-song! An ancient enemy, and honored, was joining this splendid new game!

Like some magical and deadly sprout, an arrow blossomed in the dirt between Fireclaw's feet. It was soon followed by another and another as rider after cheering rider swept past him in a swirl of engine exhaust and taunting screams.

Fireclaw, unflinching, pretended not to notice. This was different from the gunshot. They'd not harm him, this he knew. Everyone was in fine spirits this day.

One valorous warrior of perhaps thirteen roared toward Fireclaw, his gracefully curved war-club, with the smooth round river stone cemented in the end, upraised.

Grinning, Fireclaw lifted his hand, palm upward, received a tap from the club as its wielder flashed by.

This day, the young ones would go home at sundown to their

mother's houses, bragging of the wise in which they'd counted coup upon Fireclaw the Destroyer, Fireclaw the Hewer of the People.

Fireclaw the Strander of Souls.

Just as their bedtime tales, growing up, had been filled with imaginings about him, he had himself heard all of these names whispered of him many times, though ne'er to his face—save for that once, when Knife Thrower had bargained and paid for a truce.

This day, too, the older warriors, those scarred and weathered veterans who'd fought with him in the old days and lived, would, with tolerant amusement and affection, leave the young ones to their boasting and nod knowingly among themselves.

All, that was, save perhaps the war chief Knife Thrower himself, Dove Blossom's brother, his own good friend and brother-in-law. Later they'd speak of this and laugh together. His had been the first arrow planted between Fireclaw's feet. The young ones had to learn their skill and bravado from someone.

Fireclaw could think of many worse.

No one aboard the land-ship had shot at him since Knife Thrower's first whistling pass. Now the Comanche stopped their dusty circling, gathered in a line beyond what they imagined to be the range of the interloper's rifles. They'd little experience with firearms. Looking at the length of those barrels, and judging from the *crack* which spoke of rifled bores, Fireclaw realized the strangers were restraining themselves more for want of ammunition than any lack of ranging power.

Boom!

As if to prove the Helvetian correct, a single shot blasted across the prairie, spanging off the fender of a cycle. In a cloud of wheel-spinnings, the warriors disappeared into a gully, reappeared one slanting hill-shoulder further away.

The land-ship creaked to a stop, raising a cloud of its own. Silence filled the ranch yard like a thick fog. Fireclaw raised his one good hand and strode toward the vessel.

Slapping the tiller aside, the orange-bearded figure in command lifted his fist, bellowed something in a strange, harsh-syllabled tongue. At his unsubtle urging, scurrying began elsewhere aboard the ship, other shouting voices, the sound of bare feet slapping hardwood.

The gray bird squawked, perhaps in the same language, flapped, ruffled its plumage, then smoothed its wings and red tail feathers and sat quiet.

Fireclaw paused a few paces off, left hand far from the curved butt of his pistol.

He waited.

Halfway down the curving, shingle-planked hull, a door popped open, hinged upon its lower edge. Fastened to its inboard side, a short, steep flight of stairs tipped ground-ward—he could see brown hands strain upon a pair of hawsers guiding the contraption toward gentle contact with the yellow soil.

A stooped and feeble figure filled the doorway.

"Good morrow, young Sedrich," wheezed a voice from the distant past. "I've a favor I'd ask of thee, my boy."

It was the first time in two decades he'd heard the Helvetian language spoken at any great length. It sounded foreign to his ear. Down the flight of stairs, clinging to its hawser hand railings, labored a back-bent ancient in a filthy shift, supported each step of the way by the land-ship captain's countryman behind him.

Forgetting his pistol, Fireclaw jammed his prosthetic socket over the handle of the greatsword *Murderer* and swept it out. Bellowing, he charged the gangplank.

"Oln Woeck, prepare yourself to die!"

XXI:

Delicate Negotiations

. . . thou art truly among the Envoys on a straight
path . . . that thou mayest warn a people whose
fathers were never warned. . . .
—The *Koran*, Sura XXXVI

From her rooftop guardpost, Dove Blossom watched her
husband hurl himself toward the land-ship.

Though he was by nature reticent, undisposed to talk about
himself, in the fifteen winters she'd lived with Fireclaw,
sharing with him his voluntary exile at foot of what he called
the Great Blue Mountains, Dove Blossom had learned much
which would have surprised the man.

Her body tensed now, ready for the fight to come. Sunlight,
glancing from an arm's length of polished, hammer-hardened
steel, slashed past her eyes. Yet her mind was filled with
memories of a man whose back she thus defended. Fireclaw
had killed before. He would kill again this day, perhaps, or be
killed. She readied her bow, sweeping the crosshairs of its
telescopic sight along the land-ship's deck.

In the tales of her people, Fireclaw loomed fully as terrible

184

as whatever unknown majesty or horror lay beyond those ghostly peaks which fascinated him. Yet, with an unguarded utterance here, an unconscious gesture there, her legendary husband's all-too-human past had, year by year, emerged. From such fragments had she pieced together the fabric of his personal tragedies, even—this last he'd taught her, that they might have means of controlling Ursi and the other dogs which no enemy might imitate—some smattering of his native tongue. Sometimes he babbled in this language, when emboldened by the darkness, the scavenger-spirits which, sniffing out the last despairing breath of human life, devour the soul, stalked his, as they did those of all men.

There was a noise below.

At the end of the out-tilted gangplank, the ancient white man, head shaven, body draped in soiled clothing—she wondered what the dark blue markings at his temples meant—gave a feeble shout of dismay and threw himself at the feet of his fellow Helvetian. A single snarl from Ursi was enough to hold the other foreigners back.

"I beg thee," Dove Blossom heard the old one scream into the dirt where he'd buried his pinched and shrunken nose—she comprehended perhaps four words in five—"do thou not injure me, Sedrich, son of Owaldsohn, called Fireclaw! I'm prostrate before thee! I come hither upon a mission of uttermost importance to our people! I—"

A sharp report from the land-ship's center deck ripped through both the shimmering curtain of Fireclaw's rising blood-haze and the paralysis of contemplation which had held his woman uncharacteristically motionless behind him. An ugly-smelling puff of smoke, looking like a dandelion blown to seed, blossomed upon the deck amidships. Impact kicked a yellow spurt of dust into the air between his feet. Fireclaw shook his head, unaccustomed to being awakened thus from his murderous trance.

Not quite aware of what she did, Dove Blossom sent first one arrow, then another, streaking toward that cloud. Almost as one, they thunked into the cover of a cargo hatch, less than a hand's width either side of the shooter's head.

Dove Blossom was astonished.

She'd missed!

Blinking as if waking from her own bad dream, she watched Fireclaw lift his face to the rail. Perhaps the thick, foul-smelling smoke had blurred her usually unerring aim. Then again, perhaps it had been ordinary simple-minded anger: yon round-eyed young woman had discharged yet another shot at her man. A thin blue curl drifted from the muzzle of the woman's weapon.

In echo, further forward, came the *thwack* of a shoulder-bow. This time, Dove Blossom was ready. Her answering arrow, aimed for the heart, missed again, but it pinned the shooter's intervening hand to the stock of his shoulder-bow, burying itself in resin-impregnated hardwood. Meanwhile, with an almost negligent twitch of his greatsword, Fireclaw grinned and swatted the foreigner's feather-fletched bolt from its path ere it could reach his own otherwise unprotected breast.

He whistled, gave a series of commands. There was movement behind Dove Blossom as well as below as her rear guard leapt from the roof to join the rest of the great pack Fireclaw had summoned. Instantly two dozen giant, snarling, coal-black dogs, their eyes lit with the insane fire of canine ferocity unleashed, formed a half-circle about him, an arc of death, defying anyone to come and touch their master.

Dove Blossom chuckled to herself. The fabulous *Murderer* might be an object of respect, even veneration, among her people, the Comanche woman thought to herself. But without the mighty Fireclaw behind it, and the magic he brought to everything he touched, 'twas just another billet of hammered steel.

"Chinthazir taqeeqagh! Maa ghaadaa!"

The brawny red-haired figure at the tiller shouted something in a language which she couldn't follow—to her it sounded like a curse. Upon his shoulder, the strange red-tailed bird—it had mustard yellow eyes and a beak which might have been carved of jet—squawked and whistled, grimacing a different way with each new noise it made.

No one fired another shot.

Silence descended over the scene, broken when Fireclaw spat, missing the scabrous nape of the old man's bowed and dirty neck by not more than a finger's length.

He turned and glanced toward Dove Blossom, his brief look conveying, as such will between well-married couples, many minutes' worth of conversation.

Dove Blossom relaxed minutely, tension turning into curiosity.

Bending his elbow high above his head, Fireclaw sheathed his mighty blade, unlocked his wrist from off the grip—a display, his wife knew well, of contempt for an unworthy enemy—and pointed his good hand toward the rise, a thousand paces westward, where Knife Thrower's braves watched and waited upon their idling machines.

"Our people?" Fireclaw snarled in Helvetian. "Take a good look, old man; *those* are *my* people!"

Obediently the old man raised a trembling, tear-streaked face. He peered at the horizon, whimpered, and slumped back into the dirt.

Dove Blossom's heart swelled within her, she who'd been named for the blue and yellow flowers of her native high plains. She was thrilled to hear her husband's words. She'd always understood that she could never replace the lost love of his youth. Indeed, she'd been too wise to try. Instead, she'd become a willing token—numb with fear upon that first day as the gift-bride to a monster—a token of the peace which had become necessary between the Comanche and their Destroyer.

She heard Knife Thrower and his followers give a shout in answer to her husband's gesture.

Like the bow her brother had also given Fireclaw on that day—an extension upon the handle of the powerful, quadruple-limbed weapon fit his prosthetic, as was the case with *Murderer*—identical to that which she held ready now, with its magical bright-lensed sight (this came in trade from somewhere beyond the mountains), she'd served him faithfully, in the thousand ways of a wife, lived beside him, slept beside him, fed him, washed both his clothing and his wounds, at all times striving within herself to lose hold of her terror of him. Nor could she name the moment when at last she had succeeded.

Shouts from the land-ship's deck took the tone of questions now. The old man gave a muffled reply, asking something of Fireclaw. Fireclaw nodded, replying affirmatively.

The old man rose to his bare, bony knees and cuffed the nose-runnings from his chin.

Shedding fear of Fireclaw hadn't been an impossible task. Far from it. He'd shown her as much kindness and gentleness as it had been in him to show. She snorted—more than any Comanche husband would have! Nor can any woman live long with a man retaining, for good or for evil, all of her illusions about him. And Fireclaw, whate'er legend said of him—and all of it, and more, was true—was still a man.

For his part, he'd come, in his own wise, to love her; upon that she was well satisfied and certain.

The old man upon the ground grimaced, muttering something to her husband that she couldn't hear.

As for her people, they who'd at first borne the consequences of the mad Helvetian's insane rage, they'd at last surrendered to his grim determination to dwell unmolested in this place which was otherwise forbidden to his kind. Now they'd peace—

—or had until this ship arrived.

If Fireclaw was displeased, upon occasion, with certain aspects of his life with her, if she could never be for him his long-dead, pale-haired, gentle Frae—it was, perhaps, the greatest measure of that benign departed spirit's power that, over the years, and even in death, Dove Blossom herself had come to feel toward Frae something akin to sisterly love—if he felt her and her kin to be uncivilized, if sometimes he must overlook the grisly trophies of continuous slaughter—though he'd done much slaughtering himself in early days—draped in decoration upon the machinery he repaired, he never complained of it.

Not once in all of those fifteen years.

The supplicant before her husband uttered a few more

whining words. Keeping his own peace, Fireclaw looked up toward the deck again, sweeping it with his gaze. Someone beside the figure Dove Blossom had shot pulled the arrow from his hand. This untender ministration was received in stoic silence, even without the grimace Dove Blossom might have expected. Both men stood up, unarmed. The woman who was with them stood as well.

The red-haired shouter took a step away from the tiller of his ship, drew pistol and dagger from his waistband—Dove Blossom tensed, centering her crosshairs upon his broad chest—then set his weapons upon the deck at his feet. His two companions followed his example.

More talk followed, three-sided, among the old man, the redheaded man, and the man who was her husband.

These weren't, of course, the first strangers they'd suffered to visit them a while. Neighboring tribes, bearing Comanche tokens of peace and safe passage, had sometimes stopped at their ranch for water, carrying with them trade-goods, and fair-haired, blue-eyed, broad-shouldered slaves who might have been of Fireclaw's own kind.

This Fireclaw did naught about, as he did naught, for the most part, to wreak other changes to the world he found about him. From his face and eyes, the set and movement of his shoulders, she knew full well he found many such usages barbaric. Acknowledging no gods, he worshiped freedom—or he breathed it. Either expression would have served to describe him.

Nor, she knew, was his reluctance to act born out of fear. He seemed ignorant of that emotion, and would have been capable of shaping any change he wished.

Instead, he played his own game of life, seeming to want no more than to be left alone to dwell with wife and animals in peace in this place by the mountains. That there was something more to this game he played Dove Blossom never doubted, nor had she ever come to understand just what that something more might be.

Perhaps until this day.

Below, there seemed to be some argument, no longer between Fireclaw and the strangers but among the passengers themselves, who, having for the most part cast their weapons aside, took turns shouting at that one among their number who refused to do so.

It was the dark-eyed, dark-haired girl who'd shot at Fireclaw.

Beside her, yet another foreign woman rose into view—somewhat painfully, it appeared. There was blood upon her garments. She wore a hastily wrapped bandage where one of Knife Thrower's arrows, or that of one of his braves, had found a resting-place in the muscles of her upper leg. This woman looked soft and terrified. She, too, argued with the stubborn, rifle-bearing female.

Dove Blossom allowed herself another snort, this of amused contempt.

Almost, however, she admired the stubborn one. Already she perceived that Comanche women were of better stuff than these soft foreign women. She understood, despite her manner of being brought to Fireclaw, that he'd chosen her—having rejected others—only in part to establish kinship with the tribe she belonged to. There were also qualities that he admired in her, individual qualities which she, unique among her sisters and tribeswomen, had possessed. Grateful for this recognition, she placidly (though she'd never been considered such while dwelling in her mother's lodge, being considered argumentative and one who thought too much) had made a home for him.

For all concerned, the arrangement had worked well.

She'd hoped bearing him children might establish something stronger between them in time, but children hadn't been forthcoming. They'd built the ranch, establishing their machine shop, raised their dogs together, hunted side by side in the nearby hills, kept extensive gardens in the wise he'd taught her of his people.

His were strange and foreign ways, yet he'd brought much useful knowledge with him, and, better yet, a means of gaining more, a manner of looking at things which served to increase knowledge almost daily, and which he taught to anyone who asked it of him.

Always, for example, within the living memory of her people, and in tales ancient with the telling, had they received their weapons and machinery from the west, wonderful things far beyond the capabilities of the Comanche to imitiate. Now, at the least, and thanks alone to Fireclaw, had they achieved a measure of independence and understood the fashioning and operation of their bows (although the sights remained a mystery, even yet to him). Thanks to skills he'd brought with him from the east, resinous adhesives and spun-glass fibers were in general use among the tribes.

The argument below continued. Now another face appeared beside the unyielding girl, the pale, half-conscious visage of another man, propping himself against the cargo hatch not far from the spot where Dove Blossom's first arrows still stood quivering. He, too, seemed to want to argue with the stubborn one.

For the first time, she spoke.

Curtly.

The wounded man bit his lip and uttered not another word.

Dove Blossom shook her head more in sadness than disgust. E'en the men were soft and pliant among these foreigners!

Once again she looked toward her husband. With her assistance, Fireclaw maintained the machines of scattered tribes whose gods, for unprecedented reasons of their own, seemed to tolerate his presence in this land. Although the Comanche and their kind had access to many more sophisticated devices than Fireclaw's people had (so he himself had told her), the gods, it was insisted by the shamans—who ought to know—didn't trust anybody with such weapons as the pistol Fireclaw had fashioned for himself, not even, it was whispered, the manlike demon servants which, in times long past, had acted as their divine armies, wiping out families, prairie villages, whole nations who'd dared dabble in the wizardry Fireclaw made practice of each day.

Yet even the gods left Fireclaw alone.

Perhaps they knew something of the awful circumstances of

his disfigurement and exile. Perhaps even they—was this thought blasphemy?—held him in awe.

The gods, laughed the irreverent Helvetian—while she cowered deep inside herself, waiting for the lightning to strike—seemed to be a trifle sloppy about supplying parts and skilled labor. Ironically, his laughter at such moments, deeply as it shook what she believed in, was also the reed through which her sanity and courage drew breath. Many men she knew—her brother, Knife Thrower, was often one such—who held their feelings in stringent check and whose only visible emotion was wrath uncontrollable. Excepting moments such as this one she was living through, Fireclaw's most usual breach was laughter. Each time he worked upon the machinery, he told her, he learned things. The gods mightn't be human, and they might be powerful, but they were not the best of artisans. It was as if—he'd said this only once to her, although it had impressed her fully as much as anything he'd said to her a hundred times—it was as if they'd copied what they wrought from someone else whose lifelong dream the first fashioning had been. The gods knew much which he didn't— but naught which he couldn't learn, if time enough were left to him. Someday he'd puzzle out the lenses, and beyond that, who could tell?

Neither soft nor pliant was her husband, Fireclaw.

And now, with pride, he'd informed this dirty old stranger, a former countryman to all appearances, that her people were his own! This he'd intoned in ceremony many years ago, but never before within the hearing of foreigners.

Life, Dove Blossom thought to herself, never for a moment permitting the crosshairs of her bowsight to waver from the dark-eyed girl's left breast, is very good.

At the land-ship's side, Fireclaw spoke.

"If she'd have me say the words myself, tell them to me that I might say them aright."

The old man started to relay Fireclaw's request, but the giant red-haired stranger interrupted in something resembling Helvetian, with a heavy, burred, and rolling accent.

"Me understandum. Fireclaw fella sayum *'sapaagh chalhayr.'* It meanum 'good morning.'"

"*Sapaagh chalhayr* . . . what's her name?"

The red-haired one opened his mouth, but the girl spoke first.

"*Ayesha. Anah ismih Ayesha.*"

"*Sapaagh chalhayr, Ayesha.*"

A quiet, sharp command dispersed the dogs.

"Keep your weapon, girl, if you're feeling a need of it. My oath you'll not be harmed by me."

He turned to Red-Hair. "Tell her."

More conversation, strange words flitted about the ship.

"*Maa manna* . . ." one person offered.

Another replied, "*Charjooh.*"

"*Min bhatlah*" and something else Dove Blossom couldn't hear came from the red-haired man.

"*Chanaa la chabhgham?*" asked the girl.

"D'you say I mean for her to keep the gun," Fireclaw interrupted. "I'll disarm no one upon my own land, do they not threaten me or mine. Tell her now and tell her straight."

Dove Blossom heard the feeling in his voice. After what he'd suffered as a youth, his hand-fashioned nine-shot, self-cocking revolver—born of a quarter century of continuing experiment and whence came the name his wife's family had given him—served as an ever-present reminder of the trumped-up offenses which had lost him his right hand, his homeland, and his first true love. That he'd taken an entirely different lesson from the experience than most men, obedient to authority, would have, was one of the things she loved most about him.

Ne'er again would such a disaster be allowed—would he *allow* it—to come to pass.

The dark-eyed girl nodded.

She lowered her rifle.

She let it rest upon its buttplate upon the deck.

She leaned the barrel against the rail.

She took her hand away.

She smiled.

A collective sigh of relief escaped from a dozen pairs of lips.

Dove Blossom let the string of her bow relax, began to flex her aching hand and the painfully cramped muscles of her shoulders.

Below her, the land-ship began emptying itself of passengers.

XXII:

Owald

Surely We have put on their necks fetters up to the
chin, so their heads are raised; and We have put before
them a barrier and behind them a barrier; and We have
covered them, so they do not see.

—The *Koran*, Sura XXXVI

"Saracens, you call them?"

Fighting a fatigue born of suppressing thoughts of what he'd
truly like to do at this moment, Sedrich Fireclaw asked this of
the man who stood across the machine shop from him, the man
he'd dreamed of killing slowly, very slowly, for the last twenty
years.

There came no immediate reply.

"Saracens, then. What manner of people are Saracens?"

The sun of an early prairie afternoon filtered through the
resin-impregnated skins which served as windows—the pro-
prietor had promised himself for years that he'd someday teach
himself to make glass—filling the small sod building with a
diffuse light.

While Fireclaw was struggling to control himself, Dove

Blossom was seeing to the disposition of the land-ship's passengers, showing them the well, sending word to her brother that supplies would be greatly welcome and well paid for.

For the time being, the foreigners would sleep in their own quarters aboard the land-ship, whose sails had been furled by the expedient of lowering the upper booms, and whose wheels, with their brakes applied, had been further secured with large stones piled about them.

Outside the shop, the alien gabble of the Saracens' conversation filled the yard.

Oln Woeck laid a mill bastard file back upon the workbench whence he'd taken it for casual, disapproving examination, wiped a filthy yellow hand upon his filthier robe in a gesture reeking—among other things—of fastidious piety. As with aught else about the man, this infuriated Fireclaw, who by lifelong habit maintained a scrupulously spotless workspace.

Even so, he kept his peace.

With difficulty.

For the moment.

"They're those whom we once knew as 'Invader,'" Oln Woeck replied at last, turning to Fireclaw as he did. "Those unbelievers sent by an avenging God who did o'errun the Old World e'en as our forbears, steeped in sin, were rendered helpless with the Great Death."

Shaking his tattooed head, he looked round the building, taking in Fireclaw's drill-press, lathe, and mill.

"I see thou'rt still at it, boy. One would think thou'd've learned a lesson, after aught that hath transpired."

Fighting back an anger which threatened to sweep consciousness away, Fireclaw stepped forward, whispering through clenched teeth.

"What makes you think I haven't, mutilator of children and helpless cripples? I pay fire-tithe to no man now, nor any god!"

At some saner level within him, he was glad he'd not brought Ursi to the shop with them. Sensing what his master felt, the great bear-dog would likeliest have torn the old man's throat out.

"Give me a tithe instead, priest," he hissed, "a tithe of words. I stayed my hand this morning, though that looks more and more to be an unwise decision. Give me a single reason why I should allow you to live another heartbeat. I'm still at it, am I? You presume much for someone who's at the most charitable best an unwelcome visitor."

Oln Woeck chuckled, a sound to raise the short hairs upon the back of anybody's neck. Those who foolishly believed in honor and the like were defenseless puppets to him. His cowardly display had served its purpose this morning and could be dispensed with now. He'd other, better strings to jerk.

."Nor hath thy manner much improved. A wise man did inform me once that a guest is a jewel upon the cushion of hospitality. Treat'st thou all thy guests like the cushion rather than the jewel?"

He chuckled again.

"No matter. I simply observe that thou still followest the mechanic's trade, in any case, and that, like all thy worldy efforts, 'tis a wasted one and futile."

A peculiar species of embarrassment swept through the Helvetian warrior, astonishment and chagrin that a grown man could utter such nonsense and nature leave him yet alive. Still, he himself permitted Oln Woeck to go on breathing simply because of this devouring need of his to learn more.

"Have you lost hold of all caution along with your senses, senile one? Look about you at what I've built—"

He held up his steel- and leather-covered stump.

"—single-handedly, thanks to your good offices. Tell me, worthless parasite, how's the effort wasted which feeds me and mine at no expense to anybody else?"

Oln Woeck frowned, as if considering this.

"Your, um, *wife* . . . we'll pass discussing her for a time. I say what I say upon account of these selfsame Saracens. Thou'rt but one man, whose solitary efforts are inevitably wasted. They, in their greater numbers and in selfless cooperation, have far surpassed your smidgenous tinkering, young Sedrich."

Fireclaw laughed, and in the laughing felt himself relax.

Neither man knew it, but it was at this moment that the younger of the two became most dangerous.

"Oln Woeck, as e'er, you mistake me. I don't begrudge the worthy accomplishments of others, but try to learn from them. Thus I've built upon the meager legacy which you and others like you did your Jesus-damnedest to destroy for all time."

He gazed about the shop as he'd invited Oln Woeck to do, as if seeing it for the first time himself.

"'Twas a place to start from," he nodded with grim satisfaction, "the onliest I had."

He brightened and, for a moment, was the boy Old Woeck had known.

"Now I'll learn whate'er these harsh-spoken strangers have to teach me, and go on from there."

The leader of the Brotherhood opened his mouth to protest this enormity, but was interrupted by Fireclaw, who'd had another thought.

"If anybody's work's futile, 'tis yours, limb-chopper. Here these impious strangers worship different gods than yours, have for centuries by all accounts, and haven't yet been punished for it. They seem to have waxed more prosperous by far and healthier than those who've taken your advice. What say you to that?"

"I say to you that God's good time is not a man's time. I say that prosperity measureth not a man's soul, nor a people's. I say that a man's healthy aspect is a disguised curse—'tis simply that much longer he must needs remain within this illusory vale of tears and testing, before ascending to the real world."

He spread his yellow, ropy hands. "E'en did I concern myself with such worldy matters, I'd not sanction this wasteful duplication of vain effort which thou celebratest, boy. Each person hath his rightful place in God's well-ordered—"

Fireclaw drew his revolver.

Oln Woeck stepped back a step.

Fireclaw thumbed the latch below the rear sight, pressed the barrel against his thigh, and tipped both it and the cylinder forward upon the frame. Nine golden cylinders rose slightly from their chambers.

"Look here at a sample of such wasteful duplication, Oln Woeck. Here's a cartridge of my devising. The brass casing holds black powder, percussive primer, and a length-split shoe of resin which in its turn contains a tiny arrow."

He slapped the pistol shut against his leg, holstered it, and shuffled through the clutter of the bench, displaying cartridge parts which had not yet been assembled.

"My first shoes were of carven wood. I shot one of your blue-templed bugger-boys with such a load, remember?" He grinned. "No matter, as you say. These Saracens, on the other hand, push great globs of lead from out of their barrels. Both ideas are sound. I think I've got the edge o'er them for range and penetration, while their approach is best for knocking things down. Different people arrive at different answers to the same problem, causing all to benefit. 'Twas e'er thus."

Oln Woeck made a strangled noise.

There was silence for a time.

"I came here, Young Sedrich, neither to open old wounds nor to debate with thee upon the pragmatics of heresy. 'Twas my purpose for this afternoon to bring thee tidings overdue of the village thou didst abandon in thy youth."

He peered into Fireclaw's eyes.

"Knowest thou that thy mother's dead?"

The naked words were like a slap across the face. He stood a long while reeling from it, leaning on the bench beside him, while pain coursed through his body, centering on a tight, burning knot in his stomach. His eyes stung with boyish tears. It wasn't the kindliest wise in which to change the subject, Fireclaw thought when he was somewhat recovered. Why he'd expected better of the old man he didn't know.

" 'Tis true, my boy, these past five years. I came with that news for thee, and other word which concerneth all Helvetii."

Fireclaw bowed his head and closed his eyes, pressing pain away from himself.

"What was the manner of her dying?"

"The manner of her dying," Old Woeck replied, "was that

she passed away without pain in her sleep, weary with a long-carried burden of grief which was entirely of thy making."

He smiled. "One gathereth that her last thought was of thee."

A puzzled look crossed Fireclaw's face as he experienced a strange, emptying sensation. Ever had Oln Woeck had the best of him. He'd been prepared to kill the Cultist when the landship had arrived and had let himself be persuaded otherwise—though it had been the dream of a lifetime to spill the old man's guts into the dirt.

Next, he'd resolved to deny the man, exchange no words with him, refuse him whatever it was he wanted. That resolve had not lasted an hour.

Now they stood in converse, as if they still were neighbors. As if there weren't decades of bad blood between them. And now his righteous anger, the burning in the pit of his stomach which had sustained him through all the terrible years upon the plains, and for which five hundred Comanche warriors and many others had suffered, had deserted him, leaving him naught behind it but a sucking hollowness.

He looked down to where his right hand had been.

"My mother's dead. What other glad tidings have you brought me, Oln Woeck? Be quick, for I've things to do, and my patience shortens with each breath I draw."

The old man's eyes widened.

"Why, Sedrich, my boy, thou'st verily grown taller but no wiser. Look thou round thyself, at this prosperous establishment, thy fields, thy shops, thy dogs, thy . . . woman. Consider but thy formidable new name. 'Twas *I* who put thee here. Neither wouldst thou've a scrap of it, were it nor for the will of Him who worketh through me."

Sedrich felt a welcome flash of renewed rage at the injustice being spoken.

In another breath, even that much deserted him.

Oln Woeck continued. "E'en so, thou didst hurry off too soon, and hast borne with thee certain assumptions which are incorrect, concerning the final outcome of events."

"*What?*"

"I see I've thy interest at last." Oln Woeck chuckled. "Thy lady-love, young Fr—"

"Speak not her name or you shall die where you stand!"

The old man cleared his throat.

"As you wish it. She who was to have been my lawful bride, according to the customs of our people, died not in vain entire."

"What are you speaking of, you, you—"

"She bore thee a son whose life thou didst believe as lost as hers. But it was not to be. Thou art a father still, Sedrich-called-Fireclaw. Thy son's name's called Owald."

2

The slanting sun streamed into the workshop door, glinting off the metal parts and tools, dazzling the eyes. Fireclaw's head was whirling. A son! Why, in the name of aught that was intelligent and decent, had he fled? Why had he—

He turned and seized the Cultist's robe, lifting the man off his feet.

"What became of my son, old man, tell me now do you wish to live an eyeblink longer!"

"Why, Sedrich," Oln Woeck squeaked. There was a tone of triumph to him, nonetheless. "I've not the faintest of ideas."

Fireclaw set him down upon the oil-stained dirt floor.

The old man smiled, exposing toothless gums, enjoying Fireclaw's pain and consternation.

"Treachery's an inherited trait within thy line, boy. We'd a bargain, Sister Ilse and myself, a bargain which she violated at the premonition of her death."

Fireclaw raised one good hand, palm outward in interruption. "You mean she knew . . . ?"

The old man nodded. Both knew it happened in that wise with the Sisters sometimes.

"She told my son—*thy* son—*our* son about the circumstances of his birth. Fifteen years old he was by then, e'en younger than thyself, methinks, and he, too, disappeared. 'Tis rumored to seek thee out.

"He hath not been heard of since."

3

Dove Blossom found her husband where she'd thought she would, in a favorite spot of theirs, high upon a ridge above their ranch where they'd first hunted together, fifteen years before. Refusing to make Old Woeck any immediate answer—it was characteristic of the old man, she understood, to follow up on unjust calumny and shocking news by demanding a favor—Fireclaw had left the ranch overnight, heading for the hills to think things through.

To the east, the land slanted dizzily—a "hogback" Fireclaw named it, although she had never seen one of the half-feral pigs his people had brought with them from an Old World which was scarcely real to her itself—as if tip-tilted by a giant, losing four hundred paces of altitude in not much over twice that horizontal distance. Across this windswept diagonal, sage, coarse grasses, stunted pine, and cactus intermingled, fodder for the gray-brown ghostly mule deer, hares, ground squirrels, and rabbits, all drawing meager sustenance from the reddish, sandy soil.

To the west, the ridge lost half its height all at once, in a sharp, vertical drop overlooking a broad, pale green and boulder-studded mountain meadow where grew the yellow and purple flowers she was named for. Porcupine gnawed girdles in the bark of aspen trees. Beyond lay mountain forest, above that snow, blue-purple barren rock, and mysteries she had no wish to penetrate.

North and south the ridge extended, a league in each direction, until it was broken off like the brittle edges of a bit of kneaded cornmeal dough. Here creek valleys, dry this time of year, flowed from the mountains to the plains. Daytimes, one could see across these steep-sided clefts to their other sides, where the ridges took up once again, bordering the Great Blue Mountains as they marched from ice and tundra in the north to the broiling of southern deserts.

Tonight the sky was clear and still.

Coming unheard upon him, Dove Blossom saw Fireclaw sitting cross-legged before a fire no bigger than his fist. His back was toward the wind-twisted trunk of a fallen evergreen, too big to have lived upon this weather-tortured ridge, and having at last paid the price.

His sword lay in its scabbard across his thighs.

He watched the fire until a tiny pinecone she'd displaced with a fringe-moccasined foot rolled into a root-walled bed of last year's scales at the base of a tree. It made no greater noise than the breathing of a field mouse, though it brought him to alertness, and coaxed a full hand's width of gleaming, deadly steel from *Murderer*'s sheath before he saw that it was she who'd followed him.

He spoke not but slid the sword back into place, acknowledging her glance with one of his own which she couldn't read. This, more than anything else which had transpired this day, frightened her. He turned his eyes again into the blue-and-yellow heart of the palm-sized fire he'd built in a hollow of scooped-out sand.

Dove Blossom crossed the clearing, a space little larger than their bedchamber at the ranch, and, finding a comfortable bend beside her husband along the same fallen trunk he leaned against, sat down on a carpet of red-brown pine needles.

The fire crackled, sparks drifting upward where they winked and died. Fireclaw added a small branch, watched the bark-flakes curl and peel as the seasoned wood beneath it started burning.

Incense rose about them.

Of a sudden, and in terrifying silence, he was at her, seizing her sueded shirt, thrusting it off over her head. *Murderer* lay upon the ground, at the other side of the fire, unheeded and unnoticed. He tore at the waist-bindings of her skirt, breaking a thong in desperate haste. Naked save for her moccasins, she lay back where he'd pressed her, uncomfortable on an itching carpet of dried needles, looking up as he knelt over her, tearing at his own clothing.

The worst was that he'd not meet her eyes, nor even look

upon her face. His own was twisted, darkened, stony. Had it been blood-haze, that would have been bad enough. This was something else, far worse. Something she'd never seen before.

Then he was upon her, forcing her legs apart, though she didn't resist, entering against unready flesh. She bit her lower lip and squeezed her eyes shut, suffering the pain as long as she was able, feeling his lower jaw dig at her shoulder, his breath rasp in her ear, his one good hand bruise her hip. Her moaning gasp conveyed a different message than he was used to hearing from her, but, in the middle of his savage rythym, he ignored it, hurting her with every breath and every heartbeat.

He spent himself in silence and rolled away, still refusing to catch her eye, his back bent and his head low, his gaze once more upon the fire. Perhaps he was thinking, as she was trying not to, that a secret private place of theirs, this clearing, had been defiled irrevocably by his thoughtless urgency. She pulled her clothing to her breast and, concentrating hard upon the many years of tenderness between them, rather than upon this ugly moment—now blessedly behind them—of unthinking need, she laid a hand upon his sweat-sheened shoulder.

Sedrich turned to his wife, as if continuing an interrupted conversation.

"I'd believed, for all my life till that moment, that my mother's Sisterhood was benevolent, protective, a shield and a shelter against the Cult."

He shook his head, keeping his eyes upon the fire before them.

Arms wrapped close about her bare knees, Dove Blossom watched the fire also, disappointed that his thoughts were not upon her, yet understanding and eager to help her man in whatever wise she might.

"Yet, when you needed help," she offered, "the Sisterhood proved to be as bad as the Brotherhood?"

"Worse, in their own deceptive wise. Sins of omission. You know, I brought up the matter of the fletcher, the man they mutilated when I was a boy. He was supposed to have had a

Choice, as I did, 'tween that and ostracism, but 'twas complicated by the fact he was already crippled. So, in addition to the legs he'd given for his people, the Cult took his hand as well." He shook his head. "This afternoon, Oln Woeck couldn't e'en remember the incident.

"Ah, well, memory's selective. I didn't remember their burning a cross upon his lawn—as they did upon my father's when they came for me—but I remember kicking through the ashes afterward."

"What would he have of you, my husband? What has he traveled thus far to demand?"

Sedrich laughed. "This I've asked of myself from the first moment his foul feet touched our land. Why does Oln Woeck enter my life again," he reached up and touched her cheek with a gentle finger, "just when things are arranged as I like them?"

He looked up toward the unanswering stars.

"He supposes I should be grateful to him, for giving me a start upon this life we've built together, you and I, with broken fingernails and bleeding knuckles. He's shocked and hurt to learn how much I burn to spit his guts upon my father's sword."

He rubbed his temples with his fists.

"What does he want of me? He told me, after dancing round about it for half an hour. Sinner that I be, said he, I'm needed. He says the future of all the Helvetii may depend upon me, offering other reasons, as well, why I should cooperate with what he has in mind."

"What reasons could he offer, Sedrich?"

He took her small brown hand in his, telling her about the son he'd not known he had.

"My mother labored mightily the child's life to save, having within her expertise diverse and potent formulae, the distillation of them from the blood and organs of pigs and goats and other animals. These did she instill within one of the younger Sisters, who did give the baby suck as if she'd delivered him herself.

"And he survived."

Five minutes passed before Fireclaw spoke again.

"He'd be twenty by this time. He was called Owald, after my paternal grandfather—a fortuitous coincidence, since the same name also runs in Oln Woeck's family, he says, and was acceptable to him. Young Owald was raised in the belief that he was Oln Woeck's son—a 'necessary deception' to spare him the painful knowledge that his real father had 'cruelly' abandoned him."

Again he shook his head. "I think, by now, the pious son of a pig believes the lie himself."

He paused, then: "In truth 'twas my own mother did the raising, as Oln Woeck's duties with the Brotherhood—"

"Ne'er mind that." Dove Blossom insisted, "What is it Oln Woeck wants of you?"

"He's asked me to guide a party westward, through the mountains, into whate'er domain lies beyond."

Dove Blossom's sudden intake of breath would have been audible a hundred paces away, had there been anyone but her husband to hear it. Why was it, just when Sedrich had begun to open up to her after all these years, he was going to be taken away from her?

Casting aside the final vestiges of the womanly reticence held to be proper among her people, she made bold to share these thoughts with Fireclaw. He appeared to ponder them a long while before giving her an answer in Comanche, or in Helvetian when the Red Man's tongue—at least that warrior's portion he knew—lacked words he needed.

"Dove Blossom," he began, unable to look at her when he spoke thus, yet knowing that, this once, he must. More than ever before, he was conscious of their many years together, years which sometimes seemed to have flown by like days, but which also, upon occasion, felt to him as if they'd been all his life. "My wife and partner. How can it be I've ne'er told you what's in my heart about you?"

She held up a hand to silence him, anxious that her husband not humiliate himself in betrayal of customs which she herself had violated. They were her people's customs, she realized as she made the gesture, not his. Also, in his words—words she'd provoked, and now had no wish he should continue—she felt some sense of parting, which filled her with panic and an infinite sadness.

Fireclaw took her hand from the air between them, kissed it upon the palm and placed it in her lap.

"Now I've started this, contrary woman, I'll be heard. You're to me the most . . ." He struggled as if to find a word. "The most *decent* human being e'er I've known. The more that, since, unlike the innocent girl young Frae was, you're wise in the ways of the world. Your decency is a matter of deliberation."

Although she couldn't know it, the truth of Sedrich's words was in that instant demonstrated by the fact Dove Blossom felt not the slightest twinge of jealousy at Frae Hethristochter's name, but took them in the wise in which he'd meant them.

"These are words of great respect, my husband, not of love—although I thank you for them and will carry them with me till I am no more." This time her upraised hand forestalled an answer. "No, no I doubt not your love, for it has been a lifetime in the proving. Yet somehow your words, which touched not upon the subject, have nonetheless told me you will bow to Oln Woeck's wishes and go with the Saracens."

His face was pained. "I think me I must, beloved wife. I feared I was growing aged. Now the old, unanswered questions gall me as ne'er they did when I was young. P'rhaps because I know the time I've left to answer them is limited. 'Twould seem, as well, that westward's where my son—"

This time he seized her hand and held it tight.

"—where *our* son's gone."

"Good," she replied, "I'll go with you."

Fireclaw's face brightened at her answer, but, even as she spoke it, some stirring deep inside her body told her that the gods, mocking their longest, dearest held wishes, had contrived that it shouldn't be so.

Fireclaw and Dove Blossom watched the fire.

After a little time had passed in silence, he took her in his arms and made quiet, gentle love to her, as tender as e'er he'd been when first they'd known each other fifteen years—and a lifetime—ago.

This time her moaning in his ear conveyed what it was supposed to.

"Oln Woeck was right about one thing, dear my Sedrich," she whispered between gasps. "You're but one man, mighty Fireclaw. One man who can be replaced—at least for me—by no other."

XXIII:

The Sword of God

... when Our command comes and the Oven
boils ... We charge not any soul save to its capacity.
—The *Koran*, Sura XXIII

Morning sunlight streamed through a deep-bellied bay of
windows spread abaft of Mochamet al Rotshild's cabin—past a
filtering barrier of battle-splintered frames and hasty patching.

All about the low-ceilinged chamber—Fireclaw had to duck
upon entering and continue stooping to avoid braining himself
upon rafter-beams soot-blotched by gimbaled lamps of brass—
Comanche arrows had been wrenched from the paneled walls,
or simply broken off. Nor had the furnishing and fixtures
avoided similar damage. What little there was left of the
windows, after Knife Thrower's enthusiastic welcome, was
glass. The broken panes had been replaced with a material
Sedrich Fireclaw had never seen before, gray-brown, fibrous,
much like paper, only thicker.

"One gathereth that the vessel's master," Oln Woeck had
explained as they had crossed from the ranch-yard gate an hour
earlier, toward the immobilized land-ship, "hath purposely

kept her bow turned to the westward, so as to be awakened by the dawn each day."

Great black Ursi trotted happily beside Fireclaw, sniffing out unfamiliar footsteps stamped into every handspan of his accustomed domain. The animal sensed an excited bustling in the air about him, and, as often was the way of his kind, an impending voyage.

Fireclaw nodded, understanding both of his companions.

"Methinks," the warrior replied, "that anyone else would have wanted a view of the mountains to wake up to."

He raised his eyes toward them, looming like a mighty deep-stepped wall to the west.

"Still," he offered, "the sight of yon great barrier can't be a very comforting one to a seaman, looking like the very tidal wave of Doomsday as it must."

For once, the leader of the Cult of Jesus was in agreement.

"Aye, and worse, this be as far as his land-ship goeth. From here, his expedition—and your own—doth proceed afoot."

Fireclaw shook his head. The man couldn't let an opportunity pass to remind him of the coming search for "their" son—and the continuing necessity that Fireclaw permit the Cultist to go on living. Yet the voyage was vitally necessary as well, Fireclaw knew, to the Saracens, growing as it did directly out of a dangerous political situation in a broader world than he had ever known existed.

Upon returning from the nearby foothills, he had surprised Oln Woeck this morning with his curt agreement, at least to hear out this Commodore Mochamet al Rotshild, promising as well to advise the Saracens, to whatever extent he was capable, upon the likelihood that their small company would reach their goal.

Fireclaw had left it to the Cultist to wonder about his reasons for cooperating. If the old man thought he knew what those reasons might be, so much the better.

"My single condition," he had informed the astonished man upon summoning him to the ranch house where he and Dove Blossom had broken their fast well before dawn, "is that you, the wise and trusted mentor of my boyhood, must accompany me upon this great adventure, since your wise counsel is likely to be constantly required."

Oln Woeck had paled.

"But, Sedrich," he had protested, "I had planned returning eastward. I feel that I am needed there far more greatly."

Ruffling the big dog's ears, Fireclaw had laughed.

"Do you not return, Helvetia will go on existing, whereas, do you not continue with the Saracens and me upon this trek, to whatever extent its success depends upon me, to that extent shall it suffer by your absence, since it will foreordain mine."

To a far greater extent than he appreciated, Oln Woeck had brought the man he knew as Sedrich Sedrichsohn—whom others, who knew him far better, now called Fireclaw—up to date concerning the village he had left abruptly and so long ago.

Land-ships, for example, such as a younger Sedrich had been punished for experimenting with, were now in increasingly common use among the Helvetians everywhere. Oln Woeck seemed to have forgotten who invented them, treating the matter just as if they had always existed.

Or grew upon trees, the warrior thought.

"Moreover," the Cultist told him as they approached the hull of the Saracen vessel, still closed up tightly against the surprising chill of the prairie summer night—and any intruders it might bring—"contact is beginning in full measure with these rich and powerful strangers from across what they term the *Lesser* Ocean."

Raising his steel-tipped stump to pound upon the hull, Fireclaw smiled down wolfishly at the old man.

"Had it not, in fact, begun covertly many years ago with Frae's father, Hethri—"

Oln Woeck's jaw dropped.

"How could you have known that? How—"

Fireclaw paused, letting the old man sputter, refraining a moment more from awakening the Saracens.

Then: "And is there not much more to say, in full truth, concerning this 'bargain' which existed between you and my mother, which you have accused her of violating? Remember, as you answer, Oln Woeck, how dearly you want a favor of me."

The old man's mouth was a tight, straight line.

"Aye, as long as thy son, Owald, wasn't brought up in the Cult, the boy would be raised in the belief that I was his father. I was to supervise Sister Ilse's handling of it."

Fireclaw could well imagine the slow, relentless pressure upon his mother and the boy over the years, the solicitous presence, the pious grimaces, the incessant lectures, all eventually leading to suggestions about head-shaving and tattoos.

Possibly far worse, knowing the old man's personal habits.

"Ere she had, in whatever witchy manner, sensed the imminence of her death, she delivered to the boy Owald, then fifteen years old, a parcel of her highly prejudiced opinions concerning his birth, the death of—*stay thy hand, I'll not say her name!*—of his own mother, and the disappearance of his natural father."

Fireclaw nodded.

"And young Owald had never gotten along with you, anyway, believing you were his father or not."

"He himself disappeared from our village"—Oln Woeck sighed—"the very day Sister Ilse was laid to rest."

Sedrich pounded on the hull.

2

"Marghapaa, sapaagh chalhayr! Maa chajmal chathahs!"

Mochamet al Rotshild himself met Fireclaw with an engulfing hand as the Helvetian warrior and his unwelcome companion reached the top of the gangplank.

Ursi sniffed at the Saracen's baggy clothing, then immediately found a corner and lay down.

Through that companion—seemingly no more popular with the Saracen captain than with Fireclaw—they exchanged a few words of courtesy, then proceeded aft to the wide-windowed cabin where, before Fireclaw's wondering eyes, the "Commodore" began spreading map after map, each unrolled following its extraction from a tall case of pigeonholes which occupied an entire wall of the small room.

From the first such, there had clattered to the floor an arrow. In one corner swung a gilded cage, unoccupied.

"These Saracens," Oln Woeck explained, providing his own casual translation of Mochamet al Rotshild's opening remarks, "are transparently terrified of someone or something called the Mughal—I can't determine whether 'tis a man or millions—who seemeth to have decided to act upon a centuries-old grudge stemming from sectarian disagreements within their heathenish religion."

The Saracen captain kept his eyes directly upon Fireclaw as the old man spoke, but he frowned at several points within his declamation. It was obvious to the warrior that he was less ignorant of the Helvetian tongue than the leader of the Cult of Jesus believed.

Oln Woeck continued.

"That religion is called by its practitioners Islam. Its practitioners call themselves Moslems—and they are most assiduous in its practice. At any moment now, we shall be interrupted by their caterwauling prayers, which, like the ablution rituals of the Sisterhood, they perform several times a day."

"How long," asked Fireclaw, eager to plunge into the pile of maps rapidly growing upon the table before him, "will these infernal prayers go on?"

He had a second thought. "And are they so damnably obligatory as to interfere with the safe completion of this silly quest they've asked our help for?"

"Of the latter, young Sedrich, I know no more than thee. They've certainly a language well created for prayer, also for elaborate insults, curses, and—"

Mochamet al Rotshild spoke.

"The captain biddeth me remind thee that he and these other Eldworld Moslems wish to establish an alliance with whatever standoffish domain may exist across the Great Blue Mountains—they know as little about the facts of the matter as we— ere their great Asiatic rivals can. There's a battle raging 'tween the two Islamic civilizations for control of what they call the basin of the Greater Ocean which lieth 'twixt this continent and one called Great Asia."

Fireclaw nodded.

The captain, through Oln Woeck, explained that there were many rumors about the magical accomplishments of those dwelling west of the Great Blue Mountains. Wizards there had learned the turning of base metals to precious ones, it was said, or the extension of human life to immortality, even perhaps to make ships such as this one *fly*.

Mochamet al Rotshild laughed with Fireclaw and Oln Woeck at these tales, then grew serious of aspect.

"Even more fabulous rumors," he conveyed through the Cultist, "concern a weapon capable of destroying whole armies and fleets, wielded by a flesh-eating Sun-God—a notion, I might add, which both horrifies and fascinates these pious Moslems. The captain, who is not so pious—he bade me say that to you—hath his doubts about these other tales, all save the last about the weapon. He claimeth to have seen it work, and hath been ordered by his king to investigate further."

The captain pointed at a map purporting to display the entire earth. He made a short speech, then waited for Oln Woeck to translate it for Fireclaw before continuing.

"Open war is even now being waged in yet another place, here, which they call the 'Island Continent.'"

From his mother's teachings, and the crude hand-drawn maps in her many books, Fireclaw had known about Great Asia and the Greater Ocean, though in details the charts he'd seen in boyhood differed considerably from these of the Saracens.

Of this Island Continent, those same books had said nothing, not even acknowledging that it, or yet another, icebound at the bottom of the world, existed.

"Similar representations as this that he leadeth," the captain explained through Oln Woeck, pointing to the southern continent of the New World, "are even now being made among the 'Incas', here, an ancient, powerful, and subtle people."

" 'Incas,' " Fireclaw repeated, letting the alien word roll over upon his tongue.

"But I suppose," the tattooed Cultist added on his own account, unable to resist a bigoted sneer, "that the mighty Fireclaw knoweth nothing of such matters, and careth less, having been most fully occupied with the carving out of his own domain among these benighted—but so very compliant— savages for many years."

Fireclaw thrust the steel throat of the resin-impregnated leather cuff upon his severed right wrist over the oddly-shaped handle of the dagger at his waist.

There was a solid metal-to-metal click, although he did not withdraw the blade. Ursi lifted his head, whistled plaintively, then laid it across his paws again and was still.

"Priest," Fireclaw answered, gratified to see that Oln Woeck still disliked the title, "limit yourself to what the captain, here, has to tell me, and spare me your nasty little embellishments. Or I shall directly have need of learning his language for myself."

Mochamet al Rotshild chuckled, having understood a bit of what had passed between the men.

"You-fella Fireclaw tellum priest-fella good," the captain essayed in his faltering version of Helvetian. "Me-fella Mo quicky-quick learnum Fireclaw tongue, if helpum."

His blue eyes twinkled with mischief as the leader of the Brotherhood glared back at him.

Sedrich grinned back. He liked this wicked red-haired foreigner and resolved forthwith to learn the captain's language whether or not he decided to dispense with Oln Woeck's translation services by paying back the debt he'd owed the man for twenty years.

He looked from the Cultist to the Commodore and back again. As was always the case, the trouble with simply killing someone like Oln Woeck was that, within the hour of his death, there would be a thousand of his ilk—and maybe worse—to take his place.

That this was never the way with wiser men and more valiant warriors, Sedrich Fireclaw felt, constituted one of the greatest tragedies of human history.

He turned his attention to the map, where certain significant facts had begun to emerge.

From the Saracen point of view, one with which he could heartily agree, judging from the map, this expedition had already been under way a long time, demanding a weary-making and dangerous voyage across what they termed the Lesser Ocean to the shoreline of a barbaric New World, thence out of the eastern forests and across the western plains.

When asked about it, Mochamet al Rotshild told Fireclaw that Saracen seagoing ships ran on steam, a tidbit Oln Woeck was extremely loath to translate until he was once more shown a bit of dagger-blade.

This time, the captain's.

Fireclaw was of course familiar with the small, alcohol-fueled steam engines used by the neighboring Red tribes. But he had not stayed at home quite long enough to see the march of progress alter the horizon of the eastern sea. In a way, he thought he might be glad about this. He might never have found a way to imitate these later marvels, had he grown up watching for them on the ocean.

Finally, nodding his head and shaking the hand of Mochamet al Rotshild, he agreed to guide the Saracen expedition to the shore of the Greater Ocean. He was not surprised—given the one condition he'd extracted—that his fellow Helvetian was not quite as happy with the decision as he had claimed he'd be.

Inside Fireclaw the Destroyer, a much younger Sedrich, son of Owaldsohn, father, it now appeared, of Owald, had time to wonder what Oln Woeck would find to steal from him this time.

3

Some time later, after one of the prayers Oln Woeck had promised would transpire, the three men stepped out upon the deck.

There Fireclaw was formally introduced to the young

woman, scarcely more than a girl, he thought, seeing her up close, who had tried so hard to kill him just the day before.

She had been taking the occupant of the gilded cage back in the cabin for a walk. Giant Ursi threatened to knock the girl over, attempting to jump up to investigate an alarmed Sagheer more closely. Fireclaw had to order him—and sharply—to sit.

"Ayesha," he pronounced her name again.

"Fireclaw Sedrich al Sedrichsohn," she echoed, rolling the *r*'s until they each became a trill.

He laughed.

"Just Fireclaw will do. I've gotten used to it. Or Sedrich, as I was called when I was her age."

He was amused that, with the aim of sweetening their diplomatic cause, the Saracens had brought with them this fierce (although admittedly dark-eyed and pretty) child warrior. She was apparently the favorite daughter of their ruler, one Abu Bakr Mohammed VII, who claimed, among a long string of somewhat pretentious titles which did not translate at all well into Helvetian, that of Caliph-in-Rome.

Like Fireclaw, this ruler's daughter had a constant animal companion, a tiny, ancient-eyed being she called by the name Sagheer, who rode atop her shoulder.

Already last evening and this morning, Fireclaw had watched his Comanche in-laws as they had begun to bring supplies to his ranch in trade for goods Mochamet al Rotshild offered them. Like Fireclaw, they had never before seen such an animal. Unlike him, many were terrified by it, muttering among themselves that it was the spirit of an ancestor which advised her constantly by whispering in her ear.

"She is to be wedded," offered Oln Woeck, "immediately upon our arrival, to a mysterious and powerful Sun-King, purported to rule absolutely across the Great Blue Mountains."

"A prospect"—Fireclaw nodded, watching both Ayesha and the captain for signs that they understood his words—"she visibly anticipates with a truculent fatalism which apparently encourages her to risk death at the hands of strangers."

Mochamet al Rotshild guffawed, then spoke at some length

to the girl, who promptly colored, assumed a furious expression, and turned her back upon the men.

The little animal upon her shoulder scolded them.

Ursi barked in counterpoint.

Fireclaw wondered to himself what kind of father would employ his daughter as a bargaining chip in such a manner, saying as much to Oln Woeck, who, with many a frightened gulp and stammer, conveyed the question to the captain. The younger Helvetian was deciding that he did not like this Abu Bakr Mohammed much.

He was truthful—to Oln Woeck's dismay—about this as well.

"I would imagine," the Cultist translated directly for Mochamet al Rotshild, "that Fireclaw hath seen many a brutal act in his life, brought about by dire necessity."

Fireclaw nodded.

"Nor," the captain added, "can I imagine Fireclaw flinching from commission of such an act himself, in need."

It was Fireclaw's turn to laugh. The captain had him.

"Morever," the Helvetian had Oln Woeck say for him, "I have long made practice of remaining unconcerned about the fate of strangers. It has served me well. Best tend the needs of those belonging to oneself."

He shrugged.

"If the girl is being sent west for political purposes, very well, she is not my daughter, she is cargo."

Mochamet al Rotshild frowned at this cold-blooded dissertation. Still, in all, this attitude made easier the things which had to be done in the name of duty.

When in Rome, do as the Caliph. Very well, thought the red-haired Saracen, let this wise-eyed barbarian be his guide in more than just the geographical sense. He did not like what he was doing to Ayesha, and this Fireclaw had spoken of it well.

Let it remain that way with him as well.

XXIV:

Knife Thrower

No soul knows what it shall earn tomorrow, and no
soul knows in what land it shall die.
— The *Koran*, Sura XXXI

Amber flames lit the faces of the people watching him.

"And the servants of the gods were manifest in numbers
greater than the pigeons blackening the sky as they pass from
south to north in springtime and from north to south in
autumn."

Blanket slipping off his shoulders to the ground behind him,
Knife Thrower raised both naked brown, lean-muscled arms,
pointing the direction which the sparks flew from the fire
burning before him, drowning out the smaller, bluer lights of a
moonless sky.

Looking round the circle which had formed about him, he
knew that Fireclaw had heard this tale many times. Also his
sister, since the earliest days of her childhood.

This was exactly as it should be. Nor did it deter him now.
That such tales be told again and again, until each Comanche,
each Cheyenne, each Dakota knew them by heart, and learned

219

from them, was a solemn duty which the gods had placed upon them, one of many such. And the telling of the tale to strangers—those few who were permitted entry to this land—conveying the warnings it contained, was of special importance.

There were many strangers now.

The old, scarred one who never bathed.

The great and hairy one whose beard was the color of a winter sunrise.

The one who had survived an arrow through the chest (both Fireclaw and he, the war-chief of the Mountain Notch Comanche, bore many similar scars.)

Others, too, including two women and the oddly dressed servants of the hairy one.

All must be told that they trespassed and what punishment was likely to be. Ordinarily this duty fell to the shaman of the Comanche, but Knife Thrower's tribe's had died a few days ago—an omen, the People were saying among themselves now—not yet ceremonially replaced by the youth the old man had chosen for the duty.

And besides that, Knife Thrower was himself curious about these interloping strangers.

"And the servants of the gods did slay the People, scattering those they left alive from forest-frost to burning sand, mixing them again and again, until no two people in any of the villages they created spoke the same language.

"And they did give these villages each a name, and bade them take up life again, as before, yet with certain injunctions."

Fireclaw knew what these injunctions were, thought Knife Thrower. He broke them every day. His very presence broke the law, as did the fire-weapon on his hip.

And yet the gods left him alone.

"And in the times of my own grandfather did the Dog-Eaters break the injunctions, believing the gods tired, or unobservant, or passed into the not-is. And the Dog-Eaters, being not so many nor so strong as others, fashioned for themselves a weapon, using fuel they had been shown how to make for their riding-machines."

"And the weapon spouted flame, consuming men and many other things, many paces away."

Knife Thrower shuddered.

He always did at this part of the story. He knew many of the People who had personally seen the result of the Dog-Eater's experimentation. Some of them bore scars so terrible it appeared the very flesh upon their faces and bodies had melted and reset.

"And, though it had been many generations since the servants of the gods came down into our land, they did descend upon the disobedient and proud Dog-Eaters with a greater flame, and with their toothed swords and lances of unbearable glory.

"And when the servants of the gods had labored over the Dog-Eater's village for a day and a night, even the stones had slumped into themselves and run into the soil like the wax of bees.

"And the servants of the gods spoke to the People, saying, 'Behold, the Dog-Eaters are no more. Guard you the land against intrusion and hold thy injunctions. Fish, hunt, use the weapons you have been given to work the will of the gods, and all shall prosper.

"'Break the law and you shall perish horribly.'

"And an unnameable thing came in the night and swooped them up and they were gone."

He dropped his upraised hands into his lap and was still.

The hairy one spoke to the old man.

The old man spoke to Fireclaw.

Fireclaw asked, "This thing without a name that swooped them up, what did it look like?"

Knife Thower thought long before replying.

"My brother, you have asked me this yourself, many times. Tell them what I told you then."

"That it was dark," the Helvetian answered, "that no one would say what the thing looked like, even those who saw it plainly by the light of a burning village."

These words did Oln Woeck haltingly convey to Mochamet al Rotshild and the other Saracens.

"It was very large," Knife Thrower conceded.

"Yes," Fireclaw urged without translation for the benefit of the others, "and what else?"

"It made a roaring sound like that of giant bees too many to be counted in a countless number of lifetimes."

Fireclaw repeated what the Comanche war chief had told him, and waited for the second translation.

"Yes, go on."

"That its color was that of our riding-machines before they are painted. A dull color of unpolished silver."

"In other words," Fireclaw sat back in triumph, "a *machine*."

Knife Thrower swallowed what seemed to him the deepest of heresy. He was accustomed to such from Fireclaw.

"Perhaps, my brother, perhaps. I have had such thoughts myself, since meeting you. But a machine of the gods. And, if they are alike unto that machine as we are to the machines with which they have gifted us, then the gods are more than mighty, they are . . . they are . . ."

Words failed the war chief of the Mountain Notch Comanche.

This did not happen often.

Still, it seemed to happen whenever he discussed the gods with his brother Fireclaw.

2

It was a spiny land, of which the rolling hills of south Faransaa had been but a mild foretaste.

She had come to view one of the spiny ones, not this green shrub which she crouched behind with Marya, which seemed to be all spikes itself, but a clumsy brown waddler something like a European hedgehog, only much, much larger.

Its spines were deep brown at the root, deep brown at the tip, with a broad band of ivory occupying the center third.

Marya had been given something like this animal by one of

the Comanche, a fibrous handful of prickles, dry and brown. She had been told that it was the egg of a prairie creature. Ayesha had recognized the cockleburr and the joke behind it, but her servant had not truly believed her when she had explained that she was being played with.

Thus this minor expedition onto the prairie by themselves.

Ayesha was certain she could find the creature, more certain that it was a mammal which did not lay eggs. So far, the only profit from the journey was that Marya had learned to avoid the flat green ground-hugging cacti with long red-brown spines, nearly invisible against the sandy soil. The limp she walked with now was her diploma.

In Rome, the gullible Marya had once been given a flamingo feather, told to thrust it into the rich soil of the Caliph's garden. From it, she was assured by that particular joker, would grow, like a plant-cutting, a fabulous bird.

She had believed that as well, in preference to the truth a seven-year-old Ayesha had told her, each day faithfully watering the base of the thing until one of the gardeners, disgusted, had pulled it up and burned it wih the lawn-rakings.

"See, Princess, there it is!"

The servant whispered now.

"Does it not look exactly like the eggs it lays?"

Ayesha shook her head and whispered back.

"Either this is not its egg-laying season, or it bears its cruel fate with more dignity than one would credit from its appearance. Look, can you see what's happening over there?"

Marya shielded her eyes, peered at the human figure which had discreetly placed a large rock upthrust between the ranch and himself. The brown-skinned man was dressed in a leather loin-wrapping, like most of these plains people, but, even at this distance of several hundred paces, seemed somewhat more familiar than that.

Without waiting for an answer, Ayesha asked another question.

"Is that not the sailor whom the captain hired just after we made landfall back upon the coast?"

"No," her servant argued, "it is the one they call Knife Thrower. The brother of Fireclaw's woman."

"I think you are mistaken, Marya."

Marya shrugged, peered closely at the porcupine, then once again at the spiky object which she had folded in her kerchief for protection from its spikes.

Ayesha rose slightly.

"Stay here. I want to know what that fellow is up to."

"Mistress, what if he is simply relieving himself?"

"Our host has better facilities than that. Stay here."

The girl nodded and went back to looking at the animal.

It was a long while before Ayesha had made her stealthy way within a hundred paces of the native. She had been right; he was not one of the locals, but the man Mochamet al Rotshild had hired. She had always been somewhat suspicious of the man, of his intentions, caught him looking at her oddly when he thought she did not notice.

Now he was doing something even stranger.

He appeared to be speaking to a rock.

"You will do exactly as you're told," he told the stone he was holding in his brown hand. When he had finished speaking this sentence—in Helvetian—he held the rock to his ear, presumably while it spoke back to him.

"No, I'll brook no disagreement. When we've left this blasted and forsaken place, they all must die, every one. 'Tis a bargain I have made. Moreover, they can't be allowed to spread the contamination any further. Do you understand?"

There was a pause.

"Good."

The man tucked the stone into a pouch which he was carrying, stood, and walked back to the ranch.

3

And, back at the Helvetian ranch, in her snug, warm cabin bunk aboard the soon-to-be-abandoned land-ship, with Marya—who in the waking world had never yet been gifted with cockleburr or even a flamingo feather—snoring soundly in the adjoining room, with Sagheer safe and secure in his little cage, and with armed men—including the formidable Fireclaw, red-handed killer of five hundred—all around to protect her, the Princess Ayesha woke up shivering.

She sat up and wrapped her arms about herself.

"That was certainly an odd one."

"Princess?"

That, and unintelligble muttering, came from the other room.

"Go back to sleep, dear Marya. It still lacks several hours before the sun is up."

"Yes, Princess."

Looking out through the open porthole, Ayesha could see the piles, moon-silvered, of supplies around the ship. She found it difficult to believe that all of it, rough-hewn wooden boxes, furred and leather bundles, huge clay jars, rolls of fabric, everything, in fact, which had filled the land-ship's single hold, plus all of that which the natives had brought with them, could be carried by the few of them who would be climbing into those mountains in just another day.

One more day.

Beyond the supplies, she saw Fireclaw's sod ranch house. Lights still burned within it. Still shivering, she wondered for a moment whether Fireclaw, too—or perhaps his woman—found it difficult this night to sleep soundly.

Certainly Dove Blossom had everything at risk, and little to gain, concerning this voyage. She would stay behind and take care of her husband's house. The man she obviously loved would meanwhile be traveling to an uncertain fate in an unknown land which she believed was the dwelling-place of vengeful gods.

She had, Ayesha understood, no other family.

And her only brother, Knife Thrower, was going with him.

SURA THE FOURTH: 1420 A.H.—

The Voyageurs

Now We have made it easy by thy
tongue that thou mayest bear good
tidings thereby to the godfearing, and
warn a people stubborn.
> The *Holy Koran*, Sura XIX, *Ta Ha*

XXV:

The Great Blue Mountains

Some of you there are that desire this world, and some of you there are that desire the next world.
——The *Koran*, Sura III

"A small blade," Knife Thrower muttered, almost to himself. He measured the length of steel lying heavy and workmanlike in his palm. "No implement for fighting."

Nor was it broader, he observed, where it met the unguarded grip—itself a full fingerwidth longer than the blade—than the nail of his thumb.

"Truly spoken," his companion admitted, resting a hard fist upon his muscled thigh, "and 'tis but single-edged." He pointed with a steel-capped wrist. "Yet see you how the back runs straight, trued to the handle's taper, the edge curving at a leisurely rate to reach it at the point? 'Tis of such a hafty thickness"—he shook his shaggy head—"one might use it as a pry-bar in need."

"My own sister truly fashioned this thing?"

Knife Thrower looked up at the bland-faced man, asking the question once again in wondering disbelief. That was indeed what Fireclaw had been telling him. And Fireclaw-whom-some-called-Sedrich never lied.

Not without good reason.

Fireclaw threw his head back, laughing at the consternation of his Comanche brother.

The war chief sat upon his own rolled blanket, in a small, slant-bottomed clearing undistinguished from any of a hundred others they had passed by in this sparse-covered country. It lay beside a narrow trail of packed red earth no human feet had ever hammered out. Deer and rabbit tracks embossed its surface. Northeast, the land tipped toward the prairie floor from which they had started five days before.

This long a pause so soon—the sun had just reached its midday apex—rankled both trail-wise warriors, but, upon examining the remainder of their company and conferring, they had decided little help could be found for it. Some, like the Saracen Princess and her servant, were unaccustomed to the exertions which this trek demanded of them. Two were elderly—although it was hard for the Comanche warrior to think of Oln Woeck and Mochamet al Rotshild as being the same sort of animal, let alone about the same age—and required more frequent respite than at least the red-bearded pirate was willing to confess. With each step forward, the situation would grow worse, the narrow trail steeper, the mountain air thinner, their companions from the level of the ocean shorter of breath. Let them gather strength now, while the gathering was easy.

Knife Thrower gave the implement a small toss in his palm. "Know you, husband of a sister who knows not her place, that whatever name I am called by, I have never, neither in combat nor in play-practice, thrown a knife?"

Fireclaw grunted, running a hand over his fresh-shaven scalp, ending with an absent tug at the war-lock he had left, hanging braided down the back of his neck. He let the braid slip through his fingers, then lay his fist back upon his thigh.

Knife Thrower knew well that Fireclaw had heard the story before. Doubtless he would hear it many times again. With the

Comanche warrior, meditating upon it constituted a means by which other matters were often contemplated.

"A thrown knife seldom kills," Knife Thrower asserted. "I see no purpose in handing my enemy a weapon. I am called as I am for no better reason than that once, close to my name-day, I cut myself on an unsharpened blade which skidded upon a cottonwood root I carved. In temper, I threw the knife upon the ground, where it broke. For this, a war chief of the Comanche has a name which is a joke."

For a time, both men kept silent, thinking the same thoughts. Together, they watched the camp about them, paying particular attention to the younger of the pair of sailors—honing his own pair of outlandish daggers upon a smooth-faced stone he carried with him—whom Mochamet al Rotshild had hired to serve as guides and translators once the party reached the domain beyond the mountains.

Somewhat slight of stature, the fellow was, nonetheless, broad-shouldered, like an athlete, with hard, sharply defined, and rippling muscles upon his arms and legs and torso, smooth, tanned, nearly hairless skin—there was a faint yellow-reddish cast beneath the tan—and capable-looking hands.

His eyes were a deep brown, nearly black, above the arched and prominent nose. Somewhat narrow, pointed at their corners, they possessed the foldless lids which marked him, to the limited extent of what Knife Thrower knew or Fireclaw could tell him, as neither European nor Helvetian, but as a native of the New World. His straight hair, cut evenly round his well-shaped head at a level with the tops of his ears, was so black as almost to be blue where the sunlight glinted upon it.

Like his older, fatter companion, he wore a thin pair of moustaches which began nearly at the corners of his mouth, drooped around them, and tapered practically to his chin.

All in all, the outward aspect Hraytis, as he was called by the Saracens, offered the world to contemplate might have been as sinister as his plump companion's, had it not been for the obvious youth he could not disguise—he could not have been eighteen, by anybody's measure—and his open good humor. He smiled and laughed, not foolishly, nor frequently, but upon occasion with a full throat, and a rounded, self-deprecating warmth which compensated for his tonguelessness among them, the Comanche, Saracens, and Helvetians he traveled with. The women of the party apparently found him charming, for all that he looked like a little boy with whiskers painted on—and for all that he had proven a skilled and merciless exterminator of the enemies of those who had befriended him.

By preference and custom, both he and his companion dressed themselves only in breechclouts of a rough and heavy fabric they could have acquired anywhere. In the cool of dawn, when the sun fell, or when the weather warranted it, they added a peculiar garment of the same material, like a small undecorated blanket with a slotted hole in its center for the head. Once donned, it draped itself from the back of the knee to a similar height in front, and, when the weather was especially inclement, would be belted about the waist.

"They say they are from the 'Isle of the Pelicans,' upon the western coastline." Fireclaw spoke at last, then finding it necessary to explain to the landlocked Comanche what a pelican was.

He had spent more time with the strange pair over the last several days than had his brother-in-law. " 'Tis the center for a people and a way of life which require remaining at sea, sometimes for decades, individuals and families being born, growing up, living out their lives, and dying aboard ship."

Knife Thrower nodded. He knew that, caught by a storm, the pair had been driven down the western coast until, at the pointed cape of a southern continent of the New World which Mochamet al Rotshild had shown Fireclaw with his maps— and which neither man had ever known before existed—their ship had been destroyed by even more powerful storms which seemed never to abate in that region.

Whenever it was requested of them, Fireclaw explained, they cheerfully recounted the adventure at great length (though in despicable Arabic), naming places they had been, people they had met, ships upon which they had labored in an effort to return home—a home they apparently knew as little of, owing to a way of life which seemed natural to them, if to no one else, as the Saracens. From Mochamet al Rotshild's perspective, the sailors simply happened to be the only representatives available to the Saracens as guides to the mysterious western domain.

Knife Thrower turned his gaze from his odd traveling companions to the land they traveled through.

To the south lay the canyon, slashing east and westward through the foothills, along whose steep-sloped, sagebrush-littered sides they were making their first climb toward the ice-tipped peaks lying ominous before them. The sky was a mind-emptying blue. A needle-scented breeze made sighing noises among the branches of twisted, winter-stunted pines which gave it its aroma. Long ago they had forgotten how to bend with it, but they had never broken. Chipmunks scolded the intruders. A meadowlark sang in a grove of aspen. The air was clear and cold, the sun hot and bright.

A good day to be alive in.

Nearby, Fireclaw half-sat against a weather-rotted stone thrusting through the thin, acidic soil. Great Ursi lolled panting at his moccasined feet.

Young Hraytis was not alone in using this resting time to good purpose, both men observed with approval. Not far away, Mochamet al Rotshild ran a stiff brush and a cleaning patch down the barrels of the four pistols he carried with him, finishing with the tiny fifth weapon he kept hidden somewhere on his person.

Beside him, his girl companion followed his example with her rifle. Knife Thrower found it interesting—if somewhat scandalous—to watch her labor at this manly task, the many rings she wore upon her fingers glittering as she moved her hands, the bangles in her dainty earlobes chiming softly, flashing in the sunlight.

For a dozenth time, Knife Thrower frowned, turning the little hand-forged blade in his fingers. The Helvetian grinned at his brother-in-law, prouder than if he himself had fashioned the weapon he was displaying to the Comanche.

Setting aside the puzzling yet undeniable fact that a woman had transcended her natural limitations to create it—Fireclaw had that manner with everyone he met, stirring remarkable ideas into their brains as if they were so much porridge boiling over a cooking fire—the little knife was not without other distinctions. Even its handle was unique, spun as it was from lye-washed bear-dog combings, impregnated with hardening resin. When they returned again to the yellow plains, Fireclaw told him, he would investigate other uses for this clever substance. Might not war-shields or longbows be fashioned from the stuff? Even Knife Thrower found himself in this wise wondering.

At that, it was better than wondering what his own wives might be learning in his absence from the kinswoman he had given to this strange-thinking outlander long ago.

Heavy caps at each end of the handle were of needle-filed and polished trade-brass, that between the blade and handle cunningly fitted from three soldered pieces—Fireclaw pointed out the hair-fine dull silver-colored lines—supporting the blade, that the pommel cap upon the end of the handle might be twisted off to reveal a hidden compartment for small necessities such as tinder, fishing line, or hooks.

"At present, as you see, 'tis filled with the dried petals of the flower your sister takes her name from."

It was time for Knife Thrower to laugh. "As if her husband required any such reminder of the secret, loving manner in which she forged this clever implement to surprise him."

Fireclaw shook his head. "She thought it her parting gift, ne'er thinking how another, spoke in casual words, might o'ershadow such a pridesome thing as a present of one's first-forged—"

"*Sedrich!*"

It was the filthy oldster, Oln Woeck, shouting across the clearing as if the great Helvetian warrior were his bond-servant. Knowing something of what had passed between the two Helvetians years ago, Knife Thrower wondered why the younger of them didn't simply stake the older over an anthill and be done with him. Looking over his shoulder, Fireclaw took the last, wistful sight of the prairie he would enjoy until they were higher in the mountains. He inserted the gift-knife into its wet-fitted scabbard, tucked it into the rough-spun shirt he wore, where it hung by a thong about his neck.

"I mean to put yon unwashed murderous cur-spawn down for good ere this journey's o'er," he told Knife Thrower. "Today I'll be content to give him another painful and humiliating lesson in deportment."

He tapped the knife concealed at his bosom.

"Though I'd ne'er consider telling Dove Blossom, I don't hold the idea of a hollow-handled knife too practical. Weakens the tool at the very place it should be stoutest. I'll leave her blossoms there. In this wise, she'll travel with us."

Knife Thrower grunted. "You are sentimental for a blooded warrior."

Fireclaw laughed. "Only such can sentiment afford. I go now, with a different sentiment, to render Oln Woeck's day less pleasant."

XXVI:

Traveling Short Bear

Thou art not responsible for guiding them; but God
guides whomsoever He will.

—The *Koran*, Sura II

Nodding, Knife Thrower remained where he was, turning his
back toward the prairie. At another time, he might have
enjoyed watching whatever it was Fireclaw planned doing to
the old Helvetian shaman.

Instead, he watched the others lying about the clearing. The
foreigners were exhausted. Soon they would have to rest for
more than just the few minutes Fireclaw had thus far allowed
them.

Ah, well, the war chief thought, the journey would harden
them by stages. His brother Fireclaw would be a bit more
demanding of them every day until they were accustomed to
the trail. He himself would aid in that. It would not take—

"They are a soft lot, these," came a gruff, rasping voice,
echoing yet interrupting his thoughts, "but for the most part
determined of mind and, in their spirit, courageous."

Knife Thrower looked up into the broad, flat-nosed face of

Traveling Short Bear, no Comanche, this one, but a Ute, upon whose tribal territory the party of Fireclaw were now trespassing. He had big ears. And thinning hair, which was unusual among his people.

Knife Thrower nodded.

"For a company of only nine to cross the world entire requires mind and spirit, courage and determination—or extreme stupidity."

Traveling Short Bear rested his ample fundament upon the same rock where Fireclaw had sat.

"Stupid, my Comanche brother, is one thing they most certainly are not. Nor with one exception, slovenly." He indicated Oln Woeck, trading sharp words in the eastern tongue with Fireclaw—it seemed mostly a one-sided exchange, favoring the warrior. For a time they watched Mochamet al Rotshild and his companion dabbing at their weapons. "I confess," he sighed at last, "I know not what else they may be."

He lifted a short-fingered hand toward one of the Saracens.

"Tell me, Knife Thrower, what is this little girl, this Princess Ayesha they coddle so, like a baby? Among my people, the daughter of a chief is distinguished, if in anything, by the fact that she works somewhat harder than the other women."

Knife Thrower shook his head.

"Gift-bride-to-be or not, to this rumored 'Sun King' of the western gods, she is a dream-seer."

Observing the Ute's surprised expression—an alteration of his customary facial repose which few Europeans or Helvetians would even have noticed—he nodded, adding, "No one had told me this before I guessed it, but I have been well educated to recognize the look."

The Ute grunted understanding. It was, indeed, the wise in which shamans were chosen, the duty of war chiefs being to do the choosing. In turn, successors to Knife Thrower and Traveling Short Bear would be chosen by the next shamans of their tribes. Although they knew it not, each wondered to

himself what sort of leader Oln Woeck had chosen over
Sedrich Fireclaw.

"Trance-roots and other herbs are all well enough," the
Comanche went on, "but they are wasted upon the un-
talented."

"Meaning the sane?" the Ute chuckled.

Knife Thrower laughed but did not answer. That his own
tribe lacked a spirit guide at present owed to the fact no one
among them had the haunted aspect this Saracen girl carried in
her eyes.

"I confronted Fireclaw with my surmise, which he confirmed, saying that, the night before we left his place, the girl
dreamed of voyagers like us, who, having started late, and
trapped upon a mountain pass in winter, were reduced to
eating one another before spring came. The odd thing is that
she did not dream of the happening itself, but of being told as a
traveler-for-pleasure, generations afterward, by guardians of a
shrine where this had transpired. Nonetheless, her awakening
screams aroused the ranch and all else for a mile round."

"Of what use is such a dream?" Traveling Short Bear
frowned. "It does not foretell the future, neither does it reveal
the past—except, perhaps, a past which never happened."

Knife Thrower shook his head.

"Let me tell you, then, of what she dreamed last night—
according to my marriage-brother, who had it from Mochamet
al Rotshild.

"A great spirit wagon filled her dream, possessing neither
wheels nor sails, like the monster-headed Saracen land-ship I
have spoken of, and fashioned all of metal, dashing up the side
of a mountain with its tail afire. From her words, I knew this
mountain—although she could not—it is visible from the
prairie, a great peak, for a mounted warrior a full day's travel
south of here. At the peak, this spirit wagon left the mountain
and soared into the sky, headed, she said she somehow knew,
for a village upon the moon!"

Traveling Short Bear shivered, making a sign to ward off
evil.

"Perhaps the gods are calling her to come be one of them,

and your party will fare well enough through the forbidden lands. But will the rest of you be permitted to return?"

Both men shrugged.

"Well, friend Knife Thrower, I have my own education. Some of these foreign strangers are beyond me, but beware. I know the look of Marya, the female attendant of this girl-shaman."

"Yes," Knife Thrower answered, "her leg will bear some watching after, if she is not to slow us upon our journey."

Traveling Short Bear snorted.

"The gods take her leg! I tell you, friend Knife Thrower, that she is an hysteric, liable to do anything at any time to anyone in any situation, as long as it is unpredictable and destructive. This is something you and your strangeling brother Fireclaw can but little afford, do you continue trespassing, not only against your neighbors, but against the gods themselves."

The Ute allowed himself to slide down the rock until he was seated upon the ground, closer to Knife Thrower. From his beaded pouch he took a handful of jerked antelope meat, tore it in half to share with the Comanche. Chewing his own portion, he rested his fat arms upon his fatter knees and lowered his voice.

"We of the tribes owe a responsibility to the gods and have reason to remember the consequences of not fulfilling it."

Knife Thrower nodded.

"Consumed by the Breath of God, an old shaman told me once, like the Dog-Eaters."

"Yes, the Dog-Eaters—and others—obliterated by powerful and angry beings dissatisfied with their devotion and obedience. This lens-eyed David Shulieman is another matter. 'Rabbi,' your Saracens call him, whatever that is. Some sort of holy man, I gather, but not of the dream-seeing kind. Is it this one who has arranged the dispensation by which you have not yet been obliterated?"

Knife Thrower grunted.

"When pressed to it, he can acquit himself with some skill in a fight."

He began tearing little strips from the jerky to nibble upon.

"He is the teacher of the girl, and nothing more, her amanuensis. Women fashioning weapons! Men attending them as servants! What in the name of the gods is the world coming to?"

Traveling Short Bear stopped chewing, assumed a puzzled expression which Knife Thrower offered nothing to dispel.

Instead, the Comanche changed the subject.

"In the Commodore Mochamet al Rotshild, a diplomat much like yourself, friend Ute—and, my brother says, a brigand—I recognize the spirit of a fellow warrior. He is the real leader of this expedition, for all that, as long as we trudge through unknown wilderness, they take their orders from Fireclaw."

He accepted another bit of meat from his companion.

"The young ear-bangled woman Lishabha is a female 'companion' to Mochamet, whose name—if not her fighting temperament—I have just this morning discovered."

Looking past the food in his hands, Traveling Short Bear nodded in sudden understanding.

"Another unconventional soul to turn the safe, familiar world upside down? Unlike their Sergeant Kabeer, a stolid, unimaginitive dog-soldier, no threat to the gods, a fellow who would be quite at home upon any side in any fight."

"Yes," Knife Thrower answered. Having finished with his portion of the snack, he drew a small knife from his waistband, selected a pine twig from the ground. With one angled cut, he sliced the twig to a sharp point. "And he seems to be recovering more rapidly, from a far worse wound, than the woman Marya."

They were quiet for a time. Knife Thrower used the twig to pick his teeth.

"Ali, their loutish retainer"—Knife Thrower shook his head—"I do not much care for, never having clearly understood which of the outlanders he serves."

"But certain," Traveling Short Bear finished for the Comanche, "that he serves that person with hidden reservations. This, too, is a look I know, my Comanche friend. Were he one of my own tribe, I would send him many times into the forefront of the bloodiest battle, to purge himself of future treachery, or to perish.''

Both men took a small handful of the dry, sandy soil, rubbed their hands clean of the oil of the meat. Later, they would wash at the stream. Another brief silence followed, broken, this time, by the Ute.

"A strange party, indeed, you travel with, Knife Thrower. And, if he should be numbered among it, tell me of the talking bird of Mochamet al Rotshild. I heard the old man this morning teaching it Comanche words!"

Knife Thrower dug into his own pouch, extracted a small container and another object.

He shook his head.

"I know nothing, except he is called 'Po,' which, in the Saracen tongue, Fireclaw tells me, means 'mouth.''"

"A fitting name." Traveling Short Bear watched the hands of the war chief. "And 'Sagheer'?"

"The humbly fleshed spirit of some ancestor, my own people speculate, who serves out a penitence perched upon the shoulder of the Princess, whispering sagacities in her ear."

From the container he took shreds of vegetable matter, stuffed them into the crooked ceramic tube—of Fireclaw's fashioning, a gift—he also held. From another he tapped a few grains of the fire-powder which his brother manufactured, struck flint to steel.

The powder flared. The smoke-weed caught. Knife Thrower inhaled through the pipe before passing it to the Ute.

Traveling Short Bear inhaled.

"Yes, my Comanche friend, I suppose they might well be counted. One can never tell whom the gods will favor or why. Of your own group, I certainly would count Ursi, the great bear-dog of your brother Fireclaw."

Knife Thrower accepted the pipe back again. It was a strange weed these Saracens had brought with them, different from *kinikinik*. It made one dizzy, at first, sick to the stomach—although the visitors reported the same symptoms from Comanche weed. Fireclaw's powder did the flavor little good.

He puffed blue, aromatic smoke into the mountain air.

Voyaging with them also, of course, was this old, seasoned war chief of the Utes, Traveling Short Bear. While the Helvetian had been supervising preparations for the journey, Knife Thrower had been arranging for its safe passage through neighboring lands, at last deciding to escort the travelers himself.

Those arrangements had required they meet, at the ill-defined verge of Comanche territory, with Traveling Short Bear, not merely a chieftain but the ultimate link in a long line of individuals and tribes who passed along the bounty of the gods—items such as *kinikinik,* or the trade-brass his sister Dove Blossom had made use of—to the prairie tribes who guarded their ancient borders.

Such a diplomatic meeting, by long custom, had to be an "accident," and thus was delicate to contrive. Traveling Short Bear, "wandering for pleasure" upon his own tribal lands, had met the Saracen-Comanche party by "chance" this very morning. Now the group would make a polite show of accompanying him homeward. A matter of tricky protocol, this unprecedented passing through the dwelling grounds of those who had been, upon occasion, the part-time enemies of the Comanche. Such intertribal wars had become fewer within Knife Thrower's memory, peace easier to maintain. Still, it called for chiefly authority upon both sides.

Whatever the reason, Fireclaw had, within the hearing of others, declared himself to be well pleased with the presence of Knife Thrower, allowing to the dubious Saracens that he enjoyed the company of his brother-in-law, always valued his counsel. In many respects, however, the expedition was not to the personal preferences of Knife Thrower: too many they were to be inconspicuous, too few—even had all been such warriors as the girl companion of Mochamet—for an effective fighting force. He knew Fireclaw, too, had had to suppress feelings of foreboding.

This, of course, he would not tell Traveling Short Bear.

"Among their own," the Ute observed, watching the face of Knife Thrower through the smoke they both exhaled, "neither Comanche, nor yet Fireclaw his countryman, willingly number this Oln Woeck."

Knife Thrower nodded but did not reply. Among other irritations, the old tattooed Helvetian shaman had grown more openly, more vocally, disgusted at the marriage of Fireclaw to the sister of Knife Thrower with each passing day of preparation. The rasping, sneering, whining of his dotard's voice had become one with the soughing of the pines, the prairie birds, the crickets, almost a natural feature of the air— albeit in its irritation-value it was more like unto hailstones bouncing off the resined hides of one's lodgehome. By the time Fireclaw had given his final instructions to Dove Blossom upon maintaining their freehold, spoken his goodbyes with misgivings he expressed to no one but his brother, it was her placid, cautious temperament—and that alone—which kept Fireclaw from throttling the filthy ancient where he stood, or splitting him like a game hen with that great sword of his.

Thus had begun their march, afoot, through roadless hills toward a pass negotiable in high summer.

"Too many shamans." Passing the pipe back, Traveling Short Bear persisted. "Nor do the Saracens who brought the oldster here with them seem much anxious to claim him, any more than they lay close claim to the spear-throwing youngster and his squat, combative companion who you say accompanied them to the ranch of Fireclaw."

"You are a fine peace-speaker, Traveling Short Bear," Knife Thrower answered with a frown which was half jesting. He took a deep draft from the pipe, found the embers bitter, knocked them out upon the ground, where he stirred them into the sand with his fingers. "But an unsubtle spy. Mochamet al Rotshild told Fireclaw the moustached strangers are sailors, rescued last year from a wreck off a place called 'Island Continent.'" This last he rendered in memorized Arabic. "They had, hopping from one chance vessel to another, worked their way back as far as the east coast of this, our New World, where the Commodore hired them—"

"Upon the suspicion," the Ute interrupted, "denied by them, that they are from somewhere within—or at least near neighbors to—the hidden region which this Saracen party now intends to penetrate."

Traveling Short Bear laughed.

"I am perhaps indeed unsubtle, Knife Thrower, but, since you have answered my questions, not yet ineffective. If the surmise of the Saracens be true, these men are kinsmen to the gods, for all that they resemble starveling castaways."

Knife Thrower found a yellow strand of well-dried grass, forced it into the mouthpiece of the pipe to clean it.

He shook his head.

"I have never seen their like before. They somewhat resemble normal people. See, their red-brown faces are flattish, like our own—unlike those of white-faced Fireclaw or of the Saracens. But with noses like the beaks of birds."

"Birds of prey." Traveling Short Bear peered over at the strangers they discussed. The pair sat, resting in the sun, sharing some morsel of food. "Their eyes are shaped like our own, lacking the lid-folds Fireclaw possesses."

Knife Thrower put his pipe away.

"They groom their hair grotesquely!"

Traveling Short Bear looked at his companion.

"Perhaps they think we do."

Commanding but little Arabic, the sailors spoke between themselves a tongue unknown to the well-traveled Saracen captain, to Fireclaw, or to Knife Thrower, who was familiar with the dialects of several dozen tribes, although from time to time he imagined he recognized a word.

"The youngster they call 'Hraytis,'" offered Knife Thrower, "meaning a small, many-legged creature somewhat like the gray-green crawfish our village children sometimes tease out of stream-bottoms to roast or eat raw." Well could he remember doing this himself before he had been gifted with his first longbow.

Traveling Short Bear smiled at a similar memory.

"This name perhaps he has earned by being fished from the sea."

"Perhaps. In any case, the Saracens also call his companion 'Hapurya,' which Fireclaw reports is a similar creature, unknown to those of us dwelling inland, but which he himself calls by the name 'crab.' "

Traveling Short Bear folded his arms across his chest.

"Whatever their names, they carry fascinating weapons. The young one has a pair of knives the like of which I have never seen before. Their handles are set across the axis of the blade. With shank protruding between his second and third fingers, he knife-fights with exactly the same motions he would use to fight with empty hands. Fascinating."

The Comanche nodded.

"Yes, I watched him sharpening them just now. He fights also with his feet. I have seen him practice as we travel, kicking overhanging tree-limbs higher than his head, while the Saracens sweated and panted to place one foot before another."

He paused a moment.

"I watched him eating yesterday with one of those knives. A clumsy meat-cutter, with that spadelike handle, but both edges are supplied with teeth, like those of a saw, making quick work of whatever task they are put to. I would not care to be considered such a task!"

Traveling Short Bear laughed agreement.

Knife Thrower did not share the humorous outlook of the Ute. At the same time he cursed Fireclaw for the curiosity which now infected him, he burned to know more about these sailors, kinsmen of the gods or not.

He glanced westward.

High above the mountains, faint up-blown fringes of a cloud-line had appeared to darken his spirit, if not the remainder of the day.

XXVII:

Smoke Upon the Wind

"We have been sent unto a people of sinners, excepting the folk of Lot; them we shall deliver all together, excepting his wife . . . she shall surely be of those that tarry."

—The *Koran*, Sura XV

Fireclaw's dread—and Knife Thrower's—was soon mirrored by real events.

The storm-clouds, poking up just above the serried western horizon, covered but little of the sky as yet; still, they grew blacker by the hour, and more menacing.

He'd long since chastened Oln Woeck. When called to account for his words and manner, the old man had subsided uncharacteristically but had not, Fireclaw thought, judging from the veins standing out upon his blue-marked temples, taken it in good grace, being informed in front of the others—and in Arabic rehearsed for the occasion—that he was never again to shout after Fireclaw nor think to order him about. The younger man had turned upon his heel and walked away without waiting for reply.

Oln Woeck still sulked at the base of a tree as gnarled and ugly as he was.

Fireclaw had gone to inspect the blisters upon Saracen feet, the bruises upon pack-carrying shoulders. Afterwards, he saw to the rearrangement of the packs themselves, the contents of which had to be redistributed occasionally as supplies were used. From where he worked, he watched Knife Thrower and Traveling Short Bear arise, perhaps grown weary of just sitting while there was light enough to travel by.

They ambled toward the pair of alien sailors Mochamet al Rotshild had hired. The Saracen guardsman Kabeer was already speaking with them, as was Ali. Fireclaw had meant to keep an eye upon this group, who'd taken, in the past few days, to gambling together before sleep. He'd heard the money clinking, palm to palm, listened for the rattle of the throwing-cubes, heard what he assumed to be their heated exclamations over wins and losses. An innocent enough diversion, he thought, provided it remained innocent. Still, he wondered where Oln Woeck was, with his moralizing, upon the one occasion when it was, perhaps, called for.

Before the Comanche and the Ute reached "Shrimp" and "Crab," they passed by the Princess Ayesha, lying half-propped upon her elbows upon a blanket next to her maidservant, both women idly staring out over the mountain lip onto the prairie. David Shulieman sat not far away, writing something in a book he carried with him.

Knife Thrower and Traveling Short Bear stopped.

The latter appeared fascinated by Ayesha's pet, Sagheer. Traveling Short Bear spoke a word in polite Comanche. Knife Thrower, possessing no command of Arabic, waved an arm at Fireclaw, who rose, grateful of distraction, and strode to meet them. In any case, he could always use another chance to try his week-old Arabic.

Before he got there, Traveling Short Bear reached a blunt, curious hand out to Sagheer, who chittered at the man in fury, dashing his little face against the outstretched hand. The Ute jumped back with an exclamation—not quite as polite as before, and in his own tongue—held one injured hand in the other. He stepped forward again, bending, not to seize the little animal but to calm it.

His fingers were arched backward in a patting gesture, his gravelly words were soft. Yet the words and gestures of one people are not always those of another, nor easily understood across the barriers of language and culture. From out of nowhere, Marya produced a long, slender, gleaming dagger. Her hand rose over the stooping Ute, fell—in a skewed arc as Knife Thrower's own blade rose for her belly, where it had entered to the hilt, up to her breastbone, making ripping, sucking noises. The woman pitched forward upon the blanket.

Ayesha screamed.

The entire camp erupted as Fireclaw rushed toward the Saracen women. The blanket rapidly grew sodden, scarlet. He shouted at everyone—the sailors and the Saracens had weapons out, even Shulieman had dropped his writings to leap to his feet—to stay back. Fireclaw left his greatsword undrawn, but placed himself between his Comanche brother-in-law and Mochamet al Rotshild, who, despite his apparent age, had somehow appeared at Ayesha's side, his tiny pistol nearly swallowed by his great fist, as if he'd been smoke carried upon the wind.

His companion, Lishabha, was close beside him.

Mochamet al Rotshild spoke.

A cracked and whining voice intruded itself: "They want to know why this barbarian hath murdered one of their party." Oln Woeck had also joined the group.

"I know what he wants, old man," Fireclaw answered. "Shut up. Stay out of this. 'Tis a bad enough situation."

And a bad beginning for a voyage, Fireclaw thought to himself. He ran a hand over his naked scalp, wondering whether he'd ever see the ending of all this and get back home.

Oln Woeck stepped back for the moment, the fire always buried deep within his black-rimmed eyes threatening to blast forth furnace-white. An equally dangerous look from the younger Helvetian persuaded the old man to contain himself.

Fireclaw turned to Knife Thrower.

"What's happened here, my brother?"

"This," the Comanche answered, nudging the dead woman with a disdainful toe, "attempted clumsily to skewer Traveling Short Bear. Let this be a lesson to us, husband-of-my-sister. It is what comes of letting women have their own way." This time Fireclaw could see that the warrior's words were not mere humorous banter. Momentarily he sensed the gulf that their friendship usually spanned. The Comanche looked down at the blade still dripping in his hands. "I had not time to treat the offense more gently."

Fireclaw nodded. "I see."

He switched to faltering Arabic. "Girl, why did your servant strike at this man?"

David Shulieman, who had joined her, stiffened, and the Saracen Princess' eyes widened at being addressed thus, but she swallowed it with better courtesy than Oln Woeck.

"I—I think she feared for my life. She did not understand what . . . what this other man wanted with Sagheer."

Fireclaw nodded again, passing Ayesha's words along to Knife Thrower.

The Comanche warrior shook his head.

"Stupid. Traveling Short Bear, have you been offended?"

The Ute had risen, having been shoved out of harm's way by the Comanche chief, and was dusting off his knees.

"Why should I be, friend Knife Thrower? It was an accident of judgment which certainly did me no lasting harm, all thanks to you. In any case it has been scrubbed away with the blood of the offender. I am sorry that it happened. Have Fireclaw tell that to the girl."

In due course these sentiments were relayed to the Princess, who, naturally enough, was little mollified, but took them in such dignity and understanding as she could impose upon herself. Her teacher spoke with her. Her eyes were large, her olive skin gone ashen. Later, Fireclaw thought, the reckoning tears would come, but not, if he understood Ayesha, in front of strangers.

The camp began to settle into place again. He tended to the washing and bandaging of Traveling Short Bear's injured hand himself. It was a deep and ragged wound, ugly, very much like the bite of a man—of which he'd suffered and delivered many in the heat of combat—and would surely fester if improperly cleansed.

Oln Woeck sat beneath his gnarled tree again intent upon his thoughts as if, Fireclaw believed, calculating what might be made of this mishap the way a merchant might calculate the possible profits and losses of some enterprise.

Mochamet al Rotshild, having ordered Kabeer and the sailors to prepare a cairn of stones—the ground was much too hard this high in the mountains to bury Marya—and asked the rabbi to prepare to say the words which were appropriate in the circumstances, observed Knife Thrower washing his gore-smeared weapon as Fireclaw washed the Ute chief's hand.

He turned to Lishabha.

"Formidable fighters, these Red devils. I did not so much as see him draw the knife."

Fireclaw, who'd overheard the remark, turned to face the elderly Saracen captain.

"Yes, 'twas what my brother had in mind when he acted. Had Traveling Short Bear been worse injured, or considered this mistake an insult, we would now be at their mercy."

Mochamet al Rotshild raised his eyebrows.

"How so, mighty Fireclaw?"

Fireclaw pointed at the blue-tinted apex of the next range of hills, across the canyon.

Mochamet, squinting against distance and age, took in a deep breath.

"My word, have they been with us the entire morning?" He pointed out what he'd seen.

Lishabha started, snarled, placed a hand upon the hilt of the large dagger she carried, and tossed a glance toward her rifle, leaning against a tree too far away to be of any use.

Mochamet put a large, hairy hand over her tiny smooth one.

Fireclaw laughed as the entire crest of the next hill rippled, shortened itself by the height of the solid rank of Red Men who'd seen peace return to the Saracen camp and were now going away.

"So close." The Helvetian exhaled forcefully. "Too close.

Tell me if I am saying this aright in your language, Mochamet al Rotshild: I think not well of a people who send little girls into such peril for reasons of politics.''

The Saracen grinned and shook his head.

"Well spoken indeed, Sedrich-called-Fireclaw. I could not have put it better. However, we have a proverb in my native land, 'It is the water which cleanses, not the soap,' meaning that one man cannot change the nature of society nor the times, only masses of people and great events can—and that one should not destroy oneself trying.''

"My mother had a saying of her own,'' Fireclaw countered, translating an old thought into new words. " 'Tis the wave which moves, and not the water,' meaning that the only source of change is the individual.''

Mochamet al Rotshild looked surprised.

"Yes, I had forgotton, Fireclaw, that you know the sea—and that, in effect, you invented the vessel upon which we came inland to your domain. I shall try to remember better in future.''

With these words, the last of the Ute warriors had disappeared. Mochamet al Rotshild and Lishabha went to tend their own affairs.

"A lucky resolution,'' Knife Thrower offered in the special dialect private to the men of his tribe, "to what might have been a massacre.''

Fireclaw grunted agreement, answering in the same language.

"Never were truer words spoken. Daughters deserve better fathers, brother-of-my-wife. For the first time in a long while, I find myself caring whether we survive or not.''

Knife Thrower was puzzled.

"A peculiar thing to say, Fireclaw.''

"Perhaps.''

He brushed at the small knife swinging in its scabbard from the thong about his neck.

"You accused me of being sentimental. Well, learn this morning what I learned five days ago, from the lips of your own sister. In some respects she knows her place well enough e'en to suit your prejudices."

Knife Thrower shook his head.

"The mystery only grows deeper with this kind of explanation, my brother."

"No mystery at all. In the spring Dove Blossom will at last bear me a child."

On the Helvetian's face, Knife Thrower realized, he saw an expression he had never seen on the man's face before.

It was embarrassment.

"I find," he told his woman's brother, "that I wish more than anything to live long enough to see that child born."

David Shulieman began an eerie, alien chanting. Westward, yellow-white lightning lashed the overhanging clouds of indigo, and muted thunder rolled about them where they stood.

Oln Woeck sat beneath his tree and watched.

XXVIII:

Factions of the Ancients

Certainly the dwellers in the Thicket were evildoers,
and We took vengeance on them.

—The *Koran*, Sura XV

*Overhead, the sky itself was a pale, luminous frosty gray, so
full was it of stars.*

*For each solitary point of light that punctuated the
blackness upon ordinary nights, this night perhaps a thousand
scintillated above, perhaps a hundred thousand. They glowed.
Each pulsing gray-green droplet in the misty horizon-filling
canopy was enveloped in a pearlescent halo of its own: star-
vapor, composed, perhaps, of still yet other stars, too far
away, too tiny, to be seen.*

And this mist of stars which filled the heavens—was alive.

*Every moment, every quarter of the sky, was filled with
motion. Stars stirred and writhed, here and there forming
short-lived patterns which faded or yet formed another. Here,
a single star traversed half of heaven's arc, leaving behind
a tracery of itself, like dewdrops upon the invisible webwork
of some celestial eight-legged spinner. There, a spindle co-*

alesced of star-glow, reeling, throbbing with a pent-up energy which sent it dancing with a dozen other of its kind before it shattered without sound, into the mist from which it had condensed.

Ships there were, translucent sky-vessels, woven of phosphorescent luster, hurrying about incomprehensible errands. Now and then, vague silhouettes of sky-beasts hinted at a manlike form before dissolving into vapor once again.

And every bit of this, and more, transpired all at once, each fraction of a second showering down more fresh wonders upon the stunned beholder than he might take in within a lifetime's span of years. It was a profligate display, wasted a thousand times over upon anyone who possessed but a single pair of eyes to see it, a single mouth to gasp each time some new miracle flared, danced, transformed itself into yet another, or a single mind to batter into some pitiable semblance of awed appreciation.

It was the antithesis of nightmare—in its own way, far worse—a spectacle so wordlessly wonderful that awakening from it became punishment for some terrible sin no mere human being could ever have committed. It was one dream of which she never had told anyone. Words were powerless to convey more than a millionth of the whirling grandeur she beheld upon those three or four occasions in her remembrance when it had come to her.

Using words, she feared—and the fear somehow, was for her life—even attempting to, might drive this dream away forever.

It was quite dark when, exhausted yet now unable to sleep, Ayesha covered her own rich traveling clothes with a plain cloak borrowed from poor dead Marya's bundle. Taking Sagheer with her, she followed the bend of a dry streambed to see the ordinary stars.

In the west, half the sky had surrendered to a featureless blackness which defined the coming storm. Occasional lightning underlit mountainous blue-gray billows, silhouetting the peaks they towered over. The air was still and heavy and expectant, warm for the altitude and for an hour this late.

The Saracen expeditionary party had not yet climbed far into the Great Blue Mountains. This had been but the first week of a journey of many months. Yet the daughter of the Caliph-in-Rome felt she had been journeying all of her life.

More than anything, at this moment, she wanted to be alone to think about what had happened to her servant woman, lifted off the ground where she had knelt by a brutal thrust from a savage chieftain's knife. This was all she wished for, to be alone to think, free of her keepers, guardians, and mentor, free of the savages and barbarians who surrounded her, free of the malign presence which was Oln Woeck, free of Fireclaw, the very sight of whom stirred and disturbed her. She wished for nothing more than to grieve and to wonder, to look up at the stars, chips of diamond, hard and fierce in thin-aired brilliance. Yet she had been forced to sneak away, like a criminal, for they would not let her alone.

She did not blame them.

Or at least not very much.

Save for her own murderous traveling companions, no one else at all in this deserted wilderness existed to harm her. Yet they who "protected" her would have bidden her take an escort, even so. What they most feared, naturally enough, was losing her father's gift to some unknown ruler who waited for her like a spider at the end of the months of footsore toil and unknown peril which lay ahead.

Now, her eyesight dimmed by the smoky firelight she had left behind, in a borrowed cloak too large for her small frame, and upon stolen time, she was free. For a little while. And, as always—as she had always believed she preferred—very much alone.

Where the sky was still clear, a sudden blackness blotted out the stars, ovoid in shape, Ayesha thought, somewhat elongated. Before she could see more, it merged into the greater blackness to the west, and disappeared. A gust of damp wind fluttered the hem of her cloak. Sagheer chittered upon her shoulder.

"What—*maa chalhghapar*?"

There was a sudden noise behind her. The sound of gravel gritting underfoot started her heart hammering in her chest. She had stopped breathing. Almost afraid to see what lay behind her in the moonless darkness, she turned.

And felt little relief.

It was a savage—a different savage from those horrible friends of Fireclaw's—whose name meant Small-Bear-Who-Travels. This, she had first thought upon hearing it, was a good calling, for he indeed looked like a bear, short, and very broad. He had followed her as she slipped out of camp to this isolated unlit spot, a place where, if she needed it, there could be no help until it was too late.

The wind blew, rattling dry leaves underfoot. Sagheer jostled, nervous beside her ear.

What did this savage want of her?

The fat little man laid both hands—the right one thickly bandaged from the damage which Sagheer had done it—over his heart, then raised them to his lips, thrust them outward, curving down. At first, she was frightened at such an intimate gesture, then realized that he was saying something with his hands—with his pleading eyes—about speaking to her from a heart filled with pain.

She turned, nodded her head.

"*Nanam*, please go on," she told him in Arabic, stroking her frightened marmoset a bit to calm it. "*Chanaa chabhgham*. I will listen—if that is the word for it."

The savage pointed backward, toward camp, or back down the trail they had followed these five days, then placed his injured hand upon the side of his head, as if combing long hair with his cloth-wrapped fingers.

He made an abrupt gesture which could mean nothing else but a stabbing at his belly. Ruthless, he continued the imaginary cut upward until Ayesha thought she would faint or vomit from the sight of it. Then he placed both hands either side of his head, rocking it side to side as if he had a toothache.

"*Maa manna?* Are you saying, Bear-Who-Travels, that you regret that Marya was murdered upon your account?"

"Mar-ya," he echoed, repeating his dolorous gesture, then, in broken, faltering Arabic: *"Cha-naa muth-ach-as-sibh."*

I am very sorry.

Ayesha turned her back upon the Ute chieftain, hot tears seeming to boil from beneath her tight-shut eyelids. The little man must have asked someone, perhaps Sedrich-called-Fireclaw, for words in which to make this apology, carefully memorizing the otherwise meaningless syllables that they might be carried to her now.

Taking a deep, painful breath, she struggled to regain control, began speaking before she turned.

"*Sghuhran jazeelan*. Thank you, *Siti* Bear-Who-Travels, *ghaadaa min luthbhah*, there is nothing about you which is small at all. And let me never utter such words as 'savage' or 'infidel' again, for in this God-forsaken wilderness, you are an uncommonly decent—"

She had heard a thumping noise, a grunt, and whirled.

Yet another something thumped behind her. A rough-callused, foul-smelling hand tore Sagheer, screaming, from her shoulder, tossed him away like trash, then clamped itself upon her face, bruising the mouth and nose they sealed off. A loop, thrust over her from behind, tightened about her unprotected throat.

Only then did the hand leave her face. She gasped, discovered to her terror she still could not get a breath, and began thrashing. Another arm, wrapped about her body, encountered more difficulty restraining her. Tearing at its fingers, trying to bend them backward, she believed she might break free. She was discouraged by a tightening of the thong, which brought whirring blackness to her eyes and ears.

In the same frozen instant, a pair of figures leapt upon Traveling Short Bear as his own hand—rendered clumsy by the bandaged wound—fumbled for the knife at his waist, blood already streaming black down his face. Something heavy smashed his head. The Ute groaned, his skull a flattened horror at one side. Limp-armed, his blade still in its beaded scabbard, he settled to his knees. Like the servant-girl before him, he was lifted to his feet again as his naked belly was torn by an upswept curve of metal, glinting in the starlight as it entered, glistening as it ripped its way back out again. As his life spilled into the gravel, a whimper was all the man could wring from his dying mouth.

Too stunned now to struggle, weak from lack of air, Ayesha watched the same dark figures creep up upon her. One of the pair helped hold her. A third tore her robes away, slashing with the same bloody knife which had been used upon Traveling Short Bear. Sticky, crimsoned fingers imposed themselves upon parts of her which no man had ever seen, let alone touched before.

It was Kabeer!

Paralyzed with astonishment, Ayesha watched his hands violate her exposed and shivering body, his horrifying leer illuminated by a stroke of lightning.

"*Massach chalhghayr*, my Princess, good evening," he murmured, licking his lips. "Your stepmother, the Lady Jamela, asked in this manner, and from an exile somewhat less ignominious than your father planned it, to be remembered to you."

"*Limaadaa*," she forced herself to ask, "but why—"

Before she finished, Kabeer gave answer.

"*Lima laa*, why not?"

There was muted, cruel laughter, whipped away in the rising, moisture-laden wind.

She opened her mouth to scream. A gore-smeared rag, once part of her dress, was forced between her teeth. More were knotted about her wrists. While thunder bellowed above them, they forced her down against the stony ground, her arms pulled back above her head, the two men holding her naked shoulders while Kabeer knelt, thrust his hands between her knees, and forced her legs apart.

Dazzling brightness seared the sky.

From some remote place within herself, she observed her own smooth, white thighs lashed by tongues of pale fire. How like those of the marble statues in her father's gardens they were, something inside her observed with a calm which bordered upon insanity. She seized the thought. It was not as if none of this had ever happened to her before. She had known pain and terror all her life. She had killed and been killed a thousand times in dreams so real that it was the waking world about her which seemed like an illusion. And, somehow, she had survived it all.

Now, she told herself, as pain began to blot out the rest of her existence, she would survive this. Now she would become that statue.

Statues feel nothing.

Lightning flashed. Spitting upon himself for lubrication, the sergeant grunted his way inside her as the men started taking brutal turns with her.

A cold rain began falling.

XXIX:

Blood-Haze

But when the sight is dazed and the moon is eclipsed,
and the sun and moon are brought together, upon that
day man shall say, "Whither to flee?"
                                        —The *Koran*, Sura LXXV

Lightning dashed a man-shaped shadow against a water-worn
and weathered boulder. Thunder bellowed, drowning out the
hearing sense as, just before it, momentary brilliance had
inundated vision. The shadow faded as if washed away by
rainfall streaming down the pitted surface of the rock and
vanished into the darkness it was made of.

Someone else had followed Ayesha to the creekbed.

That someone else was Sedrich Fireclaw.

Outnumbered, Fireclaw feared most that the Princess might
be injured worse in any fighting he might start than even she
was being injured now. He knew, from much experience, that
the garotte about her slender throat could kill within a hand's
count of heartbeats. The streambed gravel precluded silent
approach. Each of the men was armed. As the helpless girl
resigned herself to the uses which they put her to, each kept

watch as others took her, his help no longer needed to restrain her. Fireclaw couldn't use his pistol, surrounded as his party was by Utes—soon enough to become hostile with the murder of an important member of their tribe. His double-limbed bow he'd left behind in the camp.

He chafed to wade in bare-handed.

He bunched his cloak, felted out of oily fur combed from his dog-pack, closer about his body as the downpour sizzled around him. Water dripped from his razor-naked head, from his warrior's braid and down his neck. He forced himself to watch, and to remember.

Lightning raged. Thunder coughed and grumbled in its wake.

Ursi's muzzle pleated, showing teeth, as a low growl escaped into the rainy night.

"Quiet, Ursi!" Fireclaw whispered. "Sit!"

Despite the storm, he had recognized their voices. The menials of the party: Ali, the retainer supposed to protect his princess; Crab, one of the peculiar sailors; Ayesha's guardian, Kabeer. The only one of their ilk missing, he thought nastily was Oln Woeck—but then that one preferred molesting boy-children.

Rain fell, and the wet-dog odor which rose from Ursi's oily pelt—or perhaps it was his own cloak—was the only familiar comfort in this alien place. Fireclaw watched the men rip their savage pleasure from the girl while even his missing phantom hand ached with the damp cold and the effort of restraint.

When there remained no liberty possible which they'd not several times inflicted upon her—they'd removed her gag, and, each having used her in that wise, replaced it e'er proceeding to an outrage worse, likelier to produce screams—they quarreled about whether to kill the pitiable bundle of bleeding flesh in bloodstained, sodden clothing they'd left huddled upon the wet and stony ground. Kabeer insisted she must die, Crab argued wordlessly against it.

Emptied of his appetites, weather-soaked, and fearing now some unnamed future retribution, the manservant Ali decided to settle the affair of words with action, releasing the garotte-ends he had held, grunting as he bent to pick up a large stone.

Waiting was over.

Feeling the scarlet curtain of blood-haze begin to descend about him, Fireclaw took two deep strides into the muddy bottom of the streambed. The shimmering five-foot length of *Murderer* whispered from the scabbard at his back.

He spoke softly, fighting to remain conscious long enough to finish speaking.

"If yon girl yet lives, I'll dry your nasty little pricks to hang upon her belt."

Kabeer and Crab whirled to face him, short exclamations leaping from them at the sound of Fireclaw's voice. The challenge, issued to draw the three away from Ayesha, was his last conscious act. Slipping at last into combat-madness, he decapitated Ali in mid-scream with a casual backhand swipe of the greatsword as the treacherous servant dropped the head-sized stone and straightened. Stone and head rolled separate ways, the latter wide-eyed, openmouthed, into the growing runnel of the creekbed. Ali's torso toppled, splashing into the water like a broken toy.

Before Ali hit the ground, Fireclaw was battling with Crab, their efforts spraying sheets of water from beneath their feet, while great black Ursi bared his fangs and lunged for Kabeer's throat. In this the dog was aided by the sudden appearance of a wet and furious Sagheer, who scratched and bit, ripping one of the assailant's eyes from his head.

Even had the sailor been Fireclaw's equal, a pair of saw-toothed daggers against greatsword was an uneven match. A ringing slap spun one of the shorter blades away into the rain-soaked night. Without effort, Fireclaw straightened his arm. The razor-pointed blade-tip sighed into Crab's midsection, two more feet of whispery-keen edge following on its momentum with a hiss. Wrist up, bending elbow, tucking in his shoulder, Fireclaw tore the steel through him sideways.

Crab's remaining weapon fell from an unfeeling hand. He pitched forward.

Forgetting the sailor before he had yet fallen, Fireclaw turned.

"Down, Ursi!"

He intended saving Kabeer from the animals, were it possible, if only to discover why a man he might otherwise have respected had visited such betrayal upon a harmless girl.

"Down!"

Even within his own death-dealing frenzy, the animal knew this imperative must be obeyed. Pushing the dog back by its bloodied muzzle, Fireclaw reached to pull the screeching marmoset away, bent over, seized Kabeer by a collarbone, lifted him, one-handed, to his feet. The man's still-unfastened trousers slopped about his ankles. He had, in terror, soiled himself. Blood trickled from his wounds, mingling with the rain.

Disminded, Kabeer could only whimper.

Fireclaw let go for a fraction of a second, backhanded Kabeer across the face to stop his blubbering, grabbed him once again before he could fall backward.

"Now, child-molester," he shouted against the weather, "we'll have answer from you!"

The sergeant flapped his ruined mouth and flailed both his arms. A sudden *twang* answered for him before he could speak. A shoulder-bow quarrel whistled past Fireclaw's unprotected head from the misty shadows to snatch another rapist's life away.

Stubby arrow planted in an empty eye-socket, Kabeer, late captain of the Caliph's personal guard, slumped in upon himself and became one with the muddy soil around him.

Lightning ripped the sky, thunder smashed the silence.

The rain kept falling.

2

Wet wind returned Fireclaw to himself within an unprecedented breath or two. The warrior found himself staring round at a scene such as he'd not witnessed since those first blood-drenched boyhood years upon the forbidden plains. Five bodies—those of Traveling Short Bear, Ali, Crab, Kabeer, and little Ayesha—lay about him upon the gravel, covering the mud-streamed floor of the little creek-bend.

He whistled: "Ursi! Come!"

Fireclaw went first to Traveling Short Bear, knowing within an instant's touch that the Saracen party now faced a disaster they might well never overcome. The war chief of the Utes was as dead as was possible, his head like the hollowed back of a dance-mask. With him died any hopes they owned of passing in peace through the territory of his tribe.

He rose, muscles trembling with the cold and with the drain which blood-haze always put upon him. Little point wasting time upon Crab or Ali. Had either yet lived, he'd have left him to die. Likewise, Kabeer would ne'er stir again.

The arrow Fireclaw recovered from the sergeant was of Saracen make, with feathered vanes about its nether end, not that this told him anything. There were three or four shoulder-bows about the camp, some Saracen, one Helvetian, handy to anyone who picked one up. He had seen Crab use one, and likewise Shrimp. A tool can be used for many purposes, he thought, but 'tis the intentions of the user which do the murdering.

The moment he removed her gag and the garotte, Ayesha vomited, voiding herself onto the rain-washed gravel in a much less fatal wise than her attackers had. She went on with it until naught was left to give up, and she was doubled with cramps, close to asphyxiated with the effort.

She uttered not a solitary word.

Fireclaw wrapped his cloak about her, comforted her as best he could. He'd never doubted she was still alive, having been forced by grim circumstance to watch what the others had done with her. At the same time, despite himself, he was somewhat suspicious. It had been surpassing stupid of the girl to wander off like this. Perhaps her carelessness had been deliberate, inviting the attack that she might be "spoiled," and thus unable to wed her unknown husband-to-be.

He'd known others—himself, name one—who'd performed desperate, self-destructive acts to rival this.

As for the men, Fireclaw was somehow certain, without knowing whence that certainty arose—that there was more to this, beyond the simple, ugly act he'd witnessed. Groping for an answer, he first asked himself whether it had been the Princess they'd intended assaulting. 'Twould be natural to assume, in that cloak, and in the rainy darkness, that the odd-assorted trio had mistaken Ayesha for her maidservant—save that she was dead. Or for Mochamet's "attendant," Lishabha—but everyone knew what a fighter that one was. To add to the mystery, each of the attackers carried a large cache of unembossed silver disks—like coins, but without markings—which he could have earned in no honest pursuit.

From long habit and longer prejudice, the Helvetian warrior found himself wondering what part Oln Woeck might have had in this, then dismissed the speculation, not as unworthy, but as unreasoned and unproductive.

Feeling emotions toward Ayesha he hoped were fatherly, Fireclaw began to suspect she'd wanted, abandoned by her father, simply to die. To be certain, she'd not put up a fraction of the fight she had earlier, from the deck of the Saracens' land-ship.

He gave equal consideration to the matter of her "gift" of second sight—he'd spoken with Mochamet of this ere leaving the ranch—of what the affliction had done to her. He knew the Saracens admitted of a peasant superstition—such as there'd been where he'd grown up, belied by the proficiency of those like his own mother—that such powers remained only with untaken women.

Perhaps Ayesha had reasoned at some level she could rid herself of this burdensome curse, at the same time of a marriage she rejected, perhaps even of a life she no longer wanted to live.

Fireclaw suspected she was to be disappointed upon all three counts. Ayesha still lived, thanks to Fireclaw, to play out whatever hand fortune had in mind for her. To the reckoning of some, this might make Fireclaw a hero for a time.

She herself would never thank him for it.

Still conscious of the existence of some anonymous someone out there beyond his range of vision, who'd slain the third rapist—who could as easily slay him and the girl—Fireclaw lifted her in his arms, carried her back toward the encampment. Partway there, they encountered Knife Thrower, stalking the perimeter. The Comanche war chief carried neither longbow nor shoulder-bow with him.

Knife Thrower made no conversation, his one swift glance taking in everything he might have asked his Helvetian brother about: the bloodied girl, the bloodier sword. Ever watchful, he knew who was missing from the camp. He raised an inquiring eyebrow. Fireclaw tossed his head a fraction of an inch, back toward the gravel-wash, and Knife Thrower nodded understanding.

Together, they took the Princess back to warmth and safety. Ursi followed, Sagheer not far behind.

XXX:

Lishabha

And they have made the angels, who are themselves
servants of the All-merciful, females.
> —The *Koran*, Sura XLIII

The rain had died off to a heavy, falling mist.

Fireclaw sat cross-legged beneath his stick-supported cloak,
before a bed of glowing coals protected from the weather by a
slant of short-cut logs. Locked into the socket which replaced
his missing hand, he held a tool which looked to Lishabha,
from where she half-reclined a dozen yards away, like a
complicated pair of black enameled pliers. In his lap and
scattered otherwise about him, he held supplies and other
tools.

The man had been at it an hour, inserting spent revolver
cartridges, one by one, into the small cylindrical attachment
extending at right angles from the stationary leg of the pliers,
squeezing the other leg with his good hand, opening the tool to
let the reshaped casing, its dented primer ejected by a pin, pop
out onto a blanket spread beside his knee. Threading a new
fixture into the pliers, he had then replaced the primers with

fresh ones, filled each casing with propellant, employing a tiny dipper across whose opening he struck off surplus powder with a small brass rod.

Now he sat assembling the projectiles his pistol used, each small metal arrow laid within its expendable resin "shoes," slipping each resulting cylinder into the mouth of a casing. These he had laid out in flat wooden blocks, each with holes drilled halfway through its thickness in rows of ten by five.

Lishabha was impressed. Fireclaw's cartridge manufactory took up less space than the utensils she carried for eating, a pair of metal bowls, and matching cup.

When a hundred pistol shells were thus complete, Fireclaw changed the die once more, pressing each projectile to its proper depth, crimping the brass cartridge mouth into the surface of the shoe. He wiped each casing clean of the touch of lubricant he had employed to work them, then assembled them to circular clips which enabled him, one-handed, to recharge all the chambers of his pistol with one smooth motion.

The process was interesting; watching it had occupied the rain-gloomy hours. But it was an omen that meant he expected trouble. Lishabha had concerns of her own—not unrelated to the preparations Fireclaw was making. Beside her, sweat-drenched head and shoulders in her lap, lay the Princess Ayesha, whom Fireclaw and his brother-in-arms had brought back to the camp. Knife Thrower was out prowling the perimeter now, having taken Mochamet and young Hraytis with him.

Before they had gone, they and Fireclaw had transformed this stopping-place into a real encampment.

Fireclaw's great blade, cleansed of human leavings, had easily hewn a couple of small trees into stripped branches and broad, dense boughs. These the men had assembled into a half-tent under which they had placed the exhausted, bloody young woman they had rescued. Lishabha had boiled water in her kit and, when the men had gone—all save Fireclaw, who appeared to take no notice in any case, and the holy man, Oln Woeck, who seemed intent upon some meditations of his own—sponged the girl as best she could with a scrap of cloth about whose origins she did not inquire.

It had not been a pretty sight nor a pleasant task, although Ayesha would not be long healing. Physically, she should be as ready to march tomorrow as any other of the party—save those, *thapnan*, upon whom Fireclaw's sword had taken vengeance. Yet the Princess' mind, her willingness to continue life, let alone the journey, was another matter.

Upon the face of it, no logic could explain her present state. She had arrived at the encampment, arm-borne, as one who suffers the terrifying visions of fever, seeming not to know those who essayed to help her, nor their words, struggling with subdued moans, feeble, aimless motions, as if they had been those who had assaulted her.

Lishabha had cleansed her, treated the few injuries which deserved the name, smoothed her hair, caressed her brow, realizing all the time that her real injuries, invisible, would be a long time healing—if they did not prove fatal, in metaphor or literality.

Fireclaw gathered his implements, packed them in a roll of oiled hide. He retreated to the far side of the camp, another dozen yards away, to spread his cloak and bedroll. He would watch, by turns, with Mochamet and the others. The Helvetian shaman, for some reason or another, they did not take into their precautionary calculations.

Lishabha had demanded her own turn. To her indignant astonishment, she had been rejected by one who knew from experience her capabilities in that regard. Did she believe Mochamet when he asserted that the task he had assigned her was more important, tending to this pampered palace-bred softling? Perhaps she would decide before night was over. At present, it was Fireclaw's turn to sleep.

"Chayn . . . Ham chassaanagh?"

Ayesha stirred, opened her eyes. At first they were inward, unfocused. Then, as memory and recognition returned, she rolled over, burying her face against Lishabha's thigh, and began to sob. Lishabha smoothed her hair again—this kindness had been mechanical at first, until Lishabha realized that

something in the girl's despair had moved her own heart—
speaking syllables of comfort until the sobbing died away.
Ayesha slept where she was until an hour later, judging by the
motion of the stars, when the entire process repeated itself.

She slept again.

Lishabha watched the rain.

Much later—Fireclaw had replaced Schulieman upon
watch, been himself replaced by Knife Thrower—when the
Princess stirred again, she remained awake after crying herself
dry. Lishabha offered her a cup of broth.

Ayesha accepted without enthusiasm, then was reluctant to
permit Lishabha to go from her as far as the coal-bed to
prepare it. Lishabha, sounding sterner than she felt, insisted.
While she stooped beside the fire, she reached into the well of
her experience, that which she had learned from life—for the
most part under Mochamet's tutelage—for the right words to
heal injuries of the spirit.

Returning to the lean-to with the cup between her fingers in
the still-damp cloth, she found a sentence forming itself upon
her lips of its own inane accord.

"*Charjooh,* how do you feel?"

Ayesha's nose was red, her lips and eyelids swollen. A fist-
sized bruise marred one pale cheek; her chin had been scraped.
She took a ragged breath, speaking out of a calm Lishabha
recognized as less healthy than outright hysteria.

"I have thought about this moment," the Princess replied,
taking the cup, "as I suppose every woman has, imagining
what it would feel like to be . . ." She swallowed, forced
herself to finish. ". . . violated. *Limaadaa!* Why, in all the
visions I have been compelled to suffer, did I not foresee this?
Last night—*laa,* in the name of God, it was just *this* night—I
dreamt a fantasy about stars! It seems a lifetime ago. I had
never in truth imagined, after all, how it would make me
feel."

Struggling for an apparent impassivity she did not feel,
Lishabha took the cup as the girl placed her face in trembling
hands and began crying again. She placed a free, ring-
decorated hand of her own upon Ayesha's shoulder.

"How is it, my Princess, that you feel?" It was important, she knew, to keep the girl talking. The sooner she emptied herself of the experience, the better.

Ayesha looked up, tears streaming down her cheeks. Her nose was running. She wiped it upon a sleeve. "Do not call me that, Lishabha. I am just Ayesha. *Old*. I feel *old*."

Lishabha stifled a small laugh born of sympathy, which would have been misunderstood. *"Nanam chanaa chabhgham.* I know what you mean. All terrible experiences make one feel like that. I am lucky. I was *born* old, and have been growing younger all my life."

Ayesha sniffed back tears, straightened herself, took the cup again, staring through steam arising from its surface, but saying nothing. Lishabha searched for something to say.

"You, too, are lucky."

These words Lishabha had with care selected, but, even uttering them, she knew a pang of doubt. If she were wrong . . . if she were wrong, they were but words. It was in any case too late. Swallowing her doubts, Lishabha plowed forward.

"Has your life been forever changed, forever ruined? *Chanaa muthachassibh.* What happened was unpleasant, also frightening. You knew not what was going to become of you. *Manlayagh,* no damage was done which will be visible in a few weeks' time. A normal function was forced upon you which, save in the all-important manner of consent—"

"Do you dare," Ayesha interrupted in an outraged tone, "trivialize what has happened to me? I have been . . . I have been . . ."

She set the cup aside, spilling most of it into the dirt floor of the lean-to, began crying again.

Knowing now that she had done the right thing, and hating herself for it, Lishabha placed a gentle hand upon Ayesha's bruised cheek. Her rings were cold against Ayesha's face. "You have been raped. I do not trivialize it, I describe it. I confront it. That is the way—the only way—you are going to survive its having happened."

"Nanam! Yes! Let us confront it!" Ayesha slapped the

jeweled hand away from her face, began to flail her own. "I have learned firsthand a lesson of history! Man is an instinctive, perverted animal, sodomizing his enemy by raping those whom both sides regard as property! To him, coupling is no more than an act of war which in peace he teaches to succeeding male generations with tales and jokes he tells them in saloons!"

In the distance, they heard the muted roll of thunder. Perhaps, Lishabha thought, an argument was just the thing the Princess needed. She seized Ayesha's hands. "Is that not just like a scholar? A scant few minutes of 'Woe is me,' then you begin writing a thesis." She shook her head. Fine wire twists of gold and silver in her earlobes bobbed and jingled. "I think I liked 'Woe is me' better."

She released Ayesha's hands. "This is nonsense that you speak, girl. And you have less excuse than I, for you are educated. Even I can see the fact that we speak of it at all refutes this picture you paint of men. If they were brutal out of heritage, were rape instinctive—or even in particular widespread—we would not be sitting here discussing it, for, being products of it, none would carry any gentler inheritance to make discussion possible!"

"But you have seen them for yourself, Lishabha," Ayesha protested, "strutting, posturing to one another, demonstrating their virility by regaling others of their kind with tales of butchery, child-molestation, rape—"

This time, Lishabha did laugh.

"*Maa ghaadaa?* Now who trivializes what has happened? There is no such crime as rape, Ayesha, nor any other of the things which you have placed upon your laundry list. There is only one crime, be it perpetrated upon a woman, man, or child: violent assault upon a person against that person's will. Thank our large male friend over there, with all the muscles—and his sword. They who have transgressed have received such punishment as all such who transgress should receive. She who is innocent and injured—"

Lishabha stopped suddenly, wondering if she had begun to say too much. Then, the decision made, she went on.

"The old one, Woeck, held *you* to blame. When they brought you back, he said such things never came to pass unless a woman entices a man into it."

Lishabha gazed across the darkened clearing at the gray lump of blankets which was the old Helvetian priest. Ayesha would not look in that direction, but kept her eyes fixed on the ground.

Lishabha laughed.

"Sedrich-called-Fireclaw threatened to strike the old one's head off on the spot—that sword of his makes the eeriest whistling noise when he whirls it about. Knife Thrower made an even ghastlier suggestion, and my Lord Mochamet. . . . The Rabbi David calmed them down, then promised to unleash them again upon Oln Woeck did he not desist in future with his moral judgments."

Rummaging in her pack, she removed a small white cylinder, placed one end in her mouth, lit the other from a twig fetched from the fire. She blew smoke, and regarded the sleeping form of Fireclaw.

"They are not so different from us. Their moral range is greater. The worst of them is worse than a woman could be. The best of them is better."

"I think," Ayesha answered, somewhat calmer, "I have heard this asserted before, but of women by men."

Tapping ashes on the damp ground, Lishabha grinned. "Hmm. Well, I suppose it is bound to look like that to them. We know elsewise." She offered a puff of her *thanpaah* to the Princess.

Ayesha refused with an outstretched palm, a shake of her head, and slumped back. "A normal function, you say. I see that even now you contemplate how it would feel with that savage Fireclaw. How could . . . can you possibly . . . think about . . . *doing it* with him?"

Lishabha gave Ayesha a knowing look. "I do not think that it is I who wonders what he hides beneath his breechclout. As you say, I am property—that of *Siti* Mochamet al Rotshild. I do a lot more than just 'do it' with him. Other things. Mostly because I like it. Some because he does. It gives me pleasure to see him happy, and to know that I am responsible."

"Do you love him, then?"

Lishabha smiled. "*Nanam,* although it is not that simple. He found me in a Barcelona slum. He taught me everything I know, almost everything I feel. He gave me a life I would not otherwise have had."

"So it is a matter," Ayesha replied, "of gratitude. Of obligation. He teaches you. He feeds you—"

Lishabha took a puff, adding another aroma to the mixture of rain and woodsmoke.

"The important thing to learn about love"—laughed Lishabha—"is that it is complicated, mixed up with a hundred other feelings. Some days I love him because he is gentle, some because he is ferocious. There is, as you say, gratitude and obligation. But . . . you know I am his bodyguard."

"Maadaa qulth? Chanaa la chabhgham."

"You heard aright. He was looking for someone like me. He interrupted a fight in which, untrained and outmatched, I was getting the best of four other urchins, all male, all bigger. He trained me. I watch his back. I saved his life twice within the first year, have saved it countless times since—he has a liking for dangerous places. So maybe he feeds me—loves me—out of gratitude and obligation."

As rain hissed gently into the coals glowing nearby, Ayesha considered this a moment. "You think he loves you? Did he teach you, then, to . . . these other things?"

"Not equivalent questions." Drawing deeply on her *than-paah,* she held the smoke a moment before going on. "*Nanam,* he loves me, as a woman, as a friend, as a companion in arms. I suppose as a daughter, as a man loves that which he has created. *Nanam,* he taught me 'other things.'" She laughed. "It takes so little to put a sparkle in his eyes."

"But he is *old.*"

Again Lishabha laughed. "My Lord is young enough. I am she who has kept him thus, with . . ." She moved slender fingers a handspan beneath her navel. ". . . with . . ." She brushed the same fingers across her lips. ". . . with . . ." She touched her small, firm breasts. ". . . with . . ." She turned her hips, one dark playful eye upon Ayesha's scandalized expression, then converted the fluid motion so that her fingers moved to her right temple. "Most of all, with this." She smiled, tapping her head.

"Stop it!" cried the Princess, then: "He uses you like a sheep—a whore—a boy!"

"*Maadaa thureet?* Thus I never worry about losing him to sheep or whores or boys—small chance!" Lishabha observed with satisfaction that she had been right. Scandalized indignation was a vastly more desirable emotion—and more attractive as well—than cowering defeat. And more conducive, too, to the Princess' swift recovery.

"That is disgusting!" Ayesha shivered. "It is perverted!"

"*Laa*, it is love, where nothing is withheld." Lishabha leaned closer to Ayesha, shut her eyes, her inner focus upon a vision she abhorred but which she nevertheless considered in all aspects.

"He could be rocking, bouncing grandchildren upon his knee, letting time murder him." She inhaled, opened her eyes. "Instead, he is exploring the world with the same ardor he has explored me. I keep him interested. *Pismallagh,* may he live forever—if he does, then so shall I."

A faraway flash of lightning illuminated the horizon. Ayesha shook her head violently. "*Chanaa la chabhgham!* I cannot believe I am hearing this! How could *that* keep a person alive? I have seen nothing since I came to this place but death and more death!"

"At least you are now argumentative and angry. Is that not better than the way you were? Facts of life, Princess." Lishabha shrugged. "You may not approve, they may not suit the politics or religion of the day. *Laa thaghthaam*. They suit me to perfection. The wonderful thing is that the *facts* do not care, one way or another."

Lishabha blew a ring of smoke into the night air. It drifted upon the damp breeze and disappeared.

XXXI:

The Aspen Grove

So, when they forgot that they were reminded of, We delivered those who were forbidding wickedness, and We seized the evildoers with evil chastisement for their ungodliness.

—The *Koran*, Sura VII

At dawn, the Saracen party proceeded with caution along the narrow trail to a ridge-top, where they began climbing downward again into a round-bottomed valley lined with rain-soaked yellow mountain grass.

Here, the novice travelers of the party, Rabbi David Shulieman among them, discovered what the experienced voyageurs had known all along. "As demanding as an uphill march might appear," he wheezed at Fireclaw who trudged beside him, "downhill is much more difficult!"

"Inviting carelessness and falls." The warrior laughed, not without sympathy.

"Yes," David answered.

He removed his spectacles to polish off moisture they collected every few minutes in the steady drizzle. His hair and beard had curled into a thousand tight little ringlets. Then, placing the metal-framed lenses before his eyes again, he cast an envious eye at Fireclaw's knee-length fringe-topped moccasins, comparing them to the boots he wore.

"And ramming already trail-battered feet into the toes of shoes not well selected for the task we put them to."

David studied this peculiar, savage man they traveled with. The language he spoke—his native eastern tongue, not that of the even more savage tribesmen who had adopted him—was similar to a number of extinct Old World languages, their speakers one with the dust. In addition, the Helvetian was making rapid progress in the soft-syllabled and sibilant dialect of Arabic favored in the Judaeo-Saracen Empire. He loved to exercise his growing fluency whenever chance arose.

After a period of silence, Fireclaw shifted the enormous sword across his back to a more comfortable position, and waved a metal-tipped arm at the world about them.

"We've some good luck in the matter of weather, if not in your choice of footwear. . . ." David knew, in Fireclaw's view, they owed their present relative safety to rain which had fallen almost since they had entered the mountains. "The prairie tribes greatly fear thunder and lightning—"

"This appears to be universal," the Saracen scholar offered, thinking of sky-worshiping Mongols of days long past, "with primitive plains-dwellers everywhere."

Fireclaw grimaced at David's choice of adjectives, a choice the rabbi had regretted the instant he had uttered it.

"Knife Thrower's an exception," the Helvetian answered. With words—gestures filled the gaps in his vocabulary—he explained to the Saracen how he had duplicated boyhood experiments with static electricity for the Comanche war chief, who had seen the connection straightaway between them and the displays which lit the heavens.

David was impressed, with both men. "Yet neither of you can say for certain whether the mountain Utes share this fear?"

Fireclaw shook his head, keeping an eye upon the trail

ahead of them, on occasion fingering his dagger, or the grip of the handmade revolver swinging below his left hip.

Polishing his glasses once again, David thought back to the previous night. When Fireclaw had encountered Knife Thrower, patrolling the short trail back from the streambed, the Comanche had guessed the truth of what had happened to Ayesha, but remained quiet, vowing to the Saracens to keep secret what had been done to her.

His good intentions in this regard were in vain.

Next morning, somewhat recovered, Ayesha had, as a duty, related to her worried tutor and to her father's representative, Mochamet al Rotshild, the entirety of what had happened to her. Conferring over what to tell the others, both considered omitting the rape as an accomplished fact. But it was a small party, and rumors found sustenance among them, fed especially by the cruel and strident moralizings of Oln Woeck. Those there were who felt the old man's pious blathering must be countered. In due course, something resembling the truth was known by the rest of the expedition.

They then took up with Fireclaw and Knife Thrower the question of whether any point remained to the expedition.

The rabbi's assiduous scholarship and Mochamet al Rotshild's worldly experiences, were equally useless. Nor did Fireclaw know anything about the secret civilization whose boundaries they were crossing. Gossip, passed down by generations of Knife Thrower's people, more resembled theology than geography.

The callous but pragmatic question remained: Had Ayesha been "spoiled" for her diplomatic mission? One individual surprised David by speaking his objections to the manner in which the Princess was being thus regarded.

"This attitude you Saracens seem to share confuses me," admitted Fireclaw.

It was by this time clear to the Rabbi David Schulieman that, in fact, very little in life confused this remarkable man, the oddest combination he had ever known of bloody-handed ruthlessness, astonishing compassion, and subtle intelligence.

"Among my own people," Fireclaw told him, "a woman

can't think of being wed until she's first conceived a child. How great an asset can virginity be"—this he asked much like a well-trained scholar of the ways of men, dispassionate, as if he were discussing weather or the price of grain—"in the household of a Caliph whose wives—"

"Or at least"—the scholar had gathered the direction the Helvetian was headed—"those of our present Caliph's historic predecessors . . ."

Fireclaw completed his thought: "—sometimes number, to my limited understanding, among the thousands?"

David did not reply, nor did Mochamet al Rotshild. For this, of course, as with all contradictory customs of a species which, in aggregate, seldom did things logically, there could be no ready answer, whether from a scholar or a pirate.

The Helvetian then expressed his deduction that the usual reasons for rape had nothing to do with what had happened to Ayesha in the creekbed. Otherwise, he asked Mochamet al Rotshild and the rabbi, what did Kabeer's taunt, which he had overheard, about the Lady Jamela mean? Why was so much money found upon the three? David, more acquainted with conflicting factions and palace intrigues, was in private thought inclined to agree with Fireclaw, although, following the crafty Commodore's lead, he offered no word of support.

It was at this moment that the boy sailor Hraytis, wearing nothing but his customary loincloth, a pair of odd-handled daggers in its waist, interrupted them with more words, in the Saracens' recollection, than he had used upon the rest of the journey thus far. Suspicious by association, everyone had watched him since the well-deserved death of his companion, Crab. That loss, or fear of his being connected with events leading up to it, had affected him. He had spent the night huddled in his blankets, apparently mumbling to himself, or sobbing.

"Children of my tribe"—Shrimp volunteered that he had been born into another primitive tributary to the Sun King's domain; he spoke in creditable, albeit thick-accented, Arabic—"pursue such practices as render the matter of virginity unimportant by the time a girl is of an age to marry."

Knife Thrower and Fireclaw nodded to one another, saying they themselves knew tribes of which the same was true.

"I understand the present dilemma my noble Saracen lords find yourselves in, if only that, unlike most of my people, I have left my native land, traveled the world, encountering people with different feelings about these and other matters."

"Charjooh, min bhatlah," Mochamet al Rotshild asked, "can you make no guess as to the feelings of this Sun King?"

The boy shook his head.

"Although my home is closer than this place to the seat of the Sun King, we know less of him even than the Comanches or the Utes."

He eyed the Saracen chief. "It seems the further away one starts, the more one is likely to know. Strange, but do you not find it so?"

Mochamet al Rotshild did not reply, but offered that, upon the contrary, his experience was that the closer two peoples were, the more similar their customs, although this sometimes, paradoxically, made them fiercer enemies.

The men spoke further, each expressing his opinion, realizing it was nothing more than that. Thus upon this unsatisfying basis was it decided: their voyage westward would continue, the voyageurs somewhat diminished in number, until they encountered further reason—no one added, perhaps a fatal one—not to do so.

Late the previous night, Ayesha had learned that her visions had not abandoned her. David and Mochamet al Rotshild's girl, Lishabha, their weapons across their knees, had sat up with her through them. They were worse than ever, filled with fire and bloodshed, the stench of woodsmoke and death. They seemed to center—to Fireclaw's concern and consternation—upon her rescuer and the renewed hopes David had this morning learned the Helvetian had left back upon the plains.

Morning offered no better in this regard, the Princess now insisting, just before the assault, that she had glimpsed the dark shape of a soaring god-ship such as Knife Thrower had spoken of round the campfire at Fireclaw's ranch.

"I think, despite considerable respect I feel for my pupil's powers of observation, I would dismiss this measure of her tale," David told Fireclaw later. "It is a well-known phenomenon, how terrifying events insinuate themselves backward into an imaginative memory, altering the record of what has already come to pass."

Fireclaw nodded, but resettled the revolver in his holster, loosened his dagger in its scabbard, checked the position of the sword across his back. Despite any reassurances he had offered the Helvetian, the rest of the morning David caught himself—and others who had overheard Ayesha's protestations—peering more than once into the dismal overcast. Oln Woeck practiced a silence uncharacteristic of him, although whether this arose from monkish contemplation, the stern rebuff his moralizing had received, or from concealed fear, no one offered a guess.

At Knife Thrower's suggestion, they had bundled up poor Traveling Short Bear's mutilated body as best they could, in visible token of respectful sorrow, leaving it behind with the most opulent grave-goods the party could afford to part with— the carcasses of his murderers staked out upon the ground about him.

All eyes upon trail, sky, forest, and surrounding hills—too many objects to watch for too few eyes—they had at last reached the summit of the foothills and started downward once again. The greater heights still loomed before them like an impassable wall. It was upon the gentle slope at the end of the alpine meadow that Fireclaw stopped them, taking David ahead with him for a look at the meadow-end.

"If it happens, it will happen here."

Fumbling with his still-unfamiliar holster-flap, David thumbed the breech-catch of his massive four-barreled pistol, tipped the long, heavy cluster forward, took some courage from the sight of the brass heads of the thumb-sized cartridges there. From the beginning, he thought, even to his own myopic and uneducated view, this place had looked like a trap—a trap they had no choice but enter.

To their left, their freedom of movement was confined by a low, crumbling cliff-face, not higher than three men standing upon one another's shoulders, but underslung, worse than vertical, the back of one of the sloping upthrusts where they had camped the previous evening.

To their right, a pair of soft-contoured finger-shaped hills—sagebrush-covered leavings of great rivers of ancient ice, David explained to a skeptical Fireclaw—pointed toward the cliff. That nearest them was broken into a pair of little round-topped hillocks with a low brush-filled dip making a gap between them.

At the end of the farther finger-hill stood a small copse, perhaps two dozen trees, of white-barked aspen. Their wet leaves trembled in the wind like the palsied hands of senile old women. Between this and the cliff was a broad gray gravel-wash which, a few weeks earlier, with melting snowpack, would have been a healthy stream. At present, it was nothing more than a muddy tumble of boulders, averaging Ursi's size.

Lying among these scattered rocks, the shriveled carcass of a large deerlike animal Fireclaw called *Wapiti* thrust weather-whitened antlers toward the empty sky. Ahead of them rose a naked-crowned mountain, mantled upon its flanks by a dense stand of evergreens.

David snapped his pistol shut but did not replace it in its holster.

"This we'll avoid," Fireclaw told the party, "swinging to the right round the far side of the unbroken finger-hill, down into the next valley, behind the front range of the Great Blue Mountains. Thus, we'll have accomplished our first passage through the barrier, no epic feat—doubtless there're many higher, more difficult passes ahead—but something of a milestone, nonetheless."

Well back in the meadow center, where they could see aught approach for a thousand paces, the rest of the party sat awhile, preparing their weapons, battling with bold yellow deerflies for their first meal of the morning, jerked antelope and cornmeal, taken cold. But for their color, the insects resembled houseflies. There were not many of them, but their bites drew blood. Their buzzing in the mountain stillness seemed alarming, almost painful in itself.

Fireclaw—and Ursi—had by this time moved with David into the wash, where a steady breeze blew at their backs. Given the Saracen group's small size, its consequent vulnerability, the Helvetian believed he could not afford to precede it by any great distance.

"If danger comes—as 'twill, I know—they'll need my sword and pistol, Ursi's fangs and claws."

He and David and the black animal made irregular progress toward the base of the round-top nearest the cliffside, moving whenever a damp wind arose to whisper through the grass, clatter through the aspen, covering faint noises of their passage.

Between times, they waited and watched, David laying his pistol across his thighs, removing, cleaning, replacing his lenses as they steamed to near-opacity in the damp, miserable weather.

"Look!" Fireclaw's voice was a harsh whisper.

As they skirted the hill, they saw a fat, glossy doe among the trees, nibbling at silver-colored bark, despite the fact she was downwind of them and should have been alerted. Perhaps it was the steady drizzle which masked their approach. A spotted fawn grazed beside her. Fireclaw took this as a good omen. The animals' unfrightened demeanor caused him to decide their path ahead was clear.

"At least for the moment," David offered with a growing understanding of their peril.

Fireclaw gave a snort which might have been an ironic chuckle. He rose, signaling to Mochamet al Rotshild to let the party move ahead. The pirate chieftain and his companion met them halfway back to the meadow-verge. They squatted together in sparse high grass, their clothing water-dark from passing through it, their voices still low for no reason either might have been able to name.

Pointing toward the gravel bed, Mochamet al Rotshild exercised his improving Helvetian. "Yon stone-littery would be a good place for an ambush." He loosened a pistol in his sash.

Beside him, Lishabha inspected the breech of her long-barreled rifle.

"*Nanam chanaa chabhgham,*" Fireclaw replied in Arabic. "So I thought, as well."

The men grinned at one another.

"When we've reached the bend, we'll be subject to attack at all times, for the next several leagues beyond, from those woods yonder and the flanking hill."

Mochamet al Rotshild assumed a pious expression. "Be thou valorous, Sedrich-called-Fireclaw. The All-merciful, Compassionate God loves martyred warriors well."

Fireclaw scrutinized the man's weathered face. "The Goddess despises idiots."

The pirate laughed. "*Nanam,* I am curious to discover which of the two prevails in this realm." He grunted an old man's grunt as he arose. "From the look of it, neither. No matter, *laa thaghthaam,* how would you have us dispose ourselves?"

For some time, Fireclaw informed the older man, he had been thinking about little else. The Princess Ayesha, the reason they were here, should be protected at the center of the group. She was handy enough with the rifle she carried. Her little pet, Sagheer, was a fury unto himself. But Fireclaw was unsure how her present, brutalized condition would affect her fighting abilities. Rising, with a scratch at Ursi's head behind the ears, he spoke more of his thoughts.

"You and I," he told Mochamet al Rotshild, "will precede the party by several dozen paces."

The Helvetian and his mighty warrior-dog would take the right side, until they reached the evergreens.

" 'Tween us and the party's center I'll place Rabbi Schulieman, here, whose loyalty to his Princess, I think, is unquestionable, but whose battle skills are untested."

David did not know whether to be pleased or otherwise in this judgment, above all when the sea-captain concurred. He covered his embarrassment by removing his spectacles, rubbing the spots upon his nose which they irritated, and said nothing.

Fireclaw went on.

"Flanking the Princess I'd have your girl Lishabha upon the right. Oln Woeck"—useless, he could be seen thinking to himself, but not yet expendable—"upon the left. Our rear will be guarded by my war-brother Knife Thrower and Shrimp— but here I'll reverse order, placing the sailor, of whom we're both uncertain . . ."

"Considering the events of last night," Mochamet al Rotshild suggested.

"Indeed . . . upon the right."

The rabbi stroked his weather-kinked beard.

"Where he will be first to die, should such come to pass. *Nabhwan thismaghly*, you are a hard man, Fireclaw."

The Helvetian ignored David's appraisal.

"In any event, his abilities and trustworthiness haven't yet been tried. Should he survive—should any of us survive—at the least we'll have taken his measure."

David, Mochamet al Rotshild, and Lishabha returned to the others, passing along Fireclaw's orders. In this formation they waded through the last sodden grass, placing a toe upon the margin of the gravel-wash.

They passed the round-topped hillock without event, making toward the left of the aspen grove. It, in itself, was little threat: David could see through it. It concealed no Ute warriors.

He was less sure of the longer hill behind it.

As they drew even with the overgrown gully between the two lines of the hills, disaster struck, as Fireclaw had suspected, from behind.

XXXII:

The Breath of God

O if the evildoers might see . . . that the power
altogether belongs to God, and that God is terrible in
chastisement.

—The *Koran*, Sura II

A mind-numbing shrieking filled the air.

All vision limited by the heavy drizzle, Knife Thrower
hurled a blunt, guttural Comanche exclamation at his brother-
in-law. Both warriors realized the high-pitched noise was
intended to panic them, to bunch the Saracen party up, drive it
like a herd of frightened deer into the teeth of an opposing
group certain to be ahead.

"Make left!" Fireclaw shouted, drawing his revolver.
"Make left!"

A spear-throwing stick rattled in release. Its missile struck
with a hollow, meaty thump. Shrimp had counted his first
coup. Fireclaw would worry about the boy no longer.

With some semblance of deliberation, and before the Utes
could reach them from behind, the party drifted leftward,
toward the base of the cliff, into a clutter of boulders which

afforded some protection. Here, Shrimp sent another Ute into oblivion with a spear in the solar plexus, stooped to gather up the shoulder-bow he'd also carried, discharged a projectile into the approaching Ute ranks once again.

A second party of mountain savages rounded the aspen copse, running toward where the Saracen group might have been caught had they continued for the evergreens. A storm of arrows preceded them, though all of this first volley fell short or missed. A war chief upon the mist-shrouded hill shouted orders in falsetto, raised his feather-fringed lance, demonstrating the next angle of fire to be taken.

A rifle-shot cracked, lifting the chief from his feet, rolling him down the back side of the hill. The Helvetian had no time to see who'd fired it. He found himself hoping it had been Ayesha, but it had likelier been the warrior-girl, Lishabha.

The dull bellow of David Shulieman's four-barreled pistol followed as an echo, a single load of roundshot tearing into the cluster of Utes, bloodying the lot. While they stood cursing, the rabbi killed three of them with the shots remaining to him. He removed his glasses, polished them, commenced the process of reloading.

To Fireclaw's surprise, a third party, hiding somewhere in the gully perpendicular to the wash, charged out in what would have been a well-timed rush from the side—had he permitted his own group to stay within the arms of the Ute pincer. He saw, now, how it was that he'd been fooled. As the Utes rushed by, their voices raised, the mule-doe decoy struggled in terror at the end of a long braided tether.

Her fawn danced frantically beneath her feet.

A second gun banged, without visible effect.

Knife Thrower and young Shrimp now stood side by side, blades flashing, guarding each other's flanks as a dozen enemy warriors circled them and screamed.

The younger of the two had cast aside his shoulder-bow, drawing instead the odd pair of knives he carried, fighting with them as if he were fighting with his fists. At each punch and twist, an overconfident Ute died or backed away with something of himself missing.

Knife Thrower had seized an eagle-feathered lance from a fallen Ute, fending and thrusting with his left hand while he wielded his own much shorter dagger in his right.

Fireclaw holstered his still-unfired revolver, locked his double-limbed Comanche longbow into his prosthetic, nocked an arrow, sent it flying into the face of the young sally-chief leading the Utes from the gully. The Ute stumbled, fell, lay writhing for a longer time than the Helvetian would have imagined possible.

A second yard-length arrow was upon its way—this shaft struck a warrior from the frontal assault—as Saracen firearms began to go off all around him.

The crack of Lishabha's long-barreled military rifle was distinctive, followed as it was each time by the scream or grunt of a dying opponent. A momentary glitter caught the corner of Sedrich's eye as she unsheathed the long, narrow knife she carried, affixing it with a mechanical clank to the end of the single-shot weapon. This—"bayonet" he remembered hearing it called—didn't impeded her shooting, but it kept the enemy away from her when she'd opened the breech of her rifle or was reaching for more ammunition.

Mochamet al Rotshild had a large-bored pistol in each hand. When he'd discharged these to good effect—the Utes had slowed their charge now, having discovered the party wasn't the easy pickings they'd anticipated—he reached for smaller weapons in his boot-tops, accounting for another pair of Utes.

His parrot screamed, echoing the joyous war-cries of its master.

The Princess Ayesha wasn't in evidence. The mist had thickened. Fireclaw couldn't spare the time to do more than glance about for her, then go on fighting.

At his side, a snarl.

He whirled in time to see a Ute warrior, one of two or three daring braves who'd climbed down the cliff-face to surprise the Saracens, get his throat ripped out by the bear-dog. He dismissed the situation as taken care of. He'd problems of his own: the primary war-band had taken cover now, their belly-down approach obscured by the weather and sparse brush, crawling closer.

He unlocked his longbow, unsheathed *Murderer*, his mighty sword, and drew his pistol once again.

A Ute rose in front of him, shrilling. He snap-shot the warrior in the groin, feeling the buck and slap of the revolver's grip against his palm, lunged to cut another, shoulder to waist. The great blade caught between the bones for a sickening moment. Fireclaw saw others rushing at him, two of whom he shot. A dead man's hand, given momentum by a will which no longer existed, slapped the shaven top of Fireclaw's head, grasping for a hold in hair that wasn't there.

Fireclaw thrust his foot against the dead man's pelvic girdle; *Murderer* wrenched free with an ugly noise, to hew the rest down where they stood in shocked surprise.

During a brief respite, Fireclaw discovered that the others of his party had been backed to the cliff. He, alone with Ursi, stood amidst an enemy who were learning a lesson he'd once taught the Comanches. About his feet lay the cloven, powder-burned, or broken bodies of a dozen men.

Nowhere could he see Ayesha.

Thunder rolled—he could not remember seeing lightning, but the air smelled rank with ozone, fresh-spilled blood, and gunpowder. Mochamet al Rotshild shouted behind him. A few yards away, Lishabha had a Ute down, the butt of her rifle making a figure eight as she finished him with the blade at its muzzle.

Suddenly another of the cliff climbers was behind her.

She moved to withdraw the blade—too late—as the warrior threw himself upon her back, one hand tangled in her hair, his other arm reaching round.

His knife bit deep.

Lishabha fell, her throat slashed to the spine.

"Lishabha!"

Roaring Arabic profanities, Mochamet al Rotshild rushed upon the startled man, the heavy pistols in his hairy hands both empty. Unheeding of the warrior's flailing knife, he beat Lishabha's assailant with the guns wherever he could reach.

Even at this distance, Fireclaw could hear the small bones breaking in the man's face as the massive weapons pounded him into unrecognizability.

Po, the parrot, squawked and barked derisively into the dying man's shattered face.

Shulieman was down, too, his body curled about an arrow in his abdomen. It was the furious screeching of the marmoset Sagheer which told him at last of the whereabouts of the Princess Ayesha. Through a rift between the heavy sheets of drizzle and powder-smoke, Fireclaw could see the Saracen maiden. Soaked in blood from forehead to ankle, standing over her disabled mentor, her rifle tucked into her hip with one hand, the rabbi's heavy pistol in the other.

To Fireclaw's utter amazement, Oln Woeck also huddled at her feet, reloading for her, terror and an odd sort of determination written upon his already shriveled features. Her face was that of a statue. Three warriors in succession tried to reach her, break the chain of fire she kept up.

Each warrior died.

A litter of bodies about them almost concealed Shrimp and Knife Thrower. Just as the attack appeared to slacken, fresh forces poured from between the hills.

Shrimp went down to a polished wooden war-club.

Knife Thrower stood a while longer until a Ute arrow transfixed him just beneath the collarbone. Refusing to fall, he spat blood in the eyes of the nearest Ute, carved the same face off with a single stroke. Another Ute stepped in, thrust a blade at Knife Thrower, who deflected it. Its point entered his right hip. The rest of it slid into his body e'er Fireclaw was upon the man.

His knife still buried in the Comanche chieftain's flesh, the Ute turned, mouth agape in what might have started as a war-cry. With an angled thrust, Fireclaw levered the smoking muzzle of his revolver past the man's lips, shattering teeth.

He pulled the trigger.

Flame spurted from the Ute warrior's nostrils. The back of his head disappeared in a reddened fog. Fireclaw and his brother Knife Thrower were showered with debris.

Feeling an unfriendly hand upon his blood-bespattered shoulder, Fireclaw turned, slapped the war-painted face of this new attacker with the barrel of his pistol—the front sight cut flesh—dropped the gun, and seized the warrior's throat. Both hands locked in vain about the Helvetian's mighty wrist, the man was lifted off his moccasined feet. They flapped and dangled as he danced for life and lost.

The terror left his face.

His eyes grew dull.

Fireclaw tossed the hulk away and stooped to recover his revolver.

Shrimp groaned, rolling over, injured but alert, but the three were alone for a moment. Knife Thrower coughed, covering his chest with clotted blood.

"My brother—"

He'd not time for another word. Across the gravel bed, a hundred Utes were massed to charge them. There came a hail of arrows, a worldful of screaming from the Utes. In sadness and disgust, Fireclaw knew that he and his Saracen party were doomed, almost before their journey had begun.

The savages began running toward them.

And abruptly froze.

Over a rise, from the opposite end of the broad meadowed valley, there came a terrifying roar. Lumbering forms appeared, unearthly in the masking dampness. To Fireclaw, they looked like the beach-washed horseshoe crabs of his youth, darker—a glossy black—and infinitely larger.

Traveling abreast, three of them—no, there were four, *five*—filled the meadow from cliff wall to mountainside. Lights twinkled along their flanks. There was a sound, as if a blanket the size of the entire valley were being ripped in half. Utes began to fall like the fat raindrops spattering Fireclaw's bloody shoulders.

The giant forms moved closer.

Swift was their approach.

A hurricane roared in their wake.

SURA THE FIFTH: 1420 A.H.—

The Saw-Toothed Sword

No creature is there crawling on the earth, but its provision rests on God; He knows its lodging-place and its repository. All is in a Manifest Book.
    —The *Holy Koran*, Sura XI, *Hood*

XXXIII:

The Copper-Kilts

And on the day when We shall muster them all together . . . Behold . . . how that which they were forging has gone astray from them!
—The *Koran*, Sura VI

Despite the uproar of the battle raging round him, Oln Woeck, huddled at the obscenely bared knee of the pagan Princess Ayesha, thought he heard the gibbering of a nearby voice.

Ayesha stood o'er him, as she stood o'er her wounded mentor, the false priest David Shulieman. Her demon marmoset sat upon her shoulder, screaming the Devil's epithets past its bared fangs at the Utes. As for himself, Oln Woeck tried to move, tried to peek round the girl's smooth, dark, naked—

He broke off the unclean thought ere it was fully formed.

Her robes were gore-bedecked, rain-soaked, and battle-shredded nearly to her waist. A shoulder of the garment was rent and hanging, exposing her left—

Again he thrust the thought away, looking desperately about him, seeking the source of the whining sobs.

As was to be expected, machines had failed them all. Again. Unequipped with an attaching barrel-knife such as that vessel of filth Lishabha had used, Ayesha held her unholy Saracen rifle, long since run empty of the iniquitous cartridges which had fed it, by its long, metal-banded barrel in her tiny fists, its broad, crescent buttplate glittering a brassy threat to anyone fool enough to venture too near. Her palms were reddened, blistered with the infernal heat the thing had built up doing its evil work. Yet, with the unflinching relentlessness of all souls lost in sin, she paid it not the slightest heed.

Mayhap, with His inevitable and infinite concern with justice, He whose name might not be spoken by the faithful until His Son be redeemed had visited upon the barbarous and unbelieving Saracens their just deserts. Oln Woeck discovered he was too paralyzed with fear to move. He wondered, ere he could stay himself from doubting, why a fastidious soul who took the righteous pains he did—as he had, for virtuous example, in the matter of the vile and unconsecrated mating Sedrich Fireclaw had committed—should be punished with the Saracens, as if he were but another among their blasphemous number. He discovered that, sometime in the past few minutes, he had wet himself like an infant. He discovered, as well, that the voice he'd heard gibbering earlier was his own.

He let his wrinkled face fall, tears mingling incontinently in the mud. Above him, the Princess of the unbelievers braced herself, unaware that, in the bracing, she had lasciviously spread her—

The Utes shrieked, forming for their final charge.

Oln Woeck had found much to fear in this Jesus-forsaken land. Each day he'd feared the foul and worldly tarnish of the ungodly Saracens would rub off upon his soul. Each day he'd feared the savages, who certainly could have no souls, would murder him, either in his nightmare-troubled sleep, or as now, upon this battlefield.

Now he feared greatly they'd not do it swift enough.

He feared the hidden, satanic empire upon whose bitterly defended borders they had trespassed, to their doom.

And lately, most of all, most of the time, e'er since he'd

come to that fateful, righteous decision at the ranch, then seen steadfastly to its carrying out, he feared that Sedrich Sedrich-sohn, no longer the stripling boy he'd lorded over back in familiar Helvetian lands, but one whom whole nations of bloody-handed barbarians—who trembled at the name—called Fireclaw, would find his secret out.

An unreasonable man, this Fireclaw (and in this he did indeed resemble Sedrich Sedrichsohn, the boy who had become the man), one who didn't recognize reality—nor futility—when he saw it plainly. E'en now, the fine mist falling about him, he continued to wreak bloody havoc with blade and pistol till, jammed by fouling, the unsanctified revolver quit, and he had to rely upon his father's greatsword alone.

About the Helvetian warrior lay the bodies of uncountable dead. Had he, Oln Woeck, implanted such a fury in the boy, or had it been there, like his father's blood-haze, smoldering, all the time? 'Twas sometimes said that animals came to be like those who raised them. So valiantly fought Fireclaw's bear-dog, Ursi, that his assailants, sure of victory, now sallied forward simply to touch the great beast, that they could tell about it afterward—if they lived.

Many of them didn't, their throats torn out in the attempt.

Should they be victorious, Oln Woeck understood from things he'd overheard before this trek, the Utes would take the hair from atop the animal's skull, hang it in their lodges beside the scalps of valiant human warriors. At this terrible moment, 'twas the one thing about the Utes which made sense to him.

The valor of the Helvetian warrior, the Saracen Princess, their mighty canine ally, and Mochamet al Rotshild, who'd o'ercome his grief to scream his Arabic curses once again and fight beside them, was in vain, Oln Woeck thought miserably.

All was lost.

Why didn't they have the sense to see it? Why lacked they the good sense to lie down before the instruments of His wrath with some remnant of dignity? Why didn't they give up?

He had, long since.

Of a sudden, lying there halfway upon the weather-slickened grass, halfway upon the muddy, blood-spattered gravel, awaiting the final merciless onslaught of the Utes, he'd something which resembled a cheerful thought. Through some terrible miscarriage or oversight, as may be, of justice, he was compelled to face the wrath of Him who might not be named. At least he wouldn't have to face the wrath of Fireclaw, for now the man would ne'er find out what he'd done.

'Twas at this very moment that the sun broke blindingly from behind thinning clouds in the west. The vision-obscuring mist was swept away as if by an omnipotent—if somewhat ironic—hand. Five gigantic, powerful, wheelless craft rode up upon their cushions of hurricane-force wind. From a distance they began to massacre the marauding savages, saving what remained of the Saracen party.

Likewise Oln Woeck for Sedrich's vengeance.

The objects were like great mobile barns, seven, perhaps eight times the height of a tall man. Yet, on account of their great length and breadth, they appeared to cling low to the ground they traveled o'er. Mostly black in color, their surfaces were mottled, varying in texture as if to make them difficult to see in a dark or wooded place. Here, they stood conspicuous against the yellow meadow grass, like alien mountains, their flanks steaming from the recent rain.

Oln Woeck found himself wondering what their owners felt the need to hide them from.

Toward the front of each machine, a series of sloping platforms was crowded with the forms of oddly-dressed men, directing the fury of multi-barreled weapons which had cut the Ute attackers down exactly as Oln Woeck's razor—or Fireclaw's now, for that matter—daily removed stubble from scalp.

When the machines were close enough to whip-slap the remaining tatters which the Saracens wore, they gave out a great sighing. Their motive magics ne'er altogether silenced, the machines settled a bit closer to the damp earth.

And lay motionless.

No trumpet sounded. Great ramps were lowered—or lowered themselves—to the ground. Broad double doors opened in the machines' sides. From them vomited hundreds, perhaps thousands of men-at-arms, hastening toward the recent scene of battle.

In utter, inhuman silence.

The fighting-men, if men they were, not some man-shaped variety of demon, wore skirts fashioned out of strips of rust-browned copper, waist to knee, cunningly beaten into the delicate semblance of feathers, and riveted upon a backing of ebon-dyed leather.

Likewise fashioned of black leather—or mayhap of the hardened resin such as the Helvetians were wont to use, 'twas difficult to say which—were their back- and breastplates, molded in the image of a naked human torso. Atop these, fastened at the shoulders with what may have been insignia of rank, they wore short, sheer cloaks of printed fabric, more images of feathers, mostly gray, contrived to blend into whate'er natural surrounding they should happen upon.

O'er their heads they wore hard helms, fashioned in the fierce shapes of the skulls of birds of prey or predatory animals. The warriors' faces were concealed behind the smoky tint of blistered transparencies. From the crest of each helm there projected a slender black wand, gracefully curved and bobbing like the antennae of a butterfly.

As if a floodgate had been lifted within his mind, an overwhelming wave of insectile horrors crowded in upon him, images of loathsome, crawling hordes which suffocated sanity. He heard the gibbering again and forced himself to silence.

Wordlessly—yes, and in Jesus' name like so many ants or termites—hard-armored groups of five formed up to sweep across the corpse-littered battlefield, finishing off the wounded Utes they happened upon. Oln Woeck suspected that this represented no act of mercy, but of straightforward—insectile—thoroughness. Three of each five carried drawn swords of blackened steel, milled along the edges into deadly saw-teeth. The other two, with short, peculiar weapons slung before their chests, stood watch. These also wielded some divining implement, a small black coffer to which they referred with great frequency, apparently informing themselves somehow whether or not those whose bodies they trod among yet lived—thus meriting their grim attentions.

There was a clutter of other implements and weapons Oln Woeck couldn't fathom even thus far.

One such group of five at last approached Fireclaw, who stood panting, legs spread in a combat-stance, his greatsword held before him, dripping scarlet.

Ursi growled as they came near.

The Helvetian warrior spoke a warning word as if to render the giant bear-dog silent as these strangers. Unheeding of this gesture, one of the copper-kilts raised the blunt snout of a massive pistol. It gave forth a dull cough. Ursi started, then collapsed, the ebon fletching of a tiny quarrel projecting from one shoulder.

Another copper-kilted group filed in behind the inert animal's master, that he be surrounded.

Fireclaw had raised his sword, shifted weight to spring upon the armsman who'd shot Ursi. Without a word, the leader-at-arms of both groups hailed the Helvetian, tapped upon the odd-shaped weapon hanging at his own armored chest, seized it by the handle hanging below it. Resettling its sling, he pointed toward a nearby evergreen, its scaly trunk perhaps the widest span across that which the outstretched fingers of an adult male human hand could measure. The leader raised the weapon, right hand upon the grip, left hand held beneath his forearm, clamping the receiver to it with his thumb. He peered through a tube attached to its side.

Suddenly the ripping noise came.

Oln Woeck cowered in terror. When he forced himself to look up again, the tree, shredded through its thickness, was toppling o'er. The leader-at-arms pulled at an odd rectangle upon his weapon where it projected a hand's width behind the grip. It snapped free. He cast it aside, where it struck a boulder with a dull, clinking noise, replaced it with another taken from a pouch he carried at his waist.

Turning once again to Fireclaw, he slapped at his hip, pointing a gauntleted finger at Fireclaw's revolver, stretching out an upturned, empty hand to receive it.

Fireclaw dropped the point of his sword, unfastened his weapons belt, tossed it toward the man. In his loins, Oln Woeck felt an inexplicable flush of satisfaction at the sight, one which bloomed into something resembling beatification when the Helvetian was likewise silently commanded to yield sword and dagger—and complied.

This ritual, complete with its demonstration of the destructive qualities of the strangers' powerful weapons, was soon repeated for the edification of Mochamet al Rotshild and the Princess Ayesha, who, as Fireclaw had before them, yielded their own arms.

Knife Thrower, whose life might yet have been saved, despite his terrible wounds, was fallen upon by the armsmen, his body pierced, his throat slashed with half a dozen saw-toothed knives from ear to ear, perhaps as punishment for allowing a violation of the borders he, like the massacred Utes, had been supposed to protect inviolate.

Beside Oln Woeck, the Rabbi David Shulieman lay, obviously dying of his wounds, while their captors argued with incomprehensible gestures, apparently attempting to make up their minds about him. Not a single word was spoken. Finally the remaining barbarian sailor began shouting in his native language, perhaps objecting to this inhuman treatment of his new friends, more likely currying favor by denouncing them. He was allowed but a few words ere he was seized by both arms, hurried 'tween two burly armsmen into the nearest giant machine.

Oln Woeck suspected he'd ne'er be seen again.

Two of the great machines detached themselves from the others, heading off in the direction Fireclaw had opined the Ute village lay in. Ere long, above the ridge separating this place from that, flame-lit smoke began to rise. There came to them the blanket-ripping sound again which signified death occurring in great numbers. After a surprisingly short interval, the machines returned.

By this time, howe'er, the pitiable remnants of the Saracen party had other concerns. Soldiers were coming for them, threatening them with weapons, seizing them as they had

Shrimp, dragging them toward the mysterious machines they'd arrived in.

Fireclaw himself went willingly, shrugging enemy hands away from his arms, speaking in low tones a few words of parting to his great dog who, under other circumstances, might have leapt, savaging many of the armsmen ere being cut down by their potent weapons.

In Fireclaw's eyes, when he again looked up, Oln Woeck could detect the poisonous glint of something other than grief for his animal companion: that same curiosity which had ere this led him to evil. It had murdered his father and his mother. It had driven him away from home. Now he wanted to go aboard the machines, wanted to explore them, wanted to see the greater machinery which had created them.

Mochamet, parrot flapping loudly at his shoulder, followed his example. David Shulieman, upon a stretcher the armsmen had brought, offered no resistance, but the Princess squirmed, fighting the hands which forced her along.

Till she screamed.

Following the crane-necked gaze of the girl, Oln Woeck, with the rest of the party, turned toward the ridge to which they'd been backed by the Utes. Something was there, something dark, something terrible. Something huge enough to dwarf the great machine into which they were now being hurriedly dragged.

Perhaps this was what the copper-kilts had feared.

It rose like a bloated moon, black upon the horizon, unspeakable in its immensity.

XXXIV:

Imperial Captive

Or do those who commit evil deeds think that We shall make them as those who believe and do righteous deeds, equal to their living and their dying? How ill they judge!

—The *Koran*, Sura XLV

One of the women gave a squeal, mocking him.

"I won't!"

The boy stood half inside the boat, a foot within the hull, the other on the planking where the craft lay canted. The air smelled of salt and iodine, the sun skipping from unrippled water. Scattered about were his father's tools. Clutched in his hands—one at his hip, the other thrust before him—he wielded a sculling oar.

Answered the foul-odored old man, his bony figure draped in unbleached fabric: "Stay thy hand, boy! Too young thou art to pay the penalty! Give me that oar!"

The boy complied—after his fashion—thrusting it into the man's solar plexus. The tip sighed into his midsection, two more feet following on its momentum with a hiss. The man pitched forward, half severed at the waist. He looked up. His nose was a sunburnt hook, his eyes the color of icebergs. Like his namesake, he wore only a breechclout decorated with the dried petals of the flower Dove Blossom took her name from.

"What in the name of Exile d'you think you're about, son?"

The boy recovered from the thrust, assumed a stance straddling the gunwale. He let his weapon, a length of metal high as a man's breast, broad as a man's hand, sharp as a man's memories, slam back into its scabbard.

"No more than to make the rowing easier, Father."

The big man stared at his son. "And why should rowing be made easier?"

The boy ran a hand through his graying mane, where feathers, bound at their bases with blood, replaced the braid he'd worn.

"Why, to ease thy suffering in Hell, Father, by sharing it with thee on earth."

One of the women growled.

His father's hands clenched into fists, the veins of his forehead threatening to explode. "What pigshit is this, you dung-ball? How darest thou speak to me thus?" The boy knew what was going on in his mind.

"Tell me, boy, who first thought of suffering? The idea belongeth to the community. Destroy it, thou committest blasphemy."

The boy stamped a naked foot. "This idea is mine! *Before I let you interfere, I'll make you pay a tithe, in bone and blood!"*

"Muttonhead! Fishbait! Cart-axle! Priest! What makes you think we want ideas?" the shaggy giant retorted. Foam formed upon his lips, whence sprayed gobbets. "Impious brat, 'tis your ideas've brought on every calamity your mother's suffered for a thousand years!"

The boy was puzzled. He remembered well conceiving his father, across a barrel in the shop, a pillar of two grades of steel folded under the hammer to create a hero of the western wars they daren't make trouble with.

Unable to answer, he let the sword, unequaled elsewhere in the world, drop until its blade rested on the older man's hair, bleached by exposure to the sun.

"Yes, Father."

There was a long pause. "Father, about my idea . . . I needs must start o'er again, anyway."

The boy's eyes were crafty. He reached down to tousle one of his wives between the ears. Frae nodded meekly, golden curls bobbing. He seized her by the throat with his one good hand and squeezed, letting his thumb find the thin, ribbed cartilage beneath the skin. Sweat stood out upon his forehead. She tore frantically at his fingers, but to no avail.

A few paces away, Ursula Karlstochter snarled and bristled.

It was long before the young Helvetian let her inert body slip to the ground at his feet. Dove Blossom sat beside Ayesha, the glance she gave the Saracen girl curiously intelligent and ironic.

"The women need to rotate, independent of each other," the boy told his father. "I'll make a drawing after supper."

Calculation appeared on the father's bearded face. "Be hush! You were fashioned in my forge, by tinkering. What purpose do you serve? The village won't permit you to have your way."

Bending, he took hold of his son's shoulder, wrenched him from his attachment to the gunwale. He gave the boy a casual toss.

"You're too right-handed," he called after his son. "You must put some work into your off-side."

The boy sailed out upon the estuary and disappeared with a splash.

"Now," the man declared, "a dangerous innovation's gone from our community."

Sedrich Sedrichsohn awoke with no remembrance of having gone to sleep. The bed he lay upon—

He leapt up, discovered that he had been suspended somehow in midair, wrenched his body face down as he fell, his warrior's braid slapping at his cheek. His arms folded under him, trying to tuck his knees beneath him. His bare feet tangled in some sort of netting he'd not noticed as the floor rose up to meet his face.

He landed with a jarring crash, heart hammering, head pounding, stripped of everything he'd worn—and cleaner than ever he'd been for days. Even his prosthetic, with the molded fiber-resin cuff reaching nearly to his elbow, had been taken.

He groaned as he turned over.

The floor he now rested upon was warm, but very hard beneath a generous covering of fabric. Without thinking, he reached up. His head was a stubbled ball of agony, the stiff nap he felt there telling him that many hours had passed, the throbbing hum which filled it telling him—he knew not what. The room swam round him before his eyes.

He wanted to throw up.

Instead, he pushed himself backward, every muscle stiff and protesting, leaned exhaustedly against the wall, shifted his good hand to his naked-feeling right arm, flexed the little bit of wrist-joint remaining to him there, and fought down the blood-haze rising within him before it could dismind him to no useful purpose. The room entire seemed to vibrate about him with a low, smooth buzzing he imagined he could feel transmitted through his back and buttocks.

The bed he'd been lying upon—if "bed" were indeed the word to use, or "lying"—had been softer than any he'd known since leaving his father's house.

Perhaps that was what had alarmed him so.

He looked up to where it hung now in a twisted ruin over his head. It was a strange bed, a stranger's bed, fashioned from an open lacery which might have been the work of fisherfolk, suspended at two points upon the close-spaced walls above the thickly carpeted floor. It had been draped over with a smooth, shiny fabric which now lay upon the floor beside him. The stuff was cool to the touch, caught at rough spots on his callused hand, and was of a garish brown-red color, decorated at its borders with an unfamiliar yellow pattern.

Sedrich-called-Fireclaw, son of Sedrich, didn't know where in the name of the Goddess he was, but, before too much more time passed, he swore by his mother's staff and his father's sword, he was bloody well going to choke it out of somebody!

Feeling more like himself with this resolve, he turned, shifting his weight onto his right hip. It was a small room they had put him in. He began remembering, now, the animal-helmeted warriors in black and copper armor who had slaughtered the Utes. The ceiling would likely brush the bristles of his head. Had he possessed two hands, and had he stretched them far apart, his fingertips would just have missed touching the opposite walls in both directions.

For all of that, the place was richly furnished. An oddly shaped but comfortable-looking chair with a small table beside its arm was covered in the same fabric as that which had fallen from the strange bed and now lay draped across his knee. Nearest the strange bed, where he himself might have planned a window, there hung upon a wall of unreflective featureless gray a great brassy disk, a distorted, alien face embossed upon its surface with its squarish tongue extended. Two other walls were decorated with ocean landscapes, so cunningly painted that they almost fooled the eye into believing they were windows, save that they would be dead to the touch and gave forth no light.

Mochamet al Rotshild had spoken of such an art among the Saracens, calling it— *Lishabha was dead!* Knife Thrower dead as well! David Shulieman, and Shrimp—*and Ursi!*

Breathing deeply, he seized the netting above him with his one good hand, lunged to his feet, waited out the dizziness, making an effort to collect himself. The dream he'd suffered began pouring back into his mind, along with the urge to vomit. The throbbing he'd felt had not been of his imagining; he could feel it now, in his unshod feet, coming up through the floor, and decided that it made sense—he had seen the size of the machines the copper-kilted warriors had arrived in, vaguely remembered boarding one of them.

It must be idling at the moment, going nowhere, for the

mountain terrain was much too varied not to be felt in the rolling of even so great a vehicle as this.

He glanced about.

The place boasted of no windows, but, among its other furnishings, the tiny room had been provided with three louvered doors, one upon the wall opposite the bed, two others in a third, across from the chair. Fireclaw proceeded to explore them.

The first such he tried, no different in appearance from the others, was low, slotted at an angle he couldn't, in his present weakened state, bend down far enough to peer through, and of a most peculiar shape. He would have had to duck under its round-topped lintel to pass through it, but the round brass knob in its middle resisted the opening twist of his wrist.

In the back of his mind, beneath the layers of pain and disorientation, Fireclaw's search now changed from one for clothing and an exit to one for weapons and escape.

The second door admitted him into a remarkable room, even smaller than the first, containing a porcelain sink, what must certainly be an indoor privy of the same substance, and what might be a small closet for vertical bathing. Running a hand over his freshly cleaned skin, he wondered how his keepers had managed to stand him up inside this thing and scrub him. There didn't seem to be much room.

He took time to confirm his theory about the privy. His headache peaked unbearably just afterward, then began to slacken.

The third door concealed the greatest surprise of all, a wall-built wardrobe. Inside, suspended from an iron bar upon peculiar triangular wire frames, he found his freshly cleaned deer-suede breechclout, his antler-decorated vest, likewise the felted dog-hair cloak he wore over both when it was cold——

——and *Murderer,* cleansed of the gore of battle, standing in its half-scabbard in the corner.

Stepping from the closet, he let the sword ring out upon the brass throat of its scabbard. Light from some unseen source near the ceiling gleamed along its polished, feather-hammered surfaces. The edge still made a crisp little whisper when he crossed his thumb against it. The exultation he felt at the sight of that great weapon was, atop the headache, almost more than he could bear.

If he were a prisoner, why had they left him his mightiest weapon? If not, why was the door locked?

Were men responsible for their dreams?

Further exploration only deepened the current mystery and added more to many contradictions. Pistol and dagger he found in the wardrobe, also cleaned—although he noticed with an ironically appreciative grin that someone had relieved both belt and gun of their supply of ammunition. His prosthetic lay there as well, its soft-tanned fastening straps neatly folded. Among the objects which he carried in his pack—cleaned and propped up in the other corner of the closet, behind his cloak—the only item he missed was his reloading kit.

Perhaps it and his ammunition were still out being cleaned somewhere. He doubted it. The only thing he knew for certain about these alien warriors was that they were tidy enough to please his mother. But there was something reeking of contempt in this generosity, as if the copper-kilts so trusted to the superiority of their own weapons that they feared not those they'd left to Fireclaw.

He looked forward to a chance to instruct them otherwise.

A rattle at the locked door brought Fireclaw whirling about to face it, nightmares and aches forgotten.

"Yourself now air t'come wit me," a voice pronounced, in miserable Helvetian.

The door swung open upon a helmetless copper-kilted armsman, apparently reading syllables from a penciled scrap of parchment in his otherwise empty hand.

"Yourself now will be pers'nally honorifized by audiencing wit His Imperial Dom—"

The armsman looked up.

His eyes widened.

He gasped.

He took a step backward at the terrifying sight, not of the helplessly groggy captive he had been instructed to expect, but of a giant savage, alert and raging, with a five-foot length of razor-edged steel held back in his hairy hand and poised for slaughter.

XXXV:

Audience with the Sun

But the parties have fallen into variance among themselves; then woe to those who disbelieve for the scene
of a dreadful day. How well they will hear and see on
the day they come to Us. . . . Warn thou them of
the day of anguish, when the matter shall be determined. . . . Surely We shall inherit the earth and all
that are upon it, and unto Us they shall be returned.
—The *Koran*, Sura XIX

Fireclaw's triumph was but momentary.

From either side of the startled messenger there stepped into
the Helvetian's view another of the copper-kilted warriors,
black-helmeted, armed with one of the short, rapid-firing
weapons he'd seen used to such lethal effect upon the Ute.

Their peculiar, complicated-looking muzzles were leveled
at his hairy chest.

He raised an eyebrow and grinned, lowering *Murderer* with
conspicuous care, turned back into the small room, and cast
about for its wolfhide scabbard. The messenger stood in the
spot he'd retreated to, across the narrow corridor.

"D'you imagine," Fireclaw asked, indicating his naked body with a sweep of his equally naked stump, "His Imperial Dom'll mind too much if I get dressed ere we go visit him?"

This question proved beyond the linguistic ability of his visitor. The helmetless armsman assumed a puzzled expression, referred to the rote-speech written upon the parchment, found no answer which suited him. He watched Fireclaw repeat the gesture, understood at last.

"Yes," the fellow answered, "audiencing wit habiliments."

He faced each of the other warriors in turn, speaking a few words in some language Fireclaw couldn't follow.

The muzzles of the blanket-rippers dropped.

The armsmen, however, stood watching Fireclaw's smallest movement as he took his clothes from the wardrobe and put them on. Thinking to establish himself from the outset among these people as he'd done among the Comanche, he slipped the prosthetic cast over his right forearm, adjusting it to his liking. He strapped revolver and dagger about his waist. He slung his greatsword over his back. Habiliments, indeed. It was an effort not to watch for their reaction from the corner of an eye.

Turning, he bent down, stepped through the low, arched doorway into the corridor—and caught his breath. Everywhere he looked, ceiling, walls, even the floor, artists had embellished the smooth surfaces with some kind of painting— murals in many colors, scenes of battle rendered in a style which, in their bloodthirsty enthusiasm, might have done justice to any engagement Fireclaw had ever fought.

In one scene, copper-kilted warriors could be seen, lined up, drawing the intestines from a staked-out prisoner, as if they'd been playing at a tug-of-war. Between the soldiers and their victim a low fire had been built, baking what was suspended over it.

Yet it was neither this picture, nor the many others marching along the walls and ceiling, inlaid upon the floor, which had taken the Helvetian's breath. This couldn't be one of the crablike vehicles—as huge as they'd been—which he'd seen upon the meadow! From one dim-lit end of the passageway he'd entered to another, brilliant-lit, toward which the arms-men prodded him now, at least five of those machines could have nestled, one after the other, nose to tail!

The helmetless messenger had backed himself against the garish corridor wall opposite Fireclaw's guard-flanked door. Having issued the summons to an audience, he now started toward the bright-lit end of the passageway, inviting Fireclaw to follow.

Fireclaw strode between the guards, taking a long step to catch up. As he did so, the guard to the left of the door wheeled even with the other, where both, in Fireclaw's presumption, would walk behind the giant Helvetian and the messenger.

For the briefest of moments, as they turned, the peculiar, slotted muzzles of their weapons crossed, a finger's width apart. Fireclaw's left hand snapped out, seizing both weapons by their barrels, wrenching them from the shocked grasp of their owners.

"Escorting dangerous prisoners," he advised with false solemnity, "is that serious an undertaking."

Breaking into a grin, he tossed the weapons at the messenger with a casual wrist-flip.

"Your minions'd best be better trained for it in future."

The alarmed messenger fumbled to keep from dropping both guns. The scrap of paper he'd been reading from fluttered to the inlaid floor. Fireclaw stood with his arms folded before his chest. His point had been made: he was naught here save a willing guest. He wished he could see the expressions behind the helmet visors.

When, after an awkward moment, their confiscated weapons had been returned to them, the guards—stiffer-postured than before—took up positions to the rear of the other pair. All four proceeded toward the light, Fireclaw taking deeper strides than usual so that his shorter-legged escort, losing dignity with every pace, was half compelled to run behind him. It was a long walk, during which Fireclaw revised his estimate of how many of the alien land-vehicles might have fit within whatever structure they now occupied.

Eight perhaps, maybe ten.

The deep, enveloping throbbing never ceased, never altered pitch nor volume.

For five whole minutes they strode along a polished floor embellished with pictorial representations of the painful and protracted deaths of thousands of individuals, which the walls and ceilings multiplied fourfold again. The hideous, decorated corridor grew brighter, widening until they traveled the long length of a half-cylinder, the walls upon either side stepped back, curving upward from what was, in comparison, a narrow floor, to a wide, flat ceiling above their heads.

Upon the many steps there were arranged a myriad of curious objects: animal and human statuary, garish and obscenely painted; idols of rough stone and polished metal, some with far more arms or heads—or other organs—than seemed natural to the man; lacquered cabinets; ornate Z-folded screenery; other exotic furnishings; a thousand mechanical devices, black and gleaming, whose origins and purposes Fireclaw could but guess at, and with little confidence his guesses were correct.

They halted, between the upcurved walls and flattened ceiling overhead, fifty paces short of the shadowless interior of a glaring quarter-sphere of many-paned windows. It was the bottom quarter of a sphere, the warrior observed, providing a broad-angled view of what was forward and beneath the enormous chamber.

The glass (if that was what it was) had been arranged like spaces between the webbing of some nightmarish spider. If 'twere afternoon, as Fireclaw believed, the quarter-dome they occupied was facing westward. The vehicle—for such was what it now proved to be—was traveling in that direction, at great speed, and at such a dizzying height that the wild, many-folded land visible below appeared as nothing more than heaps of sand within a child's sandbox.

They were flying!

At the center of the web reposed a figure equally nightmarish. It half reclined upon a great chair, carven from a single slab of some translucent green stone. This was suspended, by a system of taut wires, several feet higher than Fireclaw's head.

"Step forward, Sedrich Fireclaw," a voice commanded. "The windows will sustain your weight."

Fireclaw heard motion behind him. He glanced backward. His erstwhile escort had stepped forward, intending to prod him into obedience. He glowered at them and they shrank back, cowed. He turned his attention back to the figure before him.

'Twas human. He could have no doubt of this. Also male—although the object which reposed between its naked thighs was artificial, leathern, a grotesque caricature of what ought to be there. Aside from this, and from the mop of colored feathers about its base, with narrow straps which held the ugly object about its waist, the figure was unclothed—that of a wiry, athletic, well-muscled brown man—save for its jeweled and lacquered fingernails, each of them a handspan in length and curled back disgustingly upon themselves, and for the helmet concealing its head. A drapery of some sort, woven of tiny scarlet feathers, had been allowed to fall upon the chair-seat behind the figure, enveloping the buttocks.

A small, T-handled dagger hung upon the leather straps at either hip.

The helmet was not unlike those affected by the guardsmen, save that it seemed to have been fashioned of fine-beaten, polished gold. Instead of having been wrought in the likeness of some bird or animal, it resembled the disk Fireclaw had seen upon the wall in the cabin where he'd awakened: a hideous face with tapering rays zigzagging from its edges, a broad, square-ended tongue protruding from the mouth, obscuring whatever lower lip it claimed, reaching almost to the chin.

Only the large eyes were dark, fashioned of the same smoky substance as the visors of the guardsmen. Fireclaw imagined that these eyes regarded him in estimation now, as he himself attempted to regard their owner. During the long silence, the messenger and both copper-kilts had thrown themselves prostrate upon their faces. Hand resting upon the wooden grip of his holstered, empty revolver, Fireclaw stood straight, looking into the hideous artificial face, ignoring the mountains passing by a league or more beneath the transparent floor.

"Even thus suspended between the heavens and the earth you don't abase yourself."

The mild-toned voice had emanated, not from behind the hideous golden mask, but simultaneously, it seemed to Fireclaw, from all corners of the great quarter-sphere. The words themselves had been Helvetian, well formed, without accent.

Fireclaw didn't move.

There followed a brief outburst Fireclaw couldn't understand, save for some few of the words with vague resemblance to those of the Comanche. Of the origin of this second voice there could, however, be no doubt, addressed, as it had been, at the inlaid, polished floor by the messenger who'd brought him to this place. The masked figure moved as if in speech, its four-cornered voice answering in the same unknown language.

It resumed in Helvetian.

"Our faithful servant inquires of Us whether We'd have you—'the barbarian,' he calls you—forced into the customary gesture of respect toward Us. We've demurred, forewarned by Our Dreamers that your defiant posture's aught We might have expected of the legendary warrior, Sedrich-called-Fireclaw."

Fireclaw nodded but uttered no word.

The three guardsmen stayed flat upon their faces, leading the Helvetian to suspect that others—well-armed others—kept close watch from some concealed niche for the sake of their superior's safety. Perhaps such was the purpose to the confusing array of painted and polished bric-a-brac cluttering the steps of the receding walls behind him. Any number of the manlike statues might have been living individuals, frozen into postures of watchful wariness.

Another long silence reigned while the two men, proud Helvetian warrior and golden-masked enigma, regarded one another.

"Astounding!" The sourceless voice spoke again, breaking the silence. "You've outwaited Us—We who've Ourselves triumphed in many a negotiation through the simple tactic of outwaiting another more anxious than We to fill the terrifying quietude."

It raised a slender, sun-browned arm.

"But see here: would you not ask Us a thousand questions, Sedrich-called-Fireclaw? D'you not wonder where you are, what manner of conveyance we ride within, or what's to become of you? Is there naught you wish to learn from Us?"

The Helvetian let his silence last a moment longer.

Then: "I calculated you'd tell me what I want to know"— Fireclaw suppressed all expression save for the faintest hint of a smile—"or you'd not. What has become of my traveling companions—my dog? The same fate as befell the Ute?"

"Sedrich Fireclaw"—the gold-masked figure turned a long-fingernailed brown hand over, palm side up—"there *are* no more 'Ute'—nor any 'Comanche' either."

Belying the racing heart within him, the Helvetian raised an inquiring eyebrow.

The golden face nodded.

"They've been eradicated by Our personal guard—erased from the face of the earth, for failing to stop the Saracen party's penetration into Our Domain."

The strange figure gave a shrug, somewhat exaggerated by its weird attire, yet as if this were an idle matter, of little concern, they were discussing.

"They'll be replaced in due course, either by random levies from near-neighboring tribes, or from surplus population within the interior. New 'Ute' and 'Comanche' nations— provided they're allowed to retain and, um, redeem those arbitrary designations—will spring into being, each equipped with appropriate cultures, appropriate legends, appropriate sophistication in the mechanic arts."

Fireclaw snorted.

"Harsh punishment indeed, for a single, small infraction. One I can testify they were attempting manfully to correct. And little chance to learn from one's mistakes."

The sourceless voice laughed. The noise bounced round the great room, echoing from polished surfaces.

"They were attempting, not to do their duty as regards Us, but to avenge the death of their leader, Short-Bear-Who-Travels. Punishment? Oh, no, great warrior. This wasn't a punishment at all, any more than your replacing an unreliable or defective part in one of the machines which We provided your former neighbors."

Somehow, despite the exaggerated nails, the figure placed its fingertips together.

"Sedrich Fireclaw, if peoples are to survive, they must begin learning, not from their own mistakes, but from the mistakes of others. Teaching this—making the learning of it a necessity—is a task We've taken upon Ourselves. 'Tis oft unpleasant, but such doesn't render it a whit less important."

The figure paused, as if awaiting reply.

There came none.

"One thing's certain: when Our 'reeducation' of the replacement population's complete, when they've been installed in their respective territories, their languages will this time be constructed from wholly unlike roots. This regrettable incident happened in the first place because such a measure was left too long by Our esteemed predecessor. The 'Ute' and 'Comanche' came to learn one another's languages, began to operate upon a friendly, mutually beneficial basis, instead of from distrust and enmity, as is the natural order of things."

Fireclaw shook his head.

"I fear I fail to understand you—"

"Likeliest you fear you do understand Us. Their languages, those of the 'Ute' and the 'Comanche,' were of course as artificial as their legends. Dear fellow, there ne'er were any 'Dog-Eaters,' simply an implanted legend. The entire complex was long o'erdue for replacement in any event. History—and Our Dreamers, of course—inform Us that these fringe provinces are invariably neglected, almost always to the incumbent authority's eventual regret."

Fireclaw suppressed any visible manifestation of the shudder he felt traveling through his body, forced himself to listen to the cold-blooded voice addressing him.

"Of course," the same voice continued, "another reason all

this difficulty came to pass is that the current incumbent was o'ercurious—'tis a failing of Ours—philosophically interested in one Sedrich Fireclaw's effect upon the Comanche."

The near-naked figure leaned forward in his chair, placed one obscenely nailed hand upon its suntanned thigh, rested its metallic chin in the palm of the other.

At some unseen signal, a section of the shelved wall to the Helvetian's left swung aside.

From within a dark interior there stepped—at gunpoint—Mochamet al Rotshild, followed by the Princess Ayesha and a terrified-looking Oln Woeck. Unlike Fireclaw's escort, the guardsmen who brought these individuals with them suffered no doubts as to the proprieties. They were forced to the floor, to their knees.

From there they were pressed forward upon their faces.

"The Rabbi Shulieman still lives as well, although but just," offered the four-cornered voice. "Have no fear, Sedrich-called-Fireclaw, your great dog Ursi's well, having been put to temporary rest with the selfsame potion, contained in a dart which struck him, as has embraced you in its gaseous form these past dozen hours."

One of the new copper-kilts, wearing the black mask of an eagle, raised a large and awkward-looking pistol as if to illustrate the explanatory words of his ruler. Someone else, then, thought Fireclaw, possesses enough Helvetian to get by in.

A foreign word was spoken.

One of Fireclaw's escort, the helmetless messenger, climbed to his feet. From across the great hall the pistol made a snuffling sound. The volunteer went down again, this time upon his back, with a feathered dart protruding from his unarmored throat.

"He'll awaken again in a few hours," the masked figure offered, "just as you did, with little more than a headache and a few bruises to show for his unpleasant experience. 'Tis more than We can say for those in custody of your dog—who let the beast awaken and were slow in tranquilizing him once again.

Three amputations were necessary, and one mercy-slaying. He's your dog, sir, he could be no one else's!''

A metallic flash caught Fireclaw's attention. He took his eyes from the remainder of his party, let them travel once again to the figure, who'd raised both hands up to the golden mask.

"You're a remarkable man, although you've ne'er realized quite how remarkable. A warrior of astonishing repute, well justified. Something of a philosopher."

The hands came down again, taking the mask with them.

Sitting upon the elevated throne before the Helvetian warrior was the boy whom the Saracens had called Shrimp.

"Yes, mighty Fireclaw, 'tis We." The voice was human now, no longer issuing from the walls and ceiling. "Better known within Our own domain as Zhu Yuan-Coyotl, ruler of the Han-Meshika, spirit of the Sun incarnate. A clumsy appellation, to be sure, but one which, now and then, impresses even Ourselves."

The boy shook his head at these words, as if dismissing the topic with embarrassment.

"You can't e'en begin to comprehend the intellectual prowess represented by your leaping from coarse, dry-mixed gunpowder to repeating firearms in less than a single lifetime! Why, man, Our Dreamers tell us of civilizations entire who took a thousand years to accomplish what you have, all alone, within but a single generation!"

The boy-ruler leaned back again.

"Too, We've always debated privily with Ourselves the relative importance of the individual in society. Here was an unprecedented opportunity to experiment."

He sighed.

"With your capture, of course, the experiment's o'er, proving only what We expected it to prove. In the long run, that the individual—any individual—counts for naught. A sobering thought indeed, friend Fireclaw, for an absolute monarch."

The complicated mixture of feelings within the Helvetian was beginning to congeal into anger and hatred.

" ' 'Tis the water washes,' " he quoted, almost to himself, " 'not the soap.' Tell me, what's *this* individual to expect—"

He indicated the others with a sweep of his arm.

"—and these, now the experiment's o'er? Or has this already been decided?"

The youth raised his hands to shoulder level, palms up. For a moment he resembled one of the many idols in the room behind. The jewels set into his artificial nails glittered in the sunlight.

"All here will serve Us, as indeed all people upon this earth eventually serve Us in one wise or another. Like every traveler to this forbidden land, you and your expedition have been brought before its official ministers for questioning."

He chuckled.

"Unlike most of them, you've been brought before its supremest official. This privilege, though rare, makes little practical difference. Information, you will in due course discover, is always allowed to flow *into* what Our more fanciful minions call the Crystal Empire. Never out. Whatever travelers happen to learn in the process of interrogation dies with them, usually sooner than later."

He shifted upon his throne more as if the topic were uncomfortable than the green-stone seat.

"But We see what you're asking: what of your ranch, your shop, your dog-pack, your wife, your child-to-be? Were they, too, 'erased' by Our personal guard?"

Fireclaw nodded but conceded nothing more.

Zhu Yuan-Coyotl shook his head.

"We assure you, sir, that no such action was necessary upon Our part, or that of Our guard. We're afraid 'twas already taken care of—by your old friend Oln Woeck."

"Oln Woeck?" Fireclaw felt the prickling at the back of his neck and along his limbs which presaged disminded killing anger. A veil of crimson washed over his eyes.

At the side of the room, the Cultist glanced up for a moment, horror upon his face.

Fireclaw, fighting blood-haze, believed he heard a whimper.

"Yes, Fireclaw," the Sun Incarnate continued. "Ere leaving

the ranch, he used some poison stolen from your shop to con-
taminate your wells, killing Dove Blossom and the dogs, as he
tells me in some pride he did your father in his time.''

Great pain swept through Fireclaw's body as the words sank
in. He trembled in the grip of rage.

"We're afraid, b'time Our copper-kilts arrived, 'twas far too
late to save them. They'd all spent many days in the process of
a lingering and painful death. Our guardsmen gave the evil
work a decent finish—cremation, one might call it. E'er they
were through with the Comanche, they burned your establishment to the ground.''

Blood-haze replaced all pain and struggle in a single,
blessed wave. Filled with blackness, his body thinking for
him, Fireclaw whirled, drew his mighty greatsword with a
joyous ringing shout.

He leapt toward Oln Woeck.

A snuffling sound came from the pistol-bearing guard
standing over the Saracens.

Fireclaw knew a different sort of blackness.

XXXVI:

Ship of the Cloud-Tops

They say, "Why does he not bring a sign from his Lord?" . . . Had We destroyed them with a chastisement aforetime, they would have said, "Our Lord, why didst Thou not send a Messenger, so that we might have followed Thy signs before that we were humiliated and degraded?"

—The *Koran*, Sura XX

Whatever medicament was in the pístol-dart, Ayesha thought, it could make no claim to harmlessness.

She mopped at the unconscious Fireclaw's sweat-sheened face with a dampened bit of toweling from the cabin's little lavatory. In the hammock, slung between a pair of steel hooks embedded in smooth-painted walls, he swung back and forth as if in nightmare, weeping, grimacing, muttering in several languages incomprehensible syllables.

His perspiration reeked of something evil.

At her knee, the bear-dog Ursi lay uneasy, eyes closed at the moment, his square jaw resting upon giant overlapping paws, seeming to take some heart himself in her ministrations to his master. The pygmy marmoset Sagheer groomed himself upon one arm of Ayesha's low chair, nipping at imaginary tangles in his pristine fur.

He smelled of disinfectant.

Almost as if in imitation, Po ran his short, curved ebon beak through overlapping gray-white belly-feathers, ducked his head beneath his wings in short thrusts, combed his long black flight-plumes with an uncomfortable-looking stretch of the neck, twisted round in comic wise to pay similar attentions to his scarlet-orange tail.

He shook himself, wings flapping, shrieked, and filled the air with an annoying blizzard of preening-powder and little floating clots of lacy down. Sagheer sneezed, a tiny *chiff* of a noise, then glared at the parrot in resentment.

The room throbbed, as it had each second since Ayesha had awakened, with the deeper sound of engines.

It appeared proper to Ayesha that, at least in recompense for his rescuing her, it was now her turn to comfort Sedrich, in his injury if not in his grief. But, as she had already had sufficient opportunity to observe, life was seldom that symmetrical a thing. Fireclaw would recover, with or without her help.

It was Mochamet al Rotshild who was in a state of shock, and not only in reaction to the death of Lishabha.

Nearby, the much-subdued Commodore had puzzled out the secret of the golden sun-disks which decorated each of the staterooms—or cells—they had been given. The obscene tongue was a latch. Once released, it had gently lifted of its own accord upon a spring-loaded hinge. Now the reddish sun-light of a late afternoon streamed through the thick glazed porthole it had concealed.

Photographs framed and hung upon the walls of this room, hers, were of Mediterranean fisherfolk and their colorful, triangular-sailed boats, although where this "Sun Incarnate" might have come by them, she could not quite bring herself to guess.

Mochamet al Rotshild leaned against the wall beside the window, staring down and outward, as absent from the little room as he could be and still yet remain. Ayesha imagined she could discern a whiter cast to his hair and beard, more wrinkles about his eyes. Such was not possible, she knew. It required more than a single day to write the traces of tragedy, however unbearable, upon a man's face. Yet she often forgot how old a man he was, perhaps because he never seemed to remember it himself. The sudden killing of Lishabha appeared to have reminded him.

Fireclaw stirred, thrashing, his steel-and-fiberglass prosthetic all but knocking her to the floor from the arm of the chair where she sat beside the low-slung sailor's-bed. She understood but little of Helvetian, a word here, another there, recognizable from her studies of dead European languages. But the name Frae often recurred, as did fragmentary utterances addressed to the warrior's mother and father.

How very odd, she thought, considering the terrible events which had placed this warrior in her care, that Fireclaw never once uttered the name Oln Woeck.

That unpleasant individual—a premeditated murderer, if she had understood the boy-ruler's words aright—was absent altogether, having been dragged away somewhere by the copper-kilt guardsmen after Fireclaw had been rendered unconscious. They reminded her of the Roman legionnaires pictured in her history textbooks. She knew she ought to wonder what would now become of the old man.

But could not bring herself to care.

The rest of them had been brought back to this place—the animals, well tended, had been brought here then, as well— where, in one of the adjoining rooms, its round-arched door now lying open so that Ayesha could shuffle back and forth to care for recuperating occupants in each, the Rabbi David Shulieman lay in sleep induced, not by a dart-borne poison, but by wounds she feared were mortal, despite the fact that they had awakened to find him bathed and bandaged by some expert who had entered while they slept, upon first being brought aboard, and while their clothing and belongings had been likewise cleaned.

And searched.

Unlike Fireclaw, they had not been left their weapons.

She wondered which of them was being insulted by this gesture. Or was it yet another of Zhu Yuan-Coyotl's experiments? Her first, unguarded thought had startled her: that it would be a strange death for a gentle scholar to die, should, despite her most fervent wishes, David's injuries claim him. Then she remembered Archimedes—and was proud in a way that David had not fallen, a helpless victim of someone else's battle, but with a singed beard and hands blackened by burnt powder, in the exultant midst of striking down her enemies.

Barbaric!

This menacing conceit she again pushed away from herself before it had opportunity to take further shape, spreading warmth, as it did so, to recesses of her mind and body whose existence she was attempting to forget. Or at least to disregard. Scarce time had she to regain her sensibilities more than to that extent, when the beast-helmeted guards had taken them away to Zhu Yuan-Coyotl's audience chamber.

"Oln Woeck!"

Ursi's ears pricked.

He lifted his head from his paws.

Fireclaw stopped stirring, opened his eyes, and sat up, all in a single swift moment, his left arm crossing his naked chest, seizing Ayesha by the shoulder.

Mochamet al Rotshild turned from the window, blinking, then went back to gazing downward at whatever alien landscape this vast ship-of-the-air traveled over at the moment.

"Girl, where is Oln Woeck?"

Sagheer chittered a warning.

Ignoring the marmoset, the flushed and sweaty Fireclaw repeated his demand in Arabic. Ayesha clamped her jaw, determined not to cry out against the pain the warrior's clenching fingers inflicted upon her collarbone without intention.

"I do not know, Fireclaw."

Realizing he was hurting her, he released her shoulder, swung hard-muscled legs across the hammock-edge, and tipped himself onto the floor, landing with a sure-footed bounce. He put a hand to his brow, shook his head, spoke some phrase in his native language.

"He says," Mochamet al Rotshild uttered with a dispirited sigh, "that he has had nothing but one headache after another since entering this land. He makes a jest, I think."

The Saracen shook his own head.

"It is difficult to tell. He is a strange man."

"No jest," Fireclaw answered in Arabic, a twinge of humor in his voice nonetheless, "the simple truth."

He patted Ursi upon the head, picked up his pistol-belt and dagger from the back of the chair where Ayesha had laid them, wrapped them about his middle. He slung the greatsword *Murderer* over his back, then turned to Mochamet al Rotshild.

"Where are we? *Chayn . . . ham chassaanagh?*"

The Commodore stepped back from the window, weariness in his every motion, and offered the view to Fireclaw.

"I have never seen such country. It looks like the surface of the moon. I confess that it would not surprise me if it were. I had thought we Judaeo-Saracens were the richest, most progressive and advanced people in the world. I am stunned, however, at the artifices we have only thus far discovered here."

Far beneath them, the land was, indeed, barren.

To Fireclaw it resembled a burnt-off field following a cloudburst—sand-choked, washed over, deep-gullied, without a trace of greenery or a single rounded contour. Its color ranged from yellow-red to yellow-brown. It seemed to go on forever.

He pushed his face against the glass.

The flanks of the vessel in which they traveled could not be seen from so small a window.

Mochamet al Rotshild explained to the Helvetian what had transpired from the time the pistol-dart had taken him—Oln Woeck's absence, David Shulieman's condition—adding that the Princess Ayesha (who became embarrassed at this mention of her name) had for several hours watched over him, speaking to him, soothing him through his convulsions, bathing his sweat-streaked face.

Leaving the window, Fireclaw smiled, reached out, and patted the girl's blushing cheek—this liberty Sagheer also permitted, this time without a noise—with a hand whose gentleness came to her as a shock. The attention, she realized with unsortable feelings, was much as he might have given one of his animals.

"Shguhran jazeelan," he told her, searching awkwardly for words. "I am sorry I hurt your shoulder. You are a good person."

Without another syllable, the Helvetian strode across the stateroom, Ursi padding after him, toward the wounded rabbi's quarters, while Ayesha struggled once again with feelings she dare not examine, and thus could never come to an accommodation with.

Po made noises which sounded to the Princess like mocking laughter.

By the time she had gathered her wits—and her pygmy marmoset—in sufficient degree to follow the man, she received yet another surprise. David Shulieman—who had but a few hours ago lain unconscious, feverish, and weak within the netting of his own hammock—was sitting up conversing with Fireclaw.

". . . by those who experiment with kites and suchlike," she heard the rabbi tell the warrior in Helvetian, filling gaps with specialized vocabulary from scientific Arabic.

"Nanam chanaa chabhgham, I see," Fireclaw replied. "Some kite we have here!"

Shulieman smiled.

"It is true that heated gases, trapped within a large, lightweight container—tissue-paper sacking works quite well—can be made to carry it upward and away. I myself have tried that—in the process almost setting fire to the rooftops of the unfortunate neighborhood nearest the gymnasium where I was educated."

Fireclaw laughed, the pain-lines around his eyes disappearing for a moment.

He sat upon one arm of a chair, his moccasined feet flat upon its seat. No one of the Saracen party seemed willing to use the furniture here in the correct fashion, the girl thought as she watched the men. Not even herself. Perhaps this betrayed in them an unwillingness to acknowledge the permanence of their incarceration.

As if in answer to her unspoken thought, the warrior nodded, rising to his feet.

"I misdoubt," he told Shulieman, "whether the same principle's in application here. 'Twould take a walloping lot of hot air!"

The rabbi chuckled, then grimaced as a twinge shot through his body. Ayesha's first thought—for in those characteristics that we most detested in them, we are the children of our parents—was to rush between him and the warrior, ordering the latter out of the room, the former to lie once again flat upon his back.

She controlled the urge.

"Hydrogen gas," she offered instead, at which words both men looked toward her, Fireclaw turning upon his heel.

"Recall, David, how you showed me that the hydrogenic and oxygenic humors might be separated from the water they comprise by electrical current? The hydrogen rose from the receiving vessel, once we turned it right side up, burning with an all-but-invisible blue flame, well above the candle we ignited it with."

Shulieman nodded.

"So it did, Ayesha, so it did."

He turned to Fireclaw.

"Well, then, here is one Jew grateful that he has always acted in accordance with the injunctions against tobacco to which his Moslem brothers subscribe. I trust this Zhu fellow of whom Fireclaw speaks has seen to similar precautionary measures aboard his mighty vessel. To paraphrase our large friend here, it would burn with a walloping lot of invisible blue flame!"

There was a puzzled expression upon the Helvetian's face. "Hydrogen?"

Some explaining was required then, during which Fireclaw, of whom they had at first meeting shared the opinion of the

Sun Incarnate's guards, again surprised both Saracens with the depth of his knowledge of the sciences—all of it wrested out of nature's jealous grasp by his own continuous, stubborn experimentation—and with the quickness of his mind where his own discoveries failed him.

If in no other wise, the boy-king to whom she had been in wedlock promised (and who had given them such a name to call him by that Ayesha decided to keep calling him "Shrimp"—at least within the privacy of her own mind—for the sake of keeping her impressions of her future husband to manageable proportion) had been correct in his assessment of the Helvetian's genius.

Had great Archimedes himself been more like Fireclaw, she thought, one more anonymous Roman soldier's blood would have been mingled with the sand, doing no great injury to the course of history, while the ancient Greek philosopher, his studies interrupted but a moment, would have returned to the contemplation of his geometric diagrams.

Perhaps the world would have turned out a better place.

Not feeling this a proper setting in which to give such thoughts a voice, Ayesha opened her mouth, intending to add another word or two concerning her experiments with hydrogen. She was interrupted, before she could begin, by an earsplitting shriek from the next room. It was Po, the parrot, making noises they had never heard from him before.

"What in the name of God or Goddess was that?"

The question could have come from any of them, thinking in Helvetian as they were. Before any of the three reacted, the parrot's shriek was followed by a meaty thump. David Shulieman began struggling to remove himself from the hammock.

Fireclaw laid a broad, work-callused hand upon the wounded rabbi's chest, pushing him backward.

"Spare yourself, friend Saracen, lest you renew your injuries."

He turned toward the door. Together, he and the Princess rushed into the adjoining cabin. Upon the carpeted floor, they discovered the inert form of Mochamet al Rotshild, still near the opened porthole, lying upon his face, his parrot perched upon his shoulder blades, tugging at the man's clothing with his beak.

As she had often seen the captain do, Ayesha thrust an outstretched hand against Po's gray-scaled legs. The bird climbed, stiff-limbed and comical despite the circumstances, upon her finger, let her carry him across the room to a steel hammock-hook.

There he perched, his feathers ruffled, his white-rimmed black-in-yellow eyes dilating.

With all the gentleness he was capable of, Fireclaw turned Mochamet al Rotshild over, surprised to find that the man yet lived. The deep-set eyes, shut tight against some inner agony, forced themselves open to behold the younger man.

"I will be damned . . . I had not looked for something like this to happen to me for a few more years yet . . . it is difficult to breathe," he complained with a wheeze which underlined his words. "The pain within my left arm is nigh unbearable."

Fireclaw nodded, his good hand massaging the fallen man's arm which was curled up in a cramp. After a few short, gasping breaths, the Commodore spoke also of a feeling that steel bands were crushing his chest. This speech seemed to exhaust him.

He shut his eyes again.

"This thing," Fireclaw offered, thinking of his father's death, "I've seen ere now."

He looked up into the dark, widened eyes of the girl who knelt upon the floor beside him.

"Ayesha, I greatly fear—"

A noise came at another door.

The louvered panel swung aside.

From the corridor beyond, a single guardsman, like his fellows copper-kilt and helmeted, entered their stateroom, one gauntleted hand upon the pommel of an all-too-familiar holstered pistol, the other pounding once upon his breastplate in salute.

"Sir!" he announced with military briskness, in flawless, if somewhat overloud, Helvetian. "As chief commander of the personal bodyguard of the Sun Incarnate, Zhu Yuan-Coyotl, I . . ."

The man's voice tapered off as he beheld the scene he had interrupted within the suite.

"I take it"—Fireclaw looked up with a bitter expression at the black-helmeted figure—"that your child-tyrant wants to summon one of us again. If so, he'll have to wait."

The guardsman shook his head.

"Uh, no, sir, in truth it is not the ruler of the Han-Meshika who seeks you."

He removed his helmet, revealing to them a fair-complected face, surrounded by a shaggy mane of red-blond hair.

The eyes within that face were icy blue.

"It is I myself who request leave to speak with you, Sedrich Sedrichsohn, first to apologize for having shot you. Also to inform you that I am your son, Owald."

XXXVII:

The Wanderer

Do the people reckon that they will be left to say "We believe," and will not be tried?

—The *Koran*, Sura XXIX

The armored figure froze a moment, held a hand out as if to tell the others to wait, then reached down and manipulated something in the helmet he held within the crook of his arm. Insanely, he spoke a word into the helmet, then looked up with a satisfied expression.

Less than a minute passed before they had more company.

Once inside the door, the young man stepped aside for two of his copper-kilted minions, one of them bearing a bright-colored rigid box swinging by a handle from his fist.

Without a word, these two shouldered Fireclaw and Ayesha out of the way—a small movement across the stateroom caught the Helvetian warrior's eye: the Rabbi David Shulieman was out of his hammock, a curious expression on his face, leaning against the frame of the connecting door—and opened the Saracen sea-captain's clothing.

Ayesha rose, hurried to her tutor.

Letting his eyes stray now and again to the man who claimed to be his son, Fireclaw had stepped back, seating himself in a low chair to watch what happened next.

The pair standing in the adjoining cabin doorway held a brief, muted exchange in Arabic—the Princess Ayesha pointing with angry gestures several times to the man's heavy bandages—after which the curly-haired bespectacled scholar glanced helplessly toward the ceiling, perhaps appealing to some deity, and shrugged.

He allowed the girl to help him out of Fireclaw's sight, back to the sickbed he'd just left.

From the handled kit-box the guardsmen removed a number of instruments foreign to the Helvetian, passing them over Mochamet al Rotshild's supine body, along his arms, upon one occasion lifting him so that one of the objects might take the old man's measure from the middle of his back to the center of his chest.

That implement, once unfolded, firmed into a C-shape with the careful tightening of several thumb-screws, resembled one of the calipers Fireclaw used to test dimensions of a workpiece upon his lathe. The chest-end of the device held a tiny gray-green glowing window which the guardsmen watched with the greatest of concentration, here and there remarking to one another upon some esoteric point of interest.

After a short while, they turned once again to their commander, who stood leaning against the corridor-side wall with his arms folded across his black-armored chest. They uttered no more than a dozen words, in a language Fireclaw couldn't follow. If it were a question, it was not couched in the language spoken in the audience chamber.

Nodding, Owald replied in kind, receiving an answer.

To Fireclaw, he said in Helvetian: "Your Saracen friend's an old man, Fa—Sedrich Fireclaw. E'en without proper treatment, he could recover, living on in vigorous health for another twenty years. Or with it, he could expire tomorrow."

"No different," Fireclaw observed, "from any of the rest of us. What troubles him? Is it his heart?"

Owald shrugged.

Medicines were administered with the aid of barreled needles, thrust into blood vessels beneath the skin, not unlike the dart which had been used upon the Helvetian warrior. With some effort, the guardsmen lifted Mochamet al Rotshild, who was beginning to stir a little upon his own now, into the nearby hammock.

Once he was comfortable, they folded up their devices, closed their case upon them. With an alien word of permission from the man who called himself Owald Sedrichsohn, they departed.

Owald crossed the little room in two deep strides, unlatched his broad, heavy weapons belt—Fireclaw noted pouches its entire length, which he presumed carried extra drug-darts, and a short, broad dagger hanging opposite the pistol—let the scabbarded pistol drop to the floor, along with his smoke-visored eagle helmet. Finding a second chair, he seated himself without relaxing, his blue eyes fastened upon his father's brown as his father's were upon his.

Again, a small movement at the other side of the room caught both men's momentary attention.

The Princess Ayesha stood against the doorway, a neutral expression upon her features, the posture of her body—her arms were folded across her breasts—telling them, whatever propriety might demand, that she'd not leave them to their privacy.

Silence hung palpable for an unbearable time.

"You know," Owald essayed at last, "I'd planned for years the proper wise to begin this conversation, but now—"

Fireclaw interrupted. "You knew—"

"Aught there was to know," the younger man answered, "aught about you, about your work, your woman, your great dogs. I see the questions boiling behind your eyes, Sedrich Fireclaw. Perhaps the best wise to begin is to go back many years, to explain why, knowing aught about you, I could ne'er come to you till first you came to me.

"When I was but a boy . . ."

2

"Owald!"

The young man turned his head a moment, toward the calling voice. His father's latest bodyguard-companion took this as an opportunity—he had been interrupted by that voice, in mid-harangue—to teach the lad a painful lesson.

The huge, meaty fist whistled toward the side of Owald's head.

Craack!

The eunuch danced back howling, cradling a forearm in which both bones had been broken.

Baring well-formed, even teeth in what might have been mistaken for a smile, Owald lowered his own forearm—after having snapped it upward in a dynamic block which had taken the older man by surprise—but didn't relax his guard. He could never relax his guard, not in this company. For some reason he'd never understood, this man, like all the others who'd passed through their lives, resented him, jealous of each moment the boy and his father spent together.

Veins standing out beneath tattoos upon his temple, the injured eunuch lunged forward. Owald caught him with an upraised foot, not a thrust, in the solar plexus.

The man stopped as if he'd hit a wall.

Owald let his foot drop, danced for a flashing moment in a tight circle which brought the same foot slamming round again into the tattooed, shaven head.

Eyes empty, the eunuch sagged straight downward to his knees.

He fell upon his face.

Well, that was done with, the boy thought, at least for the moment.

Owald bore the scars of many such "lessons." His father (Owald was charitable enough to believe the older man was unaware of the inevitable jealous resentment) had put the eunuch in charge of the boy's deportment whenever he himself was absent.

Always he felt watched, though for what actions or betraying signs in his personality, he could never learn. He was not deaf to whisperings behind his back about "bad blood," whatever that phrase meant. Whatever crimes he or his blood had unintentionally committed, it meant cruel punishment for every least imagined infraction—or, as the boy grew taller, more skilled at a method of defense he had secretly himself invented and practiced, exchanges such as this which had established certain ground rules. The odd thing was that Owald never begrudged the times the two men, the eunuch and his father, spent together at night, after the single candle had been snuffed out.

But of course, Owald Olnsohn had never liked his father.

It took but a moment to observe that his "guardian" still breathed. Snatching up his coarse-woven robe, Owald crossed the compound, walking toward the Cult-Brother who'd called his name.

"Yes, Brother Hansl, what is it?"

Hansl Niemandsohn was a year older than Owald—and a foot shorter. His shoulders were narrow, his watery pale eyes useless beyond the length of his spindly extended arm. The surname he'd been given upon entering the Brotherhood was at once something of a courtesy and a joke, considering his unknown antecedents.

"It's the old witch-woman, Owald, Ilse Sedrichsfrau. A traveler stopped outside our gate with a message. She's asking for you, insisting you come. I don't know why."

Owald flipped the plain-fashioned cossack over his lion-maned head, wiggled his broad shoulders into the garment which, like all the clothing he'd ever been given to wear, had been too small for those shoulders within a few short weeks.

He nodded at Brother Hansl.

The "witch-woman" had taken interest in him as long as he could remember, one of the few bright lights in his otherwise grim life. She had taught him many things, suggested this method of fighting to him, had even helped him learn to read, despite his father's wishes to the contrary. He liked her, and she'd been ill of late.

Perhaps she needed him to do some chores for her.

All his short life, the Brotherhood had increasingly prospered. About him, tattooed, robed, and shaven Brothers of the Cult wielded brooms and mops and leaf-rakes, scouring the already spotless compound, sweeping up a thimbleful of soil and the few dead leaves the wind had yesternight blown there, washing ornately glazed windows, polishing the brass appointments of rich-furnished doors, watering the many decorative plantings, bustling from the cool shade of awning-draped buildings—chapel, meeting-hall, infirmary, the new dormitories—into the clean-swept, sunlit courtyard, flagged with imported green-veined marble from the far north.

The many lawns were thick and green.

The gateposts—though the gates were never closed, lest some benefactor lose the opportunity to contribute to the Brotherhood—were fashioned of wrought iron, salvaged from some abandoned smithy hereabouts, overlaid with sheets of beaten gold.

Thanking Brother Hansl, Owald crossed the courtyard, told the proctor he was going out—Owald was not a member of the Brotherhood, nor under its discipline; he'd never been tapped, nor had he any desire in yon direction—since his father was away upon one of his many pilgrimages. Once out of the compound he began dog-trotting up the road toward the overgrown ruins where the old woman lived.

The weather-grayed shack was in worse condition than he'd ever seen it before. Yellow weeds grew shoulder-high about it. Unpainted shutters hung limp over broken windowpanes of tallowed paper. The little stoop-porch was missing many of its floorboards. He knew, whene'er it rained, the unpatched roof leaked. This he'd offered thrice to repair. He'd been each time refused.

Behind the ramshackle little building lay the circular weed-grown jumble of fallen stones, of broken, fire-blackened columns which he knew—had never spoken to anyone about—was still the site of occasional clandestine gatherings by a group of women, for the most part old ones, which called itself the Sisterhood.

A strange feminine parody, it was, of the Cult his father led, the Cult which had been, for all of his short life, the center of the village's religious existence. As a boy, he'd sneaked upon the circle such nights, listening, sometimes learning. He'd come to believe Ilse Sedrichsfrau had always known of this, yet, in tacit return upon his silence, had herself told no one of his trespass.

Taking care to avoid patches of rotted flooring, Owald stepped onto the porch, rapped with his knuckles upon the frame of a door swinging upon but a single leather hinge.

"Owald? Is it you, lad?"

The voice from inside was weak, but the syllables were crisp. To the boy, after the brilliant sunlight, peering into the humble dwelling was like looking into a cave.

He stepped inside, brushing with an absent gesture at his eyelashes to remove a fresh strand of spiderwebbing which he hadn't seen stretched across the doorway.

"Yes, Ilse Sedrichsfrau, 'tis I."

"Come in, lad, come closer."

Inside, as his light-drenched eyes adjusted, young Owald could make out the old woman sitting upon a narrow cot, her bony knees draped with a patchy knitted coverlet, a crushed wicker basket of clothing beside her, her mending in her lap.

Her hands were white—he knew they'd feel icy to the touch, they ever had—the ropy veins upon them blue-black in this light. Beneath the short, well-combed white hair, her eyes, though they were surrounded with wrinkled, sagging flesh, were bright and clear.

Owald pulled a wobbling stool beside the cot.

"Are you not well today, Ilse?"

"You're right, lad, I'm not well."

She sighed, tidied up the mending in her lap, brushed at strands of thinning hair lying upon her forehead. She folded her pale hands across her thin frame.

"In fact, I'll not last through this coming night. The

Goddess, for all Her sense of humor, sets no great store in surprises. Sometimes She lets you know about these things."

A pang went through the boy, followed by a surprising feeling of embarrassment.

"But, Ilse—"

"Now, now, if I'm not disturbed about it, there's no reason for you to be. I've lived a long life. An eventful one, though, save for those precious moments spent with you, the happiest of times are far behind me. These last years are, for the most part, best set aside, not included in the count. I'll have peace now, surcease from poignant memory—from this damnable aching in my bones! I just wanted to say goodbye to you, and to give you something belonging to you."

With a twist Owald himself might not have managed, Ilse reached upward to a shelf fastened to the wall behind her cot, pulled out a small, battered leather-bound book.

She handed it to Owald.

"What's this, Ilse? 'Tisn't mine."

"By right of inheritance it is," she answered. "It belonged to your father. Well I ought to know. I gave it to him when he was a good deal younger than you are."

"My father . . ."

Owald leafed through the book. It had been blank when given as a gift; now it was full of neatly-wrought sketches free of smudges, of arithmetic calculations, of brief cryptic passages concerning the fashioning of such things as leaf-springs, the cutting of screw-threads, the mixing of caustic bluing salts.

"But, Ilse, 'tis the notebook of an artisan. A blacksmith, at a guess. My father—"

"Your father was that artisan, my lad. Sedrich was the name I gave him, son of Sedrich, himself the son of Owald, after whom you're called. You're my own grandson—don't you be looking at me in that wise! I may be old, but I'm damned well not senile! I'm that glad to be going away ere such befalls me. You're the son of my son Sedrich, self-exiled from Helvetia upon the very day I ripped you from your dead mother's body—such a fresh pretty thing she was—to see you stolen by the wormy apple who now claims to be your father."

"But, Ilse . . . ."

"Ask Old Helga, the fletcher's wife. She's an ancient, too, like me, beyond fearing any reprisal the Cult might threaten. Ask anyone in this village with the spine to speak the truth—though I fear you'll be a long time looking for one such, these bitter days. I let you grow up as you did that you *would* grow up, but the time's short now. It's past time you knew the truth."

Owald's mouth hung open, wordless.

This Ilse took immediate advantage of, speaking first of greathearted Sedrich Owaldsohn, her blacksmith husband, of clever and inquisitive Sedrich Sedrichsohn, her son—the father-in-truth young Owald Sedrichsohn had never been allowed to know.

She spoke, too, of beautiful Frae Hethristochter, of her loathing for the evil suiter Oln Woeck, of grim shining *Murderer* and the mighty and terrible deeds accomplished with it, of the ancient rise of the Brotherhood, the concomitant fall of the Sisterhood, of a lifetime of change, little of it for the better.

She spoke to Owald for a considerable time, at the end of which her voice had begun to rasp. There were salt-tears running down her wrinkled cheeks. Yet she was still in command of her voice when she pointed out a glazed bicolored pottery of apple cider sitting cool in the shade upon a rickety table beneath a shuttered window.

The boy fetched it.

They shared a drink.

"No one can say what became of my Sedrich."

Ilse spoke after a long silence. The tears had ceased to flow. They would never flow again.

"Save that, wounded as he was, believing you and Frae dead, I'd guess he pointed his face westward where his mind was e'er straying, toward the Great Blue Mountains."

Owald rose from the stool.

"I've no weapon of power such as *Murderer*, but I swear by

Jesus' suffering—or by your Goddess, Ilse—I'll slay my fa—
Oln Woeck when he returns from pilgriming in the south-
land.''

The old woman shook her head.

"Pilgriming, my wrinkled old behind! He trades there with
the Invader, as did your mother's father, Hethri Parcifal,
whose sideline he 'inherited,' to the enrichment of the coffers
of the Cult, while villagers go hungry for the merciless
tithing!''

Her voice dropped suddenly.

"Owald, hear me. There's no such object as a sword of
power. There's naught but iron, and the ordinary powers men
of power—powers of the mind, I tell you—have learned to put
into it.''

She sighed, changing the subject.

"Ah, well, I can't say 'twould be an altogether evil thing to
do, filleting yon blue-templed old—but 'twould be a waste of
effort. He'll pass off in his time, as I'm about to do, and with
less grace. And more fear, methinks. Meantime, letting him
live's the best revenge. It must be a miserable thing to be Oln
Woeck.''

"What should I do . . . Grandmother?''

Ilse smiled at the boy's use of the word. Tears threatened to
spring forth once more. Controlling them, she replied,
"Whate'er you will, lad. 'Tis what your father suffered to
achieve. Wreak whate'er of yourself you wish to—''

"I'll find him, if he yet lives.''

Ilse raised a hand to pat him upon the knee nearest.

"You please me beyond expectation, Owald Sedrichsohn. I
couldn't ask it of you, nor suggest it. There's great peril to the
westward, little hope of safety. Your father may be long
dead.''

"Then I'll find his bones—his father's greatsword—then
return to do Oln Woeck an unlooked-for mercy.''

Ilse sighed.

"Men. Find my Sedrich living, and you'll not part him from
his father's sword—though this might be the undertaking to
convince him. Tell him what I ne'er had a chance to. I loved

him as a child. I was that proud of what he grew to be, albeit most of the growing was perforce accomplished upon one single, terrible—"

"I'll tell him, Grandmother, I'll—Grandmother? Ilse!"

It was as if the old woman had nodded off to sleep, one hand resting upon her mending, the other hanging, relaxed, over the edge of her cot. A gentle smile lay upon her careworn face. Bending close beside her, he could feel no breath against his cheek, no pulse within her thin wrist, nor at the base of her neck.

Owald sat beside her in silence for a long while, watching a small spider repair the damage he'd done to its web entering the hut. Midday came, later on the lengthening shadows of the afternoon. At last he covered Ilse with the knitted blanket she'd draped across her knees. Taking with him the little leather notebook, he ducked beneath the spider's web, taking his last leave of the hovel.

Her Sisters would give Ilse proper burial.

He'd left the compound and the village before dark.

3

Unnoticed, either by the two men or the dark-eyed girl who listened past a barrier of foreign language, the engines of the airship throbbed inside the room.

"The rest of it," Owald finished at length, "is simple enough, though a long time in the happening.

"I headed west, but was neither as lucky nor as wise as my father. I lost aught I carried in the sea-wide river which divides the forest from the plains. I was captured by the Sioux ere I saw the Great Blue Mountains. In chains transported, as a slave, to their stony feet. Not a tale I'm much proud of."

Fireclaw had risen during Owald's speech. He stood staring out the odd round window at the mountains passing beneath the great ship. Now he turned to his son.

"How'd you come to soldier for His Imperial What'sit?"

Owald glanced round about to see who'd overheard the blasphemous epithet. Then he relaxed, laughing.

"Zhu Yuan-Coyotl told you the truth. Not a thing e'er leaves Han-Meshika, Father, artifices, knowledge, people—in particular that which first comes in from the outside. 'Tis our—'tis its—greatest strength. No one outside knows aught about it, while it knows aught that passes in this whole wide world."

Fireclaw dragged the other chair beside that his son occupied. Elbows upon his knees, Owald leaned forward.

"While impressed by my prowess as a warrior, the savages were afraid to keep me as their own. Far from being the model slave, I became property to a succession of increasingly dissatisfied owners, sold further and further west."

He moved closer.

"We may even have crossed paths upon one occasion. I believe I was among a number of 'guests' who stopped at your ranch for water and a rest. I never saw you, but guessed later from mutterings about our host, the mighty Fireclaw, who you might be."

Owald hesitated, then added, "Slave-runners have a potion with which they treat the only food they give their captives. It numbs the will, but leaves the sensibilities intact. I'd have given you proper greeting at your ranch, were it not for the fact I never thought to do it."

He shuddered.

"The drug also dulls the fighting-spirit, and the capacity to breed more slaves, so it is withdrawn once captives are brought within Han-Meshika. I learned afterward it's used there as medicament for certain distempers of the blood."

He leaned back again.

"I came at last into the Sun's domain, where, drawing some attention with my fighting skills, I came into his service, eventually joining and coming to lead the elite contingent of his guard."

Fireclaw, his brow wrinkled, opened his mouth to speak. Owald interrupted.

"'Tis not as strange as you might think, Father. The bodyguard entire consists of naught but outsiders like myself, an elite corps of foreigners—Saracens, Mughals, Incas,

Nubians—selected from misadventurers who've wandered in, ne'er to be permitted to leave."

He folded his hands in his lap.

"Perhaps one trespasser in ten thousand's chosen thus, men unattached to any domestic faction—no ties, no connections, no family, no friends. Zhu Yuan-Coyotl doesn't trust his own people—not e'en his ordinary standing reserves—well enough to supply them with effective weaponry. To this policy, in fact, which he didn't himself devise, is laid the Crystal Empire's long-lasting peaceable stability."

"To that, and to those Dreamers of his, whate'er they may be. Tell of those few," Fireclaw asked, "who're permitted arms."

His son produced a grim smile.

"The selectees are hated, feared by the populace. Outnumbered millions to one, they'd perish in an instant were it not for Zhu Yuan-Coyotl's official countenance.

"Upon this account they're considered safe to issue firearms. They owe their allegiance, not to mention their continued existence, to the Sun alone, the single man they serve— thus preserving themselves—by defending his life."

Fireclaw nodded his head.

"That sounds to me like an intelligent arrangement."

"As it's been," Owald answered, nodding, "some thirty generations in all. But this you'll be seeing for yourself, and soon enough, Father."

"We're bound now for the capital city—where you'll take your place beside me in the guard!"

SURA THE SIXTH: 1420 A.H.—

The Crystal Empire

Hast thou not regarded thy Lord, how He has stretched out the shadow? Had He willed, He would have made it still. Then We appointed the sun, to be a guide to it; thereafter We seize it to Ourselves, drawing it gently.
   —The *Holy Koran*, Sura XXV, *Salvation*

XXXVIII:

The Ice-Mountain

It was by some mercy of God that thou wast gentle to them.

—The *Koran*, Sura III

Her arms still folded, Ayesha cleared her throat.

Fireclaw looked up at her, where she stood leaning in the doorway. She raised her eyebrows, then glanced at Owald.

"*Charjooh*. Your pardon, Princess!"

The older of the two Helvetians couched exaggerated politeness in reasonably good Arabic.

"Have you followed aught of this—any of it within your proper concern?"

"It was not my wish to pry, sir, *chanaa muthachassibh*." She gave a shrug.

"*Laa thaghthaam,* one word in three, perhaps."

The warrior laughed.

Thinking now of David Shulieman lying wounded in the next room, of Mochamet al Rotshild breathing uneasily in his hammock, of the dead girl Lishabha, of Fireclaw's own brother-in-law Knife Thrower, of poor murdered Traveling

Short Bear, of Dove Blossom, and of too many others, dead or dying, simply that she herself might be brought, unwilling, to this place, she felt a wave of sudden anger surge through her.

"This young man," she added, "your son, would have you don the livery of those butchers who—"

Fireclaw put up his hand, palm outward.

"Those butchers who saved lately our trespassing hides from other and possibly worse butchers."

Absently he shifted his gaze to the hand he held up, turning it to see the palm.

He let it drop.

"And you forget, girl, or perhaps you do not know, that I have done some butchering in my time."

He let his eyes drop to the floor. An inward and grim expression had washed across his weathered face momentarily, then vanished. She guessed that he was thinking now upon his own ghosts.

And of Oln Woeck.

"I have some butchering left to do even yet."

Briefly, and with an explanatory word to Owald, he sketched out for the Princess much of what had been told him, omitting, she could tell, only those parts most personal or painful to relate to one who was, upon startling realization, still a stranger to him. He told her of the Goddess whom his mother had served, and in whom, he seemed to realize only as he spoke, he had long since ceased to believe. If so, she thought, then it had been a gentle parting.

". . . though why it is any of your concern, I do not know. This boy here, my son, finding him is the only reason I came along with Oln Woeck upon this foolish expedition of yours. My mother dearly wanted . . . his own mother was very . . ."

He stopped, perhaps in the belief that he had gone too far.

Yes, thought Ayesha, he, too, was thinking about ghosts, many of them dead far longer than Knife Thrower or Lishabha. From the casual utterances of others—she understood Helvetian better than she had admitted—she had pieced together Fireclaw's story during their journey and knew more about him than he was aware of.

She remembered again the ancient saying among her own mother's people: "In my weakness, I fled to the desert to escape mine enemies—and the desert made me strong."

Now she nodded, merely indicating understanding, knowing as she did so that it was the same economical gesture his dead wife might have made, communicating a deeper sympathy than any third observer might have taken from the act.

That a lifetime of tears was hidden somewhere behind the eyes of this war-shaven slaughterer, she understood as well. Another watcher might have dismissed them as a weakness or hypocritical sentiment. Yet she could see the effort he spent undertaking to stifle them. She could not, she knew, bring herself to condemn either the man or the feelings he was attempting not to show her.

An odd thought struck her.

At least, if Fireclaw were to join the bodyguard of Zhu Yuan-Coyotl, he would be staying—she doubted anyone could hold the man against his will—within the Sun's domain. For some reason—she was beginning to know the reason, but not yet ready to acknowledge it—her heart was lifted by the thought.

Something *pinged* within the room.

Owald shouted out a single word.

The door swung wide before yet another of the copper-kilted warriors, this one pushing before him a wheeled tray, its odd-shaped contents covered with a quilted swatch of cloth.

"I took upon myself the liberty of ordering a meal."

Owald dismissed the soldier, wheeling the covered cart into the center of the room.

"Our journey draws near its end. You must both be well prepared for what that will bring."

Strange aromas began invading the air around the cart.

"The truest test of courage is not the first bite of a foreign food," Sedrich observed, "but the second."

Owald joined Ayesha in laughter, perhaps rather more than

the jest truly merited, and whisked the insulated cover from the serving tray.

Abruptly, a gong sounded somewhere outside in the corridor.

Owald looked up, startled. With a ripping noise, he peeled back a section of his sleeve, apparently consulting a timepiece he carried strapped about his wrist.

"Damn!"

Rising, he gathered up his heavy pistol-belt and eagle-headed helmet from the floor where he had dropped them.

"Come with me, the both of you," he growled, then in laboriously slow Helvetian for the Princess' benefit, "We must have picked up a tail wind. I'd like to have eaten something."

He glanced wistfully at the cart.

"We go, instead, to be tourists, to witness the sight of sights. Have no fear, ma'am, for your sleeping companions. I'll send someone to care for the wounded."

"Ma'am" indeed, Ayesha thought. She had never been called *that* before! Princess she was used to being called, or at most, Your Highness. She was not some middle-aged, overweight dowager! She blushed beneath her olive complexion. Was this formality because he knew she was bound for marriage to his ruler?

Or did he take her for his father's woman?

And why did all these questions to herself fill her with a warm and languid stirring which was, somewhere at its foundations, such an enjoyable sensation?

She, at least, had forgotten about the food already.

At the young man's insistence, Fireclaw agreed, with visible reluctance, to leave Ursi behind. Although how well the dog would get along with a flock of strange nurses, Ayesha wondered with a little amusement. Sagheer, however, would not be separated from her. Of him Owald offered neither advice nor command.

The rolling serving tray they locked up in the bathroom to keep the animals from distributing its contents throughout the stateroom—though not before both men had grabbed themselves whatever came to hand to carry with them.

Tossing a hesitant and guilty glance back toward the sleeping Commodore, Ayesha followed Owald through the door.

Fireclaw followed after them.

2

Striding along the corridor outside the stateroom, they came to yet another door which, sliding open, revealed a case of skeletal metal stairs arranged in a tight spiral.

The throbbing sound was louder in the stairwell, rendering conversation impossible.

Swallowing a last, inadequate bite, Owald brushed his hands upon one another, then signed to them to precede him.

Ayesha gathered her skirt-hem and obeyed.

He followed them downward and around past several doors, then shouted them to a halt. He slid a door aside, then led them forward, toward the sunlight.

At the end of the corridor, a narrower one than that they had left above—and blessedly undecorated, the girl thought to herself—they came at last to a transparent door which Ayesha reasoned must have been immediately beneath the Sun's glass-paned audience chamber several flights above their heads. It opened into a broad, semicircular room rimmed in what at first appeared to be floor-to-ceiling windows.

Owald slid the door aside.

A harsh wind slapped them in their unprepared faces, nearly ripping the gathered skirt-hem from her hand. Little Sagheer shrieked and hid his face against her bosom. She tucked him inside her robe, where he seemed content to remain.

Owald grinned, then motioned them forward.

Ayesha was astonished. The "room" ahead was actually a covered balcony, open to the air, hanging beneath the hull of the giant airship. In its arch-fronted center, a single V-shaped pair of glassy panels breasted the main force of the wind, yet a hurricane seemed to whirl and surge about them, bringing water to their eyes, making it difficult to snatch a breath as the air rushed past.

His own hair billowing about his eyes, Owald ushered the Princess and the warrior forward until they stood upon the brink, held back by a low and flimsy-appearing rail.

Owald peered ahead.

"The pilot will turn a touch into the wind now—it waxes fierce upon this stretch—and crab a little across the course. Otherwise, the ship bobs up and down, shaking everything within it, and disturbing the digestion. Not the most pleasant of sensations."

He seized his father's arm and pointed.

"You see yon tower upon that point ahead? I've practiced mooring this vessel there myself. Except for mountain journeys, which require more experience than I've yet accumulated, I could pilot this machine, single-handed, clear across the Eastern Ocean if I had to."

Owald glanced upward.

"Nor is Zhu Yuan-Coyotl maladroit at the wheel. He's probably there this very minute. He loves to fly."

Ayesha looked down.

Judging by the angle of the late-afternoon sun, the airship had turned southwestward, crab-stepping across what first appeared to be a great, wide, convoluted river. This spread itself more broadly by the moment as they traveled over it, as if it were the mighty Nile about to meet the sea, but transformed itself, instead, into a series of bays, punctuated here and there by odd-shaped islands.

As the ship left its course over the water, Ayesha caught her breath. Beneath them lay a multicolored carpet, bathed in sunlight, a huge abstract mosaic, which she gradually came to realize could be nothing else than a city, leagues across, a city to dwarf any—even all—of those ruled by her father the Caliph.

From horizon to horizon, north to south, east to west, edifices, no two of which appeared to be of the same size, shape, or color, crowded one another, heaped themselves toward the underbelly of the airship and toward the sky above that.

Among them, not a single acre of bare ground was to be seen. What greenery there was—and there was greenery aplenty: tall grass, palm trees, thick-woven decorative hedges, ornamental shrubbery—carpeted the rooftops of the buildings. Ayesha thought she caught a glimpse of an orange-orchard before the ship passed over it, sweeping the rooftops with a shadowy footprint even longer than itself.

The city teemed with people, too far away to be discerned in any great detail, looking to the girl much like a vast army of insects milling about in a gigantic hive, crowding one another, surging, going about their everyday imcomprehensible, insectile business.

Nor did there seem to be any coherent system of avenues or alleyways. Buildings merged into one another, a squarish tapering monument becoming a rounded dome, a lacy minaret melting at its base into acres of flat, glass-covered structures. Streets—none of them straight for more than a few dozen paces—flowed over these as often as around, sometimes ducking beneath them, occasionally appearing and disappearing in a manner which made no sense to her eyes.

All such features ended, however, at the water's edge where they, and the course of the giant airship, intersected yet another shoreline, that of the largest bay of all.

Across the water—dark gray, whitecap-topped, and cold-looking—she could just make out a cliff-gapping harbor-entrance, night-lights already blinking upon opposite promontories (or perhaps they were left lit all of the time), and beyond, the razor-straight blue-under-blue line of the western ocean's horizon.

To the northwest and southeast, the great bay stretched away into the dusky infinity of the coming night.

Between the structure-crowded shoreline they now crossed and the mountain-flanked harbor-mouth, four small islands lay within the bay, all near its entrance from the sea. Three of

these, in particular the northmost, sheltered by twin penin-
sulas, were built over as densely as the endless city which
surrounded the bay they lay within.

Directly to the south, nearest the harbor-mouth, a barren,
rocky islet raised itself from the water, forming the foundation
for a mighty tower, the tallest building Ayesha had ever seen,
taller than she had thought a building could be, featureless and
gray.

Owald pointed a finger at the tower.

"There's the Spire of Dreamers, and—"

The southmost island, somewhat to the west of the tower-
isle, like the northmost, presented a disorganized jumble to the
eye.

"The Palace of the Sun Incarnate, residence of Zhu Yuan-
Coyotl," Owald shouted with hoarse excitement, "the seat of
government for the Empire of Han-Meshika!"

The fourth, and second-largest, island possessed an edifice
which glowed softly as the last rays of the sun shone through
it. The airship made directly for it. Beneath them lay what
appeared to be a mountain of ice, a solitary pyramidal glacier
standing in the midst of a bay which was itself a veritable
inland sea.

Ayesha gasped in half-recognition, the uneasy feeling she
had seen this place before.

Unlike the moldering Egyptian pyramids she had visted as a
girl, this monumental object was table-flat at the summit,
entirely constructed of the purest of transparent crystal, each
man-height block crafted into an eye-disturbing, irregular
shape, mirrored within its depths where it met, in a flawless
seam, with neighboring blocks.

"One thousand seven hundred sixty paces!" Owald
shouted, the wind of the great ship's passage slapping at his
cheeks. He pointed a finger, swinging it horizontally.

Thinking she had failed to understand what Owald said,
Fireclaw translated for him.

"Deep paces," Owald added, "those of a big man! From
base to top, a diagonal span of eleven hundred seventy-four

paces, it's the height of four hundred fifteen men. Tall men. If you could walk it—or wanted to—there are twenty-five hundred steps!"

At the flattened summit, there was what appeared to be an elaborate temple, open to sky, its floor consisting of what looked to the girl like a giant pool.

It was not its color alone—a deep and brooding red—which spoiled this illusion. Because she knew, despite appearances, that the pyramid was not made of ice, she reasoned that this "pool," in reality, was as solid and glassy as the rest of the gigantic edifice.

It was even more transparent.

As it fooled the eye, it terrified the mind. Its depths seemed to exceed even the great height of the pyramid, to plunge downward to the very center of the earth itself.

"It must have taken centuries to erect!" commented the Princess, devoting only half an ear to what the man was saying. Stunned by all she had thus far seen, she was beginning to believe that, setting her irrational fears aside, the fate her father had wished upon her was not quite the end of the world she had imagined it to be.

This was, indeed, a mighty civilization.

Hovering above the glassy mountain, they spied another airship, not unlike the one which carried them. From beneath its hull there was suspended a gigantic disk, itself not much smaller than the craft which held it in place.

"Practice," Owald told them enigmatically. "You can't see it, but upon that hill, yonder, is a crew projecting a thin light-beam at the disk. From thence it is reflected to the pyramid-top."

His father asked, "Toward what purpose?"

An odd look flickered briefly across Owald's features, as if he realized he had said more than he ought, but, having introduced the subject, he would not be let off without saying more.

"If all circumstances fall aright—if the ship's steady, and in the correct place at the correct time—if the beam runs true from hilltop to pyramid, then it will work the other way as well. Pray do not ask me more, Father, for I am oath-bound not to reveal the secrets of Zhu Yuan-Coyotl, the Sun Incarnate, at least until the one to whom they are revealed has earned his trust.

"The top's a hundred paces square . . ."

Unable to say more about the airship to his father, nor to understand Ayesha past a barrier of wind and foreign language, Owald continued with his statistics.

". . . occupying a space of ten thousand square paces, of which near unto eight thousand are taken up by the temple floor, which is called by the people the Eye-of-God."

Of a sudden, he seized her by the shoulder, the roughness of his grip surprising her. What surprised her more were the teardrops whipped from his face and splashing upon hers.

"Five thousand people at a time can be made to stand there, Ayesha! And five thousand and five thousand more! Over and over and over again! 'Tis the heart of the world we live in, girl, the world we can never quit! It is the soul of the Crystal Empire!"

He turned then and in Helvetian demanded of his father, "I brought you out here so that we'd not be overheard! How can I make her understand? Everything in, nothing out—the sole exception's those entrusted with Zhu Yuan-Coyotl's safety!"

Suddenly the young officer had Ayesha's full understanding, whether he knew it or not.

"Neither of you asked me what befalls the remainder! Ask me now! They worship *that,* here, Father!"

He pointed to the setting sun.

The other airship had begun standing off, the great reflecting-disk beneath it slowly, by some unknown machination, being drawn upward, parallel to its hull.

The flying machine turned tail toward them and sped away.

"Not merely Zhu Yuan-Coyotl, its human aspect, but an incandescent orb which they believe requires sustenance! One outsider in ten thousand joins the guard, Father—nine thousand nine and ninety die a death too terrible to speak of!"

He pointed to the pyramid again, glowing in the twilight. The "pool" in its center was by now an inky black.

"Your Saracen Princess, Father, 'tis here, in the heart of the world, that she shall be joined in wedlock to the real Sun!"

XXXIX:

The Enlightenment of
Oln Woeck

Believers, turn to God in sincere repentance; it may be
that your Lord will acquit you of your evil deeds, and
will admit you into gardens underneath which rivers
flow.

—The *Koran*, Sura LXVI

"Get up, fool!"

Naked limbs trembling, the old man lifted his face from the
grimy deckplates. He blinked, eyes watering. Some moments
passed before he could tolerate even the moderate quantity of
light entering the small room he occupied from the clattering
spaces beyond the door which had just been opened without
warning.

His breath created little puffs of vapor when he exhaled.

Before him he saw a pair of elaborate-tooled boots beneath
the embroidered hem of a brocaded robe. Pushing himself to
his bony knees, he let his eyes follow the robe upward, past
the decorative sash—a pair of T-handled daggers had been

thrust into it—past the arms, folded across the chest, resting in voluminous sleeves opposite one another, past the glittering medallion, a miniature of the solar mask he'd seen in the audience chamber, to the smooth-skinned boyish face of Zhu Yuan-Coyotl, the Sun Incarnate of the Han-Meshika.

The dark hair was concealed by a quilted cap whose untied ear-coverings flapped when the Sun moved his head. His youthful face set itself in an expression of tolerant amusement. Speaking in well-accented Helvetian, the voice fell softer now, almost gentle.

"I said, get up, Oln Woeck."

Trembling with strain, Oln Woeck attempted to comply with the demand. He discovered his unclad limbs had locked, from fear, from cold and old age, into the humiliating position of obeisance he'd assumed the instant the door had slid aside. What disturbed the old man was that his self-abasement had been automatic, a reflex performed without the slightest conscious consideration.

From behind the rich-garbed boy-ruler there stepped a copper-kilted guard, who seized the Cultist leader by one elbow and lifted him to his naked feet. Scarcely noticing the way the icy metal stung their soles, the older man gasped in the momentary belief his bones would shatter in their brittleness. Otherwise, he bit his tongue, suppressed both pent-up fear and mounting fury, and held his silence.

Zhu Yuan-Coyotl nodded dismissal at the soldier, who bowed, departing from the room.

The light still dazzled aged eyes. It was Oln Woeck's first opportunity to see the place himself. He'd been dragged from the airship's audience chamber some unreckonable time ago, force-marched along endless decorated corridors, up and down numerous spiral staircases, until he and his animal-helmeted escort had come to a huge, noisy kitchen, deep within the volume of the alien vessel.

A hundred menials had he glimpsed, milling about in the glaring light, as cookware clattered, steam hissed, unfamiliar odors assailed his already terrified senses.

There, the Sun Incarnate's guardsmen had opened a thick and heavy-latched metal door, stripped him to the skin without leave or ceremony of aught he wore, thrown him inside. He'd almost been relieved, considering this unknown land with its unknown customs, not to have been tossed straightaway into a cooking-pot. Instead, he'd fetched up against the opposite wall, losing consciousness. They'd slammed the door, casting the dazed Cultist into uttermost darkness.

Where they'd left him.

Now he could look about, the room was larger than he'd believed. He hadn't spent much time or effort exploring it, so uncomfortable and afraid had he been. Upon one wall countless ranks of drawers or lockers did he see, each with its polished metal hasp and hinges, each with a labeling plate upon which foreign characters had been painted.

The wall opposite couldn't be seen, hidden as it sat behind rows of frozen yellow-pink carcasses suspended by hooks from shining rails which crossed the ceiling.

Grateful he was not to have encountered those in the dark!

Skinned, limb-chopped, gutted, and headless, it was difficult telling what sort of animal they'd been, what sort of meat they stored in this place. To Oln Woeck, long accustomed to leaving such matters as the sustenance of his body to inferiors, they appeared to be hogs. But something gibbered at the back of his mind that his initial fears, upon seeing the kitchen, hadn't been altogether without basis.

Now the Sun Incarnate Zhu Yuan-Coyotl swept one brown, jewel-bedecked hand from the satin sleeve it rested in, indicating a small bench—an unadorned metal shelf suspended by a pair of chains—fastened to a third wall.

Upon it lay a huge, curved butcher knife.

"Seat yourself, old man. You appear surprised. Did you suspect We'd leave you here to die?"

Oln Woeck avoided answering by limping backward to the bench—for a dozen reasons he felt he daren't turn his back—lowering himself into mortifying contact with the metal. The shelf was hard, his bones unpadded by much flesh. The bench was cold. His shivering was, by now, quite beyond his control.

"The Sun"—Zhu Yuan-Coyotl passed slender long-nailed fingers across his own chest, refolded his arms; his breath, too, formed little clouds of steam—"is the sole source of light and warmth in Our World, thus the wellspring of all life."

He stepped closer to Oln Woeck.

"'Tis an impressive object-lesson to be deprived of its manifold blessed attributes. 'Let the bastards freeze in the dark' is a common curse among the Han-Meshika, as well as the cruelest, most demeaning form of corporal or capital punishment—which, of course, depends upon its duration—We practice."

Another step forward.

"In the minds of Our subjects, to be put to death by freezing in the darkness isn't just to be denied humanity—a quality all forms of punishment possess in common—nor is it just to be denied the dignity of existence itself."

Huddled with his knees against his chest, his arms wrapped about them, Oln Woeck blinked. What was this maniacal child trying to tell him? If they intended to kill him, by the Suffering of Jesus, let them do it without all this talk!

"'Tis to be denied," the Sun Incarnate stated, "in life's uttermost moments, the oneness with the source of life—which is the aim, We're certain you'll agree, of all one's strivings here upon earth—and thus the cruelest fate imaginable."

The Sun stepped closer once again until Oln Woeck, had he been capable of movement, not frozen where he sat, might have reached out, touched the rich, brocaded robe. As it was, the moisture from the Sun Incarnate's breath condensed in a light film upon the Cultist leader's upraised knees, which, to their owner, appeared as bloodless and transparent as if they'd been fashioned out of candle-tallow.

"Upon some concentrated study of the matter," the boy continued, "We've arrived at an understanding that this theology isn't alien entire to your own beliefs."

Here the Sun Incarnate Zhu Yuan-Coyotl paused, as if to let some profound lesson sink in. Oln Woeck was fervent in the wish it would, but in this he was disappointed.

At length, the Sun spoke again.

"There elsewhere flourishes an entire family of languages with which Our Dreamers have familiarized Us, in which the word for Sun also conveys a secondary meaning, 'provider of opportunities'—somewhat of the same spirit in which your people, the Helvetii, are wont to say, 'Make hay while the sun shines.'"

Zhu Yuan-Coyotl turned his back, gazing in absent idleness as he spoke at beads of condensed moisture trickling down the tarnished metal wall beside the heavy-hinged door.

"'Tis an appropriate turn of phrase, howe'er esoteric its origin. An auspicious one. We enjoy to think of Ourselves as such a beneficent provider of opportunities, Oln Woeck. Observe how We've provided you with an opportunity to sample, in a small wise, existence without the benefit of Our effulgence—"

He craned his neck about, pointing to the butcher knife which Oln Woeck hadn't touched.

"—or to attack Us whilst Our back was turned."

He laughed.

"Likewise, We're certain you heard Us explain e'er now to your traveling companions how upon occasion We provide certain opportunities for Our subjects to sink themselves in vice, that they who can't resist its blandishment might be weeded from Our, er, garden."

Oln Woeck remembered well enough, but just now he was more preoccupied with the wish that he could cease shivering. He was no longer certain whether the cold was responsible for it.

Aught about this boy-child frightened him.

"We provide other opportunities, as well, for measured advancement, unmeasured greed, dutiful obedience, self-aggrandizement, assiduousity, betrayal . . ."

He turned about again, to face the old Helvetian. Oln Woeck

hoped the boy might come at last to the point of this otherwise meaningless lecture. Its meaninglessness—he was discovering—was the principal terror of the thing.

"But We didn't visit you to prattle of philosophy or linguistics. We observe that you grow more uncomfortable, thereby less attentive, each minute. Here—"

In a single, liquid motion, the Sun Incarnate Zhu Yuan-Coyotl unfastened his sash—the paired knife-scabbards clattered upon the deck—flung the colorful quilted robe from his lithe, athletic body, snugged it about Oln Woeck.

He helped the old man tuck it into place beneath his frozen buttocks. In an instant, warmth began to wash across the old man's body, penetrating his flesh as if the robe itself radiated heat and were more than just its preserver.

Relief was to be followed by shock. He watched with widened eyes and wider mouth as Zhu Yuan-Coyotl retied the weapons-sash about his now-naked waist. Beneath the robe, the boy had worn nothing. Despite his sudden exposure to the cold, he showed no sign of discomfort. Oln Woeck confronted half a dozen conflicting feelings: relief, uncertainty, wonder, the first faint tinglings of something else. Lean, hairless, well muscled, the boy he looked upon was *beautiful*.

Showing no awareness of thoughts Oln Woeck feared written bold upon his features, the Sun went on.

"Howe'er, We did come to spin for you, Oln Woeck, the tale of an illustrious ancestor of Ours, one Zhu Yuan-Xiang, who lived some six and one-half centuries ago, also with whom We're honored to share both a given and a family name.

The boy glanced at the railed ceiling, eyes half closed, as if summoning long-unexamined memories.

"When he was a young man—he was known, at the time, by the name 'Hung Wu,' a humble monk not unlike yourself, born of a poor family of farm laborers, wiped out in one of many epidemics when he was but seventeen—his homeland languished in the iron grip of a savage foreign conqueror. Thus it had been for as long as anybody could remember. These barbaric dogs had perpetrated many terrible acts, the worst of which was opening the land to adventurers from e'en further regions, contaminating it with unsettling customs, unproven ideas, alien pestilences."

A small noise came at the door, a timid knocking which interrupted the Sun's narrative. A plump-cheeked, red-gold, oval-eyed face peeked round the metal frame.

The Sun nodded.

Many additional distractions followed as an endless parade of linen-jacketed servitors entered the tiny room, one by one, depositing numerous rich and fascinating burdens within it before departing once again to return with even more.

A floral-decorated screen-curtain, depicting, the Sun explained to Oln Woeck, wisteria and plum blossoms, willow and oleander, they placed before the hanging carcasses. Beside it, sandalwood incense smoldered in a vase of jade upon an ebony tabouret.

The cold tile floor the servants covered with a thick layer of carpeting. Over this they laid a reed mat upon which the servants placed a lacquered rosewood tea-table, its blackwood top inlaid with alternating bronze and copper tiles. Upon this they placed, to begin things, towels in a polished copper basin of hot, scented water.

Vapor rising from the vessel all but obscured Oln Woeck's view of Zhu Yuan-Coyotl.

The boy-ruler selected one of the towels, cleansed both face and hands. He invited the elderly Helvetian—to whom cleanliness was no deep-grained habit—to follow suit.

Yet he obeyed.

The steaming towel scalded the old man's frozen face and fingers, but refreshed him. The soiled towels they threw back—with some reluctance upon Oln Woeck's part—into the copper basin, which the servant removed with promptness from the room.

As the servants continued with their tasks, Zhu Yuan-Coyotl took up his topic once again.

"Yet, as Our Dreamers assure Us, naught there is which lasts eternal, Oln Woeck. Harsh oppression strengthens the weak. The most disciplined conquerors grow corrupt, bloating themselves into helplessness upon the places and people they plunder.

"There came into the land a final, terrible sickness, slaughtering conqueror and conquered alike, nine hundred out of every thousand. At the age of twenty-five, having cast aside the saffron, with clever effort Zhu Yuan-Xiang initiated a rebellion of his disarmed countrymen. As this time but one family in ten was permitted possession of a kitchen carving-knife. He o'erthrew the conquerors while they coughed and quarreled among themselves and died."

The servants had by this time hung decorative bamboo fans over the locker-doors. A string of paper lamps shed softer light than that afforded in the kitchen outside. A landscape, scroll-painted upon rattan, they unfurled upon the wall above the metal bench, itself draped in snowy damask, employed as serving-table. Platters of onion-flavored corn-cakes the servants placed there, along with bowls of fried rice, boiled yams, baked potatoes, salted vegetables, ricebowls of noodles, what Oln Woeck prayed was roast pork, something else Zhu Yuan-Coyotl told him with amusement was pickled snake and chilis.

"Taking the dynastic name Ming, he ruled his people for another forty years. The Emperor Zhu realized 'twas not enough to take the place the conqueror had vacated. Such had come to pass ere this in his land, countless times. Also, the land rotted with the stench of death. Rumors brought from other lands by the previous rulers attributed this to a disease borne by rats."

Oln Woeck's much-distracted attention divided itself between the Sun's words, a less intellectual interest in the boy beginning to tease his loins, and the food whose aroma filled the tiny room, overpowering even the incense.

Still, Zhu Yuan-Coyotl had neither seated himself upon one of the rattan stools which had been brought in for them (the old man had vacated the bench—it hadn't been difficult to persuade him) nor as yet partaken of any refreshment.

For the moment were they given candied fruit, dried melon

seeds, something which the Sun told him was a bowl of deep-fried locusts, crusted with oily salt.

Oln Woeck watched the boy, admiring the fluid grace of his movements, the unblemished smoothness of his flesh. Soon there appeared a teapot, the vapor pouring from its delicate spout smelling of jasmine and crabapple. A steward brought a skullcap for Oln Woeck, a loincloth and black lacquered gauze headpiece for his master.

"Thus did Zhu Yuan-Xiang decree a vast fleet of ships, some thirty-seven thousand in number, whereupon he, his court, aught that might be gathered up of the remaining population, might—having taken the sternest possible measures to rid themselves of disease-bearing rodents—sail off toward the sunrise, and a new land."

The Sun seated himself.

Employing a pair of slender tapered sticks as tools, he selected a moist tidbit from a platter. He waved Oln Woeck to the other chair. From outside the door there issued the mellow voice of a young woman reciting poetry. Other voices, sweeter, sang. Past the doorjamb, the Helvetian glimpsed the silhouettes of people dancing to the tune of lute, guitar, bamboo flute, silver violin.

"Thus it came about," offered the Sun, "that, fleeing the selfsame Greater Death which drove your own ancestors scuttling to what you call the New World, Ours discovered it first, in the year you reckon 718, there—or rather, here—establishing colonies which, after a time, fused with the leading native culture.

"The Han were circumspect regarding the Meshika. For them there'd be no going back. To the unstable vitality of these savages they contributed much knowledge, the stability of bureaucracy. The respective aristocracies interbred.

"What resulted—besides Ourselves, of course—was a long-lasting culture capable of a measured progress. With all due respect for my esteemed ancestor, 'twas little to the doing of it. After all, as Our Dreamers inform Us, a redheaded half-Mongol can, with the same ease, be mistaken by a superstitious savage for the Feathered Serpent as any—but you'd have no wise of knowing about that."

Agreeing in silence with the boy—that he knew not what was being spoken of—Oln Woeck accepted a cup of the fragrant infusion. Perhaps, after they ate, he could determine whether this beautiful youth might feel amenable to yet another pleasure—*no!* He mustn't allow his fleshly predilections to overpower his judgment.

Bowing his head, he muttered a few words of ceremonial gratitude to the Suffering Lord Jesus, hands trembling with the effort of controlling his voraciousness.

Zhu Yuan-Coyotl watched him with a neutral expression.

Oln Woeck took up a pair of eating-sticks.

Before the Cultist could taste a single mouthful, the Sun Incarnate appeared to change the subject. So abrupt was the change that the old man looked up, eating-sticks hanging in the air, all but forgotten, before his puzzled face.

"There are many theories, Oln Woeck, as to how one may achieve satisfaction in life. We, for example, have gone to some pains to eradicate within Ourselves any desire which depends for its fulfillment upon the cooperative goodwill of other human beings. Thus no one exercises power o'er Us. Whate'er We can't purchase, or compel by fear or force, We've learned to do without."

He snapped his fingers. In an instant, servants entered. They began removing screens, fans, lamps, tables, furnishings, fixtures, until the little room shone steel bare once again, the sumptuous food and drink an agonizing memory.

Zhu Yuan-Coyotl continued as if nothing had happened.

"Be assured this isn't the case with Our subjects, whose schooling, free of cost to them, and entertainments We've seen fit to saturate with platitudes of love, brotherhood, mutual dependence, repeated to the point of nauseation. This, too, is not unlike the theology you practice. We've observed with amusement the tendency, once one's 'seen the light'—any light, it doesn't matter—to create others with whom to share this enlightenment. We Ourselves avoid this. Truth is power,

Oln Woeck. 'Tis not in Our interests that Our subjects share it.''

The stool jerked from beneath him, Oln Woeck fought back tears of angry disappointment.

"In the name of Jesus, man—"

The Sun appeared to ignore the plea.

"Thus it may occur to you to wonder why We bother discussing these matters with you. 'Tis because, Oln Woeck, of the commendable ruthlessness with which you disposed of Sedrich Fireclaw's transgressions against what you regarded to be decency. We believe We've found a use for you. As you'll recall, We asserted that all men come to serve Us in their own wise, in sufficient time."

The Sun's hand snapped out like a striking snake, ripping the robe from Oln Woeck's body.

The old man began to shiver once again.

"The best way to rule's ne'er to let the people learn they're ruled," the Sun offered, turning his back.

This time, no butcher knife had been left upon the naked metal bench as a temptation.

"The Comanche and the Utes, Our well-spiked fence against a hostile and inquisitive world, ne'er knew who ruled them, nor e'en that they were ruled, but that they served the gods. With Saracens and Mughals set upon exploring the globe, We believe the time's come to extend this fence—and Our domination—to your own people, the Helvetii."

Tossing the robe over his arm, the Sun strode toward the door.

"As a leader of the foremost power among the Helvetii, you may have a substantial part in this, Oln Woeck, and commensurate benefit. But ne'er in the name of this Jesus—at least not in Our presence. Our scholars will determine which beliefs and practices should be encouraged among your people, which uprooted, allowed to perish. We shall discuss the details with you later.

"Perhaps.

"We shall provide you, now, with yet another opportunity—

to contemplate in some exactitude what it is you worship, the mythical ghost of a long-dead godling . . ."

He stepped outside the door, seizing the handle.

"Or the warming light of the living Sun!"

Zhu Yuan-Coyotl slammed the door.

XL:

In the Palace of the Sun

Surely for the godfearing awaits a place of security, gardens and vineyards and maidens with swelling breasts, like of age, and a cup overflowing.
—The *Koran*, Sura LXXVIII

"Now the left hand!"

One ankle crossing another, Owald, stripped to a pair of baggy exercising trousers, leaned against a marble column so green it appeared carven out of jade, bearlike arms folded, an expression of astonishment upon his fair, clean-shaven face. He'd a towel draped about his neck, still catching his breath from a session of hand-to-hand.

Sunlight poured down into the cavernous practice-hall through bright-colored windows high in the ceiling overhead, relieving the damp chill each morning's fog brought to the four islands and the surrounding city in the heart of the Crystal Empire. As Fireclaw shouted explanations—black Ursi dozed, contented, upon a carpet of brightness covering one section of the glossy floor—Owald watched his father's martial labors with professional interest.

"Head!
"Thigh!
"Head!
"Hip!
"Head!
"Shoulder!
"Head!"

Fireclaw groaned, shouting out imaginary targets as he struck them, trembling with exertion, sweat-drenched, but visibly determined to regain the speed and power a week's journey and two substantial doses of dart-drug had denied him.

Owald could see how his truncated wrist ached, bruised to the marrow from elbow to stump with what was demanded of it this morning. Nor was he any longer a young man. Yet, shifting the greatsword *Murderer* for another assault upon a man-high post of bound rattan staves planted in the floor, the graying Helvetian warrior went on and on, repeating motions he'd first learned as a youth.

Whirling *Murderer* high above his shaven head, he once again lengthened his reach with an echoing roar which was half agony, half fury, letting the gleaming steel weapon lash out. The gleaming razor-edge bit deep, showering tan-colored powdery splinters about the room, making hazardous navigation of the smooth-polished floor.

They'd have to be swept up e'er long, lest some unwary palace servitor slide upon them, breaking his neck.

Watching Fireclaw lever the great blade free, his silver-stranded war-braid bobbing, Owald reflected upon what the older man had told him in the last few days. In sun, snow, and rain, summer heat and winter cold, he'd repeated these painful motions a hundred times each dawning for the last quarter century. The man's wrists had come to resemble bundled iron staves, his forearms outsizing the calves of many another man. The practice had served him well: he still lived after all those eventful years, while many a worthy enemy didn't.

Owald suspected other, more recently acquired incentives to self-punishment were at work, guilt of a couple differing flavors, several varieties of frustration. The little dark-eyed

Princess, Ayesha, was promised in wedlock to Zhu Yuan-Coyotl, the Sun Incarnate of the Han-Meshika. Fireclaw had lost his wife and unborn child less than a fortnight since, no decent interval, in the eyes of any Helvetian, for proper mourning. Yet life gave little regard to what men considered decent. Neither seemed to realize it yet—from the viewpoint of either party, this was no time to go acourting—but Ayesha was becoming Fireclaw's woman, in intention if not in deed, which meant more trouble ahead than any sane man would wish to contemplate.

Another sudden whirl, another savage scream of unleashed power, another bite into the rattan butt. Shock sang through the blade, echoing about the room.

Yes, Owald thought, the Saracen Princess, his long-lost father, twice her age, both were in for something of a surprise. Trouble was, even he, the commander of the Sun's bodyguard, couldn't imagine how the surprise could turn out to be that pleasant one of mutual recognition which ordinary lovers might enjoy.

He shook his head, as if to clear it of disturbing notions. Life had been that simple ere Fireclaw showed up!

With each swing of the legendary *Murderer,* Owald was forced to regard the saw-toothed blade he'd carried in the Imperial Bodyguard with greater contempt. Fireclaw had practiced with one such a while earlier, flinging it aside in a few moments with disgust.

Mass-produced somewhere within the Empire, 'twas true it bit deep for its weight, creating terrible ragged wounds, which, did the victim survive, would be long in healing, if at all. The little blade spanned but two fingers' width at the haft, possessed no cross-guard to speak of. From point to pommel, it could be carried resting upon the fingertips, tucked into the armpit. Great *Murderer* must be slung across the back, handle high above one's head. The Empire's saw-toothed swordlets could be carried at the waist, like daggers.

Mob-weapons, Fireclaw had snorted, devised for close massed attack upon victims less than well prepared for self-defense. Or for finishing off the helpless wounded. Useless, he maintained, to an individual confronting enemies of equal skill.

This annoyed the Imperial Bodyguard commander, who'd heretofore taken some pride in the skill he possessed with the most scientific, deadly edged weapon in the known world.

"Now the right side for a while," Fireclaw shouted, pushing *Murderer*'s long pommel into his prosthetic, giving it a locking twist, *"and back to the left!"*

But not so much as the irritating fact that this gray-haired barbarian was right. Disgusted—although with what he couldn't say—Owald pulled the towel up over his head. He slid down the column until he was seated at its foot upon the floor.

Time passed.

The patches of colored sunlight from the ceiling crawled across the floor, somehow, as if by magic, dragging the sleeping bear-dog along with them.

At long last, Fireclaw ceased his belligerent labors, toweling his own half-naked body with linens brought by a servant while another entered, as he had each morning for a week, sweeping up the debris with a push-broom. Fireclaw glanced toward Owald, whistled Ursi to attention, began walking across the great hall toward the showers, as had been his practice every morning.

Owald stopped him with a shout, leapt to his feet, and dog-trotted to catch up.

"Wait a moment," he told his father. "There's something I want to show you first."

Ursi glanced in confusion toward the showers—he was fond of falling water, already in the habit of bathing with his master—then seemed to shrug and follow along, complacent. Together all three turned leftward, walking the great length of the empty room which at another hour would be full of off-duty guardsmen, practicing their own murderous skills, until they reached the entrance of a deep wing set at right angles to the rest of the skylighted structure, where two copper-kilted soldiers in full battle-dress awaited them.

Owald looked upon his father.

"I see you bear greatsword and dagger—also the little knife inside your shirtfront—yet you've laid your revolving pistol aside. This you shouldn't have done. 'Tis a sign of the Sun's great favor to be granted the privilege—"

"Of carrying an unloaded gun?" Fireclaw asked, adding a short, one-syllabled Helvetian word.

" 'Tis a badge of honor, Father."

Fireclaw snorted.

"Empty gun—by the sovereign's leave—empty honor. We'll speak no more upon it."

"You're held to be a dangerous man," Owald told his father. "I requested special permission for this, receiving it only under these conditions. D'you not be alarmed."

He nodded at the pair of bodyguardsmen, who obeyed by raising the short black weapons slung across their armored chests, pointing them at Fireclaw's belly.

Fireclaw smiled an evil smile.

A long, padded, waist-high counter lay in sections across the entrance to the wing. Owald removed a small key from his sweaty waistband. He bent, and from a cabinet within the counter removed another of the peculiar weapons. He pulled the long, curved, empty magazine from behind its contoured grip, slapped back the knurled charging-handle upon the left side of the dull-surfaced receiver, and peered deep into the mechanism to assure himself the firing chamber was empty.

He let the handle snap forward, replaced the magazine, handed the weapon to his father. Glancing from one of the armored guardsmen to the other, Fireclaw winked and chuckled. He accepted the deadly little machine his son had handed to him.

He hefted it in his left hand. Made for the right, it fit him awkwardly.

"Heavier than it looks," he observed, turning the muzzle toward himself to peer back along its axis.

"About half the bore-size of my pistol, I'd guess. Same sight as upon a Comanche bow, e'en to the fashioner's markings. This thing holds the ammunition."

He pushed the release-button as if he'd been doing it all his life instead of swinging a sword. He handed the empty magazine to his son, indicating the operating lever.

"This starts the first into the chamber—better idea than a revolver, once solve the powder-fouling problem."

Owald nodded, trying to disguise his amazement.

"Smokeless powder," he answered, "not much fouling at all. You want to shoot it?"

Fireclaw grinned.

"If your little friends don't shoot me first."

Owald pointed a thumb toward the far end of the hall-wing, where, a hundred paces away, cloth bags of sand had been laid upon one another to a level twice the height of a man. Half a dozen man-shaped cutouts, in the subdued colors of the sandbags, had been fastened between wooden posts in front of them.

"Just keep this thing pointed downrange," he told his father. " 'Twill keep 'em happy and your skin intact. Here, I'll start you with single cartridge."

Owald pressed a smallish cylinder—slender, copper-tipped, aluminum-cased, and bottle-shaped—into the spring-loaded top of the magazine and handed it to Fireclaw. The older man laid the short weapon along his forearm, inserted the magazine with his left hand, slapped the floorplate until it locked. He pulled the charging-handle back with an edge of his prosthetic.

"A mite awkward for a one-handed man," he observed, leveling at a target. He peered through the telescopic sight.

He pulled the trigger.

Nothing happened.

Owald chuckled. "Safety. The small lever, away at the rear. Give it a quarter-turn upward."

"Damn silly thing," Fireclaw growled, "to tinker into a weapon! What if you needed a shot in a hurry?"

Nevertheless, the warrior obeyed, resighting the weapon, and putting renewed pressure upon the trigger. Its bellow filled the hall. The spent casing leapt from the ejection-port atop the gun, spun tinkling upon the floor.

Fireclaw blinked.

"Loud enough for three guns!"

Owald nodded, grinning wide, as one of the soldiers ran forward—that small were the bullet holes they couldn't be seen from where they'd been fashioned—to examine the target.

Excited, he pointed at the paper silhouette's midsection, shouting back a single word, not in his native tongue, a Southeast Asian dialect neither Owald nor any other of the bodyguard was fluent in, but in Guard-speech, a clever, useful synthesis of the Sun's own devising, rendered necessary by the varied origins of his protectors.

"Dead center, he says, Father. He's much amazed, but I'm pleased to tell you I'm not."

Shouting, he signaled the guardsman back to the safety of the firing-line again. He thrust a gauntleted hand out, uttering more words of command in the same artificial language. The guardsman nodded, retrieved an extra magazine from a fabric pouch containing several, fastened at the small of his armored back.

With a dubious expression upon his face, he handed it to Owald, who handed it to Fireclaw.

"Thirty rounds," the commander told his father.

Fireclaw ejected and laid the first magazine upon the padded bench, reloaded with the full one, leveled the little gun, fired it five times at each of the targets in turn. Little recoil was apparent; the muzzle scarcely lifted between shots. Empty cases spurted from the weapon, several hanging in the air at once.

When the deafening echoes died from the hall and the minimal "smokeless powder" smoke cleared, there remained no need for anyone to run down to the targets. Each had a single ragged hole—five shots clustered overlapping in the center of the head.

The armored guardsmen jabbered at one another—the other man was Saracen-Irish, the sole language the two shared in common one they'd learned in the line of duty within the Empire's borders. They took firmer holds upon their weapons.

Fireclaw laughed aloud at the sight. Owald frowned, then joined him, clapping them both upon their shoulders, afterward asking for a spare magazine from the other man. This he also gave to Fireclaw, accepting the empty in exchange.

He laid it aside upon the bench.

"Rotate the safety lever yet another quarter-turn, Father. Be prepared for a surprise. And for Goddess' love, keep the business-end pointed downrange!"

Giving his son a skeptical look, Fireclaw reloaded, aligned the sight upon a silhouette, pulled the trigger. Before he could release it once again a brief moment later—with a startled expression upon his bearded face—the magazine was empty, the floor about his feet littered with aluminum cartridge cases.

Silence.

"So this," Fireclaw offered at long last, "is how the mysterious blanket-ripping sound comes to be. Impressive—"

Licking a finger—he touched it to the still-smoking barrel, listening for a hiss—he peered downrange, unable to see any further damage he'd inflicted upon the targets.

"—but somewhat wasteful."

One of the wooden posts beside a target groaned, gave forth a splintering noise. With a whoosh it toppled forward, tearing the target it had helped to hold in half.

Owald laughed again; this time his comrades joined him.

"It's an acquired skill, Father."

He took the weapon from Fireclaw's fingers, removed the empty magazine, pushed a knob upon its side, and split the receiver end for end with a tipping motion.

One of the guardsmen took a long steel rod from the cabinet. He swabbed the barrel. The other gave the exposed parts a cursory going-over with a tiny brush.

"You'll learn," Owald told his father. "You learn faster than any man I've e'er seen."

He hinged the weapon back together, slapped the magazine home, locked it up again inside the counter.

Fireclaw made a sour face and shrugged. He waved his right

arm to indicate the place they were in, the nervous guards who watched his every move, his own missing hand.

"For aught good it's done me," he answered.

As if in cosmic agreement, the earth beneath their feet chose this moment to express its own unrest. There came to them a floating, fluttering sensation, as if they stood within a boat and their breakfasts didn't sit well with them.

Overhead, lighting-fixtures swayed a few fingers' widths. A long time passed before they were still.

Although he disbelieved in omens, a disturbing tingle traveled up Owald's spine. Watching his father at blade-practice had been one thing; teaching him the use of automatic weapons could well turn out to be another. Despite a great enthusiasm for which he'd his own good reasons—Fireclaw *must* be recruited to the bodyguard; those who failed to find a useful place within the Crystal Empire were soon disposed of—the younger Helvetian still wondered about Zhu Yuan-Coyotl's judgment and motive in this regard: the trouble he foresaw couldn't be invisible to a man the likes of the Sun Incarnate. Nor was it likely much to be ameliorated by his famous warrior-father gaining yet another skill-at-arms.

Yet the next few words he intended speaking were the sole reason he'd joined Fireclaw at this morning's practice. Receiving the Sun Incarnate's permission to speak them had been more arduous by far than getting the nod about the gun.

"About your hand, Father . . ."

Fireclaw turned from a reexamination of the targets, a puzzled frown written across his face.

"What about it, son?"

'Twas the first time Fireclaw had named him thus. It added to the tingling of his spine.

"Well, if you're to join the bodyguard, you'll have to be less clumsy in the use of its issued weapons."

He pointed at the prosthetic cuff.

"Yon stump-shoe could slow you down, under fire."

Fireclaw nodded, waiting.

"That it could."

"I've spoken to Zhu Yuan-Coyotl about it, just this morning, Father. He's granted his permission. You've an appointment—another honor, I might add—with his personal physicians tomorrow afternoon. They'll be wanting samples of your flesh.

"They're going to start you a new hand growing."

XLI:

Spire of Dreamers

How many a sign there is in the heavens and in the earth that they pass by, turning away from it!
—The *Koran*, Sura XII

Firelight cast dancing shadows upon the thick furry wall of evergreens surrounding the encampment. Smoke drifted into the starless sky, filling the clearing with incense.

Sitting under the front edge of the lean-to, Ayesha pushed at the coals. For a time, the light drizzle which had followed them all week had ceased. A fresh log hissed and bubbled, the bark crackling. She tossed aside the weathered stick she had been using to stir the fire—one end was charred and smoking. She turned, her eyesight dimmed by the fire's light, to face her companion.

Fireclaw lay back to one side of the rough shelter he and the men had built for her, warming his damp-moccasined feet at the campfire's margin. His weapons lay discarded beside him.

He and his friend Knife Thrower had just returned from patrolling the perimeter of their small encampment, replaced now by Mochamet al Rotshild and Sergeant Kabeer. It was their second week upon the trail westward. They had just passed beyond the lands of the hospitable Utes, having maintained the fiction of seeing the dignitary, Traveling Short Bear, home. They were entering this new land with caution, taking long rest-periods, building conspicuous camping places, giving the so-far-invisible inhabitants of the region a chance to look them over.

Several yards away, in the outsized shadow of the Princess' lean-to, young Shrimp and his companion Crab lay sleeping. In a few hours, they would replace the Saracens upon watch.

Despite a lifetime spent tolerating the woman's failings, Ayesha felt lonelier than she would have imagined possible with Marya gone. The fourth day of their journey, she had reached a careless hand down for a dried stick for the fire, only to see the stick writhe in her hand, striking her with its extended fangs upon the tender inside of her elbow. The poison had been injected into a vein.

So quick had her dying been that it had scarcely delayed the party, despite the efforts of the Helvetian and his Comanche comrade to pull the potion of the rattled serpent from her body. Fireclaw, suffering a bad tooth, was still somewhat pale and shaky from the effort which had resulted in his own poisoning.

This was a hard land, set in the center of what she was discovering to be a harder world.

He sat up, speaking as if he knew Ayesha's thoughts.

"It is a shame, Princess," he offered in improving Arabic—the man seemed to be a sponge for languages—"that your father did not see fit to provide you with more than one female companion."

Ayesha nodded.

"My stepmother was ordered to accompany us. My father thought that a suitable, um, reward, for certain . . . but, in any event, the unhappy woman took her own life the very day we disembarked. We had no time to find anyone else we both trusted.

"Two deaths already. What is next? It has been an ill-starred voyage even thus far."

"Yet it might have been far worse."

The warrior moved closer to the girl, into the shelter—and relative seclusion—of the lean-to. She wondered what it had been like for him, living upon the edge of the vast prairie, all alone, for so many years. She was curious. Why had he not taken a woman from among Knife Thrower's people? It did not occur to her to move away. It was not cold in this place, with the fire glowing before them, yet his closeness was a comfort much like needed warmth.

He placed his hand upon her shoulder.

She reached up to remove it, then, at the last instant, placed her own over it. Breathing became difficult; an odd exhilarating, painful sensation sang through her body. Fighting tears she could not explain, she ducked her head forward, brushing his hand with her cheek.

So Fireclaw would be the one.

He placed his other hand about her slender waist, pulled her to him. She felt his palm cover her breast, travel down the contours of her body to rest upon the inside of her thigh. His mouth found hers. Without remembering how it had happened, Ayesha discovered herself lying beside the giant Helvetian, helping him to remove her garments.

With something beginning to resemble desperation, she fumbled at his clothes.

Then she did feel the cold, until she was surrounded by his warmth, breathing in the smoky, animal smell of him. He possessed her body with his mouth and hands, denying himself nothing of her, as she denied him nothing. She knew little pain—it was, after all, her first time—yet he was gentle with her, languidly slow.

When it was done with, she wanted it to begin all over again.

2

"No, my Princess?" David Shulieman levered himself onto one elbow. "Then tell me—*maa chalhghapar*—why you jump each time that Sedrich Fireclaw's name is spoken? *Maa manna?*"

Mochamet al Rotshild grunted agreement.

"Perhaps it is just that our Ayesha—who grew up in the shadow of Vesuvius—now finds herself sensitive to the trembling underfoot such as we have this morning experienced."

Both men chuckled.

The Princess Ayesha, daughter of the Caliph-in-Rome, turned her back to both of them, her face burning with embarrassed fury.

"*Maadaa qulth?* David Shulieman, you have been my lifelong mentor, but now even you overstep—"

"And what of me, then, Princess?"

Mochamet al Rotshild leaned upon the cane he had walked with since first getting to his feet after the attack aboard the airship. The sound of his breathing was now less noticeable, his coloring was better, Ayesha observed with a detached part of her mind, but he still hobbled like the old man he had overnight become.

"*Maadaa thureet!* What *about* you, Commodore?"

Ayesha heard the bitterness in her own voice. Even she was a little surprised.

"That my esteemed father, in his infinite kindness and wisdom, has appointed you my official keeper implies no obligation toward you upon my part!"

The Saracen captain turned to Rabbi Shulieman and shrugged. The rabbi would have repeated his gesture, had he not been half reclining. Instead, he allowed himself to roll flat upon his back once more, the gesture conveying more resignation than a simple shrug.

"See here, Ayesha, *limaadaa*—"

"No, you see here, Captain! David! Both of you! Have I not journeyed in humiliating obedience to this godforsaken place at the bidding of my father? Have I not suffered every horror, every indignity short-of death itself, which could have been demanded of me? Have I not done my duty, perhaps even a measure more?"

Silence enjoyed a momentary reign. Neither man could refuse her the affirmative nod she demanded.

"I shall wed this Sun-King-Coyote-Shrimp of yours, as I

have promised, *lima laa?* If, of course, he wants me—damaged goods that I have become. But one thing neither of you—nor he!—shall ever have of me is the privacy of my thoughts and feelings! I shall not be interrogated about them further!"

She whirled with an inarticulate noise, stamping out her anger upon the carpet leading to another room of the apartments they had been assigned within the Palace of the Sun.

Mochamet al Rotshild shrugged again.

With a sudden noise, the door slid open.

Owald was there, in full uniform, high-polished helmet in the crook of his arm.

"Princess"—he nodded, speaking in Helvetian, the only language they shared in common—"gentlemen, your attendance is required by the Sun. I'm to escort you to him."

Ayesha turned in the doorway she had entered, argument forgotten, a concerned expression upon her face as she looked at David lying bandaged upon the couch.

"The rabbi," she told Owald in syllables as stiff and formal as the young man's greeting, "is ill as yet. He can't accompany us. Nor do I believe the Commodore—"

Owald shook his head.

"My lady, this is no request. I'm commanded to bring you before Zhu Yuan-Coyotl this minute. I've come prepared to meet what seem to me, anyway, to be your reasonable objections."

He raised an armored hand, beckoning to someone in the corridor beyond the range of Ayesha's vision, then stepped aside. There entered the room another of the soldiers, pushing a lightweight wheeled chair. Owald set his helmet aside, assisted in getting the rabbi upright. Shulieman was stoic about being placed in the chair, although it was clear to Ayesha that the process pained him.

Owald straightened.

"I can have another such contrivance here within a moment, should the *Siti* Mochamet—"

"Not upon your life, boy!" Mochamet al Rotshild roared in Arabic.

He rose to his feet, albeit leaning upon his cane.

"When the day arrives I needs must become a human roller-skate, you may bury me, whether or not I am still breathing! In the name of the Merciful and Compassionate, let us go!"

The animals, Po and Sagheer, were left behind. Together they traveled the great length of the residential hall to one of the elevating chambers they had not quite become accustomed to.

Within it, Ayesha was surprised when the car passed by the level of the Sun's audience chamber. It continued to descend many more floors than she had believed the palace possessed.

The door slid aside, permitting entrance of an odor of dampness, iodine, and oiled machinery. Owald guided them down a metal-walled corridor which opened upon a vast water-floored chamber, lit by electric lampions of a kind only yet speculated about at home in Europe, set high in the ceiling overhead.

"Our greetings! *Heebh ghaalah!*"

The cheerful voice was that of the Sun Incarnate, standing upon a metal-mesh walkway bordering the artificial pool which took up most of the huge room. Many strange craft lay bobbing at anchor or tied to posts along the walkway. The Sun had been inspecting one such, showing it to Fireclaw, who stood beside him.

Ayesha's troubled heart—she had not seen the warrior since their arrival here, not since falling into exhausted sleep and dreaming—began racing within her, and she had difficulty breathing until she gained embarrassed control of herself.

The man had looked at her and looked away.

"*Charjooh! Ghaadaa min luthbhah!* Sightseeing this morning!" exclaimed the Sun. "Step carefully, now, this little tub's round-bottomed and treacherous."

David was taken from his wheeled chair, lowered onto a leather-padded seat within the boat, amidships, with Owald. Ayesha climbed down, settling upon the seat behind him, against the comforting bulk of Mochamet al Rotshild. Zhu

Yuan-Coyotl—and the Helvetian warrior, his back toward her—sat up forward. The sole survivor missing from their original party, she realized as the Sun Incarnate of the Han-Meshika pushed buttons which caused the little boat to throb, was the elder Helvetian, Oln Woeck.

A startled moment came and went as a two-sectioned canopy of some ribbed, glassy substance slid up from the gunwales upon each side, clanking together overhead. Something hissed. Ayesha experienced a moment of discomfort until she swallowed.

Her ears popped.

The Sun Incarnate steered the boat away from the dock.

"Despite appearances, this is not sea-level, here."

He waved a free hand at the black, oily water they traveled across toward the shadow-obscured far wall.

"We are many fathoms below it. That arched portal up ahead is a water-lock."

This portal they then entered.

Ayesha watched as heavy metal doors slid closed behind them. Inside the chamber, the water-level began rising as the Sun manipulated controls upon the console before him.

Water sloshed up above the level of the gunwales, crept up the transparent sides of the boat. After a moment of panic, she remembered her father mentioning Mughal ships which traveled under water. She attempted to relax.

At length another door opened before them. The tiny vessel scooted out into the open depths amidst a flurry of rising bubbles, into the dark, murky water of the bay.

The journey, following this alarming start, was brief and uneventful. Ayesha watched for fish, in particular the large man-eaters rumored by the Palace help to inhabit these waters, but saw nothing besides a few jelly-saucers waggling their uncertain way through the depths. She supposed the noise of the engine frightened faster animals away. Sightseeing was not much assisted by the fact that the water permitted but a few feet visibility before all became a gray-black fog about the boat. She wondered how the Sun could see to steer. A greenish light upon the console lit his face from underneath. He paid it rapt attention.

As did Fireclaw, an ecstatic grin upon his face.

At last they began angling upward. The waters brightened, although they grew no clearer. Daylight broke upon them as they themselves broke the surface of the bay, making straight into a little harborlet carved out of solid rock.

Ayesha leaned back—

—and caught her breath. Towering high above them was the tallest building she had ever seen, perched upon an island which was no more than an upthrust of barren stone. She had seen this structure from a palace window, guessing it to be half as tall, perhaps, as the Eye-of-God pyramid perched upon yet another island—not as far away as she had thought—was wide. Now she revised her estimate upward.

With a startling rumble, the transparent boat-canopy disappeared into the gunwales.

A blast of cold, wet wind struck Ayesha's face.

An attendant waiting upon the quayside assisted with pulling David Shulieman from the boat, helped to get him seated in a chair identical to the one he had left in the submarine chamber beneath the Palace of the Sun. Overhead the sky was gray and overcast. It was cold upon the naked rock, which, as if in warning, transmitted to their feet another of the silent rolling flutters—this one much gentler than before—which they had earlier experienced.

The breeze blew in sodden, salt-laden gusts which felt like sword-thrusts. Shivering, they hurried toward uncertain shelter at the base of the tower. All save Fireclaw and the Sun, who strolled at leisure, making swooping gestures with their hands, talking about the submarine vessel they had just abandoned with reluctance.

The others waited for the men to catch up.

"You may have been told"—the Sun Zhu Yuan-Coyotl glanced back at the commander of his bodyguard—"that the Eye-of-God is the heart of Our Empire. From the limited viewpoint of Our subjects, we suppose there is some truth in that."

He stopped before an entrance. Bronze doors half a dozen stories tall stood closed before him. The tower itself was of a featureless sandy-gray artificial stone, still showing the seams of molds into which its substance had been poured like a gigantic candle. Hexagonal in cross section, it rose uncounted man-heights into a similar-colored sky until it diminished in the distance to a point.

Zhu Yuan-Coyotl struck his fist upon a door which rang like the father of all gongs.

A pause, then both doors began to grind aside with a soul-disturbing rumble.

"In point of fact, however," he went on, "*this* is the true heart of Our domain. Understanding it, what it represents, you will come in due course to understand Us.

"Welcome, guests, to Our Spire of Dreamers!"

He stepped between the bronze doors, beckoning them to follow.

Inside, the appointments were as luxurious as the Spire's exterior had been severe. They were in a giant entrance-hall—its ceiling seemed to vanish into darkness overhead—paneled in jade. Perhaps a hundred paces would have been necessary to cross this room from side to side. How far back it went was anybody's guess, as most of that part was spanned—and thus concealed—by a huge, dense beaded curtain.

Casting his feathered cloak upon the floor, as if in utter confidence someone would appear to pick it up, the Sun Incarnate strode to a low table placed across the entrance hall.

He took up what appeared to be a long, slender drumstick.

Standing upon the same table, with perhaps a cubit's length between them, were four delicate-appearing vases wrought of thin uncolored glass, the outermost pair about the height of the stick in Zhu Yuan-Coyotl's hand, the innermost of differing height, one smaller than the outer two, another much larger.

The Sun struck a vase nearest him.

Its ringing was not unlike that of a cut-crystal bell. He laid a palm upon its surface, yet its ringing did not cease until he had walked a few steps, placed his hand upon the furthest jar, which had begun ringing with the same tone.

The inner pair stood silent.

"Remember this demonstration," the young man told Ayesha and her companions, "when you witness what this tower holds. It will save a deal of explanation."

He set the stick back upon the table.

Together they walked around the table, through the clattering curtain, into the depths of the Spire of Dreamers.

XLII:

The Tree of Might-Be

By the sun and his morning brightness and by the
moon when she follows him, and by the day when it
displays him and by the night when it enshrouds him!
—The *Koran*, Sura XCI

Beads clattered in the Sun's wake.

The broad curtain had concealed the semicircular foot of a
titanic case of stairsteps, like the walls about them hewn from
gray-green stone, twisting around, ever upward, from the
ground floor of the Spire of Dreamers into heights unseen
above.

At his bidding, Ayesha followed Zhu Yuan-Coyotl through
the curtain, Fireclaw holding it aside first for the Princess
Ayesha, then for slow-moving Mochamet al Rotshild, pushing
David's chair. Owald in his copper kilt and blackened armor
passed through it behind them.

Ducking to avoid entangling his sword-handle, the Helvetian warrior let the beaded strands flow through his fingers.
They dropped from his hand to swing clashing against each
other. He strode, then, to catch up with Ayesha and the Sun.

It was, she thought, an unlovely and unsettling place. Devoid of any decoration—if but in this alone, it was unlike any other building Ayesha had seen within the Crystal Empire—the giant stairwell which comprised the hollow central portion of the Spire was of itself unlit. Looking upward was like being a midge-fly trapped inside the chamber of a titanic rifle-barrel—the wall-hugging spiral staircase enhanced this illusion—looking upward toward the muzzle-crown.

In the well's center lay a low dais heaped with glowing charcoal from which the cloying smoke of incense powder issued—huge amphorae of the stuff stood open and at hand upon the floor nearby—twisting and curling toward the invisible heights.

"Ayyah!"

The Sun clapped his hands.

From out of the surrounding shadows a pair of husky male attendants, arch-nosed and red-brown of complexion, materialized, unspeaking, to accompany the visitors. The threadbare robes they wore were blackened, not by any dye within the coarse-woven fabric they were fashioned of, but from years, it seemed, of wear without being washed.

The two who wore them were far worse, their ebon waist-length hair rope-stiff, knotty and matted with some unguessable accumulation of filth, the skin about their faces and hands crusted over, crackling like the soil of some drought-afflicted land. Each brought with him his own hovering cloud of tiny insects. Larger crawling things dropped off their clothing as they passed, scurrying for the safety of the shadows. The odor of their unwashed bodies was more than Ayesha could withstand without gulping back a bitter foam—her stomach stirred, threatening worse—which rose, despite her efforts to the contrary, at the back of her throat.

The faces of her companions told Ayesha they were suffering the same reaction.

"Our priests—"

Zhu Yuan-Coyotl introduced these dreadful attendants with a wave of his hand. Even he stood well back, breathing in shallow gasps in their noisome presence.

"—will assist Us."

Together, they set foot upon the stairs.

At frequent intervals, broad archways of truncated, triangular shape appeared, piercing the smooth-polished walls beside them. Entrances, it appeared to the girl, to bright-illuminated corridors radiating outward in great number from the central well, burrowing deep into the unknown outer structure of the Spire. These spilled their light in reasonable abundance into the well.

The Saracen-Helvetian party began climbing, David's wheeled chair paralleling the path they described, locked as it had been by the unsavory priest-attendants Zhu Yuan-Coyotl had summoned upon a clever, self-powered rail which had been mounted low at the well-end of the stairs. The mechanism made no noise as it moved the rabbi's chair around and upward. Somehow the unwashed, insect-ridden servants had accomplished this and disappeared once more and as silently.

Ayesha looked about her.

Whatever insane imperial architect had conceived these stairsteps, she thought, it was certain he had not had human ease or comfort in mind. The treads were set back too far, their risers being but half the height they should have been. The going would have been easier, Ayesha reflected, had it been the other way around.

Owald, a youth at the peak of military physical conditioning, strode along well enough, his bodyguardsman's accoutrements of hardened leather and polished metal squeaking and clattering with each lifting of his muscled thighs.

The sick and elderly Mochamet al Rotshild, upon the other hand, gasped out something between wheezes about wishing now that he had accepted the offer of his own wheeled chair.

Fireclaw kept the pace in silence.

Zhu Yuan-Coyotl seemed cheered by the exercise.

Before many minutes had passed, Ayesha's own legs ached with the unnatural motions climbing the steps demanded. At the dimmer ends of the treads, away from the arches, there had been provided no protecting banister. There existed nothing more than darkened, empty space, smelling of mustiness and incense that was too sweet to abide long.

Hanging over the abyss, David appearead pale, grim, as if resisting every passing moment the temptation to look down. Unlike the Commodore, Ayesha did not envy him the novelty of the ride.

Thus did Zhu Yuan-Coyotl, the Sun Incarnate of the Han-Meshika, lead them, an assortment of adventurers from lands far away and perhaps now more appreciated, the Saracen Princess Ayesha, the Helvetian warrior Sedrich Fireclaw, Mochamet al Rotshild, counselor to kings and caliphs, Captain-of-the-Bodyguard Owald Sedrichsohn, David Shulie-man the battle-injured Jewish scholar, past many of the radiating corridors, offering neither comment nor explanation as he did so, until, several stories up, after a climb which had been dizzying in more than one sense of the word, he at last bade them enter one of the archways.

Some delay was occasioned when David's wheeled chair was disconnected from the rail, without attendant help this time—he closed his eyes, swallowing, as Fireclaw and Owald swore and sweated, jiggling the contrivance over empty space—from its rail.

When it was safe upon solid flooring, the Commodore once more took up its handles, appearing grateful for the support they offered. They then proceeded into the corridor, where they encountered an immediate branching in its course.

"Do not fear," the Sun answered their bemused expres-sions. "We have at frequent intervals wandered these passage-ways all Our life. We cannot therefore become lost."

He then lifted a weather-browned, slender hand to waist level, thereby indicating first in turn the right-hand branching, then the branching upon the left hand.

"Nor does it matter much," he told them, "which of the pathways We choose to explore. Each of them has its own minor peculiarities to divert Us. Yet the lesson to be learned in each is much the same. Let the Princess decide which way."

"*Lima laa,*" Ayesha answered. "As you will it."

She hesitated but a moment, then, remembering the habitual

human tendency to turn rightward in such circumstances, strode instead into the left-branching corridor.

Zhu Yuan-Coyotl laughed.

This branch of Ayesha's choosing they thus followed, blinking for a while at the brighter lighting they encountered, the aged Commodore half pushing, half leaning upon David's chair.

Fireclaw kept his hand upon his dagger-pommel.

As if in hostile territory, Owald took up the rear.

Ayesha agreed with the uneasy, haunted feeling that both fighting men had, all unwitting, thus betrayed. Perhaps it was the strange surroundings. Perhaps nothing more than the subtle shimmering—something no warrior's wariness or skill would be useful in quelling—they felt within the building, radiating upward from its roots.

The earth was again restless.

They had not thus proceeded twenty paces before they arrived at yet another passage branching, after that another, and another, Ayesha choosing upon each occasion, at Zhu Yuan-Coyotl's amused bidding, which direction they should take.

In a sense, he told them, they had no destination. They were at this moment where he wanted them to be, looking upon the sights he had wished them to behold.

As if in illustration of this, he pointed at the walls. As Ayesha had already observed, they were not alone. Upon either side of the branching corridors they passed along, they were shown small, unembellished cubicles, hundreds of them, glass-fronted, each with its own door, in which inmates lay upon elevated pallets.

Both genders were represented among the occupants, as well as every age, from tiny children, looking even smaller in their grown-up beds, to wizened elders. There were people here of every race.

"These subjects," Zhu Yuan-Coyotl explained, "are selected for this service when they come of school age and are tested for the talent it requires. They come from everywhere within Our domain, their families handsomely recompensed through a significant reduction in their tax levies. They are well taken care of, and live long, productive lives. Many of them have been here in this place far longer than you have been alive, Mochamet al Rotshild."

They continued walking down the branching passageways.

David remarked aloud concerning his observation that into the bared left arm of every individual there had been inserted the end of a narrow, flexible transparent tube whose origin was a large bottle hanging upside down from a metal stand beside the pallet.

The Sun explained that the bottles contained certain substances which aided the selectees in the performance of the service which was required of them here.

"Chiefly," he added, "they partake of liquid nutrients—far more efficient than maintaining kitchen services in this place—also of an expensive synthetic enzyme based upon the concentrated extracts of the hearts of the artichoke plant. We Ourselves have tried it, even to the extent of taking the drugs."

Ayesha swallowed, feeling herself pale at Zhu Yuan-Coyotl's words.

He himself chuckled, as if at the guilty memory of some minor boyhood naughtiness.

"We are afraid We have small talent for it: one brief glimpse of a pistol made of glass."

Ayesha stumbled, seized Fireclaw's great upper arm in both her small hands—then released it, feeling her breath grow short at the merest touch of him, her face begin to redden. With an embarrassed look upon his own features, the warrior cleared his throat as the party continued along the corridor.

"All else was ordinary wish-fulfillment, small dreams of Our own everyday travails. No matter, any single subject cannot tell us much in any event. It is the aggregate which counts."

They peered through the panes of glass as if visiting a zoo. Other tubes, Ayesha saw, larger than the others, stretched from the middles of the sheet-draped forms down to recesses beneath the pallets. They gurgled as they worked, dark shadows upon occasion sliding through them to disappear beneath the pallets.

In some alcoves, the supine inmates were being massaged by pairs of heavy-muscled attendants—not the filthy priests, but others, garbed in pale green—their limbs stretched and pounded, their skin chafed to stir the circulation.

Ayesha guessed that there existed no need—and no excuse—for the inmates ever to leave their beds, let alone the rooms in which they were confined.

The idea sickened her.

Wherever the massage-teams or others performing similar services were not in attendance, some second imprisoned soul was seated in a low chair beside the pale reclining figure, writing as the inmate roused from drug-induced stupor for a while to speak. To others of the cubicles sketch-artists had been summoned—the party had collided with one such, hurrying down the hallway with his tablet and colored pencils—to draw something the inmate was describing.

"Written accounts are taken to a central processing area," Zhu Yuan-Coyotl told his guests, "where they are sorted, collated together, and each day summarized. Seven hundred thousand scribes—a veritable army—supervisors, clerks, scholars, historians, and archivists busy themselves with the task. We Ourselves are each day presented summaries of the summaries. Sometimes We suggest specific lines of inquiry for further pursuit. It takes up more of Our time and energy than any other of Our duties, but it is very often worth the cost."

In many of the cubicles, both occupants—drugged recliner and attendant scribe—dozed in subdued lighting, oblivious to visitors, servitors, casual passersby, even to the tremors rattling the fixtures.

In one such, the "subject" sat up of a sudden, screamed, then fell back and lay silent.

The scribe nodding his chin beside her did not stir.

Some few of the rooms were empty, in the process of being cleaned, replastered, painted, or otherwise repaired—perhaps in response to that very rattling. In others yet the window to the corridor had been smeared over with some soapy, semiopaque substance, as if what lay within were too terrible to behold.

Ayesha could keep her silence no longer.

"They are like chickens in a coop, these poor people! *Chanaa la chabhgham! Maa manna?* What have they done to deserve such cruel, inhuman punishment?"

Zhu Yuan-Coyotl laughed.

"The 'crime' they have committed, my dear Princess, is a lifelong one, consisting of nothing more than the inadvertent possession of a certain very peculiar excellence."

He turned to take in all the visitors.

"No, foreign friends, these are not criminals, but the Dreamers, of whom We have often spoken, also at whose mention We have seen many a curious expression upon your faces."

He looked about him at the many rooms within sight, as if attempting to choose among them.

"Now," he asserted, "you shall learn more of them, perhaps, than you had wished to know."

XLIII:

Resonance

"My prayer, my ritual sacrifice, my living, my dying—all belongs to God, the Lord of all Being."
—The *Koran*, Sura VI

Zhu Yuan-Coyotl stopped, entering one of the cubicles.

Despite themselves, Fireclaw and the others found themselves crowded about the doorway, looking in.

The cubicle's occupant, a young, fragile-appearing boy of perhaps fifteen, looked up at the Sun Incarnate, blinked without recognizing his ruler. The recording-scribe beside him, a girl of about the same age, had tidied his coverlet, patted his thin shoulder, then thrown herself, face downward, upon the floor.

"We have commanded him," explained Zhu Yuan-Coyotl in Arabic, having first spoken in one of the languages of the Han-Meshika, "to tell us what he has been dreaming of."

"I d-dreamt of this very place." The boy raised an emaciated arm, answering in a weak, high-pitched voice, employing the same language he had been addressed in.

Zhu Yuan-Coyotl translated every few words.

The boy gazed with drug-dulled eyes at the ceiling-fixtures. His body was white all over, pale as tendrils of the plantlife one finds growing beneath a rock.

"Only the windows of each cubicle were without glass," he added, "fashioned from thick iron bars painted a lumpy white, with reddish rust-stains leaking through. More bars blocked access to the corridors."

The boy sighed, licking his lips as if compelled to call up a distasteful memory.

"Words were scratched or painted," he continued, "upon the cubicle walls. Terrible words. Men, all dressed alike, brooded within them, consumed with a hatred many years in the making. They looked out upon other men who carried clubs.

"I was one of those who brooded thus."

A tear trickled down the boy's face.

He stopped speaking.

The Sun stepped closer, wiped the liquid from the pale cheek, then wiped his fingers upon the sheet.

"Go on, child, tell Us more."

"Somewhere outside the cubicles a great bell sounded. The door-bars all slid aside. The men—there were hundreds of us—stepped out and stood in rows while those with clubs inspected them, poking at them with the clubs, making rude jokes. Some of their charges looked upon the others, the youngest among us, like predators, their unclean thoughts written upon their faces. Upon one occasion, I . . ."

He shuddered.

"Then the bell rang once again—much shouting by the club-carriers—we ourselves being bidden to utter and eternal silence upon pain of terrible punishment. We turned and marched along a railed walkway which clattered with our heavy footfalls. I think we were being taken somewhere to work and then to eat."

A sigh of envy tinged these final words.

As if this effort at speaking against his will to remember had exhausted him, the bedridden boy let his thin, trembling hand drop to the coverlet. With a deep sigh, he closed his eyes.

The little scribe rose from the floor without being bidden by her sovereign. Keeping her eyes averted from the Sun Incarnate, she kneaded the Dreamer's hand.

Zhu Yuan-Coyotl spoke, not this time to the boy Dreamer, but to the girl beside the bed.

"We suspect, child, that you grow too fond of him of whose words you are but an instrument of recordance. This is disruptive. It is not Our will that it should be so. At the next sleep-period, you will ask your supervisor for immediate reassignment."

"Yes, Lord."

The girl's voice, not loud to begin with, and a small sob, were muffled by the coverlet she stared at.

The Sun nodded, spread a hand to ruffle her shiny dark hair, and left the cubicle, continuing the party's journey to yet another branching of the corridor.

Here, he stopped.

"It is a common enough dream here," he told them, once well beyond being heard by the frail boy who had spoken. "A hundred thousand civilizations, it would seem, have at one time or another chosen to make a prison of this rocky islet."

He gave a sigh of satisfaction.

"We Han-Meshika, at least, have made it something other than that, something proud, to be admired."

Sickened, Fireclaw suppressed a remark which would have been a poor substitute for what, in truth, he thought to do. They walked a few paces down the corridor, entered yet another cubicle.

This Dreamer was a middle-aged man with exaggerated features and skin the color and texture of charcoal. His scribe, like the one in the previous roomlet, was a young Han-Meshika girl.

". . . was carrying a large leather bag through a great hall, amidst thousands of other travelers like myself, also carrying their possessions thus."

As he spoke, the girl took his words down in writing. Zhu Yuan-Coyotl began to translate until Ayesha informed him that the man's words were intelligible.

The Sun assumed a puzzled expression, glanced down at the scribe's tablet, then nodded understanding.

"Ah, yes, one of those rarest of outsiders who has qualified for this position. From your father's southernmost African domains, or so it says upon the form."

Oblivious, the black man was still speaking.

"Disembodied voices came out of the air, offering instruction and advice, while at a dozen glass-fronted stalls merchants hawked cheap, flashy souvenirs, clothing, colored booklets, bland food and drink costing more than it was worth."

He shook his head.

"Uniformed guardsmen there were, inspecting people and the things they carried with them, bidding them pass through arches which made noises should any of the bags contain forbidden articles."

Zhu Yuan-Coyotl folded his arms, the tolerant expression of bored amusement telling Fireclaw that he had heard tales such as this one many times before.

"I offered passage-papers," said the Dreamer, "to a uniformed young woman, very pretty, who smiled and led me to a great door which I then walked through. I experienced dizziness, a flash of blue light. I found myself—as I had expected to—standing before my own house, where my women and our many dear children came out to greet me as if I had been gone for a long while."

He stopped, as if finished speaking.

The Sun had let his arms drop suddenly, and with them, his jaw.

"Girl," he ordered, suppressed excitement in his voice, "this remarkable dream, which begins in an ordinary wise—it sounds, at first, like any of a million busy travel-terminals for wheeled or winged conveyances—nevertheless bears further examination for the method of travel itself! Do you inform your supervisor. Convey to him my instruction to let me know of any progress you may make!"

The scribe nodded, making note without speaking of the Sun Incarnate's words upon her tablet.

Observing the confused expressions upon the faces of his guests, Zhu Yuan-Coyotl sighed.

"It often begins with something simple. During the reign of an illustrious ancestor of Ours, for example, one Dreamer dreamt of turning the metal base of a small glassy 'pear,' as she described it, into a brass-lined hole in the ceiling. When it had been seated home, it lit up with a dazzling light!"

Fireclaw nodded. David Shulieman had long since explained Han-Meshikan electric lighting to the Helvetian. It was characteristic of him that he'd already begun taking it for granted.

"Our ancestor," the Sun was saying, "ordered in his wisdom that the matter be pursued, through special suggestions made before the Dreamers slept, also by a thorough search for similar references in the archives already collected. It was not long before dreams of illuminated pears led to those of wall-switches—We were lucky there, one of our Dreamers was a house-carpenter in some other existence—transmission-lines, transformers, generators."

He clapped his hands in delight.

Fireclaw was not displeased that the Princess had moved close beside him—some subtle scent she wore offset the murky odor of the place—as the Sun rambled on.

"In this manner We learned to fly, the making of sophisticated weaponry, the surest means of taxation, a billion other things which, together, comprise the civilization of Han-Meshika. We are free to choose among the most efficacious of methods, making strides of a century's progress in but a few months if We will it."

Still the looks about him were uncomprehending.

He shrugged, beginning again.

"You have seen how this hallway splits and splits again until it has become a thousand hallways?"

"A thousand twenty-four," the Rabbi Shulieman offered, great weariness coloring his tone.

"Very good," replied the Sun. "A thousand twenty-four, then two thousand forty-eight, and so on—the same being true for some five hundred levels of this tower."

Ayesha opened her mouth.

"*Maadaa qulth!* Five hundred—"

Zhu Yuan-Coyotl nodded.

"Reckon it for yourself, girl. This island—the Spire standing upon it—is five hundred eighty paces long, about a third of that in width. The Spire's height is three times the greater of those measures. In all, close to twenty-three million cubic paces, perhaps a quarter taken up by corridors and such necessities. The remainder is divided among these cubicles, three paces wide, three paces deep, three paces high. Six million Dreamers slumber here, a living sacrifice providing indispensable food for thought to their sovereign, the Sun Incarnate."

The earth beneath them shimmered once more, just at the edge of noticeability. Ignoring the unsettling phenomenon, the Sun Incarnate turned, slapping his hand upon the jade wall which formed the junction of two passageways.

"They are like the splitting branches of a vast tree, are they not? An ancestor of Ours had the Spire of Dreamers constructed in this somewhat bizarre manner to teach himself a lesson. You see, the universe itself is constructed in this manner."

He pointed a slim finger at Fireclaw.

"Suppose a moment that you'd ne'er left your home upon the eastern coast, great warrior. Suppose you'd ne'er traveled prairieward. You'd not be here now, would you, but in some other place, doing something else, is that not so?"

The warrior shook his head, a grim expression upon his face.

"Is there not enough trouble in the world, Zhu Yuan-Coyotl," he answered in the Helvetian the Sun had employed, "to be o'erworried about might-have-beens?"

"Upon the contrary, mighty Fireclaw, the Spire of Dreamers's all about might-have-beens. 'Tis concerned with naught else. For in some might-be world as real to its inhabitants as ours appears to us, you *did* remain upon the eastern coast, to suffer or enjoy whatever consequences that decision earned you."

He turned to David Shulieman, looking down at the rabbi where he sat quiet and weary in the wheeled chair.

"Likewise, scholar, in some other world you decided to become a sailor, whereas in that world, or perhaps another, your friend the Commodore, here, followed a path of religious erudition."

Light was dawning upon the rabbi's pain-seamed face. He turned his head slowly, looking about the place as if for the first time.

"I see," the Sun exclaimed, "that you begin to understand! Those worlds exist! Our other selves exist within them! Enough worlds so that everything which *can* come to pass *has*, branching out from one another, growing in their trans-infinite number as each of us makes decisions—or perhaps with each random fall of the dice."

"Is this religion?"

Fireclaw felt nothing but disgust. Six million tortured captives for the sake of a mad boy's fantasies.

"Or fact?" the Helvetian asked. "If so, how'd you come to know it?'"

Zhu Yuan-Coyotl laughed, showing them into a third cell where an old woman was dictating.

"I dreamt this period," she spoke in a cheerful, grandmother's voice, "of a blunt-nosed winged vessel stooping like a scorch-breasted bird upon the ruined surface of the moon until, unfolding wheels beneath itself, it raced upon an avenue a million paces in extent, restrained by cords across its path which brought it to a halt."

She leaned forward, tapped the already attentive scribe upon the shoulder.

"People wearing glass-faced armor—I among their number—debarked, entering arch-topped dwellings, half buried in the soil, where we were greeted lovingly by kinsfolk."

She leaned back with a contented expression.

"We were home."

The Sun Incarnate stepped outside again, addressing the Helvetian warrior.

"There are many religions, Fireclaw, some tens of millions

of which We've encountered through Our Dream-scribes and their supervisors. There's but one Fact, of which the many smaller truths which comprise the universe are but minor aspects."

With a twinkle in his eye, he repeated the old woman's gesture, leaning forward, tapping Fireclaw upon the chest.

"We know this, for Our Dreamers tell Us 'tis so."

"As I thought," the warrior snorted, "religion."

Zhu Yuan-Coyotl laughed again.

"We understand your skepticism, Fireclaw. Were We confronting this establishment, what it has to teach Us, for the first time, We hope We'd be as wary as you are. Nonetheless—"

He folded his arms, rested his chin upon one hand.

"Look you, recall the vases We struck upon the ground floor? Like Our ancestor, we, too, wish to teach a lesson, if only to Ourselves. We'd those jars placed there to that purpose. The outermost containers ring together when only one of them is struck because they're identical—they resonate with one another—while the inner ones aren't and don't. 'Tis the principle upon which many sophisticated communications devices—"

Aycsha, listening, had become pale.

"*Chanaa la chabhgham.* What has this to do with these Dreamers whom you victimize so cruelly?"

The Sun smiled upon her, switching back to Arabic.

"We are, put in the bluntest of terms, parasites. What of it? It is no more than a word. A civilization peaceful, ordered, yet—a paradox—progressive. What need of individual 'creativity'? Why tolerate the indiscipline it engenders, when you can steal its fruits from others? Yes, Our domain is advanced. But why suffer the economic or political displacements which follow in the wake of advancement, when you can control the introduction of each innovation, avoiding the eccentric prejudices of the innovators themselves?"

Noting the expression upon her face, he went on.

"In another world, Princess, perhaps you refused your father's command, remaining instead in exile, perhaps upon the island Malta where your mother once lived."

Ayesha nodded understanding of this much, refraining to ask him how he knew of these things.

"Very well, can we not make use of whatever similarities might be between the strong-willed Ayesha who refused her father—and the only slightly less strong-willed Ayesha who journeyed here in spite? There must be many, is it not possible, chiefmost of the mind? When one Ayesha sleeps, does not her unguarded mind perhaps resonate—as did those vases—with the other Ayesha's equally open dreaming mind?"

She took a step backward, away from Zhu Yuan-Coyotl.

"Is it not possible," he continued, "that, locked thus in resonance, many of the first Ayesha's experiences are communicated to—look out, somebody, catch her!"

Ayesha's legs had failed her.

She shuddered and collapsed in Fireclaw's arms.

XLIV:

Bribery

Seek you help in patience and prayer, for grievous it is, save to the humble who reckon they shall meet their Lord.

—The *Koran*, Sura I

"Ah, well."

Zhu Yuan-Coyotl raised an eyebrow as Fireclaw lifted the Princess Ayesha into the safety of his arms.

"We suppose we ought to have looked for this to happen."

Lips tight with a rising anger threatening, he feared, to transform itself into mindless blood-haze, Fireclaw spared a brief glance for the young man, athletic, tanned and smooth of skin, handsome of face and form—and, in the Helvetian warrior's estimation, more marrow-evil than Oln Woeck had ever thought to be.

"We see you disapprove of Us."

The Sun had not failed to observe the warning in the warrior's eyes.

"You think Us harsh," he offered, with an amused twinkle

in his own eyes, "o'erbearing and inhuman. You'd tell Us the measures We find recourse to are excessive."

Still speaking, Zhu Yuan-Coyotl turned his back to the man to face the wall. The older man couldn't see the sly expression upon the younger's face, nor could he have known what it meant in any case.

Oln Woeck might have told him.

"You've led a much-sheltered life, mighty Fireclaw, one most limited in its scope, learning all but naught of the universe you live in, nor of the million catastrophes an unrestrained, unguided, and uncertain humanity's engendered—"

The warrior let his hand creep, almost of its own volition, toward the dagger at his side. Encumbered as he was with Ayehsa's limp form, he couldn't use *Murderer*. Thinking better of it—another time and place, but *soon*—he drew the hand back again, supporting the unconscious girl with it.

Zhu Yuan-Coyotl whirled, staring into Fireclaw's eyes as if looking for something there. His own expression, the man noted, was an almost disappointed one.

"Why, We've lost contact entire with a hundred civilizations for no better reason than that they'd learned how to destroy themselves—and saw no reason not to use what they'd learned!"

He gazed down at Ayesha, a kindly look upon his face.

"We're patient. We could sweep the Mughals and the Saracens aside and rule the earth, Fireclaw. In some respects, We do. Yet We've wider ambitions, not just to rule one small planet, but, in due course, each globe within the realm of Our celestial aspect's attractive influence—and perhaps someday beyond."

With a gesture he'd used before, he reached out to stroke the unconscious girl's hair. Fireclaw pivoted a shoulder, taking her out of the Sun Incarnate's reach.

Zhu Yuan-Coyotl shrugged.

"Futile defiance doesn't impress Us, friend. Nor do gifts from rival potentates. We brought you to this place, for We'd heard of the girl's dreams. We realized the question would arise whether her life might be spent to greater profit as one among Our Dreamers in the Spire than as a Bride to the Sun."

He turned his head, taking in several of the cubicles and their helpless occupants.

"True," he mused as to himself, "were circumstances different, she might well provide us, in her own small way, with further insight. Howe'er, We doubt that she—or you— would regard as much of an improvement upon her lot this grim alternative."

He lifted his arms, taking in the entire building they stood within, with all of its occupants.

"At this moment We're considering a proposal put forth by the supervisors—and Our physicians—to increase its efficiency or reduce the burdens of its cost."

He peered at the Rabbi David Shulieman, addressing the injured scholar in Arabic.

"We are advised by them to amputate the legs of Dreamers when they are first brought here—they will need their hands for explanatory gestures—perhaps take their reproductive organs as well, since, as you have seen, these are a source of continuous annoyance, and there appears to be no inheritable predisposition to dream."

Shulieman shrank backward, as if this offhand proposition had been a physical blow. The Sun Incarnate shifted his gaze to Mochamet al Rotshild.

"There is some debate about the eyes. The cubicles will be wired for sound and pictures to be monitored in some central place—until We learn to wire the brain and tap the dreams Ourselves. We search every moment for means to keep them sleeping more of the day, to increase the time of useful dreaming within sleep."

Shrugging again, he turned back to Sedrich Fireclaw and the Helvetian warrior's tongue.

"It'll eliminate distractions," he explained, "the need for this vast army of scribes and whatnot, the possible contamination of gratuitous human contact."

As they spoke, the building round them began to vibrate in

the worst tremor they'd thus far experienced. The floor seemed to jump, slapping at the bottoms of their feet.

Observing the various expressions this phenomenon provoked upon the faces of his guests, the Sun smiled.

"The earth is split to the core in this region. A great crack in the surface of the globe travels westward of the city, stretching north into Our tributary domain Kwakiutl, south almost to the original Meshika capital, Tenochtitlán."

From somewhere within the depths of mortal resignation, perhaps out of nothing more than pedagogic habit, David Shulieman nodded understanding.

Fireclaw had never heard of such a thing.

"It is a scientific curiosity," the Sun went on, "at most a minor annoyance—save, of course, upon occasions when whole cities are brought down by such trembling. This came to pass within the reign of Our immediate predecessor save one."

He shrugged, returning to Helvetian.

"This little rattle-shaking's naught to worry o'er—ah, We see the Princess is already coming round. Admirable. Stoutly turned out, don't you think? Well deserving of the honor We'll bestow upon her. Shall we be going?"

Fireclaw set Ayesha back upon her feet, giving her assurances, receiving them from her. Nonetheless, he watched her until he was certain of her steadiness.

And of his own.

2

The party retraced its steps among the living dead.

They reached at last the spiral stairway, where the Rabbi David Shulieman, with an oath uncharacteristic of the retiring scholar they all expected him to be, rose grimly from the wheeled chair, demanding he be allowed to descend afoot.

"From this moment forward," the scholar hissed between his pain-clenched teeth, "and at whatever cost, I'll not presume upon our captor's *kindness*—" This last word he emphasized, although whether out of sarcasm or wounded agony, Fireclaw could not tell. "—nor let him see me help-less," Shulieman finished.

None could gainsay him.

Leaning upon the polished wall beside the stairs—in his case their odd proportions helped a little, providing space to rest upon—he gave a creditable account of himself for one that recent in his wounding, although Fireclaw saw that his color wasn't good. Nor could he move about much without trembling afterward at the effort. The Helvetian was certain that the rabbi's bandages, bulking at his abdomen beneath his clothing, would soon be soaked with blood from his reopened injury.

Outside, the sky had begun to clear, patches of blue showing through in narrow rifts between the ragged strands of overcast. The brief underwater voyage back to the Palace of the Sun was no more eventful than it had been before, Zhu Yuan-Coyotl continuing to converse, in the main this time with David Shulieman.

"I wonder what they would say," the Sun replied to a question about the civilizations revealed by the Dreamers, "did they know there were being 'scrutinized and studied,' in the words of the poet, 'narrowly as a with microscope, by intelligences greater, yet as mortal, intellects vast and cool and unsympathetic.'"

The ruler chuckled.

Fireclaw paid the conversation scant attention. Keeping a watchful eye upon the failing scholar, he was at the same time thinking about another conversation he'd been summoned to with Zhu Yuan-Coyotl at the subterranean quayside, just before the Saracens had come.

3

Zhu Yuan-Coyotl had spoken of his incognito voyage from the eastern coast. There had been, of course, no shipwreck, no deck-hopping trek as he and Crab had described. Instead, he and his late companion had been delivered by night by a vessel of the air, flying across the continent at too high an altitude to be seen, to that place where he knew Mochamet al Rotshild's surface-ship would make its landfall. In the guise of "Shrimp," the Sun had wanted, he explained, to find out for himself whether it was time his domain moved against the outside world.

"Now We've decided against it." He'd nodded, as if to himself. "Instead, We'll let the Saracens and the Mughals finish one another. But We desire mighty Fireclaw join Us in keeping Our borders closed till such comes to pass."

Fireclaw guffawed. He'd hurried to the quayside, for from the talk of palace servants, a surprising lot of it in Arabic, he'd already learned somewhat about the Spire, had believed, as the young ruler later said he might, it was a desirable alternative to the fate two empires had declared for Ayesha.

Now Zhu Yuan-Coyotl had changed the subject.

"My son," asked Fireclaw, knowing the answer beforehand, "he put you up to this, at least in part, did he not?"

Zhu Yuan-Coyotl nodded.

"Still, there's a deal Fireclaw would gain by accepting the post he's been offered. The land's rich and enlightened, brimming o'er with opportunity, its ruler generous and, given proper circumstances, inclined to o'erlook much."

Fireclaw had concealed his mounting anger, keeping his tone level. Restraint was threatening to become a habit with him.

"Enlightened? After what you ordered done to the Comanche, to the Utes, to the—"

"We often do far worse by your lights, Sedrich Fireclaw. A little human sacrifice, to put the worst foot forward, is sometimes necessary to knit Our two peoples together. This We learned the hard way centuries ago. 'Twas a matter of the immigrant Han respecting the religious customs of the native Meshika."

Zhu Yuan-Coyotl turned, placing both hands upon Fireclaw's broad shoulders.

"Besides, what's straightforward slaughter to compare with aught which other cultures do to their folk—Our own Fireclaw, for example—more slowly, more inhumanely. In the main, do We not speak aright, with the pretense of doing them good?''

Fireclaw, thinking back upon fair Frae, upon his father, his mother, himself, most recently upon Dove Blossom, could offer naught in the way of answer.

"There's much to see and enjoy," Zhu Yuan-Coyotl pointed out. "You've experienced the miracle of Our flying ships. You might learn to fly, yourself. Owald's correct, 'tis possible you can grow a hand to replace that you lost."

He stepped back, smiling.

"D'you not trouble yourself o'er our customs. The common people believe their life and livelihood come from the Sun. They must, on that account, return a portion of it. In many respects, they're correct. The pyramid gives much in return for an occasional few lives—including power to light the city at night, and means of defending it. There are also carts you've not as yet seen, smaller, more manageable than the Saracens', requiring neither wind nor steam to propel—"

"And Ayesha's dreams?" Fireclaw interrupted.

"Ayesha's dreams are familiar to Han-Meshika science, as you're about to see. She's sensitive—not uniquely so—to a myriad of other selves in other universes near to this. She therefore dreams their dreams, transmitting her own in turn to them. This is why her premonitions are that poignant—and untrustworthy."

At this moment the Saracens had arrived for their underwater ride to the Spire of Dreamers.

4

Saying he'd consider the Sun's offer, Fireclaw returned alone to the quarters he'd been given—which he now recognized were little more than an elegant jail cell.

He let the door close behind him, hearing the click of its heavy brass lock. Owald had explained this as routine precaution for the Sun Incarnate's physical safety.

"Nothing personal," the boy had told him.

Fireclaw had nonetheless taken it as personal affront to be told he was a guest and be treated as a prisoner.

There he found his bear-dog Ursi awaiting him, bathed, groomed, and perfumed. He chuckled at the unaccustomed sight. It occurred to him to wonder how many helpful strangers among the Han-Meshika the great beast had maimed this time.

The animal had wet the rug.

Likely he was even more disturbed by the morning's earth-tremors than his people, although they were no unknown phenomenon where he'd been born. Now Fireclaw knew the reason, a crack in the earth's surface. No explanation suited to calm Ursi, however.

Exploring the place about him with his body while his mind conducted searches within itself, he also discovered another token of the Sun's desire that he commit himself, and soon, to service to the Han-Meshika—or of the similar desire of his own son. He opened a door. Hanging heavy within the room's wardrobe was a full suit of Bodyguardsman's armor: copper kilt, black-polished back-and-breast, a commander's helmet in the shape of a great grizzly's head.

Alongside the armor, dangling by its sling, hung one of the black, slab-sided quick-firing magazine weapons he'd tried under nervous supervision following sword-practice. His hand went first to this, to the long, curved magazine—

—which he found to be empty.

At the window, a glimmer of light caught Fireclaw's attention.

Out upon the bay, a giant airship, not the Sun's personal craft whose shadow he could even now see being cast upon the ground about the Palace—at whose topmost tower the craft was moored—but one much like it, approached the Ice-Mountain squatting like a monstrous, hungry crystal toad upon its own patch of land.

As it did so, some large portion of the vessel seemed to swing downward from the underside, rather like the slow-opening jaw of some predatory fish. This likeness was much enhanced by the eye painted upon the bow of the craft. A shift in the wind caused the ship's pilot to steer his bow a little in Fireclaw's direction. Now the Helvetian warrior could discern that the portion opening was a gigantic, polished surface—a mirror—which, when another thirty seconds passed, would be above the glassy red "pool" of the pyramid.

He waited, watching.

Without warning, a shaft of blinding brilliance, scarlet like the pool, large as the apex of the pyramid itself, sprang with a thunderclap from the roof of the edifice, glanced off the mirror which had been unfolded at the airship's chin, lanced outward, westward, over the bay's enclosing mountains to the sea.

The airship bobbed a little in the heavy winds of the bay. Almost as quick as it had sprung into being, the dazzling light was chopped off. He couldn't see what the beam had struck far out at sea. Nor had whatever it struck likely ever seen the beam, either. He could see, where the beam had wobbled a little, a fire beginning to rage upon the promontory near the harbor-mouth. E'er long the clangor of bells and sirens indicated the fire was being attended to.

The edges of the airship's mirror were smoking.

Fireclaw shuddered.

Setting aside his own weapons, he paced the carpeted floor for a long while, his muddled thoughts, whether he willed it or no, his emotions as well, centered upon Ayesha.

He was ready now, he thought, to recognize his feelings for the girl. However inappropriate, considering the time and place—Dove Blossom had been dead a mere matter of days— however inconvenient, they were real. They appeared to be reciprocated by her, despite what he considered the great difference in their ages.

They were the same feelings, he knew with a heart which sank and took wing in the same moment, as those he'd shared with Frae Hethristochter, that long ago, feelings which no one since then had stirred in him.

He slapped his prosthetic into his palm.

The pain brought with it resolution.

He must at least *try* to rescue Ayesha from the fate Zhu Yuan-Coyotl intended for her—the Sun had been vague about this, a dire enough warning in itself—even if he himself, and every soul upon the globe, were killed in the doing of it.

Better this, he thought, than to lose love once again and once again survive the loss.

The windows rattled with another tremor. Ignoring it, he considered possibilities. Given half a chance, the girl would help herself. That was one thing—he chuckled in remembrance of the rifle-shot she'd taken at him—he loved much about her.

The rabbi and the Commodore were useless in their present state. Oln Woeck was out of the question—Fireclaw hoped that he was dead. Best leave the loyalty of his son undivided; he'd been serving Zhu Yuan-Coyotl far longer than he'd known his father.

Just as he'd decided he could count upon no one but himself for assistance, had begun prying with his dagger-point at the locking-panel upon the door to the corridor—he'd search for Ayesha, no matter where she might be in this o'erambitious pile of bricks—he heard a gentle rapping at another door, connecting this chamber to the neighboring quarters of Mochamet al Rotshild.

"Fireclaw," he offered in excellent Helvetian, "I'd a word or more with you."

The man slid the door aside and entered.

Fireclaw noticed how the aged, unwell Saracen Commodore seemed to have enjoyed a miraculous recovery from his recent illness. His coloring was back. He walked with a young man's springy gait.

Mochamet al Rotshild grinned.

" 'Twould to me appear our esteemed young host prefers his guests to be of the harmless variety, disarmed, safely locked away. You see how I've accommodated him: what could be more harmless than an old man? Why, of course, my friend, a *sick* old man!"

Fireclaw grunted, went back to prying at the lock.

The Saracen persisted.

"I see you're preparing to take your leave. Well, my Helvetian friend, I wish you God's speed. I'll not delay you long: I've a confession to make, one I'd just as soon avoid, were it not for the fact I require your assistance."

Fireclaw turned from the door, set his dagger aside.

"What is it, Mochamet al Rotshild, you require of me?"

"Why, my young friend," the man answered, an ingratiating smile upon his bearded face, "it couldn't be simpler."

Striding across the room without his cane, he placed one hardened hand upon Fireclaw's arm.

"I'm a spy, you see—and always have been—for the Mughal Empire."

XLV:

The Spy

Upon the day when heaven shall be as molten copper
and the mountains shall be plucked as wool-tufts, no
loyal friend shall question loyal friend.

—The *Koran*, Sura LXX

"I've been a spy since I was a green youth," Mochamet al
Rotshild went on, "and have come to be quite an effective
one, I might add in all modesty."

Fireclaw offered nothing as an answer, but watched Mochamet al Rotshild's face.

"My mission, what was expected from me upon this
voyage, was to prevent, at all costs, any détente 'tween the
Saracens and this so-called Crystal Empire."

He laughed, not from good humor but from irony.

" 'Twould appear, upon the other hand, that this has been
accomplished for me already, wouldn't it? My word, the
diplomatic repercussions that will arise from the fiery sacrifice
of the Caliph's envoy-in-wedlock—"

Fireclaw stopped him.

"Sacrifice, you say?"

"If I must be the first to say it in the open. Surely, you didn't—no, I see you, too, have known all along, but wished no more than I to have it spoken and out."

A pause.

"Where was I? Oh, yes: Her sacrifice to a pagan deity'll not be interpreted as a friendly gesture. Howe'er great an honor 'tis meant to represent by our little friend the Sun. Ah, me, 'twill enhance my reputation—posthumously, I'm afraid—unless you happen to have any better ideas about getting out of here than that."

He pointed to the dagger.

The earth jolted, this time moving the table the weapon he'd spoken of lay upon. Tilting at the cross-guard, the dagger rocked, the polished surfaces of its feather-hammered blade casting flickering shadows and reflections upon the ceiling.

Fireclaw seized the older man by the throat.

"'Twas you arranged for Ayesha to be 'spoiled' that the Caliph's 'gift' would be valueless!"

Even before Mochamet al Rotshild nodded confirmation, Fireclaw burned to slay the sea-trader. Yet he kept his peace for different reasons than he had upon the night when she was raped. In an instant he realized Mochamet al Rotshild's duties, as the Commodore had just explained them, might coincide with his own wishes.

"I should cut you in half, old man, this moment. Give me a reason why I should not!"

Mochamet al Rotshild rubbed his bearded chin.

"I could give you many a reason why you should. In some respects, I might be grateful for the release."

He let his hand drop.

"But, since I suspect you'll need my assistance, 'twouldn't be practical at this particular moment. Nor would it give me much of an opportunity to offer proper restitution—which, I assure you, my friend, is just this moment in the offing."

He pointed through the open door to the next room. For the first time, Fireclaw observed not just one gray, red-tailed, scaly-footed parrot, Po, perched upon the windowsill where his Saracen master had fashioned a place for him, but two.

"They're not the strongest of fliers," Mochamet al Rotshild nodded, "flap-hopping, in preference, from bush to tree to house to bush. But they remember instructions, seek home not just upon some random hatching location but upon a mate, and can better defend themselves from predators than pigeons."

Po—or perhaps it was the other parrot—began making blatant courting overtures. Mochamet al Rotshild, a little embarrassed color in his face, rose to shut the door upon them.

He cleared his throat.

"I've this day discovered rescue's at hand, some weeks earlier than I'd expected. I shall atone for what I've done by giving the Princess back her life."

He stopped, awaiting answer.

Receiving none, he went on.

"And both of you more freedom than you've e'er now enjoyed. Toward that end I shall risk—and likely lose—my own. 'Twill be up to you, afterward, whether there's any moral debt remaining which your greatsword might collect from me."

Fireclaw once again forced back his rising rage, thinking hard.

If the manner of Ayesha's "marriage" should displease her father the Caliph, destroying any hope of an alliance, her failure to appear in the appointed place at the time of sacrifice should also displease the Sun, with the same results.

"You shall yet live a while longer," he told the man, relaxing his grip. As he stepped away, he saw a grin upon the Saracen's face, looked down—in his fist Mochamet al Rotshild held a tiny pistol which had been pointed at the Helvetian's groin.

"Boy sopranos are made, not born, son." The older man chuckled. "Had either of us squeezed a little harder, you upon my throat, I upon the trigger, both of us would now be dead."

The Helvetian blinked. "Where—we were all searched."

"Concealed in the iron heel of a boot," the older man explained, "somehow it evaded notice."

Fireclaw brushed the matter aside.

"I can tell you something which might prove useful to a

spy," he informed the elderly Saracen. "The destruction of the fleet which you witnessed as a boy has something, I believe, to do with the great transparent sacrificial pyramid yonder."

Mochamet al Rotshild nodded.

"You're telling me naught I've not ferreted out for myself. Now I'll tell you something. There's a Mughal fleet waiting to pick us up once it's assured 'tis safe to approach the harbor. I believe what we saw this morning was the Crystal Empire defending itself against that fleet's most advanced elements."

He thrust out a hand, palm upward.

"Fireclaw, I owed no more, at my unwelcome birth, to the Saracen Empire where it by chance occurred than you to the Helvetian cult which ruined your boyhood. I'm no traitor, but a patriot—by choice—to a land you don't know as yet."

He folded his arms across his chest, though in truth they rested more upon his ample stomach.

"And whye'er not? What manner of loyalty do I owe the nameless, faceless Saracen father who took my mother, then left her behind? Or the family which afterward cast her out upon the street to starve—or eke her living out in the manner they'd already accused her of? Or the Caliph who'd prostitute his own beautiful, innocent daughter in a wise not too dissimilar, in the name of politics?"

He reached out to seize Fireclaw's arm.

"What do I owe any of them but my hatred? Why shouldn't I serve their enemies—to my own handsome profit—and thus destroy them? If you'll help me to discover the pyramid's secret, we can work together to rescue the Princess."

Fireclaw considered.

"Upon a single condition, old man, speaking of the Cult—that we find Oln Woeck, if yet he lives, where'er he may be within this building, and bring him along with us."

The old man laughed.

"Such fierce—and uncharacteristic—fondness you display toward your venerable mentor."

Mochamet al Rotshild's eyes twinkled. As from the first moment he'd met him, Fireclaw found he was having great difficulty hating this man as he should.

Together, they went to arouse David Shulieman. If such proved possible. The wounded rabbi, they knew, had been severely weakened by the long walk he'd insisted upon, demonstrating a pride Fireclaw well understood.

When the two men reached his bedside, they found the Jewish scholar at peace, his bespectacled features relaxed into a look of calm contentment. His eyes were closed. Across his chest he held a small, yellowed photograph of the Princess Ayesha.

He no longer breathed.

2

If there can be a good ending to life, the Helvetian thought, David Shulieman had had it. He had died with as much peace and dignity as the act affords. Without a spoken word of comment, Fireclaw strode from the room to don the armor of the Sun Incarnate's bodyguard.

"This should save a deal of embarrassing questions. My single regret's that our otherwise thoughtful host the Sun Incarnate's once again provided me an empty gun."

He looked at Mochamet al Rotshild, who'd followed him. The man seemed to have aged ten years—again—though Fireclaw suspected this time no ruse was involved in the appearance.

"Snap out of it, old man! We can't help the rabbi now, but we can save the one thing he loved above aught else. Come, now—you're a sneaky and resourceful bastard, d'you happen to have you any loaded magazines secreted about your person?"

The Saracen lifted his shoulders in a shrug and spread his arms.

"Naught but charges for my little pistol. Best take the damned weapon anyway, wear the helmet as well. 'Twill protect you and complete your disguise."

Fireclaw nodded.

"You're also a bastard of the observant kind, with a talent

for languages. How d'you say 'Where's the Sun? It's an emergency!' in Bodyguard-speech?"

With a puckered frown of frustration, the Saracen sea-captain admitted that he was not, perhaps, quite as observant a bastard as Fireclaw might have wished.

"What in Goddess' name are you good for, then?" Fireclaw asked, a grin belying the harshness of his words. "Ne'er mind, I shall find Ayesha myself. Since the rabbi no longer needs yon wheeled chair they brought back for him, I'll borrow it. You take Ursi with you, go now. Prepare our way out of this accursed place—provided you're feeling up to it—you'll find the bloated thing moored upon the roof!"

He wrapped the greatsword *Murderer* in a blanket, laid it slantwise in the chair. Ignoring certain grumbled objections from his companion—most to the effect that he didn't know how to fly the airship—he slung the automatic weapon over his chest, squeezed his head into the birdlike helmet, poked his head into the corridor.

Observers there were aplenty along its length, none of whom paid him the slightest attention.

Taking a breath, he joined them, pushing the chair, glad he'd thought of this deception as a way to keep his greatsword, which he'd not leave behind, from giving away the game. Besides, the chair might otherwise prove to be useful. It would give him an appearance of businesslike purpose. Several turns later in the complicated building, he'd lost the way, but this likelihood had never worried him. He was looking for another uniform like the one he wore.

He found it, at long last, standing beside an elevator, waiting in impatience for a slow-moving car to make its appearance. The man had his helmet nestled in the crook of his left arm, his weapon slung across the small of his back.

With a gauntleted finger, Fireclaw tapped him upon the shoulder, crooked the same finger, turned, striding to a nearby niche along the wall where he'd left the chair. He turned, but not before he arrived at the place he'd chosen. With a look which was a mixture of annoyance and puzzlement, the man had followed.

"*Mann*—who are you? *Maadaa thureet?*"

Fireclaw blinked. The words had been garbled but understandable, some dialect of the Saracen tongue.

"Where's the Sun?" he asked, mismouthing his own words in what he hoped was a similar manner. "Upon the authority of Owald the Commander. There's been a . . . a situation."

He indicated the wheeled chair, as if it explained everything. The Bodyguardsman drew an instrument from his belt, consulted it, pointed a finger at the floor.

"Somewhere below."

Fireclaw nodded, flipped a thumb, gave the man a gentle shove, pushed the chair toward the elevator. The Bodyguardsman sighed, nodded, plodded along with the warrior.

The car descended almost as far as it had before their submarine voyage to the Spire of Dreamers. When its steel doors had once more hissed aside, Fireclaw and his accidental companion marched toward another door, halting there.

The Bodyguardsman raised a fist to knock upon it.

Fireclaw seized that fist, twisted it till the Bodyguardsman turned about, slapped him once across the forehead with the steel rim of his prosthetic.

As the man slumped into the chair Fireclaw shoved behind him, unconscious, likely dying, the Helvetian forced the helmet over his head, removed the magazine from his Bodyguard-issue weapon, seized the bag of spares, rid himself of the empty magazine in his own weapon, slapped a fresh one home, and worked the operating handle.

He rolled the body aside, the bundled greatsword lying across the chair-arms, arranging things to appear that the bodyguard upon watch at the door was dozing—it occurred to him to wonder why someone was not already guarding the door.

He arranged his own uniform and accoutrements.

Only then did he raise his own hand to knock upon the door. It slid aside before he touched it.

Fireclaw stumbled through.

The sight which he beheld there stunned him.

He looked down upon a supine, undraped female figure, her

head toward him, her feet away. The rest of the room invisible to his shocked gaze, he strode closer. Upon a narrow table in the middle of the room lay the unquestionably dead form of an olive-skinned girl, not yet twenty, her smooth arms spread a bit over the edges of the table, her hands curled as if in sleep, the palms upward in a gesture betokening surrender.

A tumble of shining, raven-colored hair cascaded toward him. It lay about her shoulders as well, obscuring her face. Yet he could see that large, lash-fringed eyes, set in a soft, high-cheekboned face, were dark brown, open wide, unaware.

Fireclaw knew a moment of the blackest horror he'd ever felt.

He whispered a name.

"Ayesha . . ."

SURA THE SEVENTH: 1420 A.H.—

The Hollow-Handled Knife

You were upon the brink of a pit of
Fire, and He delivered you from it;
even so God makes clear to you his
signs; so haply you will be guided.
                    —The *Holy Koran*, Sura III,
                    The House of Imran

XLVI:

The Bride of God

And . . . Moses said to his people, "My people, you
have done wrong against yourselves by taking the
Calf."

—The *Koran*, Sura II

In a brocaded robe, Oln Woeck looked up at him without a
word, madness mingling with ecstasy deep within his glittering eyes. Beside him, in a rattan chair like the one the old
Helvetian occupied, reposed the bronzed, irresistible figure of
Zhu Yuan-Coyotl, ruler of the Han-Meshika, the Sun Incarnate.

Both men had blood upon their lips, the elder of the pair
wiping it from his chin as Fireclaw approached.

The Bodyguard Fireclaw had wondered about was here as
well, sitting upon a stool beside the door.

The slender soft-skinned torso of the helpless maiden had
been with deftness opened hip to breast—perhaps with one of
those razor-edged push-daggers the Sun Incarnate always
carried with him—her liver removed and placed within a bed
of crisp green leaves upon a golden platter which Oln Woeck

and the Sun shared between them, partaking of the warm, blood-slippery, sweet-smelling meat.

Zhu Yuan-Coyotl chuckled, brushing hair away from the dead girl's face with blood-lacquered fingers.

"You're mistaken, impetuous friend. All of the earth's people serve Us in their own wise, 'tis true. This is but a little peasant-girl, of small use to Us save as you see her here, the centerpiece of an initiation rite—our mutual friend here has determined, with commendable pragmatism, to transfer his religious faith to the Sun Incarnate. Your Saracen Princess will serve Us in quite another capacity."

Something inside the paralyzed warrior spoke for him. "Where is she?"

"At this moment, We expect she's being prepared to join the Sun in wedlock."

He pushed back a voluminous sleeve, consulting a time-piece strapped to his wrist.

"She's already at the place appointed."

"And you?" demanded Fireclaw beginning to recover his wits, "Isn't the bridegroom going to be late?"

"We shan't attend, at least not in this fleshly aspect, for 'tis neither to the body nor to the mind of Zhu Yuan-Coyotl that the Saracen Princess will be joined, but—"

Fireclaw stepped forward, seizing the Sun Incarnate by the front of his embroidered robe, dragging him to his feet. Hideous images washed through his mind, mingled with relief that it was not Ayesha here upon the table.

The young man didn't resist him.

"At the pyramid?"

"At the pyramid."

A disturbance near the door behind him distracted Fireclaw's attention. He spun, pulling the Sun with him that the younger man's body might interpose itself between the warrior and the Bodyguardsman, flung Zhu Yuan-Coyotl toward him. The Sun shouted, stumbled, a slipper caught in the hem of his robe. He fell just as the Helvetian raised his weapon. The Bodyguardsman raised his own, slapping in desperation at the operating handle, fumbling with the safety lever.

The room filled with the yammering of gunfire, the smoke of "smokeless powder" obscuring vision. Empty cases fountained from the weapons of both men. When it had ceased, the Bodyguardsman lay dead atop the struggling form of his ruler.

Fireclaw was untouched.

Another noise.

Fireclaw whirled toward a shadow creeping up on him, one of the chairs held clublike overhead, and lay Oln Woeck out with a single negligent swing of his prosthetic. Before the man had fallen, he leapt forward, pressing the muzzle of his weapon against Zhu Yuan-Coyotl's cheek.

"Lift those knives out with both little fingers—if I see the rest of your hands uncurl, boy, I'll kill you with some satisfaction here and now—toss them away!"

The Sun complied.

Finding something to do with Oln Woeck was not difficult. Bundled up in the blanket with *Murderer*, the unconscious former leader of the Cult of Jesus soon occupied the rabbi's chair.

Persuading Zhu Yuan-Coyotl to come along in peace was another matter. Fireclaw settled this, giving him a job pushing the chair. He first supervised the young man as, under the warrior's instruction, he pulled copper-clad bullets from several aluminum cartridges, filled the barrel of the dead Bodyguardsman's weapon with powder—in front of a chambered bulletless round, and hammered one of the leftover bullets into the muzzle, converting the weapon into a bomb.

Strapped across the Sun's chest—Zhu Yuan-Coyotl was by now wearing the uniform of his own Bodyguard—with a bit of the same ravelings of brocade attached to the trigger which Fireclaw had used to tie his hands to the handles of the chair, the converted weapon assured that the young man presented little problem.

2

The Sun's personal airship, the same great craft with painted eyes which had brought them all here, had been left moored, unattended, upon the building's roof. The bullet-pierced bodies of two mechanics now lay tucked behind a ladder where the gondola lay closest to the roof. In the control-cabin, Mochamet al Rotshild, strain showing upon his face, was overjoyed—no more than was the bear-dog, Ursi—to see the three men emerge from the elevator.

Still uncertain how they planned to steer the craft, the Saracen took charge of Fireclaw's prisoners, at his suggestion trussing them with strips torn from their own clothing. As the Helvetian cast them off, running from tie-down to tie-down at the roof's edge, slashing restraining hawsers with his great-sword, however, a familiar copper-kilted figure appeared at the elevator, gun in hand.

Ursi snarled, sniffed the air, whine-whistling in confusion. Fireclaw turned from cutting the next-to-last rope. The airship had begun to bob in the continuous gusty breeze off the bay. The figure with the weapon was his own son.

"Kill them! Kill them all!"

The voice was that of the Sun, shouting from the open doorway of the gondola. Owald Sedrichsohn, Commander of the Bodyguard, slapped back the operating handle. He let the bolt slam home upon a cartridge. He raised the sight to eye level.

Before Sedrich Fireclaw could ask himself whether he was capable of murdering his own flesh and blood, the young man shifted his weapon aside, aiming it at the Sun Incarnate.

"Quiet, you dirty little man," he ordered. "Don't you think you might need a pilot, Father?"

Transmitted by the last taut mooring line, yet another earth-tremor jittered through the fabric of the airship. Fireclaw grinned, slashing the rope. They leapt over the angry, writhing body of Zhu Yuan-Coyotl—a disgusted Mochamet al Rotshild had stuffed a rag into his mouth—and were safe aboard before the airship had begun rising.

In gratitude, the Saracen had stood back from the dial-crowded, bewildering console. Perhaps he might have puzzled the thing out by himself, he told the younger of the two

Helvetians—given a year or two of study. Instead, Owald seized the controls with certain hands. The engines coughed to life. The airship rose.

They made speed toward the crystal pyramid.

There, preliminary sacrifices were being offered to the sun. Hundreds of thousands of worshippers crowded about the lower steps of the crystalline monument—boats ranging in size from little bobbing cockleshells to giant vessels capable of crossing the great sea had been moored about its glassy base.

Braving the day's unsettling quakelets, many more spectators filled the city plazas across the bay.

At the pyramid's blunt apex, the scarlet Eye-of-God was obscured by the close-packed forms of thousands of less fortunate participants, standing—in what state of mind Fireclaw couldn't guess—shoulder to shoulder upon its surface. Silent they remained, all unmoving. As the sun struck the blocks of the pyramid, an incredible thing occurred.

Having finished lining their compliant victims up in satisfactory ranks over the glassy "pool," the priests stood back at the corners of the summit, their arms lifted to the sky, as if waiting—

There was a titanic pulse of light!

With a clap of thunder, a ruby-colored shaft of blinding luminescence exploded from the top of the pyramid, a full hundred paces in diameter it was, roiling the atmosphere above the bay, clawing miles into the tortured sky. Even at this distance, and through the cabin window, Fireclaw could feel its heat upon his face.

When it winked out as if it had never been—Fireclaw wiped dazzled tears from his cheeks, blinked at the yellow-green coloring the world had by contrast taken on—naught whatever, no charred hulks, not even fine white ashes, of the sacrificial victims remained behind. The "pool" was as glossy-clean as it had been to begin with.

A mighty groan of ecstasy went up from the crowds.

Movement surged along the steps.

Another group of sacrifices, thousands of them, was

brought up the side of the pyramid. There they were stood in place by the priests. Fireclaw wondered to himself—red anger choosing a strange time to rise within him—whether these apparent willing victims had ever been aught he'd have called human. Certainly they seemed to possess no human will to survive.

They too, disappeared in a blast of scarlet fury.

Heedless of the coming beam-path, Owald leaned into the controls, as if by magic tilting the entire world about them, bringing the airship even closer.

Of a sudden, from their airborne vantage, the escapees saw Ayesha being brought to the top of the pyramid in a black formal gown, steadied upon the steep-slanted pathway—rendered yet more treacherous by the shuddering earth—by a pair of priests. As with their previous victims, she seemed, however, to be climbing of her own accord.

Upon her frail shoulder, little Sagheer the pygmy marmoset was with her, even unto the end.

3

Sunlight sparkled off the water below. The sun itself was a patch of blinding brilliance upon the earth-roiled waves.

Thinking back over Mochamet al Rotshild's mysterious tale of the destroyed Saracen fleet, Fireclaw began taking note of certain details visible at the pyramid-top, employing a more practical eye than he'd exercised upon it e'er now.

"Owald!"

He shouted against the speeding airship's roaring engines, the hurricane-wind of its passage. Air sang in the window-frames, wire struts keeping harmony about the gondola.

"How long does it take yon damned rockpile to store up energy for the next pulse?"

Looking back over his shoulder at his father, the ex-commander of the Imperial Bodyguard opened his mouth—

"In the Name of God, look you!"

The interrupting voice was Mochamet al Rotshild's, his tone

incongruous, elated, bordering upon hysterical. His shaking finger pointed out the cabin window, westward.

Just this side of the faraway blue horizon, what Fireclaw presumed was the Mughal fleet the man had earlier spoken of had appeared, its tall smokestacks and high-masted rotating sails—these reminded the Helvetian of his boyhood—invisible to all within the arms of the great bay save the airborne party.

Owald nodded.

"The quakes might be slowing the priest-technicians a little Several minutes, at the least—I think!"

"He thinks!"

A grim expression settled upon the older Helvetian's face. He looked round at the Saracen—or was it Mughal now?—captain, Mochamet al Rotshild. The elderly figure danced a little with excitement. The man nodded back at Fireclaw, in wordless willingness to carry out whatever plan he'd conceived.

The Sun Incarnate Zhu Yuan-Coyotl and Oln Woeck, both trussed up, heaped without dignity into a corner of the cabin, the Helvetian warrior and his allies ignored.

Fireclaw clapped his good hand upon Owald's shoulder. None but the man's son could have taken it without buckling.

"Then I *think* I know what we shall do!"

More words were in haste exchanged.

At Fireclaw's shouted instruction, the huge, curved, polished mirror below the airship was tilted upon its hinges from beneath the hull. This process took far longer than any of them might have wished. At this speed, a supporting structure never designed to take such strain groaned against the wind, shaking the mighty vessel like a dog brandishing the rags of a fresh-killed hare.

Something like a dog as well the Sun Incarnate Zhu Yuan-Coyotl writhed with impotent fury. He bit at the gags stuffed in his mouth until the spittle foamed down his naked chest.

Fireclaw looked down upon him and laughed.

Oln Woeck cried out, wetting himself.

Squinting, measuring precious time and shorter distances

against an emerald-glowing grid set into the instrument-studded console before him, Owald dropped the mighty airship groundward while coaching Mochamet al Rotshild, sea-sailor and Mughal spy.

Together they'd inconvenience two empires.

XLVII:

The Blinded Eye

... unto each God has promised the reward most fair. ... Is it not time that the hearts of those who believe should be humbled ... ?
—The *Koran*, Sura LVII

Far below, repeated tremors roiled the waters of the bay in an insane crisscross of interfering patterns.

Grunting from the effort, a sweating, red-faced Owald Sedrichsohn shifted levers, twisted wheels. Veins stood out upon his neck and forehead. He swore at both the instruments and his encumbering Bodyguardsman's armor, dragging the great airship and its dangling mirror, almost as massive, over the top of the pyramid.

When the great craft of the skies had at last dropped low enough, bobbing in the unsteady breeze as if 'twere a child's plaything, Fireclaw slammed the door back. Timing himself against the vessel's uncertain surging motions, he leapt from the gondola, the greatsword *Murderer* locked upon his steel-rimmed wrist.

He was appropriately greeted.

Hundreds of the filthy priests of the Han-Meshika surged forward, the foul miasma of their crusted, unwashed bodies enveloping him. They carried no weapons he could see, but enough of them there were and more to crush him 'neath their dirty weight alone, did they but, in their fanatic blood-lust, will it.

Shouting curses at them, he didn't break his stride, but swung the greatsword *Murderer* from side to side—its razor-tip whistled with its passage through the air—half in warning to the priests, half to limber up an arm grown stiff with tension.

He took firm hold with his good left hand upon the greatsword's grip, just behind the guard, high above the place where his prosthetic locked upon the pommel.

Neither did the shrieking insect-beclouded mass of helpless-peasant-murderers falter, but running, mindless, stumbled into one another with their thirst to add his death this morning to ten thousand others—and one—closing their share of the narrowing distance between themselves and the Helvetian warrior.

The joy upon their dirt-seamed faces told him they believed him easy prey.

Learning different, the first to rush upon Fireclaw's gleaming blade-point screamed and died and fell, his body cloven, gutted from collarbone to crotch—severed bone-ends gleaming white in shattered flash—but not before a second and a third had rushed to join him and suffered the same fate, their spilled vitals writhing, braiding into one another upon the slickened building-top.

He killed another, and another. Still they came upon him at a run. Their mingled blood sluiced down the fuller of the greatsword, cresting where it ended halfway down the forte, showering the Helvetian warrior in scarlet until his arms, chest, and shoulders likewise ran sticky, hot, and smoking with it.

More of the screaming rent-robed men surrounded him.

He was distracted for a moment as great Ursi snarled beside him. A few feet away, one of the priests clutched at the ruined, naked skull-front which had been his face e'er the bear-dog had torn it away with a single snap of his mighty jaws.

The circle about the warrior and his dog began to close.

Bringing up a hoarse, gut-born bellow with effort, three of their hair-matted heads did Fireclaw shear off with a single blow. Still grinning, they jumped from their severed neck-stalks, fountaining with gore. They rolled over the glassy roof-lip, down the two and a half thousand cruel-edged steps below. They ended, pulped beyond recognizability, by splashing into the predator-infested waters of the bay.

In an instant Fireclaw began littering the evil temple with the entrails and disembodied limbs of a hundred others as he hacked a path through the circle they'd formed about him, measuring his progress in deaths a dozen at a time, ever forging toward the livid center of the vast altar where the Princess Ayesha still stood drugged into motionless emptiness, little Sagheer chittering upon her shoulder.

The tide began to turn. Already demoralized by the quaking building, the remaining priests of the Han-Meshika—deprived of weapons to defend themselves by generations of rulers who thought it convenient—were helpless to stop him.

Now they fell in ranks before his scarlet-streaming great-sword like scythe-gathered sheaves of grain, till it seemed to the warrior's rage-numbed mind there could be no more of them to give their lives to *Murderer*'s legend.

Still they came.

Fireclaw shifted his greatsword from the end of his weary right arm to the good hand at his left.

A priest behind him screamed. Ursi had hold of his arm, just above the elbow, but it was bleeding at the shoulder from which it was being wrenched like an uprooted weed.

2

Behind Fireclaw, still within the flying machine, Owald and the others tore their eyes away from Fireclaw's battle, the young commander attempting, as he'd been ordered, to jockey the tilted mirror across the surface of the Eye-of-God.

He was almost too successful. All too soon it cast its titanic shadow upon the Helvetian warrior and the helpless girl he'd reached at last, enveloping them.

Nearby, a blubbering priest lay face down, flopping as the mighty bear-dog stripped the backbone from his body with a savage twisting motion of his shaggy head.

Still the priests kept coming.

Shouting back at Mochamet al Rotshild, the warrior's son jumped from the gondola, racing to aid him.

At Owald's instruction, the older man lifted a red-enameled switch-cover upon the control panel, watched the three upon the pyramid-top. When he felt the time was right, he took a breath, toggled the emergency switch which fired explosive bolts, releasing the great mirror, slamming it into place over the glassy giant lens just as Fireclaw, Ayesha in his arms, raced clear of the space.

Owald was right behind them, Ursi in the lead.

At the edge, they tumbled, taken from behind by a blast of air as the giant mirror crashed over the "pool." Fireclaw rolled with it, protecting Ayesha with his body.

Owald kept his feet until his heel, slick from the priest-blood his father had spilled by the hogshead, slipped from beneath him as the building quivered.

He pitched headlong over the lip, a desperate hand outthrust for the next step. He felt his father's one good hand close hard upon his ankle. A long, terrible moment passed as the blood in which they all were bathed let the ankle slide, finger's width by finger's width, through Fireclaw's bone-crushing grasp.

Owald dropped—

—and flattened both palms against the tread of the next step. He squirmed, twisted, pulled himself back to the comparative safety of the pyramid-top.

"Die! Die! Die! Die! Die!"

Close beside Fireclaw's shaven head there flashed a shower of orange sparks. A lone surviving priest swung what had once been a decorative sacrificial axe. His warrior's sword, cast away that he might seize instead an ankle, was just beyond reach. Still watching his son's recovery, pinned beneath the semiconscious Princess Ayesha, the Helvetian warrior was slow to react.

Too slow.

Helpless, he watched the blade descend once more.

It whistled as it fell toward his face.

The earth gave a jolting shudder.

Of a sudden, Mochamet al Rotshild stepped into the way, taking the axe-bit through his unprotected skull, but gutting the priest who wielded it in the same instant with a thrust of *Murderer*'s great blade through the creature's abdomen.

The Mughal spy had made atonement.

Murderer fell.

The axe wrenched free with the verminous priest's dying convulsions and skidded, spinning butt about blade-bit, until it stopped at the fallen mirror's edge.

3

Reclaiming *Murderer*, Fireclaw carried Ayesha to the airship.

Signaling Owald with a wave of his sword to take the controls, in one mighty fist Fireclaw seized the bonds restraining Oln Woeck and the Sun Incarnate, Zhu Yuan Coyotl.

He'd sheathed his sword. Now he was assuring himself of something he carried in his shirtfront.

"Here, I've a job for the pair of you!"

He dragged them in an awkward dance toward the mirror, now lying face down over the still-warm, deadly eye of the crystal pyramid. In a blur of motion, he seized their wrists, tearing their bonds free with the doing of it, slammed them down across each other upon the metal backing of the mirror's edge. In a movement too fast for either of his victims to anticipate, he drew Dove Blossom's little hollow-handled dagger from his bosom, thrust it through the living flesh of their wrists, into the backing-plate, nailing them both down.

Ignoring yet another fit of shaking from the earth below, he stepped back to admire his handiwork. His bear-dog had leapt from the airship and was beside him.

"Tell your Lord Jesus, Oln Woeck, you died that you might share his suffering right beside him—in Hell!"

Whirling upon his moccasined heel, he ran for the airship.

Ursi followed in his wake.

"Wait, Sedrich, I beg you!" cried Oln Woeck.

The old man whined. He'd ne'er intended harm to anyone, to injure Sedrich Owaldsohn or Ilse, Frae helpless in her pregnancy, or Owald. He hadn't meant to slay Fireclaw's wife. . . .

The Sun Incarnate Zhu Yuan-Coyotl spat in his face.

Without further word, the young man set his teeth, stretching for the sacrificial axe which had killed Mochamet al Rotshild. He took a breath, raised the weapon, swung it down left-handed with all his might upon the arm pinned by the dagger.

The blade bit deep into the mirror-backing.

Oln Woeck watched, gibbering in horror, his eyes grown wide with shock. A gout of warm blood spurted over both of them in pulses, cooling in the salty breeze.

Five sharp tremors rattled the pyramid-top in rapid succession. Across the bay, the facade of a building slipped to the ground with a dusty roar. Staring at the twice-blooded axe, Oln Woeck renewed his wailing, afraid to die, yet afraid in equal measure to follow the Sun's desperate example.

Zhu Yuan-Coyotl ignored him. Holding on to consciousness by sheer will, he laid the axe aside, using a strip of cloth he'd been bound with to tie off the stump.

Running to the edge of the pyramid, he glanced down its polished, glassy side, its two and a half thousand steps looking to him like the teeth of a hungry predator. He ran back a few paces, judged the wind, which was a strong, buffeting one off the bay. Gathering as much momentum as he could, he *leapt*!

Blocked as his vision was by the crystalline monument's vast serrate-sided slanting bulk, Fireclaw, watching from a window of the slow-rising airship, never saw the end of the

Sun's leap, nor whether it ended in a watery splash far below or, as was much more likely, in his reddened, pulpy ruination. In either event the evil young man had met a fate far kinder than the one he'd intended for Ayesha, and had inflicted upon thousands more.

The water had been full of sharks, attracted by a cataract of blood from high above them.

Engines bellowing with the effort Owald demanded of them, the airship soared away, just as the next pulse of power from within the crystal pyramid gathered itself. There was a mighty roar like unto lightning. Intolerable light and heat sizzled out round the edges of the occulting mirror which nonetheless reflected most of the structure's deadly energies back into the pyramid.

Something within its substance groaned.

As Fireclaw and his companions watched, the smoking mirror seemed to hold a fraction of a second as its remaining captive screamed, roasting between knees and waist. The clothing about his middle burst into flame, showering spark-punctuated flames backward and away from him, across the heavy-lidded pyramid-top.

Oln Woeck's screams were a siren of anguish. His free arm flailed, he retched and vomited. His upper body flopped like a landed, suffocating fish. Something in his maimed hand gave way. It tore loose from the dull-glowing mirror-edge.

Legs useless, he fell upon his face, still writhing—

The bay-floor deep beneath the island seemed to give a convulsive leap, jolting the rocky outcrop and the mile-long transparent monument upon it. A titanic ring-shaped wave surged outward from the island, curling o'er at the top, sweeping away the thousands of boats, large and small, which had clustered about the island, passing by as if without notice, showering behind itself a forest of shattered planks and timbers upon the tortured surface of the water.

The ring-wave swept outward, its muddy, debris-toothed crest frothing, growing higher with each moment.

As it reached the Palace of the Sun and the nearby sheltering peninsula, the wave scooped the earth up like a gigantic shovel, turning it back upon itself, smashing, burying, drowning the millions of watchers upon the banks who'd gathered for the sacrifice.

Like a chorus of every soul condemned to Hell since the Beginning, their screaming could be heard, e'en above the catastrophe which had provoked it.

The earth gave another heave below the pyramid.

Another, great killer-wave was in this moment born to follow close upon its predecessor's wake. 'Twould find fewer victims to claim, Fireclaw thought, when it reached what had been the shore. Atop the monument, no longer resembling a mountain of ice but a living, incandescent coal from deep within the celestial conflagration it was dedicated to, the great capping mirror itself glowed hot, still turning the furious energies from below back into their source.

The mighty pyramid began to shudder, not from the tremors but in a rhythm with them nonetheless, adding power to their frequency and fury. The structure groaned. Yawning gaps began appearing 'tween the great crystalline blocks.

At the heaving, buckling summit, a tiny fire—greasy smoke rose from it and was whisked away—marked the place where Oln Woeck had fallen. It consumed itself and went out.

The earth gave one more monumental, agonized shudder—
The pyramid exploded!

XLVIII:

Flowery Death

Never a city We destroyed, but it had warners for a reminder.

—The *Koran*, Sura XXVI

The whole world tilting about it, the stolen airship whirled, slapped aside, its wire-struts snapping, lashing free, its overburdened structure groaning with the stresses, as its occupants clung, desperate, to aught within reach.

The isle of the Eye-of-God was now enveloped in a murky, fierce-glowing scarlet-centered cloud which boiled and twisted upward past the battered airship in a dense, ropy column, only to flatten into an evil-looking mushroom-cap as it met the cooler upper air.

Thunder bellowed in its heart.

Below, inside the already deep-riven earth, something gave way with a hideous noise which seemed to all about the ship like the screeching of a dying god. As if in sympathy, the surface of the great bay, extending now from horizon to horizon, churned itself in that instant into an angry, muddy foam.

Lightning flashed upon the faraway peaks.

A mighty rumbling came to them, greater than any they'd heard before, more felt than heard, like unto the end of all things, godlike and mortal alike. As Fireclaw and his shaken companions watched in horror, full half the Han-Meshika capital city, already smashed by three titanic waves, shuddered. It leapt northward in a single, terrible bound, the sudden shifting of the earth they stood upon flattening every edifice still standing for a hundred square leagues.

The wave-wrecked ruins of the Palace of the Sun swirled about themselves and disappeared, along with the island they'd occupied, swallowed by the raging inland sea. Not e'en an identifying eddy in the water marked its passing.

Likewise, nothing could be seen of any land which had once surrounded the great bay and which was now, at least until the waves subsided, part of its catastrophe-racked floor.

Aroused from her drugged stupor, Ayesha cried out.

Fireclaw followed her stunned gaze.

To the westward, the Spire of Dreamers began to change shape in some monstrous, subtle wise. Left erect by the still-quaking earth, nevertheless its great height seemed somehow reduced, its tapering sides swollen outward. Fireclaw watched great jagged cracks race one another from its base in churning wreckage and corpse-littered mud-froth, up the building's exterior, splitting, branching like the tangled corridors within, crazing the entire surface.

The mile-tall Spire began to settle into its own length, the smoke of powdered stone erupting in gray billows at its base, till nothing more remained than a pile of dust-obscured rubble a few man-heights tall upon the wave-battered barren rock.

A dull flicker of light followed, a muffled explosion which was a feeble anticlimax after the destruction of the Eye-of-God. The Spire of Dreamers vanished altogether, leaving naught but the naked stony island it had stood upon.

Already, about its fringes—the only shoreline now in sight—were heaped in man-height piles the remains of billions of dead fish, mingled with those who'd once fished for them.

Perhaps someday, the warrior thought in weary cynicism,

'twould once again be made a prison-island. Meantime, six million living dead had found their rest.

Owald shouted something, mopping at blood streaming from a shallow cut upon his forehead with one sleeve of his soiled, tattered under-armor. Wind sang round them once again, but this time 'twas more than just the shrill passage of the air past window-frames and wire braces. Alarm bells and klaxons began sounding.

The airship, its broad, fabric-covered outer surfaces slashed and tattered, had been penetrated in a thousand places by the crystalline shards of the pyramid.

It began to fall.

Trying to declare the emergency to anyone who'd failed to appreciate it, Owald turned to catch his father with a beautiful Saracen girl, many years his junior, in his arms.

He seemed to be enjoying it.

As did she.

Owald cleared his throat, a gesture wasted in the noise racketing about them.

"If you're interested," he advised, unable to resist a smile in the midst of catastrophe, "I believe I can reach the Mughal fleet ere this thing sinks not that gently, to rise no more."

He received no answer from his father.

He held up a fist. From it, upon a glittering chain, there hung a golden medallion.

"Mochamet al Rotshild," he shouted, "gave me this, ere he rushed to aid you, as token of safe passage among the Mughal. Having destroyed an entire civilization, we're assured of a most cordial welcome there—if we can make it!"

Ursi barked with joy.

Neither Fireclaw nor Ayesha heard him.

THE BEST IN SCIENCE FICTION

BESTSELLING BOOKS FROM TOR